TOMORROW BELONGS TO US

TOMORROW BELONGS TO US

LILY ZANTE

CHAPTER ONE

LANCE

The hairs on the back of my neck stand up, and my stomach hollows out.

It's the bloodcurdling screams behind me which make me turn around. A young woman sprints towards me. It's someone I know.

It's Heidi.

Heidi who doesn't understand. Heidi who always corners me after every lecture, asking for further explanations.

But now her bulging eyes are filled with terror. Unblinking, she bolts towards me.

Everything around me slows down but the movements are jerky, jagged. It's like watching an eight-millimetre movie with a projector playing and the film running in distorted slow motion. She screams again, one long ear-splitting, shrill scream, and that's when I see him. The man behind her. His expression is blank. His eyes aren't focused. He's walking calmly, his hand shoved deep into his coat pocket, and then he pulls it out from within his huge jacket. A rifle. Long and thin and silver.

It can't be real, is my first thought. It looks like a toy. It has to be, because it looks comical, and surreal and out of place on a college campus in the Fall, where the trees are a medley of golden orange and red.

For a fleeting moment, I'm relieved it's not bigger and bulkier—that it's not an assault rifle. My body relaxes as if this is a good thing. I look up at the guy, he lifts his hand, takes aim, then smiles. "Bitch!" he yells, his voice thick with venom.

This is real. My reflexes snap into action. I sprint forward, time slows down, stops, almost, and I grab the girl. I spin her around, shielding her body with mine.

A loud noise explodes in the air, like a bomb going off, a noise that is out of place here. My shoulder cracks into two, as though a meat cleaver has sliced clean through it.

And then I see Cassie, her laugh infectious and wild as she runs around with her water gun, aiming at me as she fires. She doesn't stop until I'm drenched.

My nine-year-old daughter's smile is the last thing I remember.

MEGAN

"Have you heard?" Arla ploughs through my front door like a heat-seeking missile.

"Heard what?" I close the door and watch my friend

march into my living room as if she owns this place. "You *haven't* heard?"

"Heard what?" I echo.

She switches the TV on and turns to the local news channel. It looks like something has happened, and now I remember that people at work were talking about something, but I didn't pay any attention to it because I had a report to do. I stare at the screen because Arla stands and stares at me as if I should know about this.

A reporter talks against a backdrop of police cars and officers. Groups of shocked students huddle together, hugging and comforting one another. A police officer commends college security who were able to apprehend the student but the main topic is about a college professor who was shot in the altercation.

"Onlookers say that Lance Turner, a professor at Redmond College in Boston, shielded the shooter's victim from fatal injury, but was himself shot in the process."

"That's... that's ..." It can't be him. "Is that ...?"

Lance Turner? I gasp. My mouth turns dry. The man who walked away and left me.

"The shooter, now in police custody, is believed to be an ex-boyfriend of the young woman who was targeted. Thankfully she is safe and well. Let us, once more, turn our attention to the man who is being hailed as a hero in what could have so easily become a tragic event."

"Mr. Turner!" Arla exclaims, clapping her hands wildly. "*Your* Mr. Turner. Can you believe it? He's a professor at Redmond College now." Arla's eyes are wide open, like her mouth. She reminds me of a fish.

"He's not my Mr. ..." But my words taper to a whisper. I stare at the screen as tiny explosions erupt in my chest. He's been here the entire time?

In the background, the reporter's voice is sharp and clear. "Lance Turner, the forty-three year old mathematics professor has been teaching at Redmond College for ..."

At Redmond College.

I try to process the news, struggling to make sense of it all—the shooting and the shocking new detail that Lance Turner, my high school teacher, the man I was obsessed with as a student, the man I've tried to forget, has been here the whole time. Not far away in Nebraska like the rumors I'd heard, but here in Boston.

I struggle to breathe and sit down trying to take it all in but it feels as if someone has drilled a hole in my lungs.

It's been eleven years since I last saw him. Now he's on the TV; it's a photo of him. My stomach churns, throwing up all sorts of feelings at a man who cared for me, who listened to me, who became more than just my high school teacher. This is the first time I've seen him in eleven years and it's jarring. His face is hard to forget; there's grey in his hair now, and it's short, like a buzz cut. His face is smooth, and they're still there, his high sculpted cheekbones. He's lean and wiry, and not much different in build to when I first saw him.

If I saw him in a bar or a club, I'd go home with him.

But with Lance ... the man I knew, I would want more. Not just the night, maybe more than tomorrow.

I don't know who taught me that love is hard. My mind blurs when I try to pin it down. Was it my parents and their messed up lives, or was it Lance who made me believe in the mantra I've lived most of my adult life by.

"He saved that girl's life," Arla says proudly, as if she had a hand in it. "I can't believe you didn't know. It happened a few hours ago."

"What's he doing here?" I ask, more to myself, than expecting an answer from Arla.

"Didn't you hear what they just said?" Arla shrieks. Of course I heard, but it's a total shock to my system to accept that he's been living and working here.

"It's possible that the two of you might have crossed paths," Arla says, her soft, round face flushed red with excitement. "Or you could have been at the same coffee shop, walked into the same store and not known, you could have walked across the same street."

I tune her out as I still stare at the screen, unable to shift my gaze.

"I *cannot* believe you didn't know about this," Arla repeats. "Have you had your head under a blanket the whole time?"

"I've been working," I reply, feeling dazed, as if I'll wake up from this dream. "I haven't turned on the radio or the TV." I came home earlier than usual to work on a report I'm preparing for a client. I'm under pressure to get this done and I haven't checked my email or social media. Preston and I have been trying to outdo one another at work. We both want to impress the boss because there's only one promotion coming up in our department and I intend to claim it.

I frown at the TV screen. "How badly was he hurt?"

"He's at the hospital. I don't think it's anything serious." Arla replies, with a twinkle in her eye. "This is soooooo exciting!"

"Why?"

"Why? Why? Because he's *here*! You were so broken hearted when he left, and you've wondered for years what happened to him, and now you can finally find out."

I wish I hadn't confided in Arla so much about my high school crush on Mr. Turner. But it had been much more than a crush. It was real, my feelings for him, and what he felt for me, or so I thought.

"Are you going to the gym?" I notice Arla's ultra-bright leggings and bright orange zip-up top. The sports center has become her favorite place of late.

"I was, but I can be here for you if you want."

"For what?" I ask.

"This news! I know what he meant to you."

"That was a long time ago," I push back, "and I wasn't crazy about him."

"Yes, you were!"

I ground down on my clenched teeth. Mr. Turner appeared in my life at a time when it was falling apart and when I needed him the most. He was my safety net, my safe haven. He was there for me, and he was the only one, because even Shaun failed me. Or maybe I failed him first. He was my first boyfriend. I was a late starter, you could say. We should have been friends, instead of girlfriend and boyfriend.

But then Mr. Turner came along and I fell for him. I didn't dive in headfirst. I didn't trip. At first I was too sensible to fall for his looks like the rest of my peers but later, as we got to know one another, I found someone who had time for me, someone who was willing to listen and be there and help me. That's when my eyes opened, and I began to really see him. That's when I realized why the other girls were fawning over him. He was handsome, and kind, and easy to talk to.

It was an emotional connection that we shared, and gradually, slowly, I became obsessed. Shaun and I splintered away from each other but my high school teacher became a place of comfort.

Until he disappeared without a word. It's taken me a long time to get over him, and I won't allow thoughts of him to seep back into my mind. "Nothing happened," I insist, testily.

"He's going to be all over the news now," says Arla. "He's

going to be in your face for a few days, Megan. Can you handle it?"

The news networks will carry this story for a few more days, showing the same old clip over and over again. My eyes are still on the screen, on his face. It's comforting to see, in the same way it is to hear white noise. It helps me to absorb it.

It is big news, a college professor saving a student from a shooting. But that's who Lance Turner is. He helps people. He's a hero.

And once I believed he was mine.

CHAPTER TWO

LANCE

I got taken to the hospital straightaway.

Apparently I was floating in and out of consciousness. The doctor said I was lucky that the bullet passed clean through my shoulder without hitting any arteries or bone, and because it was a small bore .22 caliber rifle, a relatively low-powered weapon, the damage wasn't as bad as it could have been.

I was very lucky. Vivian rushed to be by my bedside, but she's the last person I want to see. The woman is like a mosquito, irritating, annoying and always hovering around. I even told her as much.

"But I want to be here, darling," she said, before making a show of holding my hand, and kissing my cheek. She calls me darling when there are other people around, or if she wants something. The smell of her overbearing perfume has fused with the clinical antiseptic smell of the hospital and lingers on my clothes even though I came home a few hours ago.

Not home. But Vivian's place. I can't shower yet, and I don't have the energy to either. I can't do much because I'm still in pain even though I've been told recovery should be a few weeks rest and then physio.

"Daddy!" Cassie charges into the room. Seeing her makes my heart burst with happiness, a surge of joy blasts through my veins. I sit up too fast, then yelp when the pain hits me. I'm shirtless, and I feel as if I'm floating on a cloud. Those painkillers are strong, but I feel the pain of Cassie's jolt. Vivian's face is inches away from me, she clasps my hand harder, as if she cares.

"Let go, Vivian," I hiss under my breath as Cassie clambers up onto the bed.

"Daddy, you're awake!" she shrieks and brushes against my bandaged shoulder as she snuggles up against my side. I wince, then ask her to move to the other side, to my 'good shoulder' side.

She obliges, then scoots off the bed before running around and clambering up the other side. I'm trying to rest, but there's no chance of that with my little girl here. I'm going home soon, but Vivian insisted I come back here because Cassie wanted to see me. I wanted to see my darling daughter too.

"Does it hurt, Daddy?" Doe-like brown eyes peer at my shoulder which is covered in a dressing.

"Not as much now that you're here." I smile at her, and she smiles back. My body lights up and I float in a bubble of happiness. I love this little girl so much. I'd die for her. I was lucky I didn't get killed in protecting that student, but now that I've had time to reflect, I realize that I could have died. And then Cassie would have no daddy, and only Vivian to raise her.

Life choices.

I couldn't not shield the student from harm.

I didn't think of myself. I thought of her.

I am lucky things didn't turn out differently. With my good arm, I hug my daughter even closer to me. I want to hold her forever.

"Mommy says you're going to stay here." She stares up at me, her eyes gleaming with hope. I'm in too much pain to find a good answer. She hates me being away, but moving away from her was something I had to do to preserve my sanity.

"Oh, Sweetpea." I falter, trying to find the right words that won't shatter her little heart. It's been hard leaving her, even though it was easy to walk out of the marital home which belongs to my soon-to-be ex-wife. We told Cassie that I was leaving home and moving to be nearer the college where I teach. The innocence of childhood meant that she accepted this without question. One day I hope to tell her the truth.

Vivian and I have drifted so far apart, that the marriage exists in name only.

"Please, Daddy. You got shot. You could have died." I hate that she has already thought of this. This little girl who is careening towards her teenage years. It's only for her that I tried for so long to make my marriage work. It was hard to ignore the infidelities; Vivian has no moral compass. My lack of attention and affection over the years, because of this, made her hate me even more.

"Must you make it sound as if this is a prison for you?" Vivian gets up, displeased. "Think of your daughter if nothing else."

I smile at Cassie. "Alright, Sweetpea. I'll stay tonight."

My little girl's lips curve upwards and her eyes light up. "Can we watch a film?" she asks, getting off the bed, knowing my answer.

"We can watch anything you want."

She gives me another goofy grin. Two of her upper teeth have fallen out and she looks cute. "I'll get snacks." She disappears and Vivian, who has been sitting on a chair by the bed, leans forward and places her hand against my bare chest. I instinctively flinch.

"You don't have to stay by my side. You don't have to pretend to play the dutiful, faithful wife." I emphasize the 'faithful.'

"I want to be here in case you need me."

"I'd rather you weren't," I mutter.

"You think you don't need me, Lance, but you do. Let's face it. Who else have you got?"

"Who else have I got?" I don't need anyone but Cassie. "It's just a flesh wound. I'll survive. I'm not dying," I counter. I don't understand the fuss. The sight of Vivian wanting to take care of me makes my gut harden.

"At least you listened to Cassie, that's something I suppose. God knows you don't listen to me."

"Why would I ever do such a thing?" It's rhetorical, but Vivian will reply.

"You're going to argue with me, even when you've been shot?" She raises an arched eyebrow.

"Further proof of how much our communication has broken down."

She puts her hands on my forearm, her thumb sliding along my skin, a tainted caress that prickles. "At least you have the sense to stay the night. You can stay in my—"

I move my arm away. "Just the night, and I'll sleep here in the spare room. I'm only staying because Cassie asked."

Vivian smiles, not batting an eye, as if this doesn't matter, that I've rejected her advances. "She's so proud of you. All of her friends think you're a hero."

I look away. "I'm no hero. I was there. It was the right thing to do."

"You took a bullet for one of your students."

Heidi Byrne has been annoying lately. She's always waiting for me at the end of each lecture, claims she doesn't fully understand. I'm used to this. I have many Heidi Byrnes.

Vivian winks at me. "They're all going to fall in love with you even harder now. The Sexy Young Professor Who Took a Bullet for his Student." She motions with her hands to show that she's building a newspaper headline.

"I would have done that for anyone."

"Would you take a bullet for me?" she asks.

I study her face. It's hard, much like her personality. Sharp and pointy. There's nothing soft or warm about her.

"You know I would."

My words make her face soften. It's like I've given her the biggest compliment and her eyes turn glassy. The marriage hasn't been great. I married her for the wrong reasons, although I would never call Cassie a wrong reason, but trying to get out of the marriage has proved difficult.

Vivian sinks her claws into me even deeper now. Her father, a powerful businessman frowns upon my decision to get out of the marriage, and I can see the accusations and blame in his eyes, about being the one to break up the family even though he damn well knows what his daughter is like. The apple doesn't fall far from the tree. Her father has had numerous affairs and Vivian's poor mother, the only member of the family I have any affection for, can do nothing but stand by and watch.

"Cassie has told all her friends. We're so proud of you. You're in the papers and you've been in the news all day. My phone hasn't stopped ringing. Everyone wants to know if you're all right."

I wince. I don't understand the fuss, and I especially don't want any of Vivian's parasitic friends anywhere near me. "I don't want to speak to anyone. No friends, no press, and not your parents."

"You're going to need to rest a while, and you're going to need physical therapy to heal. You do still want to play squash and tennis, and you want to work out and hone that gorgeous body of yours, don't you?"

Before I can answer, she says, "How can you do all of that when you're trying to feed and dress yourself? You can't do it alone, Lance. You need my help whether you like it or not. Daddy suggests you move back here instead of trying to take care of yourself."

I groan. The thought of Vivian back in my life makes me ill. "I'll be fine." I close my eyes. I have to go easy on my games and fitness regime, but I'm more worried about my students and my classes.

"If you're worried about work," she says, as if she can read my mind, "don't be. I told Lesley you'd be off for a while."

My eyelids fly open. The idea of Vivian calling my good friend at the college angers me. "Why? I'll be able to go back after a few weeks."

"Someone had to let them know. Your students and faculty needed to know that you couldn't return to work yet."

My eyes narrow.

I've been shot. It's all over the TV. I'm certain everyone managed to figure it out. Vivian didn't have to go and tell them. This is what pisses me off about her, the way she tries to snake her way back into my life as if she's still a part of it. She's Cassie's mother, but that's all. That's the only link I have to her.

"Don't concern yourself with my work," I tell her, but she finds it difficult to let go of me.

"Honey," she says in that irritating, sweet-as-candy voice she often uses when she knows she's got the advantage. "Please stay here for a little longer. I'll take good care of you."

I would rather be shot in both my arms ten times over than move in with her. I struggle to sit up. "No," I reply testily, then hear Cassie's singing about the toffee flavored popcorn she's made.

"Please let us watch this film in peace," I beg. The only reason I'm staying tonight is because my daughter asked me.

Vivian isn't a part of my life, and I don't want her to ever think we have a chance of getting back together.

CHAPTER THREE

MEGAN

It's been a few weeks since Lance Turner catapulted into my life from nowhere.

Because of the campus shooting and his part in it, he's now become Boston's hero. In the day following the incident he was all over the local papers and on TV. I kept hearing the same old story of how he saved the student's life, of how he's a professor of mathematics. The media is obsessed by his looks and his brains and referred to him as the 'hunky hero.'

Even at work, my colleagues talked about him just because his story is heroic, and people always like heroes. I stayed quiet, or pretended to be busy so that I didn't have to suffer their glowing admiration for the man.

Even if I wanted to forget him, I couldn't.

But then, I've never been able to.

Arla doesn't stop talking about him, even though I've forbidden her to bring up his name. She already has a knack for talking too much, but now she's worse. She has this ridiculous theory that the universe has a grand design for me and Lance, that the chances of him ending up in the same city as me are so remote that fate must have had a hand in it.

Once upon a time it took all my resolve to rid myself of his memories. It wasn't easy at the time. I struggled, like any teenage girl would; a teen whose life had changed after her mother overdosed. I became the caretaker for my younger sister and brother.

Perhaps it was a good thing that I was stretched so thin; that I couldn't go to college, and had to stay at home, doing courses in order to make up for the college degree I'd lost out on. Because my grades had suffered, I didn't get the academic scholarships I was hoping for.

My life took a turn for the worse. I don't ever want to put myself through the pain of abandonment again. Lance Turner wasn't just a teacher to me, over time he became something more. A friend, a confidante, someone I turned to because he understood me. He could see that I was falling apart, despite my best efforts to put on a strong face.

Mr. Turner saw me.

I'd heard of Lance Turner from the moment he first started at Overton High School. It was a year before he became my math teacher, but he was already the talk of the school. The girls in my class were crazy about him.

Luckily, I wasn't one of them. Arla was tongue tied, like the others, but I had far weightier things going on in my life, and I hadn't been reeled in.

Not then.

While other girls tried hard to get Mr. Turner's attention by asking lots of questions and staying behind after class, I never did because I'd always been good at math. That is, until my grades started to drop. And that was right around the time Mr. Turner became concerned about me.

He approached me at the end of a lesson and asked me what was wrong. He'd said he was concerned about my grades falling, but I hadn't been able to give him a proper answer then. How could I have explained that my father was having an affair and my mother had fallen apart?

I didn't want him to know of my personal hell. That my parents' daily fights were becoming more difficult to bear, and that I couldn't concentrate on my studies, and that my younger siblings were struggling even more than I was with the constant screaming and shouting.

Although I didn't take his offer of help, he still tried to do what he could, giving me extra worksheets, or a textbook that no one else had, or by going over things in class that I was struggling to grasp.

I came to rely on him. It was comforting to know that someone cared. And then things changed. Over the coming months, our friendship blossomed into something else.

It was forbidden, to have such feelings for a man who was so much older and in a position of authority and trust. I didn't see his beauty, not at first. I was with Shaun, my boyfriend, and I never, ever, looked at anyone else.

It happened slowly, then all at once. I experienced sensations I'd never had before, and an emotional connection I was desperate for. It's something I've never been able to find again. Over time, especially when my family life imploded, it was to him that I turned.

I became obsessed.

Mr. Turner held back.

I couldn't. I was a mess. But he was strong, and guarded, and concerned, yet he kept his distance. At times I could see something in his eyes, that he was struggling to deny this invisible bond that was building between us.

It was in the way I caught him staring at me when he thought I wasn't looking, it was in the way his gaze would settle on my lips when we laughed, it was in the way his face twisted when he tried to hold back that night I tested his limits.

And test them I did.

I pushed him one cold and rainy night. I needed him, and I made it impossible for him to not need me back.

He was thirty-two and concerned.

I was eighteen and lost.

But that was then and this is now. I should be stronger now that I'm older and so many years have passed, but he has slowly infiltrated my thoughts again. I find myself wondering if he's back at work, or still taking time off to recover. I've become obsessed by his story and look it up online daily, hoping to find out more about him, but it's the same old story, about him being a professor, and how he saved the girl. I find little snippets from the college's website, but it's all to do with his work. Still, I get to see a few more photos of him, looking at them daily, sometimes more than a few times than is good for me.

One day when I'm supposed to be working from home, I drive past his college to get a feel for the place where he works, to catch a glimpse of him, if he's back.

How is it that he's been here the entire time, in my town, in my city, under my nose? How is it that we've never crossed paths before? How is it that he and I have ended up here? It's nowhere near Nebraska, or wherever it was that he vanished to.

Parked outside the college, I stare at the sprawling campus intrigued by the thought that he could be near. I wonder if he has a musty old office somewhere on the grounds. Then I wonder if he's here, if I might catch a glimpse of him walking in or out of the gates

My heart feels funny, and I am in a state of limbo. I ask myself what good would come of seeing him again? But, mercifully, the city's big enough that we can both avoid one another easily.

CHAPTER FOUR

LANCE

I go around the corner a little faster than I intended and slam on my brakes. The lights are green but a woman crouches on the ground frantically trying to grab her groceries which have fallen out of her bag.

Drivers are getting angry but unless they want to run her over, they'll have to wait. The driver behind me blasts his horn and I'm so worked up that I honk my horn right back at him. He honks his horn again and I give him the middle finger before getting out.

"Hey! Asshole." The guy gets out of his car and storms towards me. I ignore him and go over to the woman. A couple of oranges roll away from her as she tries to gather everything together.

I scrub my face because I'm seeing things. Even though she doesn't look my way, she looks familiar, chewing her lower lip, her expression nervous.

Time slows down just at that moment when I crouch down and start helping her. It's like a juggernaut has hit me, the way every bone in my body feels suddenly smashed.

I know that face. I know those lips and eyes.

It's her.

Megan.

Her wavy hair falls around her shoulders, but that face. That face I will never forget.

"Megan?" She finally glances up. Those large warm mahogany eyes stare back at me. Recognition skims across her face.

"Hey asshole." A guy pokes me in my back. I turn around.

"Get the fuck away," I say, my voice deathly quiet. His head tilts, he recognizes me, I think, but can't quite place me. He opens his mouth to say something, but I beat him to it. "She's getting her things together. Don't be an asshole."

The man backs away, and I pick up a jar of crunchy peanut butter and put it back in her bag.

Has she recognized me, or not? I said her name. I could never forget her. Has she forgotten me? Car horns honk louder in the background. She stands up quickly then rushes away just as I shout after her, "Wait for me!"

I race back to my car as the driver behind beeps his horn again. I give him the middle finger again. Asshole. It's not her fault her bag ripped.

I see her rushing along the sidewalk, as if she can't get away fast enough. I walked out of her life once, when she was in a bad way and I had no choice, but I've never forgotten about her.

Megan Summers is not someone easily forgotten.

MEGAN

Lance Turner staring into my eyes, so close to me, so suddenly, so unexpectedly, is surreal. My heart missed a beat or two.

I haven't been focused on my work ever since Lance Turner came into my life, and even now, as I was walking across the crossing, I was still thinking of the man. He consumes my thoughts as badly now as he did back when I was in high school. But now I've seen him, and this makes things worse. It's bad enough that I know he lives here, but for him to know that I'm here too?

No good can come of this.

I don't want to go there, back into the past again. I haven't seen him since that night when I turned to him in my hour of need, when I needed him so badly and then he disappeared. Without a word, he'd slipped away and now, he has the audacity to ask me to wait for him.

He almost has the same build. There's no excess fat, no middle age spread. He's still as lean and tall as he was back when I was in high school. Funny how I only must have glanced at him for a few seconds, but my mind has absorbed so much about him.

As I struggle to regulate my breathing, as the enormity of who I have seen dawns upon me, a car pulls up alongside me.

It's him. I continue walking, then hear a car door close, then footsteps. In the next few seconds Lance Turner is beside me, so close to me that I am forced to turn and acknowledge him. A million angry thoughts fly through my mind and my emotions tear through me like a raging hurricane.

What now? What could this man possibly have to say to

me now? I have no words for him and my breath stalls when he stops in front of me.

"Megan." He frowns. "Why are you rushing away?" It's a voice that sends shivers down the entire length of my body.

"Why are you hunting me down?"

His eyes stare at me from a face I have never forgotten. Lake blue eyes with skin that was once so smooth against my fingertips. Now he has wrinkles around his eyes and mouth. His once dark hair is now speckled with grey. He's still slim with the lithe body of an athlete. A body forever burned into my memories.

I try not to notice these things and yet, I can't help but absorb the essence of him. He looks every bit the hero from the TV screen, and he's smiling at me, curiosity in his eyes. It was bound to happen at some point now that I know we live in the same city, the same town. It's a miracle it hasn't happened earlier, the two of us meeting at some random place, at some random time.

The way he looks at me now transports me back to another place and another time to another Megan, and I find myself back in the stuffy school classroom on a hot, sweaty summer's afternoon.

He grins and it takes me back a decade. I loved that smile, and I see the teacher again. Mr. Turner, forbidden fruit. I blink and it's him, now. It's like his past and present selves comingle.

"I can't believe it's really you." He places his hands on his hips and looks at me as if I'm a piece of art he's admiring. "It's so good to see you again." He makes it sound as if he's been away for months and has only now come back. As if we are friends.

"Have you recovered?" I ask, nodding at his shoulder. It

would be rude not to mention the story that is still fresh on everyone's mind in Boston.

He sighs heavily as if the topic irritates him. "I'm getting better. It's amazing how quickly a clean shot can heal."

"You're quite the hero around here." I shift my weight from one foot to the next, juggling the groceries in my arms. The handle broke so now I have to hold it.

He frowns. "Hero? I don't think so."

"But you saved that student's life." Now that I think of it, he seems to be good at the role of saving others; of being there just like he'd been there for me. He shakes his head refusing to accept this accolade, but I don't miss the way his eyes scan over me quickly. "You look older, but good. You look really well, Megan," he says, his voice soft and tender.

Self-conscious I touch my hand to my hair. "Older, yes."

"I mean that in a nice way. You look so grown up."

"I *am* all grown up," I retort, wondering where this conversation is going. "People usually change over time." My skin turns warm, and I'm sure I can feel the rush of blood pounding in my ears. My emotions surprise me. I expected to be annoyed at him because I've been angry with him for so long, but instead I feel a sense of ease.

I'm almost happy to see him.

It's ridiculous that I feel this way when I've had such pent-up anger for this man for so long. But the anger has melted away. My body reacts to him in a way that lets me down; it's the way I usually react to a good looking guy who shows me some attention.

I can't make that mistake here. I won't let my mind go there.

When he glances away, I sneak a peek at his face. Because I've already seen him in the newspapers, his appearance is not a big surprise to me and being this close to him in person merely confirms that the years have been kind to him. He is still as sinfully good looking as ever, and I wonder if his students think the same of him; whether they are as mesmerised as us high school girls were. A twinge of jealousy courses through me, the emotion puzzling me with its immediacy and sadness.

"I never meant to startle you." He jerks his chin in the direction of the bag in my arms. "I was driving too fast when I came around the corner."

"This isn't because of something you did." I lift a shoulder, and stare at the ground, because I don't want to keep staring at him. It throws me off. Makes me lose my focus and forget what to say. Keeps me revisiting the past when I shouldn't go anywhere near there. "The handle broke."

"I wasn't to blame?"

I stare at him quietly. He clears his throat "You live around here as well?" He glances around the street.

"Yes."

He's quiet and seems to be waiting for me to say more, but I don't. He doesn't need to know my life story. He doesn't need to be a part of my life.

"I moved here seven months ago," he tells me.

From Nebraska? I'm tempted to ask, my mind buzzes with questions but I stop myself from asking them because I don't want him to know that I need answers. That for the longest time I wondered what had happened to him. It wouldn't be cool to acknowledge that I'm pissed off with him, or let him know that I cared. Whatever it was that took place between us a long time ago, it's in my past and my past is something I want to forget.

"Do you work? What do you do?" His gaze, soft and sweet like runny honey, trickles over me in my business clothes. I feel warm and fuzzy all over. "Of course you work." A shiver rolls over me and I'm surprised by my reaction to him. All these years later, it suddenly seems normal, him walking into my life as if he's always been here. In a way he has. I carried him in my heart for those first few tough years, but then I learned to forget him. I lost myself in other men, and life, and trying to forge a future so that I didn't have to depend on a man like my mother had, or run the risk of falling apart like she did when he left her.

"I'm a management consultant."

Another grin from him. "I'm not surprised. You ended up with a career crunching numbers."

"I did. I work for Roseby and Flock."

"Wow. You did very well." He looks impressed. It's a line that often impresses. They're a big management consultancy firm, and I've worked my way up the career ladder. I'm proud of myself, but now I'm feeling deflated, because being defined by my place of work is a pitiful thing. I am a pitiful thing. Seeing Lance reminds me of who I used to be and what I've become. Somewhere in the middle my dreams disintegrated and I became jaded.

I swipe a hand across my neck. "I don't know why I said that. It sounds ... big headed—"

"It doesn't—" He cuts me off.

"It's pathetic."

He looks at me quietly, as if he's examining everything about me. It's a look I know well. It's how he was able to see right into me, and why I couldn't hide so well from him in school.

We stand in awkward silence for a few more seconds. And then he says, "I never expected to see you again. I always hoped I would, but I wasn't so sure I would."

"Really?" He's never called or emailed or written to me, and now he tells me that he hoped we'd meet again one day.

I'm not going to fall for that again. I strengthen my arms around my grocery bag. "It's been good to see you but I should go."

"Already?" He sounds disappointed.

"I'm in a rush."

"Stay another few minutes, please Megan." He almost reaches out to take my arm but moves his hand away before he touches me.

Stay a minute for what?

"Are you still mad at me?" he asks as if this has slowly dawned on him.

"Mad?" I've been busted. I force a smile trying hard not to make it so obvious, but I suck at hiding my emotions. "I'm not mad." I try to casually brush off the remark.

"Not that I blame you. You have every right to be mad."

"A note would have been nice," I say, with ice in my voice. "A simple note to let me know that you were leaving." He clears his throat, and I wonder if he's masking his guilt. "I understand your anger," he replies, guardedly. "But I'm happy that we've met now and hopefully I can explain."

It's too late for explanations. Tell that to the teen who wondered where the heck he'd gone.

I have questions for him. I want to know how and why he became a professor, but questions would lead to more questions. Through he seems eager to explain the past, that sliver of time is a place I don't want to dwell in. "It's not important now."

He clears his throat. Masking the guilt? "I'm really happy that we met again, Megan."

"Are you still teaching math?" I ask, even though I know.

"Applied mathematics and dynamical systems, neural and behavioural modelling, neuromorphic technology ... that's what I teach now."

He lost me at applied mathematics. This man has the face of a movie star, the eyes of a sinner and the body of an athlete and add to that, he has brains. Some people have all the luck, as Arla would say.

"Isn't that a big jump? From being a high school teacher to becoming a professor?"

"I went back to college and got more qualifications."

"I can't wrap my head around you being a professor."

"It's still the same me underneath."

"I'm not interested in what's underneath," I toss back, letting him know of the boundaries in place.

"I can't wrap my head around the fact that you're all grown up and ..." His eyes run down my length; he looks surprised as if he still can't take it in. "Things worked out for you. I hope they did. It looks like they did."

I nod. He has no right to know of my life story. That's not a privilege he gets to learn about.

"I tell you what feels strange," he says, scratching the scar along his jaw. "To be living in the same town as you."

I agree. It is one of the oddest things to happen to me in a long time. I've gone years without hearing his name, and then in the space of a month he's shown up on TV, he's in the press, he's a local hero and now he's here, in my life.

I lower my head, sensing an undercurrent to the polite outer façade of our conversation.

"Did things work out with your mom?" he asks.

As if he cares.

"They worked out." I glance at my watch. "I really must go." I'm suddenly aware of the time, and then slowly, the muted background noises of people walking past and clutching cell phones, having conversations, laughing. Even now, being with Lance Turner has the effect of tuning out everything around me, making it feel as if we're the only two people around.

"Goodbye, Lance."

"Goodbye?" A deep line forms between his brows. "So final?" His cool, calm demeanor slips.

"What did you expect? A hug and a kiss?" I snap. It's taken me a long time to put his ghost to bed, and I don't want to resurrect anything now.

"Do you hate me that much?" He looks like a wounded animal who's been dealt a near fatal blow.

"You leave town without saying a word, leaving me to deal with all the rumors and accusations and you expect me to be over the moon when you turn up eleven years later?"

I'm annoyed that I was so specific with the time. That I pinpointed it to eleven years.

Eleven years, four months and some days. Thankfully, I stopped counting the days a long time ago, but it doesn't bode well for my state of mind that I remember to the month.

"What accusations?"

I stare at him in disbelief. "What do you think?"

"But we never—"

I glare at him. "We never ...?"

"I'm sorry."

"I'm leaving. Please don't follow me." My voice is a little too loud, a little too stern, as if I've made a firm decision. I start to move away. "'Bye."

"'Bye, Megan."

LANCE

My excitement at seeing Megan now turns to a gnawing unease.

She hates me. Her words cut me like a blade. I didn't expect her to be ecstatic, but her anger surprises me.

I'm over the moon to see her again. I've never forgotten her and I've always wondered how she was. I've always hoped life turned out well for her.

My concern for a bright student led me down a path that was not of my choosing. I didn't intend for my feelings to become so intense, or for Megan to feel so much.

A casual observer might have mistaken Megan for being a teacher's pet. But to the rest of them—the Principal and the other students—it might have seemed like something else. Something wrong, and sleazy and taboo.

It was never any of those things. It was complicated, and though I'd never set out to intentionally cross a line, there were many times I knew I ought to pare back my friendship.

With her there had been no flick of the hair, no wide-eyed staring. No flirting. She barely batted an eyelash. She'd neither looked at me, nor shown any interest.

But something happened when we met in the library—which is when it really began. We changed from being just a teacher and a student to something more.

My mind is now a tangled web of memories from the past and the young girl Megan was back then; someone I never expected to see again, even though I always hoped our paths would one day cross.

And now they have.

I start my car with the weight of misery like a boulder over my chest. The girl she used to be is gone. She's still beautiful but the natural softness has given way to hardness.

I can't blame her. It was cruel what I did; leaving town

without telling her, and then never getting in touch to explain. There were many times, especially in the early years, that I wanted to reach out to her, to see how she was, to let her know it wasn't because of her, but I talked myself out of it at every turn.

I had my own problems to deal with. I convinced myself that Megan was better off without me. Nothing could ever come of it the way we wanted.

But meeting her now, is it too much to hope that life could maybe give us a second chance?

The audacity to hope she might be single, when I am so clearly not.

I should leave her in peace. I should.

CHAPTER FIVE

Eleven years ago...

LANCE

I*'m impressed.*

There aren't many of my students, the girls especially, who are interested in a career in physics or math or wanting to major in any of these subjects in college.

But Megan Summers does. She's a clever girl, but she worries me because her grades have been slipping recently, and if she doesn't get them back on track soon she'll risk her chances of getting into college.

I don't want to see a student with as much potential as she has, fail. "Can you come and see me at the end of the lesson?" I ask her, as I hand back last week's homework sheets. Her cheeks turn crimson, and she looks embarrassed. I could have sworn I heard her friend, the chatty, fidgety one she's always with, wonder out loud what I want.

I move on swiftly, hearing the snigger from her friend. I try to keep my distance, but I'm concerned. She'd started to doze off towards the end of our last lesson and I'm certain something is going on at home.

Why do these girls think that teachers are blind, dumb and stupid? That's one reason why Megan Summers is nothing like the others. She's sensible, hardworking and clever.

She has no interest in me. She's not batted her eyelashes at me, not even once. She hasn't flirted. She's barely noticed me.

She stays behind at the end of the lesson, looking flustered. "You wanted to see me, sir?" She clutches her folder to her chest. I close the classroom door and walk back, then lean against my desk. She does the same; arms folded across her chest, hugging the folders as if they are her comfort blanket, she leans against a student desk.

"What's going on?" I ask quietly.

"What do you mean, sir?" She hugs her books even closer.

"Your grades in the last few pieces of homework have slipped. I marked the last test you all did. You got 74% but you normally average around 92%. This isn't like you, Megan."

"It's been a tough couple of months," she says, finally. There's something in her words I can't put my finger on. Her face is tense, and her lips purse into a stiff line. I can't pry too much. There's a line in this student-teacher dynamic I can't cross. The snickers in class already tell me I'm dangerously close to crossing it.

At times I ask her to stay behind and collect all the papers. It's because I trust her, because she does what I ask quickly and efficiently. But I hear the snickers. The other girls don't like it. There's nothing to it. No reason they should be nasty, but I'm wary because these things can be construed differently.

"You're in danger of falling behind." She needs to know, because I don't know if anyone tells her, whether her parents even care. "You're a bright girl, Megan, and if you want a scholarship to go to college you can't afford to drop your grades. It's not just math. I've spoken to your other teachers and your grades are slipping across the board."

She looks at me in alarm. "You spoke to the other teachers?"

"Because you fell asleep in class during the last lesson." A student doesn't suddenly drop grades over a short space of time over a lack of sleep or partying too hard.

Her head lowers and she stares at her shoes. "I'm aware of it, sir, and I'm trying to get back on top." I notice her lower lip trembling. She seems fragile, as if that hard veneer she's always had is starting to crumble. This isn't the Megan Summers I know. "I'd like to help you."

"Why?"

"Because you're bright, and you can go places. You have a determination about you that's impossible to ignore. Tell me how I can help? Would extra homework help?"

"No, sir. I already have a lot of things going on, but I've got this. I really have." She seems desperate to leave.

"A lot of things?"

She glances at the door. "I have to go."

"I can revisit certain topics again, if there's anything you don't understand," I offer. "Anything that would solidify your learning. I only want to help you, Megan."

Her cheeks turn crimson. "Thank you, sir, but I know what I have to do. I've got all the textbooks and I will get back on track, I promise."

CHAPTER SIX

MEGAN

Sifting through the debris of my feelings for Lance Turner is like walking on the bottom of a river and messing up the sediment on the riverbed.

It's upset the buried past and brought up things that were better left untouched. Ever since he burst back into my life, I've become reeled into the obsessions that I was addicted to in my teenage years.

I blame Arla. It was her fault in that Math lesson all those years ago when she knocked the pencil shavings all over her notes. If I hadn't gotten angry, Mr. Turner wouldn't have heard the commotion and he wouldn't have gotten annoyed, and he wouldn't have told me off for making so much noise even though I wasn't the noisemaker.

Arla was.

I wouldn't have had to stay behind, or collect the

homework papers at the end of the lesson for him, after everyone else had left. And Mr. Turner wouldn't have apologized to me. I wouldn't have noticed the blue of his eyes, or the scar along his jaw. He wouldn't have taken an interest in my grades, nor cared that they'd slipped so much.

We might never have met at the library all those times, or gone out to have donuts; something a teacher and student would never have sneaked out of town for.

The lines between him being my teacher and becoming my friend wouldn't have blurred.

But more than that, I would never have turned to him in my hour of need.

I would never have gone to him that fateful night.

I blame Arla for all of it, so, I call her. "I saw Lance Turner."

"Who hasn't?" Arla shrieks. "You couldn't avoid the man if you tried. He's everywhere."

"I mean I ran into him, in person." The phone line falls silent as I sink down lower on the couch.

"You ran into him?"

"I was carrying groceries when the handle of my bag broke and my things fell out—"

"Your boobs?"

"My *groceries*." I roll my eyes. What planet is Arla on? "I dropped my bag and my groceries fell out and he got out of the car to help me."

"He got out of his car?"

"Yes."

"Getouttahere!" Arla yells. "Then what happened?"

"He came over and started helping me put things back. I was so embarrassed I didn't look at him at first. Then he said my name and I looked up. But I knew that voice already."

Arla squeals in delight. "And?"

"He's staring right at me. I swear it was like being back in the classroom."

"He never stared at any of us like that," says Arla. "What did you do?"

"I got my groceries together and walked away."

"You walked off and left him?"

"What was I supposed to do? I was at a crossing. Drivers were tooting their horns. It wasn't a convenient place to stop."

"Did you speak to him?"

"Eventually. He came looking for me."

I can tell Arla is grinning. "You knew he would."

"He didn't have to go very far."

"This is so romantic!"

"You'd think a bag of chips was romantic."

"Talking of chips, wait up," she says, and the line goes quiet. I wonder what she's doing. "Shoot," she says, returning.

"Where did you go?"

"To get chips. I'm ready. Tell me more."

"We got to talking, and I asked him about the shooting and his injury. He asked me about my job etcetera, etcetera."

I can hear Arla munching away. "Is he as gorgeous in real life as he looks in the papers?"

"He—" I can't bring myself to admit to it. "He doesn't look that different to when I last saw him."

"The man has barely aged," Arla agrees.

"He's got a few wrinkles and more silver greys but he's still in the same shape." Damn that man. He's all I've thought about ever since I saw him. And it all comes back. What he meant to me. How I'd fallen for him despite trying not to.

"Are his eyes still bright blue?"

I bite down on my teeth. "They didn't look so bright this

time." But they reminded me of a lake in summer. A shimmering, iridescent blue. I have never forgotten those eyes. Or this man. Or how he makes me feel. How he made me feel back when I was cared for. My breath stalls and grows uneven just thinking about him.

"Single?" Arla chirps.

"How should I know? Why would I care?" My voice wavers.

"Why would you care?" Arla picks up on the wobble. "He's in your head again."

"He is not!"

"This could be your chance to get together with him."

"Are you crazy?" I squawk. "I don't think of him like that anymore." The idea is insane, just like Arla. But the truth is, I can't stop thinking about Lance Turner even if I tried. My thoughts have wreaked havoc ever since I discovered he was here. My imagination has wandered down treacherous paths. In my daydreams, Lance is there, haunting and teasing me with possibilities I should not even entertain.

My family would hate me if I ever considered it.

"But you always said—"

"I was a stupid teen then, with a dysfunctional family. I would have been happy if a stranger gave me some attention."

"You are happy when a stranger gives you attention."

I scratch my throat. "I don't want complications, or baggage," I say in my defense. Arla doesn't like my short-lived, twenty-four-hour relationships. I don't like the word 'hookup'. I'm not seeking spiritual peace and love. I just want to feel desired and many men have satisfied that need for me.

"You were in love with him."

"I was not." I frown, relieved that we're having this conversation on the phone. I can't remember what I've told Arla now. Time has blurred the edges of the specific truth.

My family doesn't know the entire truth either, and it's better this way.

"You talked about him all the time. It was bad enough that you were both the talk of the school—"

"Nothing happened."

"Plenty happened in the classroom, even if you never so much as touched one another. We remember, Megan."

"It was all in my head. And I blame my teenage hormones. I needed some escape and Mr. Turner gave me that." Consumed by my misery, my angst, my familial drama, I'd poured out to her my fragile dreams of infatuation.

"But you're not in school anymore and you're older now and you said yourself you would—"

"I said a lot of things a long time ago." I'd been a tangled mess of nerves at the time. News that Mr. Turner had left the school spread faster than rumors about Tillie Mullins' sexual exploits. Tillie was the class gossip and Superbitch, the one who'd helped spread the lies when everything came to a head.

His departure devastated me. He'd used me. He'd abandoned me when I needed him the most, during one of the most traumatic times in my life and now his sudden reappearance affects me more I want to admit.

It wasn't only his looks. I never fell for them the way the other girls in school did. Girls constantly fawned over Mr. Turner but not me. No. Mr. Turner grew on me slowly.

I was in the town library, squirreled away in a corner in the math and science section when Mr. Turner showed up out of the blue.

He called out my name softly, but I heard him, I could recognize that voice anywhere. I remember turning around, my heart doing that crazy little thing it does whenever he is around me.

He wanted to know what I was doing there. It was late.

Sometime after eight and he commented on it. I told him I was studying for a test.

"In the library?" he asked, speaking in whispers. He seemed surprised that I was there at this time of night.

"It's quiet here," I whispered back. "Not now it isn't. Now that you're making all this commotion." I made a hand movement between us, but he moved closer. "Is there anything I can help you with?"

"I'm studying science today."

"In which case I most definitely can't help you."

We laughed. It wasn't funny, but the laughter broke the tension in the air. He hooked his thumbs into the belt loops of his jeans. "You understand the math, though. Your understanding of the concepts is solid. You'll be okay."

I got up and walked away, needing to put a book back on the shelf. He followed me. I could feel him behind me. The scent of his cologne wafting through the air. I lifted up on my tiptoes to put the book back but I couldn't quite slot it in place because the shelf was too high. He was so close behind me I could feel the brush of his body against my back. Towering over me, he pushed the book back into place, our fingers lightly touching for the briefest of seconds before he moved his hand away. But it had already branded a searing imprint on my skin.

I turned around, and he seemed caught off guard by the movement because we were almost flush, chest to chest. I could sense the warmth of his body, and smell his cologne again, this time stronger and more potent.

He took a step back, but our gazes held. It was too late to erase the moment and pretend it didn't happen. I think it was then that I felt it first. A tingling in my core.

His gaze dropped down to my lips, a move so sinful and

forbidden. To this day I can remember how my insides were in turmoil. I was dating Shaun, but my boyfriend didn't make me feel what Lance Turner did.

We made small talk, because neither of us wanted to move away. We spoke softer than usual, different than how we did in the classroom. Maybe because we were in the library and trying to be quiet, but it felt like we were co-conspirators, even then, that we were doing something mildly wrong. It was just a conversation, but his concern for me, and the subsequent reassurance that I would be okay was a reassurance I so badly wanted and needed.

In that instant, I knew that *he* was what I needed. I didn't want him to leave, and he didn't seem to want to move away.

An awkward silence filled the space between us, in between the high wooden shelves holding the musty books.

And that was how we began.

The struggle was so real back then, to hold the family together, to be a sounding board for my desperate mother, to be the one taking care of my sister and brother. All because father took an interest in one of his co-workers.

My mother was falling apart in front of us all, and I had to be strong for my brother and sister.

That's why I started going to the library more and more, and it soon became my escape.

After that, whenever I'd go to the library–because it was always quiet and easier to study there compared to my home —I would often see Mr. Turner.

Each time I saw him, it made me happy. *He* made me happy because he cared for me. He seemed genuinely concerned. He was the only one who cared for me.

I wrench myself away from the past before I sink deeper into a rabbit hole I can't escape from.

I need to focus on now. On me and what I want: to wean myself away from one-night romantic encounters and to focus on getting the promotion because that would give me more money and more responsibility. In turn, I would feel worthy.

I can't afford to let Lance Turner into my head, messing things up for me again.

CHAPTER SEVEN

LANCE

"Daddy bought it for you. Why can't you accept it graciously?" Vivian's voice nudges an octave higher, grating on my nerves even more.

I thank the universe that I'm on the phone and not having a face-to-face conversation with her. I'm in my car, having finished a session with the physiotherapist.

"Because I don't want it. I've never wanted your father to buy me anything," I snarl, trying to soften the anger in my voice. I can't help it. This woman has made my life a misery. She is everything I didn't want in a partner, and most of my married life has been spent with me trying to forget that I made a big mistake. But things are beyond repair now, and every interaction between us is filled with spite.

I've had enough of her controlling father. He's a wealthy businessman, and has provided his daughter with a life of wealth and privilege. Vivian has always had everything, and not known the value of anything.

She's a grown woman, a pampered woman whose father has set her up in a sprawling mansion in West Newbury. It was our marital home until I broke out and found freedom. My father-in-law has also made many provisions for his granddaughter, and I suspect he continued to give Vivian an allowance the entire time we were married and living together.

My in-laws couldn't have made it any clearer from the outset that my salary wasn't enough to support the lifestyle to which their precious daughter had become accustomed. I've always felt as if I wasn't enough. Not only because of Vivian, but because of her parents as well.

"My father insists on it!" she exclaims, as if it's nothing. "You can't drive the old stick shift with your shoulder injury. Just accept Daddy's gift and take the car!"

Screw her Daddy. I clutch the cell phone, flexing the fingers of my free hand. "I don't want it. I like the car I drive. It's safe—"

"Safe?" she laughs. "That pile of junk looks like it's going to fall apart anytime soon. Don't be so ungrateful, Lance. My father's only trying to help you. The car is here and all you need to do is drive it away."

That's one of the problems with Vivian. She doesn't stop. Jab, jab, jab, jab, jab. It's constant, the way she picks and picks until I give in, and I often do, out of sheer exhaustion, and because I want a peaceful life. I often gave in, which was why I stayed in the marriage way longer than I should have. The high point of my life and the marriage was the birth of Cassie.

"I'm happy with my pile of junk. I'm not coming over to the house because I don't want the car. 'Bye."

I throw the phone onto the passenger seat and start the car. My shoulder feels stiff sometimes, especially in the morning, but I'm doing the exercises and pray that it will fully heal. The shoulder isn't as bad as my sleep. In bed I constantly toss and turn and think about the shooting, about Heidi Byrne and her ex-boyfriend, the man who wanted her dead.

When I do manage to fall asleep, I wake up in the middle of the night, terrified, shivering. Sometimes the shooter doesn't shoot me, but kills Heidi. Sometimes, the bullet hits me in my chest.

Those are the nights I wake up with palpitations. I have to get up and walk around, and I try to watch TV or read a book. I can't shake it, this fear of doom and gloom. I'm not a man who is easily scared, yet this incident affects me more than I care to admit. The doctors advised me to get therapy to talk over what happened, but I don't need it. This will pass in time.

But on those nights when I awaken with dark thoughts, I often think of Megan, and how freaky it is that we both live in the same town. This is fated. Thinking of her calms me down. Memories of our past soothe me, until I remember how it ended. My mind goes back to that night.

That. One. Night.

There were times when I wished I'd been a stronger man, that I hadn't been tempted, and then when I left I should have reached out and explained.

Seeing her again has awakened something in me. Not many men get the chance to try again but she's back in my life again and I have a chance to set the record straight. She's angry with me, and I need to fix it but I don't know what to do.

Vivian calls me again, but I ignore it and drive to Megan's

place of work because it makes sense to. She needs to know why I left the way I did.

I lean against a wall and pretend to read a newspaper. It's a tactic which has worked and one which I've used successfully ever since the shooting incident catapulted me to unwanted fame. Like an ill wind, its brought me unwanted attention; students and other professors at the campus still stop to talk to me about it. When I go out people still recognize me even though the shooting is old news now. I am no longer invisible and I long for anonymity again.

I feel like a stalker standing outside Megan's place of work. Every so often I lower the newspaper, keeping an eye on the revolving doors of the building whenever someone walks out. I catch the eye of a group of women who gawk at me as they walk by, smiling at me. There's a flicker of recognition in their eager eyes. I push off the wall and walk away, not wanting to indulge in conversation.

That's when I catch sight of Megan in the distance, walking away with a man by her side. I rush after her, a hard knot forming in my gut as my gaze fixes on the guy she's with. "Megan?"

She turns around. "Lance?" I like the way she has her hair now. It used to be straight and silky before, and now it has a gentle wave in it. The schoolgirl is gone, and in its place is a grown-up beauty, looking as if she means business in her smart dark pantsuit.

"I'm sorry to interrupt you both," I say, sensing the tall, gangly guy's displeasure at my interruption.

"I'll see you back at the office," she tells him and he scowls as he walks away. "Are you stalking me?"

"I don't stalk."

"Then how do you know where I work?" Her voice is hard and unwelcoming.

"You told me where you worked."

She opens her mouth and groans. "Me and my big mouth."

I smile and am aware that I have less than a few seconds to get her attention. "I'm sorry for showing up like this but I had to see you."

"Why?"

"To explain."

"Explain what?"

"Why I left the way I did."

"That's not important. Not now." Her lips are set in a line, and her unsmiling face tells me this is going to be harder than I thought. I'm not one to give up easily.

"I want to."

"I don't *want* you to explain." Angry eyes glare back at me. She has the right to be mad at me, to hate me even. The Megan I remember was fragile, and vulnerable, and defiant all at once. She was a chameleon. Smart, strong, yet like a wilting flower. I was drawn to her, and I couldn't help myself. She was wise beyond her years, maybe being the oldest child in a dysfunctional family enabled that in her. But I'm not used to this Megan, the one who seems bitter and unwilling to hear me out.

"That may be but you're mad at me and you need to listen." I reach out for her arm, desperate to quell her rage, hating that she feels this way about me. She glares at me in disbelief.

"I *need* to listen? We're not in the classroom anymore, Mr. Turner."

"Lance," I say, remembering the classroom all over again.

"*Lance?*" She eyeballs me. "Just Lance?"

I clear my throat, preparing myself for a battle I don't want. I'm so happy to see her again, and she isn't. "I didn't mean to sound condescending. You're angry, justifiably so, and I need ... I *want* ... to tell you something."

"I'm over it now. Let it go."

"You don't look like you're over it." I refuse to give in. "You hate the sight of me. I don't want this bitterness between us."

"There is no 'us'. Why does it matter to you so much?"

"It would give me closure."

"*You* want closure?" she snorts, pinning me with a stern look. "This must be a joke. I'm not going to turn up on your doorstep at midnight in the pouring rain again, in case you're worried."

"I'd be happy for you to turn up at my doorstep." I've revisited those memories more times than is healthy. "You're pissed off, Megan. I know your moods."

She raises her chin and holds it there, her eyes burning through me, fiery, feisty. It puts ideas in my head. I remember her moans and mewls, the way she opened herself up to me.

"It's not good to delve into the past too much," she announces, completely oblivious to the internal hurricane that ravages through me.

"But you need to know so that we can move on."

She laughs. I cringe. She sees me as an old fool. "I *have* moved on."

I thought I had, too, but now that I've seen her again, I can't. She has stoked something deep inside me, a longing that I'd been forced to deny. She's stirred the deepest of my desires, something I can't move on from and now it has awakened again.

It's not closure I need as much as connection. Even now, talking to her, it's there—the invisible force that vibrates between us. "Give me this one chance to explain, and then I'll never hassle you again."

She seems to consider it.

"We could go somewhere for a drink," I suggest, before she comes up with a good reason to get away. "One drink and one conversation and you won't ever hear from me again."

How can she refuse that?

"Coffee," she answers.

Coffee, it is.

CHAPTER EIGHT

Eleven years ago ...

MEGAN

My sister's piercing shriek tears through the house.

"Meg!" Erica's voice is hysterical. "Come quickly! It's mom!"

I fly off the bed and race into the hallway. I freeze on the spot. My mom's lifeless body lies on the floor. Erica and Jensen are crouched beside her, crying.

"Mom, wake up!" Erica taps my mom's face, then prods her chest. Jensen hugs his knees, sobbing.

Erica glances at me, her face wet with tears. "Do something!" Her scream pierces through me. I rush to her side, noting the empty bottle of pills. Erica moves out of the way and I lift my mother's upper body.

"Mom? Mom?" I check her pulse. It's there. A sliver of hope worms its way into my body. It's faint, but it is there.

She's alive, and I see the rise and fall of her chest, but guilt now pours over me that this has happened. It's my fault. I'm the oldest and I should have seen this coming.

In the periphery of my vision I see Erica and Jensen huddling together, arms wrapped around each other. My heart breaks.

As if this family hasn't suffered enough. I wished I'd been the one to find my mother, not them. I should have paid more attention to my mother's moods. To her bouts of drinking, to her inability to get out of the bed after my father walked out.

"Mom! Mom! Mom, wake up!" I beg. Her eyes are closed, her mouth open. "Call 9-1-1!" I yell to my siblings. It feels as if the walls of the room have caved in around me. This is my fault. I've been so engrossed in studying for my final year exams, I missed this. I should have seen the warning signs: the wine bottles, the way my mother couldn't get out of bed, how she was constantly crying. How she fell apart after my father left.

A few hours later, I'm at the hospital. My mom is asleep. Her stomach has been pumped and she is resting.

I'm grateful for Aunt Cherie coming over to look after Jensen and Erica. She wanted to come to the hospital to see her sister, but I'm in charge of the family now, and it's my responsibility to make sure my mom will be okay. I need to be here, and someone needs to be with Erica and Jensen.

The nurse comes in from time to time and checks the monitors, then tells me that my mom will be okay. I've been sitting by her side for hours, trying to study math but the formulae and theorems aren't sticking. My brain is thick with fog.

"Try to get some rest," the nurse tells me. She looks

concerned, her soulful eyes somehow seeing deep inside me, as if she can see my pain. I manage a smile I don't feel

"I will." But I can't rest any more than I can study for my exam tomorrow. I've called Shaun many times, needing someone to lean on but he's not answering his phone. My best friend Arla is probably fast asleep, and I don't want to disturb her.

It's almost midnight and I feel more alone than ever. It leaves me with only one place to go to, with only one person to turn to. I kiss my mom on her forehead, and stroke her cheek, willing for her to get better, desperately wanting her to know that she is loved and needed by the three of us.

In the falling rain I run. The rain with all its wretched coldness soothes me, the water trailing down my face like fresh tears, soaking my clothes until they cling to me like cellophane.

It's wrong to do this, to go to him now, but I don't care. I can't feel. I can't think. Being with Mr. Turner makes sense in this wretched moment. By the time I arrive at his place, I am soaked through to the bone. I bang on the door, my hair falling over my face like wet spaghetti, my feet squelching in wet sneakers. I try to keep it together, I try to be strong, the way I tried for my siblings as I left them to ride in the ambulance to the hospital, cursing my father for walking so carelessly out of our lives.

Mr. Turner opens the door, his face immediately twisting with worry.

"I'm sorry." I can't stop shivering. My plans to look composed disintegrate. I must look like a wretched lab rat.

He steps out, takes my arm and pulls me gently inside, away from the rain. No hesitation, no questions asked. "What's wrong?" Concern etches the tiny wrinkles around his eyes.

"I didn't have anywhere else to g-g-go." I rub the wet

sleeves of my sweatshirt, and feel colder now that I've stopped running.

"What happened?" His hands frame my face for the tiniest of seconds, before he pulls away.

But I can't hold it in anymore. I can't be strong. I fall against his chest and put my arms around him, and then I sob uncontrollably as I fall apart. He holds me close, his hand closing around my head as he reels me in against his body. Chest to chest, his heartbeat rises and falls with mine. I can't get the words out. All I can do is cry. He doesn't press for information. He waits, his big hands firm against my back.

We've done something we've never done before, standing with our arms around one another, touching like this, our bodies pressed together. A boundary we've never crossed.

When I can cry no more, I stop and sniffle into his chest. Rain trickles down my back. He smells of wood. Of pine. Clean and fresh. I don't want to move from this safe harbor.

"Tell me what happened." He slips a finger under my chin, tilting my face up. Then he cups my face with one hand and wipes away the rain with the other. He gazes into my eyes intensely, and electricity shoots through my body, making me feel all kinds of crazy.

I open my mouth to say something but where do I start? A dull ache starts to build between my legs. I press my face against his chest again and take a deep inhale. It grounds me. I want to stay like this all night.

"You're soaked all the way through," he whispers, his voice soft like a lover's caress. The veil between the real world and ours lifts. He's not my teacher. He's a friend. He's someone who I can't stop thinking about. "Hey." He strokes my face softly. This is another first; his thumbs on my skin, something I have only dreamed about. I reach for his hand and hold his palm against my cheek.

Coming here is wrong, and falling into Lance Turner's arms is more wrong, and standing pressed against him feeling his hardness is forbidden, but my mind has already played out this scenario and after a day of heartache, I'll take all the wrongs just to be with him.

He is the one thing I need the most right now because he's the only one who makes everything better.

He cares for me. It's in the way his fingers wipe away my tears and in the way he holds me, so close that I've made his own clothes damp. "Tell me what happened, Megan."

"My mom..." Even saying the words, recalling the moment I saw her lying on the floor, when I'd feared the worst, it makes me burst into tears again.

"Megan," he coaxes, his voice so low I feel it in my chest rather than hear it. "Megan." He hugs me even closer, holding me tighter, making me feel wanted in all the ways my eighteen-year-old body needs to feel wanted and held.

"I have my math exam tomorrow," I whisper. "My mom took an overdose of pills and now she's in the hospital—"

"What?" His fingers caress my face, and down below a fire builds. I can't stop staring at his lips, and I want him to never stop stroking me. "Is she okay?"

And then, in between racking sobs, I tell him everything; that my aunt has come over to look after my brother and sister, and that I've been at the hospital by my mom's side, that I've tried to study but I can't take anything in. I sniffle again and burying my face into his chest makes heat course through my veins. He shifts, and his hardness pokes against me, causing my skin to break out in goosebumps.

I want to press against him. I want to grind my hips against him.

I want him.

But maybe I shouldn't have come here, because I've

overstepped a boundary and I'm in danger of going into no man's land. But the truth is the hurt in my heart is so deep and only this man can fix it.

Shaun isn't there for me much. I can barely get a hold of him. We've drifted apart without breaking up.

I examine Mr. Turner's face, and try to read his expression. Does he feel what I feel?

Before I can stop myself, I tiptoe up and press my lips against his. I mistakenly thought he'd been waiting for it, just like me, that he'd been desperate for this, but his hands go limp. He pulls away, steps back, then folds his arms.

He closes off to me. "We shouldn't..."

It throws me, losing his warmth and comfort. Getting back into reality. He doesn't mean what he says. I can tell by the hungry look in his eyes that he is torn. His words say one thing but his body says something else.

His hardness tells me all I need to know.

"I need you." I step towards him, because this is the truth. My heart and soul do need him more than I need air to breathe.

He seems frozen in place, and makes no effort to move away. Slowly I slip my arms around his shoulders, then snake my fingers around the back of his neck. I smell his desire, so potent, so heavy, so thick. "You've always been here for me, but tonight I need you to hold me." My mouth is barely an inch away from his and I can't stop myself from doing this.

In the middle of the crisis that is my life right now? It doesn't make sense, but I don't need sense. I need something to pull me away from the nightmare of my existence. I dart out my tongue and lick his lower lip.

He groans. His hardness teases and pokes, a symbol of the truth, of what he really wants. Empowered, I brush my lips against his, or maybe he tilts his head forward an inch. It's lost in a blur, who made the first move, and it doesn't matter because we both want this. Our lips mesh together and I am lost in a soft, wet kiss that grows deeper, more sensual and more sinful. Heat spreads through my veins, the promise of something more hangs in the air like a dandelion fuzzy waiting to take direction.

Our kiss lingers and time suspends. I forget who I am, where I am. I only feel, his lips against mine, his hands around me. And that is enough. It's all I want.

This is wrong, and yet it isn't. I press harder against him, my hungry body yielding to his hard one and wanting more than just a kiss.

"We... can't... Megan," he groans, pulling away slowly, as if it is torture. He has the haunted look of a God-fearing man who has committed a crime. "I'm sorry, I shouldn't have done that."

"You didn't." I swallow hard, my knees buckling, my brain short-circuiting. Waves pulse below my belly and fire pools between my legs. I'm desperate for comfort, for release, for Mr. Turner to be that release.

I unzip my sweatshirt, and I'm about to unbutton my shirt when his hands grab me. "Stop." His voice is strange. Thick. Strangled. "We can't do this."

"I want to."

"I can't."

"Please, Lance."

"It's Mr. Turner," he says, his voice hoarse.

"But I thought ..."

"You shouldn't have come here."

He might as well have slapped me. I step away, stumble almost, while an icy fissure forms in my heart. A cry chokes in my throat like a fist stuck there.

Hasn't he heard what I've been through? I'm wet and cold and drowning in misery.

I'm desperate.

I don't want to be alone. I want to feel something. "Please let me stay, at least until the morning. Please."

I take another step away from him, to let him know that I won't make any moves. I won't go there again, to that forbidden place.

Creases form along his forehead. His eyes take me in from top to toe. Desire paints a wretched picture over his face. My eyes lower and fall to the bulge in his pants.

"I'll get you a change of clothes, and you can sleep on the couch." But it's a while before he moves away.

CHAPTER NINE

MEGAN

I marvel at this surreal moment, that Lance and I are sitting across the table and reconnecting as if we are old friends.

Pouring sugar into my coffee, I stir it slowly before checking the time on my watch. "I don't have long."

"It's past six. Isn't it the end of your working day?"

"I've got things to do for a client, and it's going to be a late night at the office."

He looks disappointed. A fragile silence stretches out between us as if each of us is afraid to start talking first. Clasping his hands, he sits forward. He looks tired. Not as vibrant as he did the last time we met. He seems worn down, by life, by things I know nothing about and I am a little curious.

He's got a milkshake which he hasn't touched. He takes a long slow breath, looks uneasy, looks away momentarily before his gaze falls on me again. "It might have seemed to you that I vanished off the face of the earth—"

"You *did* vanish off the face of the earth. It didn't *seem* like it. You *did*." I lower my head, remembering that time well. Lance dropped me home in the early hours of the morning and I went straight to bed wearing clothes that clearly weren't mine. Arla heard the news about my mom from her mom who was a nurse working the shift at the hospital when my mom came in. Arla told Shaun and the two of them rushed to my house early the next morning.

By then, Aunt Cherie had left to go to the hospital, and I was rushing around trying to get Erica and Jensen ready for school. I was also panicking about my exam which was later that morning. When my friends arrived I was still wearing Mr. Turner's clothes. They didn't know that at the time but would find out a few days later when Mr. Turner arrived at my house to return my clothes. I was at school but Aunt Cherie answered the door and she accosted me when I returned home. Arla and Shaun were with me at the time. We'd had an exam, another one that didn't go too well for me, and the two of them were determined that we would study together. They were good to me, they were there for me, but Aunt Cherie mentioning that Mr. Turner had returned my clothes meant my little secret was out.

I insisted that nothing had happened, but my explanation wasn't plausible given the circumstances. Rumors had already gone around the school that Mr. Turner and I were 'close' and him returning my clothes was too much for Shaun to take. He was angry with me, and he didn't waste any time in ruining my reputation further.

"Megan?" Lance clicks his fingers in front of me, trying to get my attention. "You zoned out. Am I boring you?" He attempts a smile. I hate his smile. It's a cheesy lovely dovey smile that makes my insides turn to mush.

"You don't need to explain anything. It's been so long. What difference will it make?"

His face turns serious. "Are you afraid of the truth? That it might give you a reason not to hate me so much."

"I resent that you're here, taking up my time, demanding to see me and explain things that have no relevance in my life anymore." There's a wobble in my voice which I'm guessing he's picked up on because his shoulders relax. He sits back. "It's important you know."

I scowl and wish I hadn't come here. "I'm busy. I have two meetings tomorrow, and I have work to do."

"Then hear me out, just this once, and I'll be out of your life forever."

I fold my arms and slouch back against the cushioned booth, huffing quietly, willing him to hurry the hell up because this is torture, facing him and staring at his beautiful face. I try to keep my eyes from dipping to his chest and shoulders, but it's not easy. I'm aware of my deep attraction to him.

"You were in the middle of your exams, and there was a lot going on behind the scenes that you weren't privy to."

I jolt at this. "I suffered the humiliation and the rumors. Tillie Mullins had a great time making up stories. Shaun was no better. *I* had to deal with it all, not you. You went AWOL."

He swallows, and my gaze drops to his neck before rising to his lips which are pressed together. He looks guilty as hell. "Principal Fielding had spoken to me a few weeks earlier," he says, finally. "He gave me a warning, said he'd heard rumors."

"About what?"

"About us."

"But we were careful. We ..." I don't want to revisit that

time. We had started to be careful. We avoided talking much at school, but I'd see him at the library. It became our meeting place. Again, nothing happened. But it was illicit, and taboo, in a way that teachers who met their students in a place outside of school, outside of school hours, would be.

We didn't touch or hold hands, or do anything inappropriate. But we talked. Mostly about my studies, at least it always started that way. He'd ask if I needed help with anything, he was always eager to explain topics I was finding difficult. But after that, we'd talk, mostly about his life, his sister and his new niece. That had been all he'd shared. I'd found out that there was no girlfriend. He found out about my parents and the stress at home, and with my father gone, and my mother a mess, I learned to lean on him more than ever.

I studied in the library often, but knowing that he might show up at any time was always a thrill. Then somehow, we left the library and went to a donut place way out of town. He drove.

But who does that?

With a teacher?

And that's when things changed. Lance was a good listener, and he became my friend and my go-to when times were tough. He was always careful.

Once, right after we'd had donuts, he drove all the way to his place just to lend me a couple of textbooks. He told me to stay in the car, and refused when I asked if I could go in with him. Then he drove me back and left me at the library.

There was no impropriety then, just lingering glances, a yearning I found harder to hide. Shaun and I were very much off and on then. I can't remember if it was because I seemed to come alive at the mention of Mr. Turner, or if he got closer to one of the cheerleaders. It didn't matter.

I snap back to the present. "Principal Fielding gave you a

warning *weeks* before that night, but yet you chose to leave soon after. Were you worried that I could cost you your job?"

"It wasn't like that," he says.

"You could have said something to me. You could have told me before you left. You could have had the decency to explain why you were leaving."

"I didn't think it would be a good idea to see you, what with your exams going on, and given your home situation."

"You helped the rumors grow by returning my clothes while I was at school."

He looks away. "It didn't seem appropriate returning your clothes at school—"

"And you think giving them to my aunt was any better?"

"I told her I'd seen you standing by the bus stop in the rain soaked to the skin, so I gave you a change of clothes and drove you home. Your aunt told me that your mom was recovering in the hospital and that she'd be home in a few days' time. I thought it best to lay low."

"Lay low?" I hiss.

"You didn't need more complication in your life."

"Who were you to decide what I did or didn't need?" I snarl.

"I'm sorry I wasn't there for you, to take the heat. I wasn't thinking." He fixes me with an apologetic stare.

"Yeah, you left, unexpectedly, and without warning. You. Just. Left."

Like my father had.

"How is your mom now?" he asks, not answering my question. Probably because he has nothing else to say.

"She recovered, and we all lived happily ever after." My mom would be furious if she could see me now. Lance Turner's name is as bad as a curse word in our family.

I take a sip of coffee so that I won't have to meet his eyes.

It's unsettling, sitting here opposite the man who's consumed so much of my life by not being a part of it, a man I've built up into some mythical god and who, by his absence, has turned into something bigger than the man he is.

It's been emotional, a fantasy in my head, and I've often wondered if he has wasted as much time as I have in thinking about us. I try to tune out the fact that I'd become so emotionally embroiled in my feelings for him; that I'd stopped seeing him as my teacher, and instead started to see him as a friend.

I notice the scar along his jaw. It's still there, if a little fainter than I remember. Lance had told me how he'd gotten it while he was trying to save his younger sister from hurting herself. He'd been around ten years old, and was helping her to learn to ride a bike. It got to the point that she was confident enough for their dad to remove the training wheels and he'd been encouraging her to cycle forward and get over her fear of falling. She'd come towards him, then veered towards the fence. He rushed towards her, throwing himself in front so that she would hit him instead of the fence. She did, and fell with the bike, on top of him, the bell hitting his jaw hard and slicing it.

I still have unanswered questions. "Why didn't you ever call me? Did you not understand what had happened to my family? That's all we ever talked about. You always seemed to care, but the way you left, the way you never got in touch with me tells me they were just words. I didn't matter to you at all."

"That's not true."

"It is true. You knew where I was. I'm the one who didn't know where you disappeared to."

"I had to stay away. Megan. You know we couldn't be together."

Heat crawls along my cheeks when he says it like that,

bringing my past into my present and holding up a mirror to my advances that night. He doesn't need to remind me.

"Where did you go?" If he's ready to give answers, I want to know.

"To Nebraska."

So, it was true.

"I got a job out there." His words punch into my heart like a blow from a hammer. He'd moved halfway across the country in order to save his career and forget he ever met me.

"How nice for you. How easy for you to put Overton High behind you and move on."

"It wasn't like that."

He'd like me to believe that, but I won't fall for his words again. All that pretending to care for me, all that concern over my failing grades, none of it had been real.

Eleven years I've waited for an explanation, and he gives me this? A warning from the Principal, and what happened that night was enough for him to pack his bags and go.

I take another sip of my coffee and curse when the drink is too hot to finish quickly because I'm desperate to leave. "I need to go." I put the lid back on my coffee cup so that I can take it back to the office.

"Already? We only just got here."

I hear a low beep. It's my cell phone. "Sorry." One look at the caller ID tells me that it's one of my clients. "I have to take this."

He nods.

My client starts talking and I fumble around in my bag for a notepad which I set down on the table. "Just a moment." I rummage around in my bag some more. "I don't have a—" But Lance holds out a pen in front of me. "Go ahead." I take the pen and scribble down the details and ask a few more questions. I steal a quick look at Lance who watches me with a bemused look. "Great, thank you." I hang up.

This encroachment on my life with clients' calls coming at all hours is a high price to pay. I need to find a better balance, to not be so fast to respond to client calls. I need to defer and delegate, but I can only do that when I reach the next rung on my career ladder. I apologize to Lance for the intrusion, then check the time. "I must go. I didn't realize I'd been here that long."

"But I haven't finished." He grabs my hand, as if he doesn't want me to get up. "Wait, Megan. Please." It's the same plea I heard in his voice the last time. I move my hand away, determined not to give in. "We're done here."

"You haven't heard all of it."

"I've heard enough."

"My sister died," he cries. The shock of his words hits like a wrecking ball. "Anna."

His little sister that he helped teach how to ride a bike.

"What?" Horrified, I slump back against the booth, my fingers spreading like a fan against my breastbone. "Your sister?" I pray I've misheard.

"They were in an accident. A pickup truck collided with an eighteen-wheeler on the highway and my brother-in-law, Brett, couldn't stop in time. Their car hit the collision head on. My sister didn't stand a chance. Brett was in a coma. Luckily, their daughter Sarah had been at home with Brett's parents who'd been visiting. Sarah was only a baby, not even a year old at the time, and my parents flew out to Nebraska and both families rallied around but everything fell apart when Anna died.

"She—" I can't say the word.

Lance scratches the lid of his milkshake cup. "I had to be there for Brett and Sarah."

Shivers roll all over me. I reach for his hand. "I'm so sorry." Something melts inside me. "Nobody ever said a word about it. I never knew."

"Principal Fielding had already given me a warning. He'd told me he didn't like what he was hearing and to watch out." Lance wipes a hand across his face. "I didn't leave because of my job, or because of the rumors. I didn't leave because of what happened between us that night. I left because of the accident. Because my sister died."

I thought he'd left me to save himself, but he'd left to go to his family, and he'd stayed because of the tragedy. All that time I'd assumed he'd left to protect himself, worried that somehow the word would get out about us. I believed he was protecting himself.

"I hadn't intended to leave. That night ... I shouldn't have... but ..."

"I tempted you. I couldn't help myself." I make my confession in a lowered tone.

"I couldn't have kept away from you. I couldn't have stopped myself. I wanted you, I did, because my feelings changed the more we got to know one another. I tried to keep my distance but then ... that night happened." He looks like a man racked with guilt.

I shake my head. "You remember how it happened, don't you?"

"I can't ever forget it."

"Then you should remember that it was me, not you." I'd been a young girl desperate for connection. He's quiet, cut off from me. It doesn't seem right to dwell on that night. "You left, and then?"

"With news of the accident, I rushed to be with them, but when Anna died, it seemed like the perfect solution to stay there and help them cope. How could I not be there for my niece? She was only a baby."

How selfless of him. "Your sister would have been so proud of you." I choke up just thinking about it.

"We helped as much as we could. Sarah was very young and she missed Anna so much. It was difficult to settle her and take care of her, but we managed. Brett was in a coma for a month. It was touch and go. I hadn't intended to stay there forever, but within a week of Anna's death, it was obvious that my parents couldn't look after Sarah on their own even with Brett's family helping. We did the best we could but there's no replacement for a mother."

At last I understand. "How is your niece now?" I whisper.

"Like any other young child on the verge of becoming a teenager. She's fine. She was too young to understand the gravity of her loss. In time, Brett recovered, but his parents couldn't stay there forever. Neither could mine. They all returned home once Brett was released from the hospital, but I stayed on. Anna and I were so close. She was my baby sister. I felt responsible for her child, for her legacy. It was heart breaking to see Sarah and to know that she would never know her mother. Something like that changes you, it wasn't only the way Anna died and the tragedy of it all, but the real sadness was in the day-to-day, of knowing she wouldn't be around to see her daughter grow up, and would never know what she had left behind. That she'd never see the milestones of her daughter taking her first steps and ..." His voice dies to a whisper. "I wasn't in the right frame of mind to contact you. I couldn't do it. I couldn't deal with that, as well as with things happening in my own family. I meant to, but I couldn't, so I didn't. We managed to get through those early dark weeks, and I resigned after Anna's funeral. A new life for me in Nebraska beckoned."

I look down to find our hands are joined together on the table. I don't pull mine away because I can see the suffering this man has endured. "You should have told me." My voice is croaky. "One phone call is all it would have taken. I could have tried to help you. I could have been there for you like you'd been there for me."

"How could I have told you?" he asks, our fingers still touching. "You had your own set of problems. It wasn't the right time. It took months for Brett to get better and then I thought you'd be off to college and that you'd be starting over. You would forget about me. What we had back then was a moment, Megan. I got caught up. You did too, maybe, and then it passed. You understand that, don't you?"

It hadn't been like that for me. If he thought it was a moment, then the moment had dragged on for me. I'd been caught up in it for years. No way could I now bring myself to tell him that he'd left me broken. Feeling abandoned and unwanted. It confirmed to me love is ugly, and hard and twisted.

There's no point in me telling him that my mother recovering was the start of my problems. That my father never came back. That I never went to college but took a year out and worked. That it was up to me to keep the family together while my brother and sister went to school. I can't tell Lance any of this because it would make him feel worse than he already does.

"Isn't it strange how we've ended up in the same place?" he asks.

I stay silent.

"Who's the guy? The one you were talking to?"

"Someone from work. Why?"

"No reason."

"Thanks for the coffee." I move my hand away. "I really must go."

"Don't be like that, Megan."

"Don't be like what?" My cheeks heat up at the way he stares at me, and deep down inside my body turns fluttery.

"Cold and distant, like I can't reach you."

"Reach me?" I ask, curious, then jump at the sound of a beep from my cell phone. It's a text from Preston. "Drinks," I groan. I'd forgotten.

"Drinks?"

"Work drinks."

"You said you had a late night at the office."

I notice the tightness around his eyes, the crinkly wrinkles that fan out from the corners. "I do, but there are work drinks later. I was going to grab a sandwich. I haven't had lunch, unless you count a bar of chocolate as lunch."

"You shouldn't skip lunch," he tells me. Something of the old Mr. Turner returns with those words.

"You always used to tell me," I reply, remembering.

"That's because it annoyed me, the sight of so many pencil thin schoolgirls going without meals. '*Not hungry, don't want to eat,*'" he bleats, making a pathetic attempt to mimic a young girl's don't-care-attitude.

I stand up. "I'm grateful for your ..." The exact word eludes me. Honesty? Advice? Guidance? What? I hold out my hand for him to shake.

"Shaking hands? Is this what we do now?" He expresses surprise but takes my hand anyway and gives it a firm shake. "Can we meet again?"

Anticipation thrums through my body. He wants to meet again. So, naturally, I shut it down. "I don't think it's a good idea."

"You're very cautious."

"I'm not a risk-taker." I want my life to be safe and secure.

"It must be part of the job."

I shrug. It's better to leave things where they are. My cell phone beeps again and it's another text from Preston. "Thanks for the coffee."

"Is he your boyfriend?"

It's a direct question, asking something so personal. "Would that bother you?"

His eyes glitter like hard granite. "What do you think?"

CHAPTER TEN

Eleven years ago...

LANCE

If I'm not careful, Megan's going to get me in trouble. It's bad enough Fielding has his eyes on me.

I shouldn't be doing this. I should tell her to leave, but I can't. Her mother just took an overdose, and her father left home months ago. This girl is broken, fragile, and she's come to me.

For help.

Not for sex.

Fuck.

I rifle through my closet picking out a pair of tracksuit bottoms and a sweatshirt that shrunk in the wash.

These will still be too big for her, but she needs to get out of those wet clothes.

I rush back, wanting to get this over with, so that I can retreat to the safety of my bedroom and jerk off in peace.

I knock on the door. "These might fit you—"

Fuck.

She opens the door and she's naked. There's a sheen to her skin, the damp, the rain, her nipples are like pink bullets.

My cock springs to life. I try to look away, holding my arm out to hand her the clothes. "Don't ..." Strangled words die in my throat. She takes the clothes, then takes my hand and puts it to her breast. I groan.

"What are you doing?" I hiss. She's tormenting me and I can't hold it in any longer.

"You're the only one who makes me feel good. You make me happy. You're the only one who makes me want to live."

I snap my head towards her. "You haven't ..." The thought of her wanting to end her life is too much to bear.

"No. But sometimes, the thought crosses my mind. I would never do anything silly, though. I have my family to think of."

I don't even know I'm doing it until she moans, until the nipple I'm rubbing my finger over peaks to a hardened tip.

"I just want one night where I can forget who we are. One night where we can lose ourselves in each other."

"We shouldn't."

She reaches down and grabs my cock through the fabric of my sweatpants. It's enough to light the dynamite stick.

I pull her to me. My hands rake all over her body as I kiss her. She groans and moans and that's when I hitch my hands under her thighs and pick her up. She wraps her legs around my waist and with my tongue still down her throat, we finally get the connection we've been starved for. She tastes sweet and soft. I don't want to come up for air. And her moans, her soft little hands skate around my neck and face, as if she can't get her fill of me, as if the access to this new way of touching and being is too much. We kiss as if this is the only time we will have. It is.

I throw her onto the bed as if she's an electric shock that could be the death of me. But she stares up at me with mischief in her eyes.

Lust teases me as I stare down at her pert, smooth, toned body. She's naked, and beautiful, and I am so aroused. I reach and pull down my pants.

She spreads her legs, hitches herself further up the bed so that her head is now on the pillow and she's in the center of the bed, Ready for me to fuck her.

What am I doing?

I can't.

We can't.

"No one needs to know." She lifts her foot and presses it to my shoulder. And in the lifting of it, I see her glistening pussy. It's enough to get me on my knees and plant my face between her legs.

She's dripping wet, the smell of her arousal speaks to the most primal of my senses and my cock hardens even more. I devour her, feasting on her as if she's the most delicious thing I've ever had.

Her legs give, falling apart at the knees, and her back arches. She moans again and I thrust my tongue inside her.

CHAPTER ELEVEN

MEGAN

"His sister died?" Arla asks. A gasp follows.

"Yes, and his brother-in-law was in a coma. It was a bad car accident. They had a young daughter but, luckily, she wasn't with them."

Arla looks distressed. "That's so sad."

"Lance said she hadn't even turned one yet." Even thinking about it now makes me sad; I haven't been able to get it out of my mind and I asked Arla to come over because I needed to tell someone, because the weight of his tragedy is so heavy.

I feel distraught for Lance, for what he's been through. All this time I've blamed him for abandoning but the real reason is so sad. I feel like a whiny fool.

"It's Lance now?" my friend asks, her tone playful.

"We're not in school now." We're adults now. Our status and age gap no longer matter. Or get in the way.

"That poor man."

I've tried to imagine what it would be like to lose one of my siblings, but the thought is too dark, too painful to hold. "I had no idea what he'd gone through at the time."

"How could you have? We were knee-deep in exams," says Arla. "And your mother had gone and taken an ... I mean, she was ill, and in the hospital. Your dad had left you and things were hard for you."

"True." My world had crashed to pieces but spending that night with Lance had given me a few hours away from the ugliness of my life. He'd made me forget. Now that I know the truth, a heavy weight has been lifted from my chest because up until then I'd felt abandoned, discarded.

Used.

I thought he'd left because he wanted to forget about me, but now I know that he didn't desert me willingly, that maybe he wanted to be with me, and that he, too, might have entertained the idea of a future together.

I've held so much resentment for him over the years, for him taking away the promise of what might have been. I hated him for not being there, I hated him when Erica and Jensen would come home upset. I didn't have to suffer the rumors for too long because I left school that summer, but my brother and sister were teased all the time, and my mom hated the things they were telling her.

Only Lance and I know the truth.

That one night, that one time, gave me a memory I've held onto forever. A scorching, steamy, sexy memory I turned to many times over; a memory as vibrant and as real as the night it happened.

Lance was the older and more experienced man. He was the best I'd ever had, not only then—I was so naïve and sexually inexperienced save for Shaun's fumbling attempts—

but even now, in my adult years. Maybe I've held onto the memory of that night and immortalized it, and have turned Lance into some sort of God-like Svengali figure, made even more potent because he left soon after.

One truth remains, I've never had anyone work magic with his tongue the way Lance Turner did.

"At least now you know why he never got in touch with you again," says Arla, her big eyes sparkling with excitement. "Mr. Turner had his own problems to deal with."

I refill our wine glasses. "We've already established that."

"But imagine if that tragedy hadn't happened," Arla continues, "the two of you might have ended up together. You might even have had babies and—"

"It was a high school crush." I fix my gaze on my deluded friend. "It was nothing more than that." My guilt makes me look away. I harbored ideas as crazy as that. The possibility of a future with him wasn't so fanciful. We could have made it happen. He liked me, he wanted me, he needed me as much as I needed him.

"You talked about him for years afterwards—"

"That is not true." A year, maybe, tops.

"He was all you ever talked about. You were so angry that he'd left—"

"Because I flunked my exams."

My friend eyes me pointedly. "I don't recall you ever complaining about his teaching. I still don't understand why you went to him that night, when you could have come to me."

"It was late at night."

"That didn't stop you from going to him," Arla retorts.

"He was a good friend to me by then. Someone older, wiser, someone responsible. A caring grown-up. I needed that. My own parents had failed so miserably."

"You've always denied it," says Arla slowly, "And I've never pushed it because it was a traumatic time in your life but ... something did happen. It doesn't make sense that you'd go to him so late, and then a few days later he brings back your clothes."

I huff out angrily. "I've told you before. I was soaked. He gave me a change of clothes. We talked. He knew about the situation at home. I used to talk to him about it."

"And you couldn't talk to me?"

Her refusal to give this up is beginning to grate on me. "He was worried about my grades, and it was just easier to talk to him." I take a sip of my wine, still thinking about what Lance told me earlier. I take another sip, because his explanation changes the landscape of my past. "All this time I thought it was his guilt which drove him away. I thought he felt guilty about what we'd done—"

"What had you done?" Arla leans towards me, her mouth agape and staring at me with new eyes, as if she's reassessing everything she's ever known about me.

"What *he'd* done," I say, quickly, scrambling for an answer. "Trying to help me all the time, and always being concerned. After the warning from Principal Fielding—"

"He was warned?"

"There were rumors flying around the school," I remind her. "Tillie and the other girls—"

"Who all wished he'd noticed them," adds Arla. "Mr. Turner only had eyes for you."

"That's not true. He helped me."

"He liked you."

"I was falling apart."

I shift uncomfortably, then lift my glass to my lips. While it has been liberating to discover the real reason Lance left, my thoughts are once again in more turmoil where he is concerned.

"At least tell me that you shared a kiss that night?" Arla begs, giggling. Her cheeks flush as she clasps her wineglass. "What I wouldn't give to have his lips on my—"

"Nothing happened," I state firmly. "He's a very noble man."

I should know how far I had to go to break down his resistance. I made it impossible for him to resist me.

"And the clothes?"

"I've already explained about the clothes."

"Did he see you undress?" Arla asks, grinning like a naughty child who's said something provocative.

"No. Don't be silly. Can we stop talking about this now? Otherwise I'm going to bed, and you can see yourself out."

"Are you going to see him again?" Arla breaks off a chunk of chocolate from a huge bar.

"Why?" But I haven't been able to stop thinking about him.

The piece of chocolate between Arla's fingers hovers in mid-air. "You haven't stopped talking about him, is why."

I open my mouth in protest, consider my friend's words, and know that she's right. I've been talking about Lance Turner for most of the evening. So what if he's fourteen years older than me?

"What are you going to do about it?" Arla persists.

"Nothing."

"But he bared his heart to you. He told you his tragic story. It should have moved you. Aren't you moved?"

"I am moved," I reply, haughtily. "I'd have to be a statue not to be moved, but what am I supposed to do?"

"What do you want to do?"

I've been wondering that myself for the past few days. I

have something of his to return. The pen he lent me the last time we met. It's an expensive one, not a Bic which can be easily replaced.

It would be an excuse to get in touch with him again.

"What have you got to lose. He's hot, he's older, wiser, and he's back in your life. What are the chances that of all the places he could live in, he's here, in this town, near you? Surely even you must know that means something. This is fate!"

"You are such a delusional romantic. I can't be with him."

"Why not? This man is a keeper."

"He's old."

"He's better looking and fitter than some of the losers you end up spending the night with."

"I am a woman of needs."

"You're a loose woman."

She's right, and I don't want to be so reckless. I'm trying not to be so reckless. It's a good thing that I have so much pressure in my job and that I'm competing with Preston. I have to be on the ball, alert, at my best. Still, it irks me when Arla calls me out on my sexual habits. "You're supposed to be my friend."

"Mr. Turner would be good for you, now that you're older and supposedly wiser."

But my family would hate it, for one thing. My mom even to this day hates any mention made of that man, and Erica and Jensen have forbidden me to ever bring up his name.

"You're not going to let this go, are you?"

"You're a grown up now," Arla continues, setting down her empty glass. "You get to make your own rules. Principal Fielding doesn't get to set boundaries for you anymore."

CHAPTER TWELVE

LANCE

"What did they want?" Lesley asks as I walk into my office and collapse into my chair.

Her office is directly opposite mine, and we see one another daily, even if it's just to wave across the hallway. She usually has her door open, as do I. It helps, especially when it comes to young female students wanting to seek my help on something.

I've learned to be cautious.

Lesley is the only person here that I feel close enough to, that I confide in. She's older, much older, and she'll be retiring soon.

I will miss her.

She welcomed me into this department. Academia can be cutthroat. Nobody thinks of it like that, but Lesley is wise and gracious, and she took me under her wing from the start.

I trust her, and so I tell her why the police wanted to see me.

"It's not how it was, the shooting," I say, ripples of tiredness coursing through me. I've been interviewed but I'm not worried because I have nothing to hide, but still, the news is unsettling.

"What do you mean?" She looks concerned and gets up to close the door. "What do you mean it wasn't how it was? Stop talking in riddles, Lance."

I sigh loudly. "The shooter wasn't after Heidi. He was after me."

Lesley blinks three or four times, processing this news. "What? Why?"

"Because he thought that his girlfriend and I were together."

She gives me that look. The stern grandmotherly look would make me shrink in my seat, if I were guilty. "Lance ..."

"Of course we weren't. She's my student."

"Did you help her?"

Her line of questioning annoys me. Lesley should know better. "Just like I help any other student who comes to me seeking help."

Lesley scrubs her forehead as she paces the room. "I've always told you to be careful."

"I am. Always. Why do you think my door is always open?"

I am all too aware of the hormones flying around as far as my young female students are concerned. Years later I have the same problem. It still hasn't stopped. I'm in the wrong profession; I love to teach, but the admiration from some of my students makes it a chore.

"You should have false teeth—stained and yellow—and maybe get one of those prosthetics which make you have a great big beer belly. I have a friend whose grandson works in the makeup department at his college. Want me to have a word?"

"You might have to," I tell her.

"Did you give her preferential treatment?"

"I told you, no. She was coming to me for help, and I honestly don't know why her ex would implicate me or why he would want to shoot me. There was never anything more."

"More?"

Like it was with Megan. I took an interest in her because I wanted to help her. She looked so lost and vulnerable, like she was drowning in a sea of hopelessness. "I was careful not to become her friend," I clarify. It perplexes me. When the police told me the news it hit me like a bullet.

"You could have been killed. You have a daughter to think about."

"I know." The shock of the news hasn't quite sunk in that I was a target, not a hero. The alleged so-called hero who saved a girl from a bullet, and now it turns out I was the intended target. The police wanted to know if there was anything inappropriate between me and the girl.

I denied it. There was nothing. She would have said the same.

"Why would her boyfriend know about you?" Lesley asks.

"He's not her boyfriend. He's her ex."

"But how does he know about you enough to want to put a bullet in you?"

"I don't know. Maybe she mentioned me to him a few times. I don't know."

"Oh, Lance." When she looks at me, Lesley's eyes are full of pity.

Will this come out in the press? I hope not. The shooting was a while back and I'm hoping people will be sick of it and in time it will all be forgotten. The girl lived. I lived. End of story.

"There are farewell drinks next week, for Professor Coyle," Lesley says. "Are you going?"

"I'm not sure."

"Do you have Cassie?" she asks.

"No, but I might go and see her. It's not my weekend, but Vivian doesn't mind if I spend time with her on 'her' weekend." Cassie's feeling a bit insecure every time I leave her. She's scared I'll get shot and will die. It kills me that this fear is already planted in her little mind.

"Is Cassie okay?" Lesley's eyes shine when talking about my little girl. She has grandchildren and she loves them. She loves my Cassie, too.

"I'm worried about her, but I think she's going to be fine."

"Is Vivian still trying to take care of you?" There's a mischievous glint in her eyes. She knows about my 'marriage'.

I don't even bother giving her an answer.

CHAPTER THIRTEEN

MEGAN

I don't want Lance to get the wrong idea, but I need to see him to return his pen.

I call the college where Lance works and ask to be put through to the Department of Mathematics.

How can he get the wrong idea? I'm only returning his pen, but the quiver in my stomach belies my calm outward exterior.

"Lance Turner?" the receptionist asks. "Putting you through."

I bite my lip, anxiety coiling through my body as I fiddle with my earring.

"Lance Turner's office." A woman answers, in a sing-song voice, and it completely throws me off guard.

"Uh." I'm startled to silence. "Uh, I was hoping to speak with Lance Turner. Is he there?"

"He went home earlier. Don't tell him I was in his office."

I laugh and assure the woman that I'm not about to tell Lance any such thing. "Uh. I-uh, I have something of his that-uh, uh… I need to return … uh … his … uh … pen." I seem to be unable to string together a sentence. I was calm and collected when I was a student. As a grown woman I'm falling apart and getting ridiculously tongue-tied and it's not even him I'm talking to.

"*You* have it! He was complaining about it going missing the other day."

"I forgot to give it back."

"You can call him on his cell phone. I'm assuming you're not one of those blood sucking reporters? If you have his pen, you can't be. He wouldn't let any of those people within a couple of meters of him."

"Uh—" I bite my lip again, feeling embarrassed by my lack of composure and for using Neanderthal grunts as a form of communication.

"Do you have his number?"

"Uh, no." I don't want his number. I really don't. That would make him think I'd deliberately called his college to get it. "I can call back another time."

"It's up to you but he's in and out at different hours. It might be better if you just call him direct."

I'm about to protest but the sweet lady at the other end rattles off Lance's cell phone number. I hastily write it down, before thanking her and hanging up. I stare at the number before me. It's a direct link to him. Shivers scurry along my spine. My nervousness takes me off guard because I don't understand it.

I twiddle the pen around in my hand. I've read the inscription many times. "Love, Anna." His sister. This pen has sentimental value. No wonder he was complaining about losing it.

I make the call and hold my breath, which doesn't help the way my stomach is churning. "It's me, Megan," I announce when he picks up.

"Megan!" His voice is a joyous exclamation, like he's incredibly happy to hear from me.

"I have your pen."

"I know."

"Oh." I'd assumed, from the way that his friend mentioned it, that he'd been looking for it. "Why didn't you call me to get it back?"

"I didn't have your number, but I do now."

"You could have stalked me at work like you did the last time."

"You didn't like me stalking you," he reminds me.

"You're admitting that you did stalk me that last time?"

"I wanted to see you." His voice loses its playfulness. There is meaning behind those words. Meanings I could project into them. He. Wanted. To. See. Me.

I have pleasured myself at night since we last met. His voice, his face, him in my life; it was enough to get me to do that. I clear my throat, hoping to clear my mind of its thoughts. "I read the inscription."

He's silent.

"You're not in a hurry to reclaim it?" He had a good excuse to seek me out, but he chose not to. The thought grates on me like a fingernail on a blackboard. Maybe this is all in my head. Maybe he has a girlfriend. Maybe he isn't interested in seeing me.

He doesn't feel the way I do.

There's me thinking I have to keep this man at bay in case I get reeled into another attraction to him, but there's no danger of that because he's not interested in me.

What made you think he would be?

"I would have gotten it back, eventually. It was in good hands."

"Well, I have it." I dangle the suggestion like a winning lottery ticket.

Come and get it.

"Do you want me to come and get it?" he asks. "Or you could drop it off ..."

A part of me is tempted by the idea of going over to his place and seeing him again. I don't need to keep this man at bay, because he's not interested in me otherwise he would have used the pen as an excuse to see me. "I can come by quickly and drop it off," I offer. "If you give me your address."

"Do you have a pen?"

"I do now."

We giggle, and a tingling feeling spreads all over me. Excitement and anxiety bunch together into one big lump in my stomach.

"Jamaica Plain?" I ask, staring at the address I have scribbled down. "You're not far from me. I'll see you in ten."

"I'll be waiting." His words are a promise that Lance Turner is waiting for me. That I am going to his place to see him. That we will be together again. A quiver of excitement shoots through me.

A short while later, I'm outside his door and I'm reminded of how different it is compared to that last time when I'd been a scared and distraught schoolgirl, soaked to the skin, my world collapsing around me with my mom lying in the hospital.

I ring the doorbell but then hear his voice, loud and angry, on the other side. My nerves tense up, like violin strings pulled taut.

"No comment," he growls, opening the door, his face twisted with anger. As soon as he sets eyes on me, his expression softens and he beckons me in. "Why can't you people stop hounding me?" His nostrils flare. "I have no comment to make, and I don't do interviews."

I walk in and glance around, noting the bare walls and sparsely furnished interior. I steal a sideways glance at him. He's in dark denim trousers and an open neck checked shirt, looking just like I imagine a hot professor would look.

He's still as sexy as ever.

And he still has an effect on me. I'm supposed to be stronger than this. No sooner have I stepped inside than I start to feel nervous about being alone with him. My eyes rake down the length of him, taking in his tight, lean build, his wiry forearms that I'm itching to kiss.

"Please don't call here again." He slams the phone down. I giggle at his politeness.

"What's so funny?"

"You. Trying to be rude."

He throws his hands up in exasperation. "I wish they'd find another story to write about."

"Reporters?"

"Goddamn everywhere. Not a single day goes by where I don't get hassled by these morons. Not a single day."

"You're the hottest new hero," I say, rambling off a headline I remember reading. Then I blush, because he looks at me a moment longer than is comfortable.

We eye one another like mistrusting strangers. Maybe he's trying to reconcile the person I am now with the high school student I was then. I did this the first time I saw him, and now, I just see *him*. Not as a teacher or a professor, but just as him. I don't jump back to the past because that is not who we are now. I want to forget that we were forbidden.

My mind tries to connect the dots and show me that he is a possibility now, that he is not forbidden any more.

"I did what anyone else would have done."

"Take a bullet for someone? I don't think so." Of all the things he is, Lance Turner is a man who always does the right thing. He did it the night of my mother's suicide attempt, he'd done it for his niece, and he did it for the student he saved on the campus.

The man is a guardian angel.

"Anyone would have done it," he insists, his tone nonchalant.

I don't agree. "No," I whisper. "They wouldn't have." Why am I whispering? Is it because I don't trust my voice to not waver? Because the air feels thicker, the room warmer. I become aware of my skin starting to heat, and my desire to take off my coat becomes ever more pressing.

"If someone came running towards you, and behind them was a crazy guy with a gun, wouldn't your first instinct be to protect them?" he asks, as if what he did was the most normal way to react.

"I would think of my own safety first," I say slowly, considering the scenario. "It's a basic human instinct to want to survive."

A flash of pain flickers across Lance's face. He seems to be reliving the moment. "I saw the fear in her eyes," he tells me, as I see the anguish on his. "It was one of the most wretched things I've ever seen." His face turns ashen. "It was raw fear. She looked like a hunted animal, as if she knew that this was the end, that she was going to die. I wasn't going to let her."

He runs a hand through his short hair, the color draining from his face fast. Then he closes his eyes. "I can still see her face, and I can still feel her collapsing into my arms." His eyes open. Dark blue orbs of anguish fix on me. "I saw the rifle, and all I could think was that she couldn't die. She was so young."

He has a faraway look as he speaks, and I wonder if he's

thinking about Anna. I move towards him. "Lance." I take his hand, my fingers instinctively stroke the back of it, trying to comfort him. His skin is harder than I expected, his hand big and smooth. Protective. I felt protected that night when he held me. "You saved her life. You should be proud of yourself." I take a few steps towards him wanting to take away the pain I see in his expression.

There is a moment of silence and I have the chance to back away, but I don't. My heartbeat quickens as we stare at one another, the way we're standing, it's eerily similar to that of eleven years ago.

I would give anything to know what he is thinking. But then his eyes fall to my lips and heat snakes around my body, twisting and coiling its way into my secret crevices. A throbbing sensation starts low in my belly, stretching to the place between my legs. I hunger for his touch. I crave for his hands around me. I want him to hold me like he did before.

He licks his lips, and I feel the pull again. It's a spidery, sensual, invisible yearning that only this man can invoke in me. My heart hammers away in my chest. My knees are like jelly. My breasts tingle and there's a fire starting low in my belly. Everything from that night, everything forbidden and off limits, is now within my grasp, ready for the taking. Looking at Lance Turner standing in front of me now, the lost connection reignites and the longing from my youth resurfaces. I lay my hand flat against his chest.

His arms slide around me.

"We shouldn't," I say, not meaning it at all.

"Why not?" He presses against me, and he is hard again. I groan inwardly at the promise of what is to come, of what could be, of where we could pick right back up again. My hands climb up and rest on his shoulders. Heat from his body warms me as our chests press together. I stare up at him and our lips are barely an inch apart. There's a suspended moment where time stands still, where we can still make a clear-headed decision and pull apart but before I can collect my thoughts or process what's happening, he dips his head and our lips touch.

It's like our first kiss all those years ago; the memory of his touch, his smell, the way he feels against me, it all comes back. He growls appreciatively, low and soft in his throat. I feel the reverberation deep in my chest.

"I've got your pen," I manage to say. The sentence sounds misplaced in the sea of emotion swirling around us.

"I don't care about the pen."

The insides of my body are in upheaval and I'm not sure if it's because the past has come into my present, or if it's because Lance's searing gaze has melted my panties, or whether it is both these things. I can't help but tilt my face up towards him again.

This time his mouth comes down hard, as if he's done with pussyfooting around, as if it's impossible to keep things at that level. His desire for me pokes against my body, igniting my senses. I try not to moan back but it's impossible as I sink into his mouth. Our bodies press together, they have their own secret language, and I don't want him to move away.

I give in because ... oh ... this man can kiss. He claims my lips as if they belong to him and I give myself willingly. Yet, my memories fight through the lust-laden haze and recall another time. A time that was dark, and hopeless and lonely for me. But I drag myself away, not wanting to make another mistake.

He frowns, his lips wet, his expression incredulous.

I'd be lying if I said I hadn't thought about it, but falling into bed with him would be a mistake. My family blame him for the mess I was in at the end of that school year, what with me failing my exams and having to suffer the rumors around school. They also see him as an older man, a teacher, who preyed on me. He didn't, but they believed the rumors because I will never tell them the truth.

I want closure. That's what I want, but kissing him wantonly, giving in, will only make me a prisoner to the memories I can't stop thinking about. The truth is Lance *did* leave me, and while I understand the reason he went to his family, I don't understand what stopped him from getting in touch with me.

"Why didn't you ever contact me?" I ask, dragging my hand across my lips, needing to wipe every trace of him away.

"What?" he asks, disorientated.

"You left the school to take care of your niece, but that didn't stop you from getting in touch with me."

He swipes a hand across his hair. "We've been through that."

"One phone call, or even a letter, would have been enough to put me out of my misery."

He steps towards me. "I didn't want to mess up your life."

"You did it anyway, by disappearing."

"I couldn't think about anything but my niece and my brother-in-law. He was in a coma. My sister had died. My family was grieving. What part of that don't you understand." He's angry.

"I was a mess. You left me to fend for myself. Do you know what it was like having to hear the rumors?"

He looks confused. "But you left school."

"I still lived in the same small town. Erica and Jensen got picked on at school. The rumors didn't stop just because you left town and because I left the school. They suffered the humiliation of their sister having a relationship with the teacher—"

"But we didn't tell anyone," he points out, naively.

"Even in town, I had people point fingers at me, people whispering and saying that you'd been forced to leave because of me, otherwise you were going to get fired. People looked at me like I was the town whore."

"Don't say that."

"They did."

"I'm sorry. I didn't know." He tries to frame my face with his hands, but I wrench myself away.

"Well, you do now."

My emotions are in tatters, conflicted thoughts poison my mind. I want him in my bed, I want more of him, all of him, but it will be a minefield of regret to go there. Not just because of my family, but because the past should be buried and stay in the past.

He's so much older than I am. We can't do this.

"I wish I'd been there for you." His gaze dips to my chest and lingers on my thin shirt, which will give away evidence of my arousal. My breasts feel heavy. I pull the edges of my jacket together.

"You left me." I step back. His eyes glint dangerously.

"I told you why."

I'm deliberately picking a fight. It's what I do sometimes. But this is warranted. "You used me."

"That's not how I remember it, and I'm sure you don't, either." His palm folds around the back of my neck and he claims me possessively. "Don't you remember what you did, Megan?" he rasps, his breath hot and sweet in my face. He presses against me, poking my stomach with his steel hard cock. Liquid heat melts between my legs and I huff out a ragged breath. Excitement courses through me. Delicious angry sex beckons.

I do remember. My clothes were wet, and I took them off. I knew what I was doing. He's not to blame, but ...

"You wanted me," I whisper.

"You were naked in front of me, offering yourself to me. I tried to resist you and I couldn't. You made it impossible. You knew what you were doing."

"You were too scared to act on your emotions."

"I was responsible." The Adam's apple in his throat bobs. "I did want you, just like I want you now. I never forgot you, Megan. I wanted to reach out to you, but it would have complicated things. You were on the cusp of a new start, a new life and a new adventure in college."

"You left me, and I was in love with you."

His mouth falls open, the hand on my neck loosens. He steps away, looking confused.

I've revealed too much.

"Love?" he asks, softly.

I get my wits together. "Lust would be a better word for it. It's a good thing you stayed away. My family hated you so much. They would hate you now if they knew you were talking to me." Luckily they won't have heard of his heroic exploits because they don't live here.

He shakes his head. "From hot to cold, in the blink of an eye. Did I do this to you? You can be so cold and so distant, like you can switch off in an instant. You were never like this."

"It's called survival."

He peers down at me as if he can't work me out. "Is that what you've been doing?"

"That's what all people do."

Another nod. "I want to make it up to you," he says, decisively.

I laugh. "Make what up to me?"

"For leaving you the way I did."

The hell I'll let him back in my life. "Stay away from me, that's how you can make it up to me."

He takes a step towards me. "My sister died, Megan."

"My mother overdosed."

"Tit for tat?" he asks. "Is that what we're doing?"

I'm just about to give him a snarky answer when his phone rings, and I briefly catch a picture of a young girl on it. His niece.

"Stay away from me," I snarl.

CHAPTER FOURTEEN

LANCE

"**Y**ou have to come quickly!" Vivian sounds distraught. It takes me a few moments to shift the focus from Megan to the banshee shriek of my ex-wife.

"What's happened?"

"Cassie's hurt. She had an accident."

I feel a pinch in my chest. "What?" Cassie is my life. My world. My everything.

"She bounced off the trampoline and went headfirst into the wooden bench. She's got a gash on her head. There's blood everywhere."

Fuck.

"I'm on my way."

"I'm taking her to the hospital."

The pinch in my chest becomes a vise, clamping on to my heart and not letting go. "I'm coming."

. . .

They used glue instead of giving her stitches.

"Does it hurt, Sweetpea?" I ask, examining Cassie's head carefully.

"No, Daddy." Cassie shakes her head super slowly. Thankfully the cut doesn't look too bad. I blanket her with a gentle hug and bend down to kiss her cheek, grateful that the injury isn't worse.

"I'm going to move that trampoline away from the bench," I tell her, and while I'm at it, the fence and other objects which could harm my little girl. I hold her tightly in my arms and stay like that for a while. I miss her so much. It's soul-crushing, how I can't see her smiling face every day.

For years the thought of not being with her kept me shackled to a miserable marriage. But a few years ago, still trying to make things work for Cassie's sake, I moved into an apartment around the corner from the family home so that I could remain a big part of her life but I realized all too soon that it was a mistake. Vivian thought she could convince me to change my mind. She pleaded with me to try couples counseling. I did. I was open to trying anything, but she was the one who often didn't turn up for the sessions. She didn't think she was in the wrong. Couples counseling with just one half of the couple attending was never going to work. There was also the truth of our situation; that when you no longer love someone, you can't start to fall in love with them all over again. It's impossible to feign it.

When moving nearby didn't work, I moved to Boston, and it's been the best thing.

Before, the long commute to work and back in the heavy traffic made me even more resentful and frustrated with my life. Now I am only twenty minutes away from my college. While I love having the physical distance between me and

Vivian, not seeing Cassie daily, or having her be around the corner, is tough.

But Vivian has become worse since the shooting.

Clingier.

She and I are such different creatures; different people with different interests, and while this isn't a good reason to go our separate ways especially when we have a child, her roving eye and interest in others makes it impossible for me to look the other way.

My mistake was to fall for a woman who had it all; she was feminine, pretty, easy to get along with, and she made me laugh. I was instantly smitten. It was a year on from my sister's death. I'd changed my life to be there for my niece and my brother-in-law and in this respect Megan is right. I did abandon her. Maybe I poured myself into helping my sister's family to get out of the mess that would have been me and Megan because I often wonder what might have happened had I stayed on at the school after that night that changed everything.

Outwardly, Vivian and I looked perfect together, but things slowly fell apart. My feelings began to fade, the shiny glint wore off. Worse, I was no longer in love. She made it difficult to love her. I sensed that Vivian didn't love me. She *lusted* for me. She liked having me on her arm, liked the way other women stared at me, liked that she was the one who had me. She often commented that I was like a magnet when I entered a room, attracting women like iron filings as I walked around.

I could turn a blind eye to her cheating because our daughter was my life. I wanted Cassie's world to be perfect and untainted. A couple of times Brett and Sarah came to stay, and I was able to take Cassie to stay with them. At least the girls know one another. I miss Anna, but having Sarah and

Cassie in each other's lives, albeit once in a blue moon, meant something. I often wonder what Anna would have made of Vivian. I wonder if she would have prevented me from making such a monumental mistake.

"Can you stay today, Daddy?" Cassie asks.

I look at her chubby little face and my heart melts. "I've got work tomorrow." Her eyes turn sad. "Maybe I can come over on the weekend?" I suggest, hating to see her look so unhappy. Cassie sheers up instantly but my smile turns to stone when Vivian sashays over to my side. Her top with its deep-plunging neckline seems oddly inappropriate for day wear.

"Poor baby," she coos, gingerly touching Cassie's hair. "I hope that cut won't leave a big bald patch on your head."

Vivian is tactless. "That's a war wound, obtained in the line of having fun, right, Sweetpea? Like mine," I say, pointing to my shoulder.

Cassie smiles proudly. "You've got two, Daddy, This one," she touches the scar along my jaw.

"So I do, but I don't want you to try to catch up with me, okay? We're not having a competition to see who gets the most scars." I gently place her on the floor. "One war wound is enough. Don't you worry about this either." I gingerly lay a finger a few inches from her wound. "Your hair's going to hide it."

Cassie squeezes my hand, cheered up by my words.

"It's time to get ready for bed, Cassandra," Vivian says. She always finds a way to ruin things when we're bonding.

I toss her an irritated stare. "Can't you let her stay up a little?"

"Please let me, Mommy!" Cassie whines

"She's got school tomorrow."

"Pleeeease, Mommy." The more my daughter pleads, the

more Vivian's reluctance to relax the rules annoys me. "Don't be so difficult, Vivian." I try to keep my voice level. "She's been to the hospital. Surely you can find it in that heart of yours to relax the rules?" Cassie and I could watch a movie, and have popcorn, a blanket and cuddle up on the couch. Now that I'm here, it would be a shame not to make the most of it.

"Baby." Vivian rests her hand across the back of my neck and I try not to flinch. Her closeness is claustrophobic. "I can absolutely relax my rules around you."

I step away, freeing myself from her claws.

"You can stay up another half hour, Cassandra," she says. It's hard to miss the wave of disappointment that rolls over my daughter. I struggle to rein in my anger. Vivian is a manipulative shrew. I would walk away from this woman and have nothing more to do with her were she not the mother of my child.

"Half an hour?" I spit out.

"You know what she's like in the morning," says Vivian, defensively. "You're not the one who has to deal with waking her up the next day and taking her to school."

"I'll stay and then I can take her to school." I weigh the pros and cons of being closer to my daughter at the cost of tolerating her mother. If I take Cassie to school, Vivian won't have a reason to complain.

Cassie squeezes my hand even more tightly. "Please, Daddy. Please stay."

"I would love to, Sweetpea, but—." I look at my daughter and my heart melts. All the love in the world wouldn't be enough to describe what I feel for her. "I can stay a few days, how's that?" I suggest, overcome with gratitude that her injury wasn't worse.

"A few days?" Cassie shrieks. "Yay! But you don't have any PJs ..."

I grin, bemused by her worries. "It's okay. I can make do."

"I could find you something to wear in bed." Vivian's voice is silk and seduction and very much wasted on me.

I tap Cassie's nose gently, ignoring Vivian's remark. "I am staying, even if I have to wear stinky clothes to work tomorrow." I've got a small stash of clothes here in a closet in one of the spare rooms.

"We can have Wheaties in the morning, Daddy!" Her eyes light up and I examine in awe the wonder on her face, at how young children have so much gratitude for the smallest things, while we are weathered and damaged by the years, grateful for nothing, and complaining about everything.

I jam my hands into my front pockets. Cassie pleading like this always cuts me to the core. At times like this I realize just how much our divorce will eventually hurt her. She has no idea about our separation and she doesn't seem to think there's anything odd about our arrangement, about us not living together. I've begged Vivian not to tell her yet. Cassie doesn't need to know. I want her to be a little older before she finds out.

It's decided. "Okay. I'm staying!"

"Yay!" Cassie jumps up and down with excitement.

"If I take her to school tomorrow, you'll let her stay up with me and watch a movie?" I ask her mother.

"You're watching a movie?"

I look at Cassie and wink. "If you pick the movie, can I pick the popcorn?"

Cassie vibrates with excitement and runs towards the door.

"Slow down!" I yell after her.

"You can sleep in my bed," Vivian whispers as soon as

we're alone. She's like a cat in heat, the way she creeps around me.

I fold my arms. "Why would I do that when you have so many spare bedrooms?"

"It's just an offer. A man has needs, and I do, too. I miss you, baby."

"Is the pool boy away on vacation?"

She raises her hand to slap me but I grab her wrist in time. "We were separated then."

I let go of her and step away. "Hmmm. I recall a certain personal trainer who had a very personal touch." I give her a big grin because I know how much it angers her. "We both know how closely he liked to instruct you."

I move away before her hand tries to connect with my cheek again. She toys with a lock of her hair. "We weren't married then."

"But we were engaged." I should have broken it off then.

"So, I've had a few indiscretions," she says, trying to grab my hand and failing, "but I love you, Lance." She walks after me as I step into the huge hallway. I glance up at the spiral staircase waiting for Cassie to come bounding down the stairs.

"Do you have to ignore me so blatantly?" Vivian's scent wafts into my personal space. It's the one she always wears, spicy and overbearing, and suffocating my senses. She slips her hand around my waist.

Here it comes. My gut turns hard, like ice, as I prepare to ward her off again. The divorce papers can't come fast enough. "Let's try to get along as best as we can, Vivian," I say, removing her hand. "For Cassie's sake." My daughter is my Achilles heel and Vivian knows it.

"Is that perfume?" She edges closer and sniffs around my neck. The woman has the scent receptors of a bear.

"Perfume?" I joke and move away.

"Are you fucking someone?"

"Are you kidding me, Vivian? Cassie's had a head injury and this is all you can think of?"

"Daddy! I got the film. This is what we're watching." She thrusts a DVD in my hand. It's Beauty and the Beast.

We've only watched it about ten times. "Awesome!" I say. "Let's make some popcorn."

She slips her hand in mine and we walk towards the kitchen.

It will be awesome. I get to spend time with my daughter though I'm slightly unnerved that Vivian is on to me. But it's not her who is in my thoughts as Cassie and I snuggle on the couch, a big bowl of popcorn on my lap.

This is the best feeling in the world, spending the evening with my princess, but I can't help thinking about Megan. That kiss was dangerous. That kiss brought it all back.

CHAPTER FIFTEEN

MEGAN

I was a bundle of nerves by the time I walked out of my interview.

I messed up a few times. Tripped over simple things, especially when I was asked about my experience in this job and what qualifications I had. I always seem to lack faith in myself. Not being able to go to college has been a huge hindrance, even though I've worked so hard getting similar qualifications in other ways.

Seeing Preston after his interview, with that slimy big grin on his face unsettled me. He thinks he's better than me, just because he's got more qualifications than me. Because he has a college degree and I don't.

The fact is, I've been here longer, and I know more than he does. He's had to ask me about things he isn't sure about. I've never had to go to him. There's something to be said for having experience and getting your hands dirty by doing the actual work.

But I messed up when the interviewer asked me why I didn't go to college and why it took me so long to get my accreditations. I stammered and stuttered, recalling the real reason my life didn't go according to plan because everything changed for me when I became my mother's carer and head of the family.

Thoughts of Lance completely messed up my head. That was even before I went into the interview room. Maybe if I hadn't gone to his apartment and we hadn't kissed, I wouldn't have had that searing hot kiss stuck in my head, replaying on auto all the time.

It happened so quickly. Spontaneously. Just like that. I was only supposed to have returned his pen.

My problem is that a good-looking man is always my downfall.

———

"How was it?" Preston comes over to my desk later. The creepy cockroach has come to gloat.

"Good." I start putting away my paperwork.

"Mine was, too," he says. "How about we go out to celebrate?"

"Celebrate?" I frown as I stare up at him. He's too confident. He knows something. "Did you get it?"

"Not that I know. They're still interviewing people, so we won't know for another week." He's extremely smug and it grates on my nerves. "Let's at least go for a few drinks?"

"You do know something." I want to get out of here, away from him.

"I do not!" He squints. "It didn't go well for you?"

Get lost.

"I don't know. I can't tell." No, it didn't. I don't want to go for drinks, or be with him, or spend time talking about work or looking at his sanctimonious face. If he gets the promotion, I'll explode in a fit of fury.

I've spoken to the other candidates. Out of the five of us, I'm the only woman, but I have the most experience. I've worked here at this firm the longest. They're college graduates. I shouldn't be riled up about it, and it shouldn't matter, but these things do count more than they should.

"I'm sure you were amazing as always. Lighten up, why don't you? We just have to sit tight and wait it out. Let's end the week with a bang?"

I fidget with the top button of my blouse. "The week isn't over yet. It's Thursday, for crying out loud."

"Or we can go and get something to eat. I've heard that Carluccio's is good." Preston's eyes are bright with anticipation.

"Carluccio's?" I press my lips together, desperate to get him to leave. He doesn't seem to take the visual cues that I don't want to do anything or go anywhere with him.

"I can book a table."

God, no. My insides tightened as if I'm getting ready for a second punch to the gut.

"I'm meeting a friend tonight," I say breezily, switching off my computer. I had planned to stay late tonight and catch up on my emails, but they no longer seem as important as my escape.

"*That* friend?" he asks. "The old guy who was waiting for you?"

I smile at him sweetly. "Your jealousy is showing." I decide to visit Arla on my way home.

"You've become a fitness addict," I say, eyeing Arla's outfit.

She's in her bright orange Spandex top and black yoga pants which look as if someone's thrown up on them. "Are you going to your spin class?"

"Nah, it's okay," says Arla, letting me in. "I didn't really feel like going anyway."

"No. You should go." I hate the idea of interrupting her plans to see Scott, her spin instructor she has mentioned more than a few times. I'm not silly. Arla's only exercise until a few months ago was changing channels on the TV remote. This is a new Arla I'm seeing transform in front of my eyes. "I don't want you missing a class on account of me."

Arla smiles happily. "I can give up Scott for one evening."

My suspicions have been justified. "I thought as much."

"He's the spin instructor."

"I know who he is."

"He's hot!" Arla squeals and her eyes go round and wide with excitement. "You should see him. He looks so *good* in his shorts. You should see his legs, *soooo* firm, like steel. I swear he could crush walnuts between his butt cheeks." A loud sigh of contentment falls from her lips.

I make a face. "*That* turns you on?" In my mind's eyes, I see Lance's naked body, his slim hips and flat stomach ...

Heat warms my face.

"When he sweats, the back of his muscle T-shirt drips with sweat," reveals Arla, fanning herself with her hand, "I can't keep my eyes off him."

I imagine a scene, because my mind goes there, Lance in a T-shirt, streaks of sweat rolling down his chest.

"Looks like you're getting hot and bothered just hearing

about him!" Arla gives me a playful shove, her laughter echoing around the room. "You need to get laid, and fast."

It's no secret that I've not had sex for a long time. It's been months. "Your instructor is the reason you're so excited about the class?" I ask, desperate to change the topic.

"I could have an orgasm just sitting on the bike."

A burst of laughter shoots out of my mouth. Arla is funny, she's frank and honest, and she has a heart of gold.

"I'm serious! Cycling away, with that hard saddle between my legs—"

"Stop it!" I beg.

But she doesn't. "A ripped, sweaty guy in front of me. Hell, yeah! Don't laugh at me," she shrieks, when I fall about in hysterics. "I'm in danger of falling off my bike if I'm not careful."

"That would be dangerous."

"You should come. It's full of hot men."

I shake my head. "I'm not going to your gym to scout for men."

"You're making a mistake." She throws her knapsack to the floor. "To what do I owe this visit?" She slips her sneakers off. We both fall onto the couch and when I say nothing, she continues "If you ever change your mind, let me know. I get a discount on my membership for introducing new members."

I immediately dismiss the idea. "I don't have time to go to the gym. You know how busy I am."

"Hot men..." Arla waggles her eyebrow. "You're not tempted even by incredibly hot men?"

"I might have a hot man of my own," I say in a mysterious voice. It's too late. I've said it now, the morsel of news I wasn't going to share with her just yet because I'm still processing it for myself.

She tilts her face towards me and her eyes go even wider. "Preston?"

"NO!" I clutch my chest in disgust. Preston's been trying to make moves for a long time and I've managed to keep him at bay.

"Then who?" Arla's eyebrow lifts.

"Lance Turner."

"Getouttahere!" She slaps my arm in jest. "Can't say I'm surprised."

"It was just a kiss. It was a mistake. It just happened."

"*It. Just. Happened?*" Arla asks slowly, as if she were trying to remember the phrase in a foreign language. "You stuck your tongue down Mr. Turner's throat, and you expect me to believe that it *just* happened?"

"I did not ... do that."

"Then he stuck his tongue down yours," Arla concludes. "You've been good lately. You've even kept Preston at bay. He's been trying to get into your panties for a long time and the poor guy only managed to get a kiss off you. Now superhero Lance turns up and bam! You kiss him. This isn't just a random guy you meet in a bar, Megan. You have history with Mr. Turner."

"It just happened."

Arla rolls her eyes. "That's what you always say. Where did it happen and how? I need all the dirty details."

I tell her everything, about the pen and the reason for my visit.

"What's his body like?" she asks. "Does he have any saggy bits?"

"It was just a kiss."

"But you were obviously close enough to him to feel him."

I press my lips together at the thought of him. "No saggy

bits." The man is hard and firm, and has a better body than most men my age that I've dated.

"How old is he now?"

"I don't know. Forty-one, I think." *I think.* I know perfectly well how old he is, because I'd lamented over our fourteen-year age gap as a student. At the height of my infatuation, I often fantasized about how our lives might turn out once I graduated high school. He is forty-three, and I've shaved off a few years already.

"Forty-one?" Arla shrieks in astonishment, as if I've said 'a hundred.'

"He was our teacher. How can you not remember?"

"*Because* he was our teacher and we're not supposed to ask such questions." She gives me a perplexed look. "How did you end up with his pen?"

"He came to my workplace last week and we went for coffee."

Arla snorts. "You kept that quiet. You've been acting as if nothing happened when he almost ran you over at the crossing."

"Nothing *did* happen."

"But since then he's been to your workplace, you've been for coffee and the third time you two meet, you end up with your lips stuck together."

My insides churn. "I didn't mean for that to happen."

"Uh-huh." Arla sounds as if she doesn't believe me." "So, you're at his apartment and?"

"Do you really want a blow-by-blow account of the evening?"

"I don't know. Is there any *blow-by-blow* account you want to share with me?" Arla collapses into laughter while I sit there, my face burning.

"No!" I reply emphatically. "I don't know how, or why..."

"You're such a bad liar!"

But I do know how, and I do know why. It was because I felt something. Maybe it's true that past loves are hard to forget. Something between us has reignited. Something shifted since the day of the campus shooting, when Lance Turner reappeared on my TV screen. Those memories from my school days came back with a vengeance. They infected my mind and my thoughts, creating a fog I couldn't cut through. Slowly, the feelings returned, those pointless, heart-wrenching feelings for a man I could never have. When I saw him at the crossing, things had shifted some more.

One look into his eyes and I was transported back to that time in my youth. Every memory, every emotion, every tiny feeling I'd ever had for him that I'd buried has now come to the surface and opened a Pandora's box of bad things—lust, misplaced attraction and forbidden desire.

But this is all it will be. We had one crazy kiss in one crazy slice of time. It's a huge mistake, even I know that, and now I feel uneasy thinking about him.

After the type of day I've had, I want to go home. I shouldn't have come here. I make a move to leave, and Arla looks at her watch and decides she can still make her class. She says she'll only be a little late for Scott.

I let her go, because she is excited and happy, and Scott does that for her. Who am I to stand in her way with my silly little problems?

CHAPTER SIXTEEN

LANCE

I almost jump out of my skin when I see a missed call from Megan.

Damn.

I've just set my princess down and tucked her in. She fell asleep again watching a Disney film. I rush home earlier than usual after work and our evenings are full of movies, popcorn and fun—which has meant late nights, and I pray she wakes up easily tomorrow otherwise Vivian will give me hell.

I examine my phone. Megan called me a few hours ago when Cassie and I were watching a film, and I had my phone on silence.

Double damn.

I've been so heavily preoccupied with Cassie, that I've pushed Megan to the back of my mind lately. I rush back to the spare room where I've been sleeping, and call back.

She doesn't answer.

I'm curious, and delighted, because ... she called me.

She. Called. Me.

My cock twitches. I haven't had sex in two years and the thought of Megan makes it come to life again.

Sick man.

I would hate for Cassie's teacher to ever think of her like that, at the age Megan was when I tried not to fall in love with her. It's wrong ... it should be wrong ... it *is* wrong ... but it never felt wrong at the time. I never set out to have any romantic feelings for her. I was a good teacher. I am a good teacher. I love my profession but, as Lesley often tells me, I don't have the face of a teacher.

I call Megan again, and it rings but she doesn't answer. I could kick myself. She might have been in trouble. I don't know what to do. I don't know where she lives. And it's late.

I strip off my shirt, and I'm about to climb out of my pants when my phone rings. I snatch it, seeing Megan's name come up. "You okay?" I ask, worried that something might have happened, because why else would she call me?

"I have two missed calls from you," she says, her tone is accusatory, and at first I don't understand.

"What? You called me."

"I did? Oh ..." A few silent seconds pass when she's probably looking at her phone to check, instead of taking my word for it. "I must have butt dialed you by accident." The words come out like short, sharp arrows.

"Butt dialed?" I call her bluff.

"Yes, accidentally. Why else?"

There's silence.

"I didn't expect you to call," I say finally, keeping my voice lowered, my ears on alert for Vivian prowling outside my door.

"Why are you talking quietly?"

Now's not the time to tell her, especially not on the phone. I want to come clean with Megan and this is not how I want to do things this time around.

"Because it's late," I say. "Were you asleep? I hope I didn't disturb you."

"I was in the shower."

"Oh." My voice has an odd wobble to it. Was she in the shower now because she's been for a run, or because she's had sex or ...what? It's illogical, the reasons my mind runs through, the place where my mind is right now. I clear my throat. "How are you?" I want to start the conversation all over again.

Silence seeps into the airwaves but she doesn't say she's going to hang up. I like that we are both somewhat comfortable hanging on the line despite the quiet.

"How am I? Don't even start."

"Bad day?" I pause for a few seconds. "What happened?"

"I don't need to tell you anything but you're on the phone now, and it's late." It's sounds to me as if she's justifying it to herself.

"Just tell me, Megan," I implore softly.

"I had an interview and it didn't go too well."

"Sorry to hear that. Why do you think it didn't go too well?"

"Because the other guys who went for it are smug confident assholes."

I chuckle.

"It's not funny."

"No, it's not. That's not why I was laughing."

"Why were you laughing?" she asks.

"Because you're all fired up and mad."

"You're weird," she says, but there is no malice in her voice. I am just thankful that she's still on the phone and talking to me.

"What happened in the interview?" I nudge her gently.

"I tripped up."

"You tripped up?"

"Are you going to echo every single sentence I say?"

Feisty. Bad tempered. She wasn't like this before. The transformation of the girl I knew into a woman isn't only physical. I'm seeing a new side to her personality. The girl in high school was fragile, battered by life and her home situation. It was one of the things that drew me to her. She was broken in little pieces that only the trained eyes of a teacher could see and I wanted to help put her back together again before it was too late.

I could see that this girl had the brains and the mind to do well given the chance. She had a lot of potential and I wanted to help her before she fell apart. It wasn't her fault what was going on with her parents. "These things happen," I tell her, wanting to put her mind at ease. "You shouldn't worry too much about one interview. There will be others."

"You don't understand how badly I wanted the job."

She has a point. I don't. "You don't know yet whether you got it or not. Sometimes what we think is our worst turns out to be our best."

"You sound like Mr. Turner again."

"That's because I *am* Mr. Turner."

I hear a soft giggle from her end and it makes me feel relieved. Makes me think that she's talking to me and enjoying our conversation as much as I am. "Don't beat yourself up about it."

"How's your niece?" she asks. It takes me a moment to interpret her sudden switch to a new topic.

"She's good. She's good. Her dad remarried and now she has two younger siblings. A brother and a sister. Just like you, if I remember correctly."

"Not like me, I hope."

"How are they?" I ask tentatively.

"They're ... good."

She doesn't elaborate and the silence stretches out even longer. I sense that she doesn't want to talk about them.

"Who's the bozo? You said the other guy at work went for the same interview. Is he the guy I met?"

"It's him. A guy called Preston. He's really feeling confident. I've been there longer than he has, but he has more qualifications. "

I want to bolster her. I have an image of her being all alone and downcast and I want to do all I can to make her feel better. "In my experience, personality, grit, hard work and a go-getting attitude—all of which you have—matter more than expensive college degrees."

"Says the man who is complicit in getting students to rack up mountains of debt just so that they can get those pieces of paper."

"So, uh ..." It's on the tip of my tongue to ask her. My head tells me not to, but my heart pushes me into it. "This Preston guy. Is he ... are you two ...?"

"Are we?"

"Are you two entangled?"

"Entangled?" she scoffs. "That's an archaic term. What century were you born in?"

"Ouch," I groan loudly. "You talk about him a lot."

"I don't. You're the one who always brings him up. Are you jealous?"

The idea of her with him is a knife twisting in my gut. "Am I allowed to be?" It's a vague question. A feeling, probing, putting-it-out-there question. She and I are in a strange situation. I have feelings for her and now that nothing is in my way—no teacher student barrier, no marriage barrier —I'm free.

But I am old, as Cassie would say. I am older, and I'm probably not a great prospect for someone young, gorgeous, intelligent and focused like Megan. Yet the thought of her with someone young, a better catch, a better proposition, fills me with fury.

Still, she kissed me. *We* kissed. There are feelings involved on both sides. It can't just be me. Megan *is* attracted to me, even though whenever we talk she sounds as if she wants to rip my eyes out.

"We kissed at a dinner and drinks event one time."

My gut hardens at the news. "And ... then?" I don't want her kissing anyone but me.

"Then nothing. I don't want to become *entangled* with anyone. I was a little tipsy and I should have known better."

"You weren't tipsy the other day, when we kissed," I challenge. I want her to say she wanted it. My heart stops and splutters as I wait with bated breath for her to say something. Something good, and positive, and meaningful about it.

"I don't know what that was."

I wait for more, but she doesn't speak. "What do you mean you don't want to be entangled with anyone?"

She says nothing.

"Who hurt you?" I ask, a gnawing feeling eating away at my gut. I hope life hasn't scarred her. I hope her parents haven't fucked things up completely for her. I hope I didn't fuck things up even more.

But still she says nothing, and I press the handset closer to me, as if it's a way to get close to her. Eleven years of nothing, and now I want all of her. I want to make things better for her because even I can see that there's a sadness she tries to hide.

"Megan? Say something."

"It's late, and I have an early start tomorrow. I butt-dialed you by mistake."

She hangs up.

CHAPTER SEVENTEEN

MEGAN

"More money will be good," my mother says when I tell her how my interview went.

"I don't think I'm in the running, Mom. Don't get your hopes up for me."

"Why not? They love you at that place."

I wish I hadn't told her about it now. I tell her that it doesn't matter how much they love me, and that they are looking for other things.

"What other things?"

"Don't worry about it, Mom. It doesn't matter."

"Of course it matters. It matters to me. You sound upset, Meg."

"I'm not," I lie.

Ours has been a rocky relationship over the years, but she's fine now and she's stronger. Our roles have reversed again so that she's the mother and I'm the daughter once more, but even though I'm all grown up, she still worries about me.

It was strange, that previous role reversal. Nursing her, making sure she was going to be fine, and taking care of Jensen and Erica, while letting go of my college dreams made that year after high school brutal. Losing the safety of school and stepping into the real world, working shifts at the ice-cream parlor and then waitressing in the evenings and on the weekends made me grow up fast.

Exhaustion was my friend. It numbed me to the pain of abandonment that I might otherwise have languished in. I didn't pine for Mr Turner for too long. I was too weary when I came home and fell asleep in front of the TV.

"You've been there for years," my mother protests.

"That doesn't matter. For management positions, employers want qualifications."

"Fiddlesticks."

"It is what it is."

"I wish I'd been stronger for you instead of falling apart..."

"Don't, Mom." I don't want her blaming herself more than she already does. She sees what I did, the sacrifices I made and hates that it was because of her. "Don't go blaming yourself. All of that is in the past now."

"All those rumors flying around the school, you and that teacher," she scoffs. "As if you didn't have enough troubles to deal with what with that teacher, and then I added more to your load."

"Let's not go back to the past," I plead. She would hate it if she discovered what I'd been up to with Mr. Turner.

"It was probably a good thing he left the school; else I'd have done something nasty to him."

I can't help but suppress a smile at that.

I didn't get the job. I've just read an email telling me the news I knew was coming.

I sink back in my chair feeling defeated. Even though I suspected my interview was weak, the confirmation burns like a hot poker.

It better not be Preston.

I hope it's one of the other guys. The older one, the man in his fifties. Experience and wisdom, and probably a good college education is what he'll have going for him.

Please let it be that older man.

Preston is insufferable at best. I dread to think what he'll be like now. I get up to leave, not wanting to burn the midnight oil in a company which doesn't value me, but Preston swarms in, rubbing his hands together with the most hideous smile on his face.

He did get it.

I almost slap a hand to my head. The douchebag. This guy has always come to me when he's stuck at work. I am better than him, and most everyone in my department would agree.

"I got the job!" he says, in a sing-song voice that makes me want to slap him. He does a little jig, and I resist the temptation to throw something at him. I force a smile.

"But you already knew that. You assumed it. Congratulations."

"Let's go and celebrate."

I pin him with an icy stare. "I'm not really feeling the vibe."

"I'm sorry you didn't get it," he says, sitting in the chair opposite.

"No, you're not, because that would then mean that *you* didn't get it."

He bobs his head, agreeing.

"And if I'd gotten the job, you'd be unhappy." I stand up and slip on my business jacket.

"I would be, but I would still help you to celebrate." He stands up and looks disappointed that I'm not taking him up on his offer. "Help me to celebrate, Megan. Don't be a sourpuss."

It's a man's world.

An unfair world.

A rich and privileged person's world.

"I'm not in the mood to celebrate, not even for you. Sorry. But I am happy for you," I tell him. It's me I'm not happy for.

"At least now I'll have you under me," he grins as if this is really funny. My insides almost empty. Did he really say that out aloud?

"Careful there. I could report you to HR for sexual harassment." I sail past him and rush out of the office, eager to get away. But I don't want to go back to my empty home, and I don't want to socialize with people.

A short while later I'm knocking on Arla's door. She stares at me in surprise because I didn't tell her I was coming over. Instead, I hold up a bottle of red wine.

"More hot kisses with Lance again?" She grins as she lets me in. I can see that she's dressed up and not in her signature workout clothes. She looks nice. As if she's going out.

"Where are you going?" I ask, suspiciously.

"I have a date with Scott!"

"You do?"

Arla beams happily. "We're going for drinks."

I move towards the door. I should ask her where she's going, and what she's doing tonight, and I should be happy for her. I *am* happy for her; I just don't feel happy. "I didn't get the job. I was hoping I could drown my sorrows here."

"You didn't get it?" Arla squeezes my arm. "Those idiots. They don't know your worth."

I set the bottle down on her coffee table. "You have a good time on your date. I want to hear all about when you—"

"I'm not leaving yet. Scott's picking me up at eight. Let's have some wine. I'll help you drown your sorrows."

And that's what we do. She tells me about Scott and where they're going, and I ask her lots of questions because it's better than talking about my problems. I don't want to foist my misery on her. It seems that I always have problems. That's the story of my life.

"Who did they give the job to?" Arla asks, refilling my wine glass again.

"The asshole. Preston."

She scowls. "He hasn't been there long."

"He hasn't." I take a big gulp from my glass.

"He started after you did."

"He did." And to think that he wanted me to go out and celebrate with him. The wine tastes good. Slightly bitter, yet full of flavor. It's warm and spicy as it slides down my throat and heats up my belly. My shoulders relax, and the bitter edge of my anger softens.

"It's a man's world," I say, taking a big gulp, then another one. I want to numb my senses, revel in the warm fuzziness that the alcohol induces.

"It is not!" Arla retorts.

"It's an unfair world."

"It can be, but there are better things in store for you. Maybe it's time you left this place because they don't appreciate you there. You're always working late and you bring your work home, and they don't recognize it. Maybe you can find somewhere else where you will be valued."

I slip off my shoes and curl my legs under me on the sofa.

"I was perfect for this job. I know more than Preston does. I don't understand why he's got the job and I don't?" Even as I say the words, I'm aware that I sound like a sore loser, still whining about it. I can't snap out of it.

"I'm sorry," says Arla. Why she's apologizing I don't know. It's not her fault. "Why don't we get you to go on a blind date?" she suggests, the sudden change in topic is so fast that it takes me a few seconds to let the meaning sink in.

Her infatuation with Scott has her stupidly believing that men are the answer to everything. Has she not been listening to me? Am I not making any sense?

"I don't want to go on a blind date." I chug some more wine then refill my glass. Arla's is still full.

"I saw an ad for speed dating," she says. "You remember that speed dating event I went on a few months ago? The one you refused to be seen at?"

I do remember. Arla came back complaining that the banker types didn't even notice her. She might as well have been a ghost. "You hated it," I point out.

"At least I went. It made me appreciate that there are other men out there. Worthy men."

"Worthy?"

"Scott is wonderful. I wish you'd come along to a class and meet him one day. You would like him so much. He's just ..." she clasps a hand to her chest. "He's just amazing."

Is this what infatuation looks like? Is this how I was with Mr. Turner towards the end? Is this why I went to him in the rain that night my mother took an overdose?

Because looking at my friend in her dark satin dress—something I've never seen her in before—tells me she's made an effort and crept so far out of her comfort zone. I mostly see her in loose gym clothes, but she's becoming more daring with those as well now. She's always been conscious of her size, hence not wearing dresses or skirts, but today she looks different. I'm shocked and happy and in awe. Arla is head over heels in lust or love or something. I just hope this man doesn't break her heart.

"Scott has good-looking friends," Arla remarks, oblivious to the doubts swirling around in my head the way the red wine swirls around in my glass. I stare down at it, thinking what an awful day it's been, then I take another sip. "Slow down! Are you trying to get drunk?"

"I'm enjoying unwinding. Let me." I make a pouty face.

"Come with me and you can meet some new people. You might even like someone."

"I thought you were going for drinks?"

"It's a spin class night out."

I raise my eyebrow. "They have things like that?"

She nods excitedly. "Come. I'll introduce you to everyone."

"I don't want to meet anyone. Men aren't the answer, Arla."

"You're miserable because you haven't had sex. What you need is for someone to screw that anger right out of you. If it helps, then go out and find someone."

"I'm trying to be more discerning." She's not wrong about not having had sex in a while. I'm not angry about that. Frustrated, maybe. Coiled up with desire after the kiss with Lance. I am filled with pent-up frustration. But hookups aren't the answer. The next day is awkward. Especially when I get their names wrong.

"A good sex session would get that anger out of you," Arla insists.

"No."

"Let me hook you up with someone—"

"Again, *no*."

"That's the only word that comes out of your mouth."

"Men aren't the answer to my problems."

"You just said it's a man's world. A man beat you today, and you were the better candidate."

"He's got all the qualifications. That's the problem. He just doesn't have the experience. He has all these accreditations and the bosses obviously have faith in him, but he's still going to ask me about things because I've been there for years longer than he has. It makes my blood boil."

"Then listen to me! Come out with me and Scott tonight."

I sense her impatience. "And be a third wheel?"

"We're meeting the spin class friends and then we're going to watch a movie. You can come to the drinks."

"Thanks, but no thanks."

"Miserable, frustrated, angry. You need a good lay." Arla gets up and smoothes down her dress.

"You look really nice in that. You should quit wearing yoga pants and loose sweatshirts."

"That's what Scott says," she replies, happily.

"That's what Scott says." I mimic her words, and roll my eyes.

"Why don't you call Lance?" she suggests.

"Why would I call him?" The anger in my voice is hard to hide. Arla raises an eyebrow. He's yet another man who is causing me frustration and untold angst. I don't need to think about him last thing at night. I don't need to think about him first thing in the morning.

And yet I do.

I don't need to get aroused just thinking about the kiss we shared.

And yet I do.

He's like a virus in my brain infecting every thought, puncturing every feeling, reminding me of what he is, and what he was, what we had, and what we could have been.

"Angry, much?" Arla frowns at me.

"It's not a good day. I came here hoping you would cheer me up."

"You made out with him last time," Arla says, ignoring my comment. "Maybe you just need to do it again."

Do it again?

"I never did anything with him," I say, "At school ..." My guilt trips me up.

Arla shakes her head. "I believe you. I'm not like the others. I stood by you, remember?"

She goes on to remind me of that time when everyone looked at me like I was a whore. Only Arla stood by me. I feel bad that I lied to her because the truth is, I was in love with Lance Turner by the end; when the arguments at home had gotten too much. He was my safe place. My fantasy figure. My hero.

"What are you going to do tonight then?" Arla asks, glancing at her wristwatch. She looks restless and I feel like I'm in the way.

She has a life, and I need to go home.

I get up, feeling a little unsteady. The sudden rush of blood to my brain makes me feel light headed. "You have a good time. Don't worry about me." I walk to the door.

"You should have gone out with Preston. Why didn't you take him up on his offer?"

I grunt, unladylike. "Because Preston is the last person I want to see tonight." The man makes my blood boil. "He said, 'at least now I'll have you under me,' and he grinned."

Arla makes a face as if she's smelled horseshit. "He said *what?*"

"Right?" I shake my head. "Why are men so disgusting?"

"Because they think with their dicks," replies Arla, wisely.

Preston is the last man I want to see. "You have fun. I want to hear all about it later." I see myself out. But I no longer contemplate going home because Lance Turner is in my head again.

Maybe Arla has a point. Maybe I should use him the way he used me that night when I was at school?

Arla doesn't know what happened that night when I went to his place and offered myself to him on a plate. I don't blame Lance for what he did. I led him on. I didn't know much about how hard it is for men to hold back. Over the years I've told myself that he wanted me as much as I wanted him.

Maybe it's time I got some sort of closure with the man who's been living in my head rent free these last few weeks.

CHAPTER EIGHTEEN

LANCE

Lesley wanted me to attend the department drinks evening but I can't stand having to answer the same questions again and again. Months have passed and people still want to know about the shooting. It irritates me. I'm over it. It's in my past; something I would rather forget.

I just want to slouch around, drink a couple of beers, and watch TV. I flick the TV channels on the remote, looking for something that might catch my attention, but after flitting around for a while I still haven't found anything. I'm still channel surfing when I hear a knock on the door.

I groan loudly.

It's Vivian. She did this a few days ago and turned up unannounced with Cassie. Ever since she smelled a hint of perfume on me, she's been acting suspicious. Goodness knows the amount of times I've smelled men's cologne on her. She turned up last week, just like that, for no reason, and blamed it on Cassie claiming that she wanted to see me.

My stomach muscles tighten as I go to answer the door. I pray it's not her. But to my utter shock and joy, Megan stares back at me, looking sexy as hell in her work clothes. Her face wears an impatient, slightly hardened expression that I've come to know so well. It's not the softness of the teenager I once knew, but the hardness of a woman who is mad at me.

"Hey," I say, bracing myself for whatever it is I've done this time to offend her, because her expression tells me this isn't a social visit. "Come in—" I start to say, when she marches straight past me, forcing me to catch a hint of her perfume again.

Damn, she smells good.

My body warms in an instant.

I'm happy to see her. My twitching cock is even happier. She glides past me and I catch a whiff of alcohol on her. This can't be good. "What have I done now?" I close the door and fold my arms as I face her.

A tiny muscle flexes along her jawline, confirmation of her irritable mood. "It's not you." The words are forced, as if she has trouble getting them out.

I'm relieved to hear that. "Have you been drinking?" I ask. It's not the ideal starting point for a conversation, but I'm at a loss as to what to say. I'm confused as to why she's here.

"I had a couple of drinks with Arla, you remember her?"

"Arla?" The name rings a bell. I place a hand on the doorhandle, expecting a second knock. "Where is she?" A thought flies through my brain, that this might be a reunion. Maybe Megan wants to introduce Arla to me.

"She's out with her man."

"She's not coming?" Relief floods through me.

"Coming here?" Megan scoffs. "She's out with Scott, her

spin instructor. He has butt cheeks that are as hard as steel, apparently."

"Butt cheeks that hard, eh?" I grin, but Megan doesn't. Her cheeks are flushed.

"To what do I owe this pleasure?" I try my hardest not to let my eyes slide down the length of her body, but I fail miserably. She looks so goddam sexy in her work clothes. A smart skirt, silky blouse, and a fitted jacket. Heels, too. The synapses in my brain start to fire. My skin begins to tingle. Blood rushes to the surface of my skin.

"Nothing. I had nothing to do on a Friday evening." She starts to pace around the room.

She has nothing to do on a Friday night and she's come to me? My heart starts to sing.

"I didn't get the job."

"You didn't get it? I'm sorry."

But I'm not sorry that she's come to me instead. On a Friday night. That means something. It also tells me that she is lonely, too. A flame ignites inside me, that maybe she also is looking to reconnect.

I walk towards her. "What happened?"

"I didn't get the job. Preston did. The other guy..."

"That guy?" I hate him even more.

"He's a smarmy little asshole." She goes off on a rant about how he hasn't been at the company for as long as she has but he's more qualified. I almost roll my eyes.

"Are you still blaming me for not going to college?"

"I don't blame you for me not going to college," she snaps. "It's circumstances isn't it? Life throws you curveballs and we end up having to deal with our circumstances."

"How can I help?"

"You can't." Her lips purse shut. She throws me an angry look and I don't know what it is about this woman, but my underused cock suddenly hardens. I shake my head, hating that I'm thinking like some dirty old creep. Maybe it's because two of her buttons on her blouse are undone and I catch a fleeting tease of her pastel pink bra. I force myself to look away. She places a hand across the back of her neck and stares at me sheepishly before looking around. It's like she's wondering what she's doing here.

I'm wondering, too.

I sit down on the couch because it's better for me to hide the growing package between my legs. Megan paces around in front me, then flings off her jacket. She's not helping. My gaze drops to her stilettoes and I'm about to tell her I don't like people wearing shoes on my rug, but ... fuck ... I kind of like her in those heels.

"I'm sick of getting passed over for these promotions," she cries, hands on hips, walking around. "I'm sick of life throwing me curveballs. I'm sick of all the shit in my life." She stops and looks at me. My hands are clasped over my cock. Hiding from her. "Sorry," she says. "I don't know why I'm venting at you but ... Arla suggested I come and see you and now I'm here I feel silly for being here. The wine is wearing off and I ..." She swipes a hand over her face.

I have Arla to thank for this visit?

"I see," I manage to say. My cock throbs inside my boxers. "Anything I can do to help?"

What a sleazy, cheesy line.

You can do better than that, Turner.

She gawks at me as if I'm talking in a foreign tongue. "Like what?"

I shrug. "I don't know. I just feel bad for you. Sounds like you really wanted this."

"I did."

"You're smart, and driven, and you'll get the right job at the right time."

"It's not that easy." Something about what she's said tells me that things haven't been so great for her.

I let her down, and so did her father. This is my chance to tell her that I feel partly to blame. I was so devastated after Anna's death, that I threw myself into trying to make life better, in any way I could, for my niece while her father was still in a coma. There was so much going on; my family was falling apart. We'd lost Anna, and my parents were grieving. I was, too, but I blocked off everything to take care of the baby. I didn't have time to think and worry about Megan.

I meant to get in touch with her at some point, but a part of me truly believed it was the best if I stayed out of her life. How was I to know that things might not have gone so well for her? I wait for her to say more, wary of saying the wrong thing, asking the wrong question given that she's already feeling so worked up.

It seems that both of our lives went to shit at that time, but I somehow managed to build a life of sorts. Not a completely happy life, but I have a child I love with all my heart.

I gave marriage a try. I have a great job. I'm happy.

I'm lonely, but mostly, I'm ... not so sad.

I'm still looking for someone.

And she's right there in front of me.

I look at Megan Summers and I try to shake the thought out of my head. I can't get involved with her. I can't mess her life up again. Last time, it was forbidden because of who I was and who she was. But this time I have a child. I have a problematic wife. Hopefully soon to be my ex. I've been shot. I'm recovering. I'm on the road to mending.

But Megan is still starting out in her life. She doesn't need the excess baggage that will come with me.

That is, assuming she'd ever contemplate the idea of wanting to be with me. Because it's all I've been thinking of ever since I met her.

But being with her?

Not an option.

She's already mad about the promotion. She's already hurting and me being in her life will only complicate things further.

"Arla suggested I get this anger out of me. She thinks I need to have it fucked out of me."

I almost choke at her words. "She said what?" My dick springs to life, and I flinch. Those lips... they give me ideas I hate myself for entertaining. I fidget uneasily, feeling uncomfortable and preyed upon as she comes towards me. She kicks off her shoes and eyes me like a hungry jaguar, her movements slow and stealthy, her eyes all lit up and fiery. I swallow, and my stomach muscles harden as I attempt to put my hands over my cock.

Offering a sly smile, she kneels on the floor.

"Wh-what are you doing?" My voice is uncharacteristically weak. She stares up at me before placing her hands on my inner thighs. I hold back a growl. My thigh muscles quiver.

"Don't ... don't d-do th-that ... "I try to tell her, even though my mind has other ideas. She leans forward, the open buttons of her blouse make it gape allowing me to see down her bra and the tempting flesh spilling out above the cups. I wriggle uncomfortably. "You need to ... to ... to ... meet someone," I say.

What a stupid thing to say.

She licks her lower lip. "I have met someone. I've rekindled a connection from my past."

Rekindled?

Is that what this is—a rekindling?

"How are you with your students now, Mr. Turner?" She slides her hands slowly along my thighs and I jerk. She's a provocateur and she knows exactly what she's doing to me. Her gaze falls to my cock—or rather, my hands covering it. It throbs and engorges under her heated gaze.

"Wh-what are you doing, Megan?" I manage to bite out as I fight for composure. I don't understand the shifting dynamics. I don't understand what's happening, but the appendage between my legs approves.

"Do your students flirt with you, Mr. Turner? I imagine you're still a fantasy for them, a good-looking math professor like you."

"I don't prey on my students. That's not what we had."

Her eyes well up in tears, and it's like cold water pours over me. I sober up and lean forward. "You're upset." It's the last thing I want. "Why?" I place my hands over hers and try to shift them away from my hardness but she doesn't yield easily.

"You haven't answered my question," she whispers.

My brain has ceased to think. "What question?"

"How are you with your students now?"

"What do you mean exactly?" I despise the insinuation.

"Are you nice to them? Like you were to me? Are you concerned and caring?"

"What I felt for you was genuine concern. I wasn't preying on you, Megan. What is this?" I shift as far back into the couch as I can, which is not much, but I'm cornered by this woman on her knees who's trying to imply that I am some sort of philanderer when it comes to young female students.

"All the girls had the hots for you. You haven't changed much, even all these years later. It makes me wonder what your students think of you. The Hot Young Sexy Professor."

There are some who seek me out. Like Heidi did. She's not been coming to the lectures much lately. She's been having counseling. The dean of the college wants me to have counseling as well. He says I need to because of my position. I can't be seen to be 'messed up' when I'm teaching.

I'm not 'messed up'. Not so much by the shooting. I still can't sleep easily, and I do wake up, but what I'm messed up about is staring up at me.

Maybe I messed her up, leaving her without explanation. I wonder if that's why she doesn't respect boundaries. She's kissed her work colleague one drunken party evening, and now she wants to pleasure me.

It's not what I expected of her. I cup her face with my hand and stroke her cheek, my finger resisting the urge to shift down and stroke her lips. "I want to help you, Megan. I want to set things right."

But this beautiful, fragile but feisty creature lays the flat of her hand over my hardness. I gasp because it feels so good.

"You can help me to get closure," she whispers, stroking me slowly. A smile spreads across her face.

"Closure?" I manage to say, just about catching the drift of her conversation. I need to move her hand away, but ... I am unable to.

It feels so good.

"Let me vent my anger tonight. Let me get closure with you by doing to you what you did to me that night when you went down and ate me out. Shaun had never done that to me, not the way you did." She presses her palm against me even more firmly, before moving her thumb over me, exploring, feeling, teasing. "Sometimes I can come just thinking about what you did. It's so vivid in my memory."

I moan softly as her hand slips into my pants and she tugs down my boxer briefs. My cock springs up; hard, and purple-ish and veiny. It's ugly, sticking out like a great big appendage that looks odd.

Her eyes widen. "My God, you're so beautiful." Her lips part and she looks ravenous. "Now I want you to come, like I did. I want you to remember me, like I have you."

I open my mouth to protest, but she's starts to work her magic, sliding her thumb over my silky tip. I squirm. This is killing me in the most pleasurable way. I'm having difficulty keeping myself composed. She bends down she licks the tip gently before swallowing it whole.

I'm in danger of coming right now. Of exploding all over. She grips the base, her soft, warm fingers sliding up and down my shaft.

"Megan ... no." My voice is a feeble protest. Weak and pathetic.

"Don't fight it, Mr. Turner."

I hate that she keeps calling me Mr. Turner. We're equals now.

"I want to suck you off and make you come hard." She licks her lower lip suggestively, grasping my shaft as her lips work all over it. She holds me prisoner but it is the best way to be held captive.

I can't answer her, not in words. I grunt when she swallows more inches of me. After a while she pulls away, her cheeks are flushed, her eyes shiny. Her lips are wet and swollen. "I want to have that power over you like you did over me."

"It was hardly like that," I say, biting out each word. My self-control is in danger of erupting.

"The way you worked your tongue and fingers, you left me spent. Utterly wasted, helpless and undone." She makes it sound as if I seduced her.

I remember it differently.

"You teased me, Megan." I recall how I walked into her room to give her a set of clean and dry clothes. But she slid down her panties and I couldn't look away. She was already topless. What was I supposed to do?

I couldn't help myself. I tried not to do anything, but she moved toward me. She took the pile of clothes and dropped them onto the chair, and then she took my hand and cupped her breast with it.

She slides her finger over my silky tip again, making me shudder. "I need to feel something, Lance. Only you can make me forget the bad things."

"I find it hard to believe that you don't have anyone."

"Ditto."

She sucks me again, and I wrestle with guilt and appreciation. Now is not the time to tell her the truth—not while she's sucking my cock with such vigor—but I will. Soon.

"Preston wanted me to go for celebratory drinks with him," she says, moving her mouth off me, giving me a little respite. She slides her fingers up and down the length of my shaft.

"You should have ..." Its difficult to form a sentence as her thumb grazes my penis.

Jesus Christ. This feels *so* good. It's been so long since I was intimate with anyone. Megan, here doing this is like a fantasy come true. I'm ashamed to say it's what I've been thinking of ever since we met.

"Do you know what he said to me? He said at least now I would be under him. Can you believe that? He's such a creep."

It makes things even worse because now I wonder what it's like to have her under me. "He said that to you?" Why is she telling me this? Why now when she's grasping my shaft and her mouth is inches from it?

"Why do you men say such things?" she asks.

"He's an asshole."

"Yes, he is." Her eyes meet mine. "Do you ever think of me underneath you, Mr. Turner?" She strokes me harder and faster, and I'm certain my cock is about to explode.

"Stop. Megan," I beg. "I don't want it to be like that this time."

"This time?"

"Why are you doing this?" I ask her.

"Because I want to. I haven't had anyone for so long, and maybe Arla is right. Maybe I just need to get my frustration out of my system. Like this." She suctions her mouth over me again and I jerk as pleasure shoots through me. "Your cock is so beautiful, Mr. Turner. "

"Stop calling me Mr. Turner," I bite out. "It's Lance ... we ... are ... adults." But now I want to fuck her. I so badly want to lift her up, turn her around, throw her against the sofa and shove myself inside her.

But she laps at my dick like its food she hasn't seen in months. I love it. Her lips seal around the head and she sucks in long and deep.

Jesus. Christ. I want to warn her. I can't control myself. It's the best head I've ever had. If she keeps up this pace, I'm going to shoot my load inside her mouth.

"Slower ..." I manage to say, and put my hand on her head, trying to get her attention, but she sucks even harder, the mewls and sighs coming from her are dirty. I love those sounds. It's like she's enjoying a delicious feast. I'm so lost in the heat of the moment that I forget to warn her. I shoot my load inside her mouth.

I feel so bad. When I raise my eyes to hers, she is triumphant, her lips wet and messy, her tongue darts out; streaked in white.

I blow out a breath. Where did she learn this? A trail of white trickles down the corner of her mouth. I wince and wipe it with my finger, but she sticks my finger in her mouth and sucks it.

She wipes her lips across my thighs and then puts me back into my clothing. I get another good look down her bra and I feel like a dirty old man.

Slumping back against the sofa, I try to get my brains and thoughts in check. "Let me do something for you," I beg, desperate to devour her the same way. I want to sink my face between her legs and eat her all up.

"What did you have in mind?" she asks.

"The same," I offer, but I also want to take things slow. To get to know her all over again. To not fall into lust headfirst, though it might be too late for that. I want to talk to her. I want to be her friend.

"I'm sticky between my legs," she says, and my brain goes into overdrive. I let out an involuntary groan and frame her face with my hands. I want to taste her so bad. So fucking bad, it makes my cock hurt. I stroke her lower lip. But that can wait. It must, if we're to do things slowly. "Dinner," I say.

"It would be a feast for you," she says, naughtily.

"I meant real food, at a restaurant, or a takeout." She looks confused at this, and I continue stroking her lips, try to exercise restraint but it is barely there, hanging on by a thread.

"Why?"

"Because ... because I would very much like to see you."

"Why?"

To my dismay she stands up before I can answer and tucks in her blouse, wipes her lips with the back of her hands again. I look up at her with gratitude. My mind has been blown and I'm desperate to have more of her. If I've tried to stay away from this woman, it's going to be near impossible now.

I can't. I won't.

I have to make things right for her, for what I did, for how I left but, fuck. I'll never forget what she just did to me. My cock throbs and begins to come back to life again.

I want more. I want to strip her naked and fuck her hard. All night. I want to get rid of my pent-up frustration. "Because I want to get to know you all over again." I mean it with my heart.

A knock at the door breaks the spell. I'm not sure if it's my mind playing tricks, but another knock soon follows. Dread fills me as the thought slowly registers. The only other person that comes here is Vivian.

CHAPTER NINETEEN

MEGAN

The air is musty, spliced with a saltiness that hints of my actions.

Lance looks spent, as if I've drained the life energy out of him, which, technically, I just did. It's empowering to know that I have taken him over the edge.

He wipes the corner of my mouth tenderly. I wonder if he thinks I'm a slut.

I hope not. I feel sticky between my legs and I'm so hot and horny and all I want is for him to reciprocate, but instead he says he wants to take me to dinner and wants to get to know me again. He says he wants to take it slow.

I don't understand. He might as well be speaking a foreign language.

Then the doorbell rings and Lance looks like he's seen a ghost. "Fuck," he mutters under his breath. Now I get worried. An unease makes the hairs on the back of my neck prickle. "Were you expecting someone?" I assumed he'd be alone.

"No." But he doesn't look too happy as he opens the door. A woman stands on the other side and beside her is a young girl clutching what looks like a dog-eared rabbit.

"Daddy," she cries.

Daddy?

My insides plummet.

Daddy?

"Surprise!" says the woman.

The news punches me in the face and I stumble back a few steps.

He's married?

And has a wife?

And a child?

I feel like the contents of my stomach have poured out into a puddle around my ankles.

"Who's that?" The little girl points at me.

"Don't point, Cassie," Lance's voice softens as he bends down and kisses the girl on her cheek.

The woman walks in, glides in, more like, as if she's a mannequin on wheels. She's thin, tall, spikey. A skeleton draped in clothes. Her face twists as her hard gaze travels slowly across my face and body. She is evaluating me. Trying to figure out what has happened.

He. Is. Married.

He's off limits. Just like he was before.

How is it that we're making the same mistakes again? Though in my defense, I didn't know this time around.

We're both adults he told me. The lying creep.

I grab my jacket and fight the urge to sprint out of the door but I need to find my shoes. Panic constricts my chest. Where the heck are they? I have to be cool, act as if we are just friends, as if nothing happened here.

"I'm Vivian." His wife sails right past Lance, who looks angry. Furious.

If anyone has a right to be angry it's me, and his wife.

The little girl holds his hand and she looks up at me with her great big eyes. Lance's eyes. She has her mother's hair and her father's eyes. She is a product of their fucking.

She is also adorable. Frustration shoots through me now that I see this man with new eyes.

He is a father and a husband.

"So nice to meet you." His wife holds out her hand. "Did he not tell you?" She comes right up close to me, invading my personal space, but I hold my own and stay rooted where I am. Then she leans in and takes a sniff near my neck. Her icy look freezing every nerve and muscle in my body.

"Tell me?" I ask, confused and frantic and suffering a brain fog of epic proportions. I clutch my bag tighter, determined to leave. I hear Lance and his daughter talking. This is a surprise, he says to her, then tells her he wasn't expecting her.

"That he has a family," his wife states in a flat voice. Words fail me. My voice fails me. Rage bubbles beneath my calm surface and I am filled with hatred for Lance.

I feel for this woman, for what she must be going through. Thankfully the girl is too young to be suspicious. But the wife can clearly see me for who I am.

"Are you Daddy's friend?" The little girl asks me, then, without waiting for an answer, "What's your name?"

I feel compelled to reply because this child has done nothing. His wife has done nothing to me. I'm the one who has done wrong. Lance even tried to stop me. He did, but I didn't listen. I forced myself on him.

It's my fault.

"I'm ... I'm Megan ..." My voice wavers.

The slut.

"Another one of your students?" The woman turns to Lance smiling. But it's a smile filled with a threat. The question is loaded with something dark and dangerous and in the deepest recesses of my mind I smell danger.

"I was just leaving." I rush towards the door, then realize I am shoeless. I look around the room.

"What were you doing here in the first place?" His wife's words are like grenades and I feel like any moment now she's going to take out the pin and cause an explosion.

"Enough!" Lance bellows, confusing me even more. He is angry when he has no right to be. His wife is calm when she has every right to be furious. This doesn't make sense.

I notice my stilettoes just then. They're strewn on the floor; one is around the side of the couch and the other one somehow ended up under it. They are a sign of our guilt and were it not for them I could have salvaged this. I could have said I was a door to door saleswoman. I might even have convinced her.

She knows. She knows just like any wife would know. Just like my mother knew.

I have become the other woman.

"Was it extra tuition?" his wife sneers. I will have it out with Lance another time because I need to leave. "Was it?" she asks when I don't answer. Her eyes assess me. "You're too smartly dressed to be a student."

I try honesty. "I'm sorry. I didn't know ..." Surely, I can't do any more damage than I've already done.

"He didn't tell you that he had a wife?"

I glance at Lance but his face is impassive. I wait for him

to deny it and to say that this has been a big joke. I wait for him to say *something*.

He fails me, again.

I move towards the door, my heart in pieces. It wouldn't hurt so much, but I was starting to believe the bullshit lies he just told me about how he wants to buy me dinner and see me again, and get to know me.

The consummate liar.

I glare at him. He opens his mouth as if he's about to say something, then his eyes go to his daughter.

I storm out.

CHAPTER TWENTY

LANCE

"Who's that, Daddy?"

"Just a ... friend ..."

"A friend?" hisses Vivian.

I can't begin to imagine what thoughts are going through Megan's mind. She must hate me, and she has every right to, but I couldn't say anything. I couldn't defend myself. I couldn't tell her the truth because Cassie doesn't know the truth. And I can't have it out with Vivian with my daughter being here.

I crouch down to Cassie's level again, aware of Vivian's dagger eyes on my back. "So, you wanted to surprise me, did you Sweetpea?"

"It was Mommy's idea."

"I'm sure it was." I stand up slowly to face the woman who makes my life so difficult. "Like the surprise last week, huh, sweetie?" I ruffle her hair. Vivian turned up on my doorstep then, as well. "Go and look in your room, Sweetpea. I've got a surprise for you."

Cassie's face lights up like a firework. "A surprise?"

"Go and see." I watch her bounding away, bouncing with energy. I bought her some toys and books that I'd intended to surprise her with the next time she came over for a sleepover, but instead she surprised me.

"You did that last week, Vivian." It takes all of my restraint to keep my voice level. "How long are you going to keep turning up unexpectedly?"

"I smelled something on you," she hisses in a low voice. "It was her, wasn't it? How many times have you fucked this one?"

"I haven't fucked anyone." Vivian has a dirty conscience and she's always suspicious of other women around me. But I don't sleep around. I've never cheated on her throughout our marriage. I've never encouraged my students, nor gotten involved in anything inappropriate.

It's only on this one occasion that I'm at fault. Though, we are almost divorced.

"Did you fuck her?"

"No, I didn't. And, despite what you think, I don't do that. I don't invite interest from other women, least of all my students."

"But something happened here." There's a dangerous glint in her eyes. "How long have you been sniffing around her?"

"I haven't." She doesn't need to know that Megan and I have history.

"I can smell it."

"We were talking." I'm about to turn away when I force myself to stare back at her. I can't look weak or guilty, even though I feel it.

"Talking? You and that floozy? You were just *talking*?" Vivian roars, just as Cassie comes running. My little girl stops, her plush rabbit falls out of her hands. I bend down to pick it up.

"Why's mommy shouting at you?" Her bottom lip wobbles. I steel my stomach, a part of me is sad for Cassie, and the other part is indignant for Megan. If I yell back, tell Vivian not to talk about Megan in those terms, she'll know Megan means something to me. I bite my tongue, grinding down on my teeth so that I don't answer back.

"Mommy didn't mean to," I say tenderly, stooping down to Cassie's level once more. "Did you find the things?" My little girl shakes her head. "Look under the bed." I wink at her, and she goes running off again.

I raise myself to standing. "You're snooping, trying desperately to find something, but there isn't anything to find. I know you so well, Vivian. Your little spontaneous visits to me, hoping to catch me in the act, will amount to nothing."

"I've been invited to a spa weekend with my friends. You never got back to me about it. You were supposed to check your diary and let me know if you could have Cassie this weekend."

I slap my hand to my forehead. She told me. She mentioned something about this weekend, but that was only a few days ago and I completely forgot.

"Are you free? You've got no choice now. You have to be because I'm packed and I'm going straight to the spa hotel from here."

"She's my daughter. I'll always make time for her."

Unlike you. Cassie is my weak point, and Vivian knows this.

"Your slut better not come over to visit you while my child

is at your place." The pungent whiff of Vivian's scent assaults my senses before her words strike me like darts.

I make myself look into her eyes. "Don't call her that." I shouldn't have said anything, because Vivian tilts her head, her gaze assessing and analyzing me in that shrewd and villainous way she has. I have already said too much. Her twisted women's instinct has made her suspicious.

But I must lie. For Megan's sake. For mine.

"Did you fuck, just now?"

"No." Technically this is the truth. Technically, we didn't do that. I look around for Cassie, not wanting her to catch any snippets of this conversation.

"Do you have any idea what it must do to Cassie to see you with another woman?" my adulterous, cheating wife hisses. "We can't mess up Cassie's life anymore—"

"If anyone has messed up Cassie's life it's you with all your affairs."

"If you satisfied my needs ..."

She's a gorgeous woman. She has it all: wealth, money, privilege, but these are not the things I care for. Inside she is empty and fickle, and has the warmth of a cold brick.

I want, I *need*, someone with heart and with whom I can have a conversation. Someone with whom I can have a shared emotional connection. Someone who is on the same level as me. Someone I can appreciate life with.

I shake my head, not wanting to be reeled into a conversation I don't care for. "Don't you have someplace to be?"

"We will always be together, Lance. We'll always be bound together. You won't ever be rid of me."

"What are you saying?" I don't plan to be rid of her. She's the mother of my child. I'm not sure if it's real or imagined, this subtle warning in her tone.

"Cassie will always be the link between us," she says softly.

Alarm makes the hairs on the back of his neck creep up slowly. "We will always have Cassie. I'll always be in your life," I tell her, as fear mushrooms inside me. I touch her arm wanting to make her feel better, even though I no longer want to be with her.

"Why can't we try again?" she asks, desperation taut in her voice. "We don't have to divorce."

"It's too late to try again."

"But this is a mistake. Let's try again."

"We did try." I remind her of the counseling we've had numerous times. It was always short lived.

She and I are so different. It's a regret I will always have, that I didn't see it sooner. That her beauty masked the ugliness beneath. That I succumbed to her body, so easily. She doesn't ignite my heart. She doesn't make me feel anything.

Cassie throws her arms around my waist, catching me by surprise from behind. I turn and face her.

"Daddy! Thank you!" She is bright and vibrant like a sunflower and in her hands is the artistic paint set I bought her.

My chest constricts and I struggle to take in air. I know what Vivian is up to. She wants to have a good time, but she also wants me in her life. Getting her hooks out of my back will be the bane of my life, but for Cassie's sake I have to put up with whatever this woman throws at me.

Vivian bends down and gives her a big kiss and a cuddle, making a show of her going away. "You be good, Cassandra."

"You have fun, Mommy."

"Can you bring her back?" Vivian asks, straightening.

"I'll have her back by late Sunday afternoon. Does that

work for you?" I had plans to go to the gym, and mark some papers, but I will put all those plans to the side and make sure I have quality time with Cassie.

"I'll let you know if I'm running late," she says. She's always thinking of herself.

"Do you want to do some painting?" I ask Cassie. "Or shall we watch a movie?"

"Can I do both?"

"Both." I chortle to myself. "Bring your paint set in here and I'll put the TV on. Want some popcorn?"

She nods. Of course she wants popcorn. I make her favorite and we settle down, me on the couch and Cassie on the floor, with her paint set on the coffee table, but my mind isn't on the Disney film.

I wonder what Megan is thinking. What's she doing. What she's feeling.

I wonder how she is.

I left Megan Summers once before, and now we've been thrown together again. This is a second chance and I'm not about to turn away from it. If only I knew where she lived, I'd march up to her home right now.

But I can't do that because Cassie is here. I text her instead:

We need to talk

There's no reply. I wait a while to see if she's read the text.
She hasn't.
I leave Cassie watching TV and walk into my kitchen for privacy, and then I call Megan.
She still doesn't pick up.

I've spent the weekend with my favorite girl.

Yesterday we visited a local museum; I had to bribe her to go to that in exchange for taking her bowling afterwards. Today we went to the park and now we're at her favorite eating place—a sushi restaurant.

We've almost finished, and she has demolished a big meal. It makes me happy. I love spending time with my girl. We've had a great weekend. I can make a life with just me and Cassie, and sharing her fifty-fifty isn't ideal, but it will do. Having Cassie one hundred per cent of the time didn't work, because Vivian was there. I tried my hardest to stay but for my own sanity I had to leave. I hope one day when my little girl is all grown up, she will understand why I did what I did.

It's always in the back of my mind, trying to figure out the best way and the best time to tell her. Vivian wants me to tell her about the divorce, and to tell Cassie that I instigated it. I have no qualms about doing that and I will, when it's official.

"Are you ready to go, Sweetpea?"

She looks pensive. There's a glob of sauce on her chin. I tell her and she tries to wipe it away, misses, so I wipe it away.

"Mommy is sad a lot."

"She is?" Cassie doesn't normally talk about these things, so my attention is on high alert. "Why do you think she's sad?"

"She says you have lots of girl friends."

I almost choke on the sip of water I've just taken. "She says *what*?"

"She says a lot of the girls at your college are your friends."

While I'm used to Vivian poisonous remarks, and I'm aware of her ability to plant things in Cassie's head, this is a low strike, even for her. "I have a lot of friends at the college—

men and women," I say calmly, while trying to still the raging storm in my chest.

"She says that girl we saw is a good friend, and you don't love Mommy anymore."

Suddenly it becomes harder to swallow the water. "She said that?"

Cassie nods, her face sullen. "Do you love Mommy?"

"I love you both very much."

"Then why was that girl with you? Mommy says *we* should be with you."

I touch my heart which is being punctured by my daughter's words. I never, ever wanted to hurt her, but pain is a symptom of a break-up. "You are with me. In here." I tap my chest. "You and Mommy are always in my heart. Do you know how much I love you? A million time more than the sky is wide and the ocean is deep."

"Then why don't you live with us like before?"

"Because of my work, Sweetpea."

"Mommy says that's not true. Are you telling lies?"

Vivian, that manipulative witch. I hate lying, and I've omitted things from Cassie rather than tell blatant lies, but now she has me cornered.

"Sometimes, especially with the traffic on the highway, it takes me a long time to drive to work and back. I wouldn't see much of you because you'd be in bed by the time I left and by the time I got back. This way, my work is a short ride away, but the best thing is that we get to spend more time together."

"I want my Mommy and Daddy to live together, like my friends' Mommys and Daddys do."

"I understand that, Sweetpea. But sometimes moms and dads can't live together. Sometimes, they have to live apart. Sometimes it's better that they do."

She frowns at me, her thin brows slanting together. Her

little rosebud mouth forms a pout. "Mommy doesn't stay at home a lot. She goes out, and Mila takes care of me."

"Mila, huh?" Mila is the live-in nanny and housekeeper Vivian's father employed when Cassie was born. I had no say in the matter.

"That's why if you come back we can have fun, Daddy. I won't be by myself."

It hits like a punch to my gut, and I'm still winded when she tells me she's going to the washroom. Whenever Cassie is with Vivian now, I will worry even more.

I keep an eye on the washroom. It's always tricky when I take Cassie out because being only nine years old, I'm hesitant to let her go by herself and I can't accompany her, but the washroom is in my line of sight and it's for one person only so I pick up my phone and check for messages and emails.

Nothing from Megan. I was hoping she would have calmed down enough to give me a chance to say my piece. On the spur of the moment, I call her and wait for it go to her voicemail again so that I can hear her voice but, to my shock, she picks up.

"Don't hang up," I say quickly, thrown for a loop that she actually answered. Maybe she's cooled off.

"Stop calling me and texting me. I don't want to hear from you again."

"But you answered the phone." She's obviously playing difficult, and I decide to humor her.

"To tell you to leave me alone."

"I need to talk to you, Megan. Please."

"Talk about what? Your wife? Your daughter? Or did you want to show me pictures of you all on vacation?"

I can't hear her too well and it sounds as if she's in a busy place because I hear people laughing and talking in the background. There's music playing, too.

She's not too upset.

"Where are you?" I'm not about to explain anything on the phone.

"Somewhere nice." She sounds oddly aloof, and happy. "On a date, depending on my next move." Ripples of laughter break out at her end. My jaw muscles clenches.

She's ... out ... on a ... date?

But why not? She's young and I'm an old man. I take a deep inhale to ground myself and regroup. "I want to explain."

"I'm sure you do, I'm sure you'll have a foolproof excuse, but I'm not falling for your lies anymore."

"When have I ever fed you lies?"

"Oh, I don't know," she says, airily. "Where should I start?"

"Why don't you start at the beginning?" I snatch at the opportunity to keep the conversation going.

"At the beginning ... when you pretended to be worried about my grades slipping? When I look back on it now, I wonder."

"Wonder what?" What does she mean? I'd been genuinely concerned about her. I'd started to care about her and I'd done my best to help her. "I want to explain about the other evening." I swallow hard. "I know how it looked when Vivian showed up—"

"No more lies, Mr. Turner," she says, smoothly. "I want to ask you one thing."

I'm ready to answer any questions she has. "Anything."

"Are you married?"

"I'm—" I hesitate because this is not the way to tell her. I need time. I need to meet her in person.

"Are you married? It's a simple question and it requires a simple answer."

I pause. "Yes, but—"

"Yes, *but?*" Her abrasive tone stops me.

"You need to hear me out, but not now." I don't want to have this conversation in front of Cassie.

"Not now? Is your wife hovering around you? Are you finding it difficult to juggle both of us?" Raucous laughter follows. She hisses at someone to keep quiet. "Listen to yourself," she snarls at me. "You can't even get your story straight. I don't want this... I don't need this—"

"This, what?"

"The complications you cause. Don't call me again. Ever."

This can't be it. "Give me a chance to explain," I beg.

"No more chances. You have a pattern, Mr. Turner, that's what you have. We have this thing, I fall for you, and then you leave and you—"

Fall for him? She *does* feel something for me. I haven't misheard. This is my second chance and I'm not about to let it slip through my fingers. "Megan—" But I stop, because a man's voice, loud against a backdrop of laughter, taunts me. Is he talking to her? Is that her date?

"Will you be quiet?" I hear her say to someone and I'm more curious than ever.

"Who are you talking to?" Jealousy pricks me like a needle and when I see Cassie walking towards me my anxiety spikes.

"I told you—I'm on a date ..."

"LuLu's cocktails are the best!" A woman yells in the background.

"Goodbye, Lance," Megan says. "Don't call me again."

"Don't do this, Meg—" but it's too late. She's hung up.

Over a decade ago, when she'd only been a blip on my radar, I'd been unable to do anything about Megan Summers. She was a schoolgirl I was worried about, and even when the warning bells sounded loud and clear, I hadn't heeded them.

But this time around I'll do no such thing. This time around there's more at stake. This time around she means more to me and I won't mess up.

CHAPTER TWENTY-ONE

MEGAN

"And then his wife walked in."

Arla almost spits out the sip of cocktail she's just taken. I've wallowed in self-pity all weekend. I've ignored Lance's texts and phone calls.

"Getouttahere!" Arla yells. "He's *married?*"

We're in LuLu's, a popular bar not far from where Lance teaches. Why she has picked this of all the places, I don't know. Why I agreed to come, I have no idea.

"I don't want to talk about it."

"I want to talk about it! You've just dumped a huge bombshell on me!"

She doesn't know the worst of it.

When Arla suggested we meet for drinks and news, I jumped at the chance. Only, I couldn't keep my dirty secret to myself. I blurted out what happened, and like the genie that's escaped from the lamp, I can't put the secret back in.

I blurted out that I went to see him and ended up going down on him. I couldn't keep it in any longer but telling her in a crowded student bar is a big mistake. I've been stuck inside all weekend, marinating in my own miserable thoughts, my bad luck with men, the complications in my life, the state of my love life. Wondering why I do things like this; seek instant gratification from a guy I'm attracted to, but this is different. Not only is Lance Turner still as handsome as ever, we have history. He's been in my head and my heart through my darkest times.

I shouldn't have gone to him, and now all I've done is read and reread Lance's desperate texts to me and listen to his voicemails. He wants to talk to me to explain everything, but I am done listening to that liar. I've met his wife and child, for crying out loud. He can't explain them away.

"Tell me about your date with Scott," I say.

"Forget about Scott. My news is boring. I want to know more about Lance's wife, and you giving him head." Arla's voice carries a little too loudly and the two guys at the table next to ours—who've been eyeballing us ever since we sat down—now gape at us with curious expressions on their faces.

I wish I hadn't told Arla. "Will you hush!" I hiss.

"You've mentioned a wife, and you said you've gone from 'hello' to kissing to giving him head. That's crazy, even for you. You do the stupidest things when you're around Mr. Turner."

"He's not Mr. Turner anymore." It's now legal for me to have feelings about this man and act on them but it's not good for my mental health. News of his wife leaves me feeling sick to my core. "There's more," I say, the cocktails have loosened my tongue and my guardedness. "He has a child, too."

Arla looks as if she's been slapped. "He ... *WUT?*" she screams.

"Will you keep your voice down?" I look around me, and

the nosey guys next to us quickly look away. "He has a wife and child," I hiss in a whisper. "They arrived unexpectedly."

"They *both* walked in on you .... while you were ... on ... your ... knees?"

My cheeks turn red at the thought of it. "I'd finished."

She jolts back and almost falls off her stool, only just managing to grab the edge of the table to save herself. "Thank God."

"God had nothing to do with it."

"She didn't catch you ..." Arla pretends to lick an imaginary lollipop. From my periphery I can tell that the two guys are staring at us.

"Will you stop being so vulgar!" I wish I hadn't come here. She's making a mockery of what happened.

Arla leans in closer. "You waited to tell me this news, *now*. In a public place? What have you been doing all weekend?"

Feeling sorry for myself.

I look at her helplessly.

"Start from the beginning and tell me everything," she urges. So, I do. I proceed to tell her in detail what happened, and she listens, like any good friend would, but in the retelling of the story, I am forced to relive it and confront it, in a way I've successfully managed to avoid it by pushing it to the back of my mind each time that thought arises.

It's not what I did to him, the power I had over him, reducing him to putty like that, but I felt good making him come undone. And now I get glimpses of the tender Lance, the one who wanted to try again, who wants a second chance; the man who wants to take me to dinner. They were nice things for him to say. They were sweet, until his family showed up. With hindsight I see him for the sleazeball he is.

A leopard never changes its spots, and now I question everything. Has he always been this preying monster? Should

I believe what he told me about his sister? Is there a niece? Because the picture I saw on his cell phone isn't the niece. It's his daughter. Did he leave the school suddenly because of his career and because of the warnings from the school Principal, as I suspected? Or was it because of the tragedy that beset the family?

I am none the wiser.

Lance hasn't texted or called today. He's probably busy playing the part of the dutiful husband and father. I'm such a magnet for the worst kinds of guys. Arla signals a server and orders another round of cocktails. "This will help," she assures me.

"They'll leave me face down on the floor," I reply, feeling miserable as I wipe away the condensation on my tall cocktail glass.

"It was buy one get one half-price, so if you hurry and drink up, I'll get another round in."

I raise my glass, grateful that Arla is the dependable, reliable, good friend who is always there for me. Unlike the men in my life. "Thanks for always being there for me."

She smiles and raises her glass, touching it to mine. "That's what friends are for."

"I don't want you getting depressed over that man all over again."

"I don't have the emotional energy to get depressed."

"To worthy men and happier love lives." She touches her glass to mine again.

We are perched on high stools around a circular bar table, one of many dotted around. It's Sunday evening and the place is abuzz with electric energy. The large open-plan room is laid out with long benches and small high-tables; laughter ripples out, people chatter, and the tinkle of glasses and cutlery all melts into the background noise.

There is no such thing as Sunday evening back-to-work blues here.

"He has a wife and daughter?" Arla examines my face for signs of trauma. I school a hardened expression, not wanting her to know how deeply it's hurt me. After what happened in my own family, this is one of the worst sins, to break up a family. "It must have been painful to see them."

It was. Like a shark's bite.

"Look at you," Arla pats my hand softly. "I've never seen you so broken up like this before, especially over a guy. But this isn't just any guy, is it?"

I don't meet her gaze. I don't want her to see right through me. A part of me hoped that we could have gotten to know one another all over again. Lance is a romantic, wanting more than just the physical stuff. Most men want the physical over the meaningful stuff. I've almost become acclimatized to it. Lance is gentlemanly in a world where many aren't.

I stare at the bright orange umbrella in my glass of Pina Colada and trace my finger around the rim. Lance might have only been a teacher on whom I'd developed a crush a long time ago, but the old emotions have soaked into my soul.

Getting over my schoolgirl crush on him at eighteen was hard enough, but to experience the humiliation this time around is even more crushing. Some men aren't to be trusted. Some men aren't the heroes they pretend to be. I blame my father because he let us all down. It's no wonder that every man I've met ever since has been nothing but a disappointment to me.

I watch Arla finish her cocktail in record time.

"Did you know cocktails are loaded with calories?"

"I'm not counting calories tonight," she replies. "Tonight, we're going to take your mind off Lance Turner."

"As if a cocktail's going to help," I mumble.

"One cocktail won't, but three or four might."

"I have a day of meetings tomorrow," I insist with a frown. "I can't go to work with a hangover." Getting drunk on a Sunday night isn't wise; getting drunk generally isn't wise. It gives me a headache the next day.

"Don't waste any time thinking about him, Megan. It's not as if you're exactly short of admirers. This is just bad timing."

"Bad timing?"

"After Mack, and now you're keeping Preston-at-work at bay."

My face twists. Mack was a guy I really liked. It was a hookup which lasted almost a month. It almost had the potential to become a friends with benefits type of relationship, but he wanted commitment, so I messed it up and argued and made it so that he wouldn't want to be with me. And, he didn't.

Preston isn't even in the running. He has the depth of a pancake. "I'll be keeping Preston-at-work at bay for the foreseeable future."

"We have company." Arla's eyes dart to the side, to the guys on the table nearby. She raises a hand to her hair, brushing her hair back from her face and tucking it behind the ears on one side. She turns and gives them an inviting smile.

"Can you not make that face?" I snap.

"What face?" asks Arla, making the face that I now know to be a part of her routine; a pout which looks like a fish struggling for air.

I point at her. "That face."

"It's exactly the kind of attention you need," Arla insists.

"I'd rather go home." I glance at the table quickly. Both guys give cheesy grins back.

"We're not going home." She sounds adamant. "You need

to take your mind off Cheating Turner and this is how we're going to do it."

My phone vibrates on the table.

It's Lance.

A shiver charges through me. My fingers hover over my phone until Arla reaches over and hits the button to end the call. "You're not falling for his lies all over again."

CHAPTER TWENTY-TWO

LANCE

I checked that Vivian had returned home before I dropped Cassie back.

Leaving Sweetpea was hard. I love having her, and I promised to have her for longer during the next school holidays. Maybe I'll take her to visit Sarah and Brett. I want Cassie to know her cousin and, had Anna been alive, the girls would have been so close because Anna and I were close. Brett's wife and their children are wonderful, so I'm thinking about visiting them with Cassie around springtime.

I park outside LuLu's after dropping Cassie home only when Vivian had returned.

I know this place. It's mostly popular with students. Darkness bleeds into the evening sky, and I peer through the windows, trying to seek her out. At first I see only the shimmering hanging lampshades and a kaleidoscope of people filling the place to bursting point.

Megan won't like it when I turn up like this, crashing her date, but I'm not going to leave until I've had my say.

Some fucking date. She didn't waste any time.

She thinks you're married, bozo.

But as soon as I step inside, the heat hits me, warm and sweet. Then the noise; the chatter and low rumbling of laughter. I scan my gaze around the large open bar, scouting for Megan. I find her in less than a minute, locating her with almost GPS precision. It's as if I'm programmed into her frequency.

Bracing myself I walk towards her. Another woman and two guys are with her—one has triple chin and the other is heavily inked. Both are big and have beer bottles in their hands. They don't look like students to me and it wouldn't surprise me that they're here to try their luck with the clientele.

"Hey." I tap her gently on the shoulder. She lifts her head, swivels her neck, recognition and surprise flicker in her eyes, and then her lips form into a thin line. Just as I predicted, she's not happy to see me.

"Can we talk, please?" It sounds like a weak request, and I immediately feel outnumbered, sensing hostility around me.

"Hey." A rough tap on my shoulder forces my attention to the side. "Hey, buddy, you're interrupting us."

"I'll be gone as soon as I've had my say." I turn back to Megan and everyone falls silent. I'm not going to leave until I've had my say.

"I told you I didn't want to see you again," she snarls. "Why do you keep stalking me?"

I'm taken aback by her accusation. She'd always been such a meek and gentle girl at school and it surprises me, how much anger comes from her. "I don't stalk." The words grind out. I didn't mean to be angry, but seeing her here with other guys, having fun, irks me. I remind myself that I'm here for a reason. "I only want a chance to explain."

"Get lost, buddy? Can't you see she's not interested?" The man behind me pokes his hard finger straight into my shoulder, near where I've been shot, and pain shoots through me like a spear.

"Don't fucking touch me again," I growl, trying not to look at his heavy chin.

"Fuck you, asshole." But then recognition dawns on the man's face. "You're the... the ..." He turns to his friend. "He's that guy, the college teacher in that shooting."

I ignore him and plead with Megan. "Give me five minutes of your time. That's all I'm asking for. Please."

It seems to be enough to embarrass her. "I wish you'd leave me alone."

"Hear me out, and I will." I take a step away, hoping she'll hop off that stool and follow me outside, but I accidentally jostle the tattooed guy. He's sitting on a different table but it's so fucking close, it's like they shoved both tables together.

"Look, buddy. I don't care if you're on TV or some hotshot, I don't care what you did, but this lady doesn't want to talk to you, so why don't you piss off?" he growls.

I ball my hands. "Why don't you?" What this asshole needs is for me to shove my fist down his mouth. I can't believe that Megan's on a date with him.

The man sets down his beer bottle, his nostrils flare and he pushes me, jabbing me in my injured shoulder again. I see red and I'm tempted to swing a punch at his face, but I can't lose my cool no matter how much I hate that he's with Megan.

"Stop!" she cries out, pushing herself between us.

"Grow up and stop manhandling one another!" her friend yells. I stare at the short, plump woman, and a flicker of remembrance goes through me. I know her. I glance at

Megan, because time is running out. "Please." I'm desperate for her to hear my side of things, and in a pathetic last-ditch effort, I urge her. "I'm in the middle of a divorce. I was going to tell you everything, eventually, when the time was right."

"Do you expect me to believe that?"

"It's true."

"Why don't you piss off?" says the neanderthal who just poked me. I turn around and resist the urge to hit him, even though he's asking for it.

"Why don't you sink back into the swamp you crawled out from?" I holler back.

Megan's eyes are round and fearful. "If you really want to help me, you should leave."

I survey the environment. We've attracted attention. People are looking our way and whispering.

"Sir, you need to leave." A man smartly dressed in a suit beckons for me to follow him. Since when did they have bouncers at a place like this?

Hell.

I shove my hands into my pockets, give Megan one final parting look, and leave. I've tried and failed, and there's nothing else I can do.

CHAPTER TWENTY-THREE

ARLA

The man is a psycho. After what I've just seen and heard, I'm starting to feel worried about Megan.

He's obsessed with Megan, but then, Mr. Turner always has been.

"We need more drinks," drawls one of the guys. "What do you think?" He directs his question to Megan.

They kept looking our way and in the end I asked them to join us, against Megan's wishes, even though she's the one they're interested in. Megan hated that I did that. I didn't do it because I needed them to fawn all over her and to forget I was even there. I did it because Lance sounds like a psycho and his actions now prove it. I was hoping these guys would be a distraction for her and help her to get Lance Turner out of her head, but now I'm worried that they'll mistakenly think we're spending the evening with them.

"I think you're right," I say, but he ignores me. I would

have fallen off my stool if he'd noticed me, but he doesn't. Most guys don't. It's always been like this for me. I'm used to living in Megan's shadow. She always gets the attention. I never do because I'm short, and plump, full-figured, though cruel people would say I'm overweight. Women like me don't get noticed, that's why Scott is such a diamond. He's such a rarity that I keep trying to look for what could be wrong with him.

Because there must be something wrong with him, to want to be with someone like me, right?

I didn't expect Mr. Turner to show up here the way he did. The fact that he followed Megan here tells me he's a creep. I wish I hadn't encouraged her so much when he first came on the scene. I wasn't to know he was married.

Now that he's been told to leave, Megan has gone quiet.

"Another round?" Triple-Chin asks, winking at his tattooed friend. The man is built like an army tank and when he lifts his arm to get a server's attention, I get a chance to read and admire the ink on his bulging biceps.

"Let's go to the bar and order," his friend suggests. I sigh with relief as both men walk off. I consider leaving the bar with Megan, making an escape while we can, but I wonder if Lance might still be loitering around outside. It might be better to wait a while. Megan sits quietly, a dangerous sign given the circumstances. "What are you thinking about?" I ask, even though I can guess.

"What Lance said."

"You shouldn't believe anything he says."

Megan is reckless when it comes to guys and relationships. She's not had much luck and I blame a lot of it on her parents.

"I'm not sure," she replies, but her voice is so quiet, I strain my ears to hear.

"You need to wise up and stop falling for everything that man says to you."

"I didn't give him a chance to explain."

I narrow my eyes at her. "After you've met his wife and daughter, you still think he needs to explain?"

She chews her lower lip. "Why did his wife knock on the door?"

"What?" I'm starting to worry even more about her.

"If it's her place, she would have had a key. Why didn't she just walk in?"

"Who cares. She came, didn't she? His *wife*? Whom you saw in the flesh. She's not a figment of your imagination. Why are you wasting your time analyzing the situation? You saw the evidence with your own eyes." If Megan isn't careful, she's going to fall for Mr. Turner's words all over again.

"I'm trying to make sense of it," she argues.

I huff out a loud breath. "Let me make sense of it for you. He's cheating, and he's lying, and you're a fool."

She sits with her shoulders hunched over, a perfect picture of misery and before either of us say anything, the guys return with a new round of drinks.

"How do you guys know that jerk?" The tattooed guy asks.

"Long story," I reply, not wanting to steer the conversation into those murky waters again. "Thanks." I raise my glass. "Drink up," I tell Megan.

We haven't made introductions yet, and I'm hoping it stays that way. These two will get annoyed if me and Megan leave now. At the very least we'll have to buy them a round of drinks to even the score, but Megan seems lost in her own little world. She's not engaging in conversation, and I'm not that much of a sucker for punishment that I'll keep talking to guys who clearly don't care if I'm alive or dead.

She turns to me. "His place was more like a bachelor pad. There were no pictures up, no homely touch, no woman's touch. No photos of his wife and child. Maybe she was lying."

"About being his wife?" I really am getting worried about her now.

"Something's off," Megan murmurs to herself.

My blood begins to boil. She's becoming obsessed by him again. "You'll make yourself ill trying to make sense of it."

"Are you still sad over that sonofabitch?" the inked guy asks. It's even obvious to them that Megan is thinking about Lance and nothing else. "I can help you forget him," he murmurs invading her personal space so closely that he's only inches from her face. Stupidly, he puts his hand over Megan's.

"Don't do that." Megan shoots back at him, visibly irate. Removing her hand, she turns to me. "It makes sense, don't you see?"

"You'll make yourself sick trying to make sense of it all," I tell her.

"But she, his wife, didn't give me the impression that she was coming home."

"You want to believe your fairy tale, but this isn't going to end happily ever after, Megan. Stories with married men never do."

"It seemed like she was passing by," Megan continues.

I lower my chin to my chest and inhale. Megan is good at concocting alternative facts when she just needs to believe what she saw. *That* was the truth. When a man's wife and daughter turn up unexpectedly, that's proof.

Lance Turner is up to no good.

I attempt to simplify things for her. "The wife and child might have returned from a sleepover at Grandma's because of   some-other-reason-that-I-can't-think-of-right-now. Grandma might have had surgery and come home from the hospital, and they went to visit her. Who knows, Megan? Who cares?" I yell, much to the shock of our new acquaintances. I throw my hands into the air in exasperation. "The woman said she was his wife! That's what you told me. You heard her! You saw her!" I'm so annoyed I could easily do a two-hour spin class. "You've got to stop this, and you've got to stop it now. Otherwise, you'll get hurt all over again. Why can't you trust your instincts?"

She pisses me off more than she knows. I want to slap that hopefulness, that obsession out of her.

"I *am* trusting my instinct. He said he'd moved to the area to be closer to the college where he teaches. There was nothing homely about his place; no evidence of children's toys or anything."

"That's because if they'd recently moved, it takes people a while to settle in. You're trying to make things fit when the truth is plain to see."

"I am not," Megan insists.

I have now officially lost the will to live. I drink my cocktail as if I've come upon an oasis in the desert and this is my first glass of water.

"I'm giving him the benefit of the doubt," she opines, causing me to slap my hand to my forehead as I try to regain my frayed composure.

"No, sweetie." I shake my head. "You're trying to fix it and make it something it isn't." If these guys weren't here, I would tell her that she's desperate for sex, for connection, and she's making Mr. Turner to be something he isn't.

Much to my dismay, Megan has that determined look on her face, as if she wants to believe her theory, even if it doesn't make sense. I'm not prepared to stand by and let her make a fool of herself again. Lance Turner is good-looking. He was the hottest teacher in high school, but this ridiculous obsession she has with him has to stop.

"The guy's a jerk," Three-Chin snorts.

"Sounds like it," his friend agrees.

"Where are you going?" I ask as Megan hops off her bar stool.

"Yeah, where do you think you're going?" Tattooed Guy blocks Megan's path. "We just got you ladies a round of drinks. The least you can do is sit here with us."

Megan gives him a thunderous look. "I'm going to ask you nicely. Please move."

"I ain't moving, sugar. And your friend thinks you're making a mistake," the man winks at me, grinning.

"Move." Megan snarls.

I put my hand on her arm. "Even I think you're making a mistake."

"I don't care what you think," she snaps.

The friendly joking disappears and talk turns serious. The air grows taut with friction.

I clench my jaw, sensing the animosity oozing from the guy who's not moving out of Megan's way. He seems defensive, suddenly pissed off with her. It's none of his business. He barely knows her, but he's brought her a drink, so he thinks he is owed something from her. Guys have always gone head over heels crazy for Megan and all I can do is watch and wonder if anyone would ever feel that passionate about me. This guy's an obvious jerk because Megan isn't interested, but the determination in his voice is something to marvel and it tickles my romantic notions. It's like he would fight to the death for her.

Scott is good to me, but would he ever feel like this?

"You can't go home yet," Three-Chin says. "Like Ronny

says, we've only just got a round of drinks, and we're only just getting better acquainted."

"What's a nice-looking chick like you doing with that dumbass anyway?" his friend asks. "Or do you have the hots for him because you think he's some hotshot hero?"

"I need to leave," Megan insists, brushing the guy's hand away and attempting to walk around him. He grabs her hand. "I'm a big hotshot. I'm a *really* big hotshot."

"Let go of my hand!" Megan yells.

"She said let go of her hand, asshole." A man's voice, loud, and authoritative, comes from behind, and before I can turn to see who said it, a fist lands on Tattooed Guy's face. I hear the sound, flat and dull, before he crashes backwards.

Lance Turner stands over him, his face red with anger. "Stay the fuck away from her."

"You asshole!" Tattooed Guy shouts as he just about manages to regain his balance. Like an angry bull, he charges towards Lance who then stumbles back and crashes into a table. He regains his balance and lurches towards the guy. "Touch her again and I'll fucking kill you."

The other man snorts. "Oh, yeah? Is this another student you—"

Before he can finish, Lance lunges at him like a fiend and the two men fight like vicious pit bulls. Tables are knocked over and people rush away and make room for the brawling men who are stumbling around, arms locked around each other.

It's hard to see how the thin and wiry Mr. Turner is going to get out of this in one piece, especially when the big guy has his arm around Lance's neck. But in a few lightning-fast seconds, Lance's elbow shoots out like a machete, striking his opponent on the nose. Blood waterfountains from his face. Lance smacks his fist into the man's gut, and he lands on his back on the floor. Then Lance throws a kick to his balls. I cover my nether regions protectively and wince, imagining a pain that isn't mine. That was uncalled for.

The man howls in pain as blood gushes from his face. An angry red puddle balloons on the floor.

"Lay another finger on her, you fucker, and see what I do to you."

"Get out!" Two burly security men appear and escort Lance out of the bar again.

Three-Chin is on the floor tending to his friend.

I witness the scene, the blood, the bodies on the floor, the crowd, and see the awe on Megan's face. Her eyes are on Lance as he's being shown the way out.

"Jesus. What the heck was that?" I'm in shock at what just happened. A staff member is tending to the injured guy. Blood is all over his clothes. It looks like a murder scene.

"I can't stay here another minute," Megan cries. She gets up to leave and I follow her. If she's going home, then good. But if she's going to find Lance, I need to stop her.

"It's been a long evening. Let's go home," I suggest, as we start to walk out.

"No." She has that same determined look on her face. I know exactly where she's going.

"You're making a mistake," I tell her, then realize that I've left my purse on the table.

"That's some crazy dude and she's his crazy bitch," Three-Chin says as I return. His friend's face is bloody, his lip is cut and there's still a trickle of blood coming out of his nose. A staff member is cleaning the mess on the floor.

"Don't talk about my friend like that," I snap, swiping my purse.

"The guy's a jerk. Didn't you hear the rumors?" Three-Chin shoots back.

I look up sharply. "What rumors?"

"He had an affair with that student he saved." He swipes a hand across his mouth. "Some fucking hero."

"What?"

"Yeah. It's all over the college."

"You're a student?" I ask, shocked.

He grins. "No, but I had a pretty fine threesome a few weeks back. Girls talk, and that fucker is the talk of the college right now."

My heart sinks and sinks down into my belly like a stone in water.

"I don't blame her boyfriend for wanting to shoot the fucker," the injured guy retorts, wiping his nose with a bloodied tissue.

The two men laugh.

The air in my lungs empties with a whoosh.

CHAPTER TWENTY-FOUR

MEGAN

The evening has quickly descended into a drama of epic proportions.

I rush past the heaving throng of people filling the bar to bursting point. Many turned around to watch Lance be taken outside by the burly security men, and now they part as I rush past.

I need to know. I need to be sure. Something Lance said made sense. I recall the absence of family photos, the woman's touch, the sparseness of his apartment when I was there. It didn't seem at all like a family home.

I rush out into the warm night air but it's dark now and I can't make anything out in the inky darkness. I look around frantically for him but there's no sign of him. I fish out my cell phone to call him.

"Megan?"

His voice comes at me from behind. I turn around as he steps out from the shadows.

He's my protector, a little voice inside my head tells me. I can't help but look at him, take in his body and admire the sheer hardness of his muscles. There's not an ounce of mid-life softness on him. "Didn't they tell you to leave?" I attempt to sound casually unconcerned, but he steps towards me, I want to shrink inwards to protect myself from him seeing the truth; that I am drawn to him. That he saved me, again, that he is always saving me. But should I be worried that he's always following me around?

"They did." He walks into my view, his face bathed in the light from the lamp above us.

"Then why haven't you?"

"I wanted to make sure you were okay."

"This is obsessive, stalking, creepy behavior." My heart which was starting to fill with appreciation, pauses.

"What is?" He scowls. "Making sure you're safe?"

"Following me."

"I was looking through the windows to make sure." He takes a few steps towards me. "What are *you* doing out here?"

I fold my arms defensively. "I came looking for you."

He's no more than a few inches away from me now. My breath hitches and my body starts to react to him in a way that is at odds with the logic of the situation. I have tasted him. I've been on my knees and pleasured him. I've made him come. And I want more of it. I want to be close to him, I want to kiss him and touch him, and have him do those things back to me.

What is he doing here? What does he want? This man has a family. I should get the hell away from him. "I don't need saving." My brain wins the fight between logic and romance. He might think he's an action hero, springing to women's defenses, but I don't need to be saved, least of all by him.

"You don't, but—"

"You saved the student, and now you've come to my aid. I'm capable of handling guys, even the ones who are complete idiots."

"That jerk was being an asshole."

"I've met a fair few of them. I can handle them. Why are you here, anyway?" I ask.

"We need to talk. It's important."

My armor hardens. The walls of the brick wall protecting my heart go up. "You're married."

He tilts his head, as if he doesn't agree.

"You're not married?" My hopes rise like bread dough.

"We're separated."

I am deflated again. "Then you're still married."

"The marriage was over years ago."

He's talking in riddles. I sigh loudly. "Arla doesn't think I should believe you."

"Arla? That name rings a bell."

"My friend, Arla. Arla Strasburger from high school."

"Strasburger?" He tries the word out, repeating it a few times. "I remember now. She used to talk a lot."

"That's the one."

"She hasn't changed that much," he remarks.

"She doesn't think I should give you a second of my time. She doesn't trust you."

"Then she's a good friend," he agrees. "She obviously has your best interests at heart."

"When were you planning to tell me?" I pivot to the more important issue.

"I wanted to tell you, but the timing was never right.

We're getting divorced. It should come through any day now. We've been living separately for a while."

My heart tells me to swallow his words but my brain is more cautious. He was silent that day when his wife showed up.

"Why didn't you say anything in front of your wife?"

He stares at me as if I've said something silly. Men lie. I know this sad fact well. A lot of the guys I've been with have lied to me; their lies ranging from the little white ones to the big, fat, soul destroying ones.

"Because Cassie doesn't know. She thinks I'm living away for work. When we first separated, when I moved out of the family home and moved into an apartment nearby, we told her that Daddy had to work long hours and it was better for me to live near the college rather than spend hours traveling back and forth. The traffic on the highway during peak times is atrocious."

I take a few long, slow, and deep breaths, making time stretch out, trying to think, because I'm not sure I can trust him, even though I want to.

"I don't want to make things harder on Cassie. Vivian is a good mother, most of the time. We're trying to do what's right for our daughter."

"But telling her lies isn't going to help."

"We're not telling her lies, we're just not telling her the truth yet."

I think back to the time when his wife turned up, and the look she gave me. "She was quite insistent about being your wife. She made sure I understood."

"Vivian doesn't want a divorce. I've been wanting to tell you, but the timing hasn't been right. I didn't expect you to show up that night. I didn't expect you to ..." He looks away.

Poor man. He was having a quiet evening at home,

drinking beer and watching TV. He hadn't expected me to show up any more than he expected me to give him the most amazing head. His wife and child turning up unexpectedly not long after was just pure bad luck.

Poor man.

"Are you complaining?" I ask, taking in all of him again.

"No ... yes ... no." He wipes a hand over his face. I still remember his appreciative groans and the pressure of his hand on my head when I went down on him. I want more of him now. A slow, rhythmic throbbing starts to build between my legs. I wonder what it would be like to have all of him. To spend the night and wake up with him. I've been thinking about this again, hard not to now, but I thought about it eleven years ago. I've been so consumed with need and lust and desire for this man, that the rekindling of it is too much to bear. I only have to look at him and I'm reminded of what we were, forbidden and taboo, and hiding from plain sight. "I didn't expect Vivian to turn up, but I can't say I was too surprised when she did. She's been suspicious for a while now."

"Why?" My inner alarm system goes off and the blare of screaming sirens tells me to back away.

"She doesn't want us to break up. Well, it depends. Sometimes she's okay with it, and sometimes she's not. I'm the one who instigated the divorce."

"Why?"

He's looks uncomfortable. "Irreconcilable differences." A vein pops out in his neck, I can see it clearly under the light from the lamps. Is he telling me lies?

"Why should I believe you?"

"Because it's the truth, and because I would never—I *have* never—set out to hurt you intentionally, Megan. Not then, not now."

I consider his words.

"I know you don't believe me, Megan," he says quietly. "My life is a clusterfuck, I made mistakes—although Cassie isn't a mistake. She's the best thing to come from this. I try to do the right thing, always, but life has a way of backfiring on me. And now you've showed up and it complicates things even more."

I'm confused. "How do I complicate things?"

"You give me a glimmer of something good."

I shake my head, trying to dislodge his words before they can imprint in my brain and replay at night when I find myself thinking of him. Glimmer? Something good? This man is living in an alternate universe.

"It seems ..." I hesitate. "It seems like a pretty big thing to omit, that's all."

He frowns. "How many times have we met? I never found the right time to mention it. I never thought things between us would happen so fast. I wanted to tell you about Vivian and Cassie, but you told me you didn't want to see ever me again. I didn't think we'd ever meet again, and then you showed up again that night. And now I don't want you to walk out of my life again. We seem to take one step forward and two steps back."

I force a laugh. "You're being presumptuous with your steps. What exactly do you think is the endgame here?"

He swipes a hand over his brow. "I don't know. You're the one who came to me. Megan."

He's right about that. I did. I could have gone home but I went to him. I was attracted to him from the moment I saw him on TV. I don't have much control around good looking guys, and I hate that I'm like this. But with Lance, it's different. This is scary, because this has the potential to be something more than one night.

He could be my tomorrow, my forever, my always.

"I thought she was your niece," I say, remembering my confusion when I first saw Cassie. "Your daughter, when I saw her."

"My niece? Why would you think that?"

"Because until your daughter showed up, I had no idea you were married and had a child."

"I'm not married—"

I set him straight. "You *are* still married, because you are not *yet* divorced."

"Noted." He folds his arm. It's only then that I see his t-shirt is ripped at the sleeve. He fought a guy, for me. I might have pushed back on him earlier but, secretly, I'm thrilled that he came to my rescue. I like that he was there for me. I'm all for women's rights and feminist ideals, but having someone stand up for me and protect me, it's the fairy tale every girl wants. Who doesn't like a protector being there for her? My father walked out on my mother and left us all to fend for ourselves, so I will take a man standing up for me any day.

I drag my gaze away from his arms. "When I came to give you back your pen, your phone rang and there was a picture of a girl on it," I explain. "I thought it was your niece."

"Ah... that picture on my phone ..." An easy smile spreads across his face, and the contrast could not be more stark. This man loves children. He loves his niece, and he lives for his daughter. "That's not Sarah, but it's one of my favorite photos of Cassie taken on her last birthday. She's got a splodge of cake on her nose and she's beaming the widest smile. That's ... that's my girl..." His voice chokes up and he seems lost in thought, lost in traces of his little girl. When he looks up, my gaze has softened.

He looks around. "Can we talk?"

"We are talking."

"Someplace else, not out here."

I can't do that. I've come out here because I wanted to hear what he had to say, and what he's told me sounds plausible, almost as if it could be true. *But it's too plausible*, a little voice inside me whispers. I don't believe things are that simple. Love is ugly. Life is hard.

Yet, this is easy, having Lance Turner back in my life. We have a chemistry that is impossible to ignore. I don't feel with anyone else what I feel with this man, it's like he imprinted on my young mind and ruined me for others.

It's wrong of me to blame my bad romantic relationships on him, especially when what we had wasn't anything like that. My teenage mind used that night to get me through the bad times; those crushing, soul destroying moments where I hated being stuck in my small town, resentful that the future I had envisaged for myself had been swept away.

In those dark days I leant on Mr. Turner, I grasped and grabbed and held tightly onto his wise words and his care and concern for me. I believed that I was worthy, that I deserved to be loved.

Now the man is back, and he says he wants a second chance with me. He seems to think my actions the other day prove that that's what I want, too. What I wanted was closure, but giving a guy head is a strange way to go about getting closure.

We both want something, even despite the complications in his life and mine. I need to be more careful because he has a past, and responsibility, and I will always be second in place.

"Can we go someplace else to talk?" he asks.

"I—" Before I can finish my sentence I hear Arla's squeal.

"I knew I should have come out straightaway, but I got talking to someone from the gym," she wails, looking from me to Lance, then back at me again. "What are you doing?"

"Talking," I answer.

"Hello, Arla."

Her gaze slowly returns to Lance. "Hey."

I wasn't prepared for her iciness. This evening she's been subtly dismissive of Lance where in the beginning, she was my biggest champion of getting together with him.

"I see you two really are inseparable." He's trying to make conversation, trying to be friendly but Arla is as hard as glass.

"I'm her friend, and friends always look out for each other." She hooks her arm in mine. "C'mon, let's getouttahere. I'll call a cab."

"Then let's wait here for it," I say, trying to figure out what's happened to her.

"No, let's wait over there." She points to the parking lot. She's acting weird. I shrug at Lance. There's no way we're going to be able to talk now. "I'd better go."

"You'd better."

CHAPTER TWENTY-FIVE

MEGAN

"How about we go together?" Preston asks.

I find it harder than ever to tolerate him. The company has its annual party for its employees next week. It's a black-tie affair. A dinner and dance event with everything laid on by the company. It is here that awards will be given for outstanding contribution. It's a feel-good evening to remind us how lucky we are to work here.

I don't want to go, but I can't *not* go, even though I'm more disillusioned with the company than ever. To not go now would mean I'm sulking. Preston is super smarmy and super smug, and he mistakenly thinks we can go together, the way we always have in the past.

Not 'together' as in being a couple, but we've ended up sitting together. Maybe this is another thing that makes him believe I am interested in him. I'm not.

"I'm not sure I'm going," I say because I really don't want

to go.

"You're still not over it, Summers?" he asks. "You're taking it very badly. Can't you at least be happy for me?"

"This isn't about you." It's not just my work life, that's in turmoil. My personal life is all over the place. And Lance entering it has just confused and complicated everything. "I'm happy for you, Preston. I really am." Though to hear me say it without a smile, I'm sure even he can tell I'm not.

"We can have fun," Preston insists. "I remember that time we had fun, hidden in the shadows, away from the dance floor."

That kiss was such a bad mistake. He'd been trying to make moves on me for a long time and I'd managed to keep him successfully at bay. But I made a mistake and opened up to him that night. I was feeling down because I'd recently split up with Mack, a guy I really liked. Things were still raw after the breakup and though the split had been mutual, the hurt still lingered. Preston was a good listener and as the party continued into the early hours of the morning, and we talked and watched the revelers dancing away, it just happened. I only kissed him to shut him up when he confessed that he'd always liked me. In my defense, I wasn't thinking straight, but I left soon after and the next day, at the earliest opportunity, I told him that an office romance wasn't a good idea. He told me that he was willing to wait.

For what?

Ever since then he's had the wrong idea. He leans closer to me. "If it makes you feel better, you'll enjoy working for me. I'll make sure you get all the best projects and the best clients."

I jerk my head sharply at him. "What are you insinuating?" I see this man for the scumbag he is.

He seems affronted. "You're good at what you do, you're

the best at it. I just want to reward you."

Am I really that messed up that I can't even differentiate between people being nice to me and people wanting something?

I walk out of my office, and he follows. "I'm bringing a date," I say just to piss him off.

His brows push together. "This is new. Since when do you have a date?"

"I don't need to tell you everything, Preston."

I was stupid in the early days when I willingly offered up my personal news, but I stopped telling him everything a long time ago because I realized who he really was.

"If you have a date, then I'm bringing Marilyn Monroe."

"I can't wait to meet her." I smile sweetly and climb into the elevator. "Goodnight."

Now I have to figure out how I'm going to ask Lance to be my plus one.

***

LANCE

She wants to meet me, at the same coffee shop where we met before.

That's not entirely true. Megan offered to come over to my place, but I stopped her. I don't want things to get out of hand like the last time.

She moves fast and that troubles me. There's something not quite right about the vulnerable and fragile girl I once knew, going from zero to a hundred by our second meeting.

While I'm ecstatic that she called and asked to meet, I'm

not okay with her coming here. I'm also cautious because, as much as I want to forget her, I can't. In my haste to see her, I arrive early. To pass the time while I wait, I check my emails and text messages. I read a text from Vivian where she reminds me about the concert at Cassie's school. I text her back and tell her it's in the diary.

"Who are you texting?" I look up and see Megan.

"Vivian."

"Ah ... your *wife*."

She's entitled to her barbed comments. "Not for long," I reply. "We still have a child. We still have to be nice and civil to one another."

"Has your divorce come through yet?" she asks, sitting down, pulling off her coat. I can't help but gawk at her off-the-shoulder woollen top.

I drag my gaze away. "Should be any day soon."

"If at all," she says, smoothly. Given that she's the one who called for this meeting, I don't know what to expect but I didn't think she'd be so thorny.

"Nice to see you." I examine her face for clues. It's blank, like she schooled herself to remain neutral and not give me any clue as to her mood.

Does she not feel anything? There is something between us. She's sucked my cock, for crying out loud. There's no way she doesn't feel anything.

My head is all over the place. Too much drama, too much angst, too many complications. Megan isn't a complication, but Vivian complicates everything. Now that she knows about Megan, she will be an even bigger bitch than before. Tangled up in this web of thick emotions, is my little girl. Cassie doesn't deserve this.

"She was reminding me of my daughter's concert at the school."

"Awesome." Megan takes the lid off her coffee and tips in some sugar. "How old is your daughter?" she asks, stirring.

"She's nearly ten."

"Nearly ten? Your daughter's nearly *ten*?" Megan's burst of anger catches me off guard.

"She's nine, for now," I say, in case that helps. I have no idea why she's so angry.

"You didn't waste any time."

"On what?"

I've been out of her life for eleven years. I don't catch her drift.

"I used to think about you, all the time after you left. For years ... How stupid I was. You'd already moved on!"

"I've explained—"

"I was fresh out of high school, living in a small town, having to listen to the rumors. I was looking after my mom, I was there for my brother and sister, because my father vanished. He left us. He didn't care about the family he had. We didn't matter to him, even after my aunt told him what my mom had done. Life was awful and you were my escape. At least, in my head you were. You were the fantasy I turned to when things got tough."

I slide my hand towards her, across the tabletop, aware that people are looking at us, but pull it away when she flinches. I'm unsure of whether I should sit beside her or not. "I'm sorry. I'm sorry I wasn't there for you."

"My life fell to pieces, but you didn't waste any time finding someone and starting a family. You were supposed to be taking care of your baby niece. Or is that another lie? It must be, because it doesn't add up how you found the time to get married and start a family. How could you do that if you were taking care of *your* sister's family?"

"It didn't happen in that order, and we didn't have

anything, Megan." I stare at her, needing her to understand this. "We didn't have a relationship."

She throws me a look of pure vitriol. "You worm yourself out of so many things. I feel sorry for your wife."

"Soon-to-be-ex-wife." I suck in a breath. "You and I weren't together." It's harsh, but it's the truth. Megan and I weren't a couple. How could we be when I was her teacher? I don't deny that it was emotional, but we weren't *together*.

That night changed things, and I can see now that she's held onto that longer than I did. I wish I hadn't given in to her. I wish I hadn't succumbed, but she was irresistible.

We weren't together. I didn't give her ideas that we ever could be. We both knew it was forbidden, and yet ... I failed and gave in and pleasured her.

"You were a student, and I was your teacher. Just because rumors spread around about us, they weren't true." This isn't the conversation I thought we'd be having, but I need her to remember how it was back then. "I didn't owe it to you to stay single. There was no us."

She looks at me, her eyes filling with pain. Then, she giggles. It's so out of character, that it alarms me. She slaps the table playfully. "It was all in my head. I was a silly giggly high school teen, and I used you as my fantasy to help me get through the bad times."

"You were never silly, or giggly." She was the opposite. Too serious, always working too hard, bright, smart. And worn down by life. Even I could see that. She didn't have the carefree attitude to life that many of her peers did. Megan Summers used to walk into the classroom with the weight of the world on her shoulders.

"Is this why you asked to see me?" To talk about the past, to have me explain? I hate that nothing between us goes smoothly. Not even something as simple as a conversation.

She falls silent and she looks so broken that I'm worried. I scoot to the seat next to her.

"Don't," she cautions, but her voice is weak.

"I'm sorry. That's harsher than I intended. I cared for you Megan. I still care for you now. I didn't care for the rumors, or the warnings from Principal Fielding and the other teachers. I didn't let that stop me from caring about you, but the rumors going around the school weren't true, were they?" I whisper, lowering my head, watching her stare at the fabric of her skirt.

"You felt ... nothing?" she asks, softly.

"I did feel something for you. You know I did. I just couldn't do anything about it. It was a fine line which I tried so hard not to cross. I almost succeeded, until that night when I gave in."

"I needed you that night."

"You tempted me," I clarify.

"But I needed you."

"And I was there for you," I reply. I wish I'd been stronger and not caved in. That night flashes through my mind, wreaking havoc with me even now. "You were so gorgeous, but you were also vulnerable, and I was weak."

She looks hurt. Injured. Like a wounded bird who can't fly. "That really makes me feel good."

"I don't want us to argue about it," I tell her. "I did care about you. I did want to be with you, but I couldn't think about the future. I couldn't think about anything because it was wrong. Things were so intense. Teachers were watching me, and the girls sniggered every time they walked past me. It must have been incredibly tough for you. I recognized that. My intentions were to stay away. You were going to graduate, and I fully expected that you would get a scholarship and go off to college to start a new life. I didn't know until now that that's not how your life turned out."

"And in the meantime, you got married and had a child."

"You can't blame me for that." She sees the past as different to how it was. "You can't think of it as you and I being an item, because we weren't. We weren't."

"You sure know how to make a girl feel good."

"If there's anyone who should feel bad, it's me. Knowing what you've suffered and what you went through, I hate that I did that to you. Now that I know what really happened, that you didn't go to college, that you failed your exams and you didn't get your scholarship, I hate that you went through this alone. I hate that I couldn't be there for you. I hate that I didn't reach out."

She lets out a sigh. "Life conspires against us. Maybe that's how it was meant to be. I'm sorry your sister was in that accident. I'm sorry your niece lost her mother. I'm sorry your whole life was derailed and I'm sorry mine was, too." She looks at me with understanding in her eyes.

"How are things at work?" I ask her, wanting to talk about something else. Something safe and uncomplicated.

She sighs. "Preston takes over next month."

"You'll be working for him?"

She appears to consider this, before answering with a "Yes ... no. I'm looking for another job."

"It's a shame you have to move." I don't want her to, and she shouldn't have to, but I completely understand why she feels the need to. "It's a shame when the company doesn't value you, but when one door closes, it's a stepping stone to somewhere else."

She gives me a look which I can't decipher. "I'm looking out of state."

"Out of state?" It's like a punch to my gut. I don't want her to go. I like the idea of her being close by. I like that we have come full circle and have met up again. All I want is for her to be happy, but there's still a sadness in her eyes. She's told me that her mother is okay now, and that her family is fine, but some wounds never fully heal. The scab might have gone, but the scar remains.

"I want a new start."

I was hoping we could try again and have a new start together, but she's not thinking about that. "You wanted to see me," I prompt, hoping to discover what this meeting is about.

She nibbles the corner of her lower lip. "I don't know how to ask." Her mask slips and she's no longer poised.

"Just say it."

"I need to ask you for a favor."

"Anything," I say quickly, relieved to finally be of service.

"You don't know what the favor is," she points out.

I lean forward and hold our gazes. "Then tell me."

"Are you free next weekend?"

For her, I will be. "Yes."

"I need you to be my fake date for an event my company is holding. I really don't want to go this year but that would make me look weak and sulky about the promotion." She speaks quickly, as if she can't get the words out fast enough.

"Aren't you sulking?" I play devil's advocate.

"I have every right to be, but I don't want to leave the company by quietly tiptoeing away."

"You want to hold your head up high."

"I just need you to get Preston off my back."

My gut involuntarily flinches. "Is he making moves on you?"

"When isn't he?"

She rolls her eyes in a way that confirms my suspicions. My muscles tighten. I don't want that slimy rat anywhere near Megan.

"He thinks I like him because I kissed him once."

I try not to react. "I don't blame him."

"I'd had a bit too much to drink."

"Does that happen often?" I ask, before I can shut my mouth and stop.

"Are you judging me?"

"No."

"Then why the question?"

I'm at a loss. I want to be her fake date, but I also don't want to ruin my chances. She's asked me for a favor, and it's one I very much want to do. Answering her question might get me in a whole heap of trouble I don't need. "No reason."

"So, do you want to do it or not?" she asks, taking a sip of her coffee.

"I can do that. Sure. I would love to."

"It's only a fake date."

"I heard you. I'll be glad to be of service."

"Thank you. You can scoot back over to your side of the table now."

I raise an eyebrow. She looks more relaxed, and there might even be a hint of a smile on her face. Was this why she wanted to meet me, to get me to come to her work event?

"Are you scared I might make a move?"

"You'd be stupid to do such a thing. We're not getting up to anything."

"You're sure of that?" I ask her as I move back to my seat.

"I'd place bets on it."

I nod. I'm grateful that she has asked me for this favor. "Give me some background. How long have we been together?"

She swipes a hand across her cheek, contemplating my question. "I didn't think this through. I told Preston I had a date but nothing else."

"You tell him it was me?"

"I did not."

I don't like that reply. "I see. Do you have a list of potential fake daters to go through?"

She shakes her head. "You're the only one I've asked."

My insides do a little tango in celebration. There might be a chance that Megan wants this, even as she pretends not to want to have anything further to do with me. "I'm sure he'll remember me," I say, already looking forward to seeing this scumbag.

"You're hard to forget. You leave an impression wherever you go. The security guys at LuLu's aren't going to forget you anytime soon."

I wince. "Sorry about that."

"You stood up for me. You were concerned about me. You looked through the window and you made sure I was okay." Her cheeks color as she says this. "Thank you."

My heart swells at her words. "You're welcome. You must get a lot of attention," I counter.

"From a lot of idiots, mostly."

"Always leave it to the wise, older man to set things right."

This makes her smile. "Don't get into a fight, please," she begs.

"I'll be as good as gold. What should I wear?"

"Dress smart. Do you have a tux?"

"Of course I have a tux."

"It's just a fake date," she reminds me.

"How fake can I be?"

"As fake as you need to be to convince everyone that you're insanely in love with me and that you have eyes for no other woman."

She has no idea that I've been falling in love with her the entire time. "I think I can fake it."

CHAPTER TWENTY-SIX

MEGAN

"**B**ut you recently bought a whole heap of new dresses," cries Arla.

"I want something a bit more ..." I rifle through the dresses on the clothes rack in the upscale boutique.

"All this effort just for Preston?"

The truth is, I have many dresses, and did recently buy some lovely ones that would be perfect for the awards night, but there's something different about going with Lance. I want to look extra nice. Sexy. Sophisticated.

I want to outdo Vivian.

"I'm not going with Preston." I pull out a mid-length slinky dark red dress with a low neck. I sense Arla staring at me. I can feel her eyes on me.

My motivations are at odds with my resolve. I'm trying to fight the attraction I feel for him, but I also want to 'Wow' him in my new outfit. "I asked Lance."

"You did what?"

"I asked Lance to be my fake boyfriend."

"You asked Lance Turner to attend your company's event as your date?"

"I did." I can't bring myself to look at her.

She lets out a groan. "Why would you do that?"

"Why do you not like him anymore? I thought you were all for this?" I put back the dress and rifle through the rack for some more.

"I should have come out straight after you that night when you left the bar. I shouldn't have left you both talking. That man gives you ideas."

I turn and face my friend, trying to get a handle on her sudden dislike of him. She hates that he has a wife, and that he lied to me. I like to think of it as him withholding the truth.

I know now that he didn't lie. He simply didn't get a chance to tell me. I believe him. I witnessed the way he and that woman interacted, and I could see that what they have isn't based on love and respect.

"His divorce is coming through any day now." I pull out another gorgeous dress. It's stunning, slim fitting and with a slit to my thigh, but I'm worried that it might be too sexy. I want Lance to want me more than he already does, but at the same time, I don't want to put it all out there. This slit to my thigh isn't appropriate for a company event.

But screw the company. In this I'd be making a statement.

"You're really going to see him again?" Arla moves to my side, her tone demanding, her expression not happy.

"To make Preston jealous."

"Which wouldn't be a problem if you hadn't gone and kissed him!" she cries.

"We all make mistakes."

"You make a lot of mistakes when it comes to men, and this, with Lance Turner, is the biggest one."

"You don't believe me about his wife, but I'm trusting my intuition. He and that woman didn't talk like a happily married couple. She was so cold."

"Why do you think that might be?" asks Arla.

"Huh?" I pull out another dress. It's a hot red number, long, with sequins and a low back.

"Why do you think his wife isn't happy?"

"Because she is an uptight, insecure woman who doesn't want to be divorced."

"I wish you wouldn't do this."

"Can you please try to be happy for me?" I snap. "I didn't get the promotion, I need to get Preston off my back, and if Lance is going to be my plus one, just for the one evening then—"

Arla snorts. "Are you going to have sex with him this time?"

"Shuush!" I glance around, hoping no one has heard. "Nothing else is going to happen. Let me have this one evening to bow out of the company with my head held high. Everyone knows Lance in this town. He's my trophy boyfriend." I hold up the dress to show Arla. "What do you think?"

"I think you're making a big mistake."

CHAPTER TWENTY-SEVEN

MEGAN

I suggested we can get a cab to the hotel and back, but Lance offered to pick me up from my place.

So, I let him.

I have butterflies in my stomach when he arrives, even though I remind myself that this isn't a date and that I have no feelings for him; that I'm not attracted to him.

Who am I kidding?

He's super punctual, arriving dead on the hour, and when I open the door, his jaw tightens. His eyes sweep over me fast, but don't make it down past my waist. My heart dips in dismay as I wait for a reaction, for a compliment, for his words. For anything, but he hovers in the doorway refusing to come in.

He doesn't like what I'm wearing.

His eyes lock with mine and I search for approval. Desire. Lust. Instead, I find a blank slate.

"Come in," I urge him, as I scamper around the room, looking for my heels. I'm so nervous, I rush around the living room, my insides sinking. I try not to compare myself to Vivian, but I'm aware that I lack in the glamour department. I can do slutty, or business. There's no in between.

"I'm fine where I am."

I glance over my shoulder, and that's when my breath fists in my throat. I see him properly for the first time. He's wearing a tux, and his blue eyes are glistening. I'm sure he knows just how good he looks.

Because he looks so *amazing*. I've never seen Lance in a tux before and so I am blown away. "You... you clean up well," I manage to say, sliding into my heels. I think that's what I said, because common sense disappears.

"Thank you."

My ears are still straining to catch the compliment.

He really doesn't like what I'm wearing.

I didn't wear the slit-to-the-hip dress in the end. Arla said it made me look like I was a high-class hooker. It was too sexy and I didn't want to project that kind of image. Not with Lance. I was aiming for elegance.

Like Vivian, but better.

I ended up buying a dark blue full length dress with a jewel studded high neck at the front and a cut out diamond shape on my back. Nothing too revealing, just a little bare back. It's classy and elegant and I feel like a million dollars in it. Or I did, until Lance showed up. He's not said one word, and I start to feel uneasy.

He still doesn't come inside. It's like he can't trust himself to. And it makes me even more self-conscious. He's coy.

Distant.

Different.

This isn't the Lance I've become used to, the one who

until recently told me he wanted to get together, he wanted a second chance. He's being careful. Restrained almost.

Or maybe he's moved on.

I'm sure he has many pretty students batting their eyelashes at him.

We make small talk as we drive to where the event is taking place. I tell him about the people he will soon meet, about my boss, Remy Brannock, and the others in my department we're probably going to end up sharing a table with.

Lance is quiet, to the point that I ask him if he's bored already. No, he answers. Then I ask him if he's worried about his daughter, or something? Again, he answers no.

I question whether it was a good idea to bring him, but then I catch sight of Preston mingling with a few of the secretaries, and I am glad Lance is with me.

We walk into the upscale fancy hotel where this event is always held. There's a room swimming with servers and beautifully dressed guests. Sparkling chandeliers hang like jewels from the high ceilings and servers stand at the doors with thin long champagne flutes on their trays.

I know the place well and this time, it feels so good to be here with Lance, of all people. I take a champagne flute, but Lance opts for a non-alcoholic drink. I tell him he can have a few drinks; he won't be driving us back until after midnight which is when this thing ends, but he shakes his head, and takes a pastel colored fruit drink.

My co-workers are standing around in their little cliques and I steer us towards them. My boss stands with his back to us, in a group which comprises Preston and a few other managers. "We'll have to say 'hi' and talk for a bit," I mutter under my breath.

Lance looks in their direction. "Let's get it over and done with."

Most of the people in my department are here but they look different, all dressed up, slick, smooth, shiny and new. A couple of the girls from the admin team catch sight of Lance and I see the admiration and awe on their faces. Their gazes shift to me then Lance, then back to me again.

"Can I hold your hand?" he asks, whispering against my ear. His fingers brush mine. In answer, I slip my hand into his. It's warm and firm. He wraps his fingers around my hand like a glove.

I've never attended any of these company events with a date before, which is why Preston and I usually have ended up hanging around together. Laughing at other people. I flinch in embarrassment. Was I really so cruel and judgmental, making comments about other people's partners and their relationships just because I didn't have anything long lasting of mine?

Not good.

As we approach my group, I feel as if I'm with a celebrity because, even though the shooting is no longer 'news', people know Lance's face because it was plastered all over the papers.

Linda, one of the receptionists, smiles at me, and the girls beside her can't seem to take their eyes off Lance. As we join the group, I make introductions, but it's not warranted because people know Lance, and they seemed dazed by his appearance at this of all places.

With me, of all women.

Murmurs of 'You didn't' tell us you were dating,' greet me as my colleagues start talking to him. Lance is gracious and charming. I watch him in action. I'm embarrassed for one of the women when she whips out her phone and asks him for a selfie.

He obliges, oozing charm like James Bond.

Then Linda asks the same, and soon, other women come over and want pictures taken with him. I stand and watch. It pinches, seeing him with other women. I wonder if this is what Vivian feels and why she doesn't want to let him go.

He rubs his hand over his hair, mussing it up, looking even sexier than ever. He's eye candy, and every woman he comes across, is eating him up greedily.

Other people join our group, I smile and make small talk, but I am not friends with these people, and only know them by face.

They're here not for me, but for Lance. They ask him about the shooting, and smile and preen and flick their hair, even those shameless women who have come with their partners. They desire him, but he takes it in his stride, as if he's used to the attention.

"Here you are." Preston slides over to me with a drink in his hand and a cocky smile on his face. He turns to face us, his eyes shifting to Lance at my side again now that the photo shoot is over. Lance's grip tightens around my hand and I instinctively move closer to him, my body brushing against his. Then he slips his hand out of mine and slides his arm protectively around my waist, his fingers stroking the silky fabric of my dress. Sparks scamper up my back and legs.

"You remember Lance, don't you Preston?" I say, cheekily.

"Yeah, I do." Lance turns to acknowledge him only briefly, before turning his attention back to his captive audience of groupies.

"This is my date," I whisper to Preston. A muscle in his jaw flexes. We make idle chitchat before my boss comes over to me.

The slimy little snake. He's obviously seen Lance and that's the reason why, because he's been avoiding me ever since we had a showdown. After Preston got the job, I asked Brannock for feedback. He gave me nothing. I asked him what more I needed to do to prove myself. He didn't have an answer.

No one here knows that I'm looking for another job, but I have a third interview next week at a company I really like.

Brannock doesn't seem impressed by Lance and barely glances at him. Maybe because it's obvious that he and I are together.

So, we move away and mingle with other groups, wanting to get away from my boss and from Preston. Lance's hand is either holding mine, or on my waist. And we've developed a strangely easy and comfortable togetherness. This is who we were meant to be. This is the future I used to imagine all those years ago.

After some more mingling and small talk we make our way to the beautifully dressed tables for dinner. People still stare at Lance, and I feel as if I'm gliding on air. I did the right thing. This is a great impression to make on my last appearance at this event. It's a good way to leave the company.

We're soon seated and it's with relief that I find I'm not sitting with the boss. But Preston is at our table and so is the rest of my department. Preston is on my right and Lance is on my left. I'm sandwiched between them.

Soon the speeches begin, and I groan. Wine is poured. It will be flowing for the rest of the evening.

It will help.

I lean closer to Lance's ear, and am hit by his scent; clean, fresh and zingy. A scent I have come to know so well. A scent my body responds to.

"This has the potential to bore you to death. You'll need to drink." I start to pour him some wine, but he puts his hand over his wineglass and shakes his head.

"I'm not bored. I'm with you." He leans in and speaks directly into my ear, his lips may or may not have brushed my ear lobe. A charge of electricity jolts up my spine. My insides melt. Possibly my panties, too. "I don't need to drink to get through this. It's my privilege."

My insides turn gooier than they were. He's doing it again.

I told him to pretend he was insanely in love me with and that he had eyes for no other woman, and he's been doing just that.

He can't be pretending, can he? Because I want this man so much. I need him. He smiles at me. His gaze dips to my lips and we forget that we are in a room filled with a sea of tables.

"Can you pass the wine?" Preston nudges my arm. Asshole. I hand it to him without turning to look at him. Then I hear a wail and I'm forced to turn around.

"You've knocked over a glass of water," Lance says quietly.

"Oh, God, no!" I see the river of water spreading outwards on the table.

"Clumsy," mutters Preston, because some of the water dropped onto his pants.

"I'm so sorry—" I grab a napkin and start to soak up the liquid.

"Excuse me." Lance has summoned a server who takes over from me. He takes my hand. "Look at me. Breathe," he instructs me calmly. When I'm looking into his eyes, I feel calm and in control. "The server's dealing with it." His voice is gentle, almost hypnotic. I forget that Preston is annoyed with me, or that the other guests were staring at me.

I just see blue.

Lance's eyes.

Cornflower blue.

My heart misses a few beats. I reach for my glass of wine, but my hands are shaking. Lance takes the other hand and places it down in the space between us. Now he's holding both my hands and I've turned in my seat to face him, with my back to Preston.

"It's okay. It's only water. It's being take care of. He'll live." His hands are warm and comforting and I don't want to let go. "Shall we go?" he whispers so close to my ear, his scent washes over me. I look at him in confusion.

"You can't just leave. We haven't had dinner."

"I mean, go for a walk in the grounds. They look nice. Wouldn't you rather be outside than in here?"

That is a brilliant idea. We get up and leave, and heads turn to stare at us. I don't even tell Preston what we're doing. Remy looks over at us, but I don't care. I don't care, because Lance is holding my hand and stroking it.

He's been so good to me.

As we step outside away from everyone, he lets go of my hand. I turn to him in disappointment and reach for his hand again, but he doesn't let me grab it.

"How did I do?" he asks, looking straight ahead.

"You're good, Mr. Turner." I want to get a reaction out of him. "You're very good. Everyone in there thinks you're madly in love with me."

He looks straight ahead of him as we continue to walk. As if what I've just said means nothing.

"They loved you," I tell him.

He makes an agreeing noise in his throat.

"Are you having fun? Or is this killing you?" I'm becoming slowly worried that I might have ruined his Saturday evening. "Did you have a better offer from your wife?"

"She's now my ex-wife."

The sentence hangs in the air like damp. I stop and face him, forcing him to stop. "It came through?"

He nods.

"When were you going to tell me?" I ask, not understanding why he hasn't shouted this from rooftops.

"Did you need to know?"

His words sting. I try to compose myself. "Did you not think I needed to know?"

He doesn't answer.

"How did ... how did she react?" I ask.

He sighs, his chest rising and falling. "As I expected." He starts to walk again, making it obvious that he doesn't want to talk about it. I don't push it, but my heart jumps like an excited child in a toy shop.

"Congratulations." It's what he wanted. "How did your daughter take the news?"

"She doesn't know yet."

"She *still* doesn't know? Don't you think you should tell her now, before she hears it from someone else?" I feel sorry for the poor child. It's not fair on her, believing that her parents are together.

"We will." He shoves his hands into his pockets and lowers his head.

"Thanks, for tonight," I say, wishing he would look at me, wishing he would touch me, wishing he would say something. *Do* something. He's been the perfect date to bring tonight, so good to me, and such a hit with everyone. I like being with him. I place my palm against his stomach and instantly, it hardens. I splay my fingers out, exploring the tautness as I slide my hand over the dips and valleys.

"What are you doing?" His voice is husky.

"I can't help it." I slide a finger through the gap between

his buttons and hear him suck in a breath. His stomach is rock hard. "Megan." His voice sounds weak.

"You've been such an attentive boyfriend." I stroke his warm skin expecting him to respond. I've come to read him well. He pretends not to care, to act as if he doesn't want me, as if I don't matter to him, but one touch, one stroke can undo all his hard fought composure. He presses his lips together and looks away.

He wants me, but he's trying his hardest to hide it. He slowly brings his face towards me again. "You asked me to make them believe. Do you think they believe?"

I tilt my face upwards. "They believe it."

I believe it. Staring up at his face I see the silver orb of the moon high in the night sky. It seems like an ending, or a new beginning.

I know what I want, and I want him.

"But it's only fake, right?" He moves my hand away from his stomach. His eyes glitter under the moonlight. They're dark, not blue, in the hazy night.

I swallow. "It doesn't have to be." He is free now. We can fall into this thing headfirst. I'm partway there, back in the thick of all that angst and emotion my teenage hormones riddled me with.

But now? What now at this age and at this time in our lives?

An electric charge fizzes between us. It's so strong that I can feel it even out here in the dark night, out in the open. The voltage sparking between our bodies.

I wish he'd kiss me. I wish he'd make a move.

I wish he'd forget what I said to him about not wanting a second chance.

"We should get back," he says, quickly taking hold of my hand and leading me back the way we came.

CHAPTER TWENTY-EIGHT

LANCE

Knowing that she once kissed that asshole makes my blood boil.

But who am I to judge Megan? I have my own baggage with the woman I married.

Megan doesn't want to go back inside just yet, but I can't stand out here any longer with her stroking and touching me the way she is.

I am in danger of getting a hard on whenever she's close by. It doesn't help that she's so forward. I wish she wasn't, but I feel it too—the chemistry between us. It's a heated, heavy ball of want and desire—a culmination of the feelings I tried to hold at bay all those years ago, emotions which festered and simmered. Now that she's in my life again, how am I supposed to resist her?

It's impossible.

She's had too much wine, and she's in a gilded little

bubble of happiness, though maybe she's also a little jealous of the attention I'm getting from her colleagues. These people are something else, nothing like the academics I work with. They're loud and rowdy, but I had a mission to accomplish, and I took note of what Megan asked me to do. I've been attentive to her and I haven't left her side. I hope I've convinced people that I'm in love with her, that she's the only woman for me, because she is.

Because I am. There's no pretending on my part. I only had to do that when I needed to put some distance between us just now. I needed to show her that it was just a ruse—like she wanted—but I'm the one who's suffering. I want to show her what she's missing, what we could be, and what I see, from this evening, is that we could be pretty good together.

I think she sees it too because her expression sobers when I tell her that we are faking it.

There are many young guys here. Loud, confident, good-looking. I've been watching them all. Watching them watching me, with her. She hasn't noticed the looks she's gotten. The way these men stare at her, with longing and lust. But she's mine. She was mine first.

"I'm not even hungry," she complains, as I take her hand and lead her back to our table. Her skin is soft and velvety. I can feel this pull between us, but she's looking to move away, find another job in another state. She's already putting up another barrier between us. She wants a quick fling, not a future. I've got a messy divorce situation. I have a daughter. It's complicated.

Heads turn once more, and I nod at people. I catch Preston's eyes and give him a yeah-that's-what-we've-been-up-to smile, even though we've done nothing. Even though there are things I want to do to Megan. My mind hasn't stopped racing with ideas.

She is a temptress of the worst kind; she doesn't value herself. She puts it out there, her body, her suggestions, what she wants. I was in trouble from the minute I saw her in that dress.

She looked amazing.

And all I could do was just stare and shut my mouth. I had to hold back because she's only asked me to be a fake boyfriend. It's a favor, just for one night, so I can't get my hopes up.

I can't do a thing about it. I can't show her. I can't make a move. I'm not calling the shots. She is. All evening I've wanted to tell her she looks gorgeous, but I've managed to keep my mouth shut.

MEGAN

Lance leads me back, but I'd much rather have stayed outside with him alone.

At least most of the speeches and awards are over with. Preston looks at me expectantly, but I don't owe him an explanation. Dinner is soon served, and Lance is deep in conversation with the person on his other side. I eat quietly, preferring that to talking to Preston.

People start mingling by moving to other tables once dinner and dessert are over with and Lance is soon surrounded by a group of women.

"Jealous?" Preston asks me.

"He doesn't stray." But something in my gut twists. Mara, a friend from another department waves me over, so I go to her. She wants to know all about Lance; how long I've been hiding him, why I've been hiding him, and how we met. She wants all the gossip, so I slowly and carefully make up a story. She keeps looking over my shoulder at him, and I get to witness first hand the effect this man has on women.

They all think I'm lucky to have him.

If only I could be so lucky ....

She tells me he's a catch, and she swats me playfully, asking why I've kept him a secret to myself for so long. Then she tells me about her relationship, and I listen, then commiserate when she tells me about her breakup which happened last month.

A warm hand rests on my shoulder, and fingers gently knead my bare shoulders. The nerve endings in my body crackle with anticipation. But when I look up, my disappointment crashes over me to find Preston staring down at me.

"Come and dance." He offers his hand. "Sorry for interrupting," he tosses over his shoulder to Mara. We're both sitting, and he's rudely inserted himself in the space between us.

My insides harden at the offer.

"You're so rude," Mara retorts.

"Sorry." He winks at her. "I'm taking my chances while I can."

I try not to wrinkle my face up too much, but the thought of dancing with Preston, especially to this slow, smoochy song, makes me want to retch. I look back at our table, but Lance is no longer there. I gaze around quickly, needing to find him.

"Come." Preston takes my hand.

I want to go home. Now.

"I'm not ... I'm not feeling up to it ..." I start to tell him, but he doesn't like my answer.

"It's just a dance."

"I believe she's taken." The scent of familiar cologne tells me I am safe. Lance is here by my side. My body softens.

Preston attempts a light laugh. "I asked first."

"She's clearly not interested." Lance is so confident, so assured, that he doesn't even look at Preston. His eyes are on me. "Care to dance?" His is the hand I take, willingly, gladly.

I would never have a slow dance with anyone at a company event, but this is Lance, and this is my last event here. A slow song plays as we walk onto the dance floor and his hands slide around my waist. I inhale a shaky breath. His touch makes my insides freefall, and my heart turns soft and liquid. Goosebumps pop up all over my skin.

"Cold?" he asks.

I shake my head. He has no idea of what he does to me. How much he makes me want him. "Not cold."

"I was never going to let Preston dance with you."

Joy shoots through me. "Possessive Alpha," I retort, feeling ecstatic. He's jealous.

"Call me what you want. You don't like him. I don't like him. I don't want you to do things you don't like."

"Thank you for rescuing me ... again."

"Any time." His gaze settles on my lips and his fingers wreak havoc with my skin. His nearness is intoxicating.

I place my arms around his neck and fall into the thrum of excitement which zips between our bodies. I'm in a happy place; somewhere I haven't been for a long time. My body starts to heat up, blood pools to my nether regions. I feel a tingle in my breasts. All this just because Lance is holding me close.

CHAPTER TWENTY-NINE

LANCE

Why did I ask her to dance?

I didn't want her to dance with that prick and I could tell from her face she didn't want to dance with him, either.

But now I find myself in a precarious predicament. All evening I've tried to remain cool, I've tried to avoid making body contact, and yet here I am. Doing all the things I wasn't supposed to do, like holding her in my arms and staring at her as if she's coming home with me and to my bed. As if she's mine.

All it takes is just the brush of her body against mine and the sparks fly between us. She looks up at me through thick lashes, and I can't stop my gaze drifting to her lips. She has the most luscious lips. They make me want her even more desperately.

I want her. I did then, and I do now.

This is so messed up. It's all backwards, how we started. There's a gleam in her eyes, mischief and pure want. My crotch hardens, and it's obvious that she can feel it because the little minx presses against me, teasing, knowing, tempting.

Driving me insane.

She has the audacity to give me an innocent smile. Lifting up slightly, she whispers close to my ear. "Let's go." Her breath is hot and sweet and dangerous. "I don't want to stay here. Take me home."

"You sure?" I manage to croak out.

"Yes."

I can do that. I'm relieved that we're leaving. Her work colleagues are okay, and the venue was nice enough and the event has been interesting. It's been a great evening and it's been the most pleasurable favor I've had to do for anyone, but I'm also in trouble. I'm in lust with her. In love with her. I'm trying to erect a boulder between us, but our slow dance disintegrated it.

I need to drop her at home and get the hell away. I park outside her apartment and pray she slides out of the car fast, but she doesn't move.

"Come up." Her voice drops an octave. It's soft and suggestive and it speaks directly to my dick. I stare ahead, knowing that it's my best chance to avoid getting sucked into her spell. I have to tread carefully here.

"That's not a good idea."

"Says who?" She gives a surprised laugh. "We've had a nice evening."

"Let's keep it that way."

"We don't have to."

"Stop it, Megan. I need to go home."

She giggles and snakes an arm around my neck, and all the cells in my skin jump. "Stop what?"

My mouth dries up. Words abandon me.

"Do you think about it?" she asks, her fingers stroking the back of my neck. "About what it would be like to give in ..."

"To give in? To what?"

This seems to confuse her because her fingers still. I grab her wrist. "You know exactly what you're doing."

"You like it," she maintains, a smile curving on her lips. "Tell me you don't think about it." She tries to free her wrist, but I don't let her. I need the contact, the warmth of her skin, the softness. I need her and right now I don't want to let her go. It's like fate put us together and wants to see what we do with our second chance.

"I think about you all the time." My voice is rough and croaky. "I think about you day and night. I've thought of you through the years and ever since we met again, I can't stop thinking about you." It's a fucking stupid admission to make, given that she's only inches from me, but she's here and she wants me, and she's doing it again. Teasing me and tempting me, and now my cock is ready to party.

Fuck.

"Then why don't you come upstairs and show me just how much you've missed me?" she purrs. She'll be my undoing.

I make the mistake of looking at her. "Why do you talk like that?"

"Like what?"

I let go of her wrist. "Like you want sex and nothing more." She's twisted her body and is sitting more forward, leaning towards me. I catch the dangerous scent of her perfume and look away.

"We both want it. Don't tell me you don't want more?" She reaches for my cock again. Just her touch makes me jolt. She moves her hand away and I miss it instantly. She can be such a tease. "You want it," she says softly. "We could go all the way ..."

Every muscle in my body tightens.

"There's no need to make such brazen moves." I sound like a monk, and my words don't agree with my body.

She giggles. "Brazen moves? You're sounding ancient again."

"You don't have to move so fast. You don't have to make yourself so readily available."

"So fast?" she cries. "We haven't seen one another for eleven years."

"Do you want to be with me, Megan? Or do you just want me to fuck you?"

"I love it when you talk dirty, Mr. Turner."

She calls me that when she wants to get a reaction out of me. I stare ahead of me, fighting the urge to give in to her.

"We can fuck now," she offers. I hate that word coming from her lips. I grit my teeth together, trying to not think about her offer even as my cock strains inside my pants.

Because I do want to fuck her. I want to fuck her so badly. But I also want to make love to her. I want to cherish her and treat her with the respect and understanding she deserves. I turn to her with a heavy heart, my emotions thrashing with my reasoning. I turn to her. "Do you want to be with me?" It's my turn to play the devil's advocate.

"Be ... with... you?" Her brows push together as if she doesn't understand.

"I want to be with you. Even though you say you want it to be fake, that tonight was fake, you must have felt the chemistry between us."

"I felt something." Her mischievous smile sends shivers through me. I wish she wouldn't make everything be related to sex. I wish she'd stopped using innuendoes. This isn't how she used to be.

She goes to reach for my hardness again, but I grab her wrist, preventing her. "Just go, Megan." With much effort, I move her hand away.

She slides towards the door. "Just think about it. In five minutes we could be naked and—"

"Go."

"Grumpy guts."

I do want her. I want us to try again. I want my second chance with her.

But not like this.

She climbs out of the car. "Wait." She bends down and looks at me. "Why don't you come in?"

"I want to do things properly. I want to see you again, and you can lie to yourself and say you don't want me, but you do—"

"Of course I do. I'm ready to—"

"Not. Like. That."

She pouts.

"Let's try it and see. Let's try a few dates."

She swallows. The shimmering jewels on her dress glisten under the interior car light. "A ... date?"

I nod. "A date, talking and getting to know one another, slowly. We don't have to take it anywhere but slow and steady."

She seems to consider it. "Well ... I don't know."

At least she didn't shut me down.

"I'll call you."

CHAPTER THIRTY

MEGAN

I've taken Arla up on her offer.

She's given me a free pass to her spin class with Scott. I walk into the room a few minutes late and am met with the sight of slim people in second-skin lycra tops and shorts, sitting on their bikes. Arla waves at me, and in the sea of lycra and metal, I navigate my way to her.

Almost at once the lights dim and disco music comes on. For the next forty minutes I'm in a dark room with flashing strobe lights, surrounded by people who are furiously spinning the wheels of their stationary bikes.

Scott instructs us. He tells us when to change gears, how much to increase the load by and when to change the incline.

From my vantage point I now have a chance to get a good look at the man who has become the center of Arla's life. I'm finding the new gear change hard, and I ask Arla if I'm doing it right but she doesn't answer me, because she doesn't hear me, because she's busy ogling Scott.

After the first ten minutes, I don't talk much anyway. I can't. My lungs feel as if they're on fire and I can't feel my legs. My butt hurts, and a quick glance at the clock tells me I still have another twenty-five minutes of hell to get through.

I struggle to keep up, and shock hits me to see everyone around me cycling fast and furiously. We are not cycling uphill, apparently. Arla manages to keep up, and this I find rather shocking.

This is what love does to you? It makes you forget your body is screaming for release, and makes you want to prove yourself in your lover's eyes.

I am never doing this again.

My jaw drops. I can't close my mouth anyway, because I need to take in huge gulps of air. My lungs are screaming for it. What I really want to do is fall forward and hug the handlebars.

I am so out of shape. But I have a fast metabolism which means I don't look out of shape. Lance doesn't think I look out of shape. I didn't miss the way his eyes raked all over me in the dress on Saturday night. I didn't miss the press of his hands on me when we danced, or the electric touch of our bodies. I certainly didn't imagine the way his hardness poke through the fabric of my dress.

No wonder he stopped dancing. No wonder he looked relieved when I told him I wanted to leave.

That night when he took me home, I had other ideas, but he ... he has a sense of nobility.

Scott yells at us to increase our speed and to add more load on the gear. I fiddle with the settings but can't figure out what to do.

A strong, hairy arm comes over. It's the guy from the bike next to me. "Like this," he adjusts it for me, then winks.

"T-thanks."

He nods then starts cycling like a maniac, sweat dripping from his face. I can't move the pedals much, so I adjust the gear back to what it was before.

I really need to get some sort of fitness routine going. I used to swim a lot, but work turned hectic and I was so dedicated to my work that I neglected myself.

They're all climbing an incline in the hardest gear, but I'm cycling happily, at the lowest gear, on a flat road.

This I can do. My thoughts go to Lance again. Going to the company event was a mistake, because now he's been imprinted even more fully in my head than ever. If I had a remote chance of forgetting him before, it is now gone. I want his arms around me, I want his lips on mine, I want his body pressed against the length of mine.

I want all of him.

The lights come on, shocking me out of my reverie. People around me are climbing off their bikes and standing in between them, stretching out their bodies. I'm still cycling like an idiot. Arla frowns at me and I stop cycling but remain seated.

This is what happens whenever I think of Lance Turner. I forget time, and where I am.

As we leave the room together, and Arla asks me what I thought of the class, I lie and tell her that I liked it, and that, yes, this was fun and of course I'll most definitely come again.

There's no hope in hell of that ever happening.

We shower and get changed and decide to get lunch. She wants to know all about the company event and Lance. I try to keep it brief, not give too much away, hide my feelings about how I really feel—and hide from her that we've sort of agreed to try going on a few dates.

Not that he's called me.

It's already been over a week.

Maybe I misheard. Or misread the conversation. Maybe his ex-wife has her teeth in him again. I feel sorry for him.

"I hope you didn't kiss him again," says Arla. Her eyes run down my length before she rolls them "Or do something worse." She hovers around in the lobby of the sports center entrance and is working the vending machine. Lately she's become very anti-Lance and even though I've explained that Lance is getting divorced, she doesn't seem to buy it.

"I did not. What a stupid thing to say," I mutter.

"It's not stupid. You turn into an idiot around Mr. Turner." She grabs her bar of chocolate, then punches in another number. A packet of chips falls.

"Are we going somewhere for lunch, or are you going to fill yourself up on snacks?" I ask the back of her as she bends down to retrieve it.

"Megan?" That familiar voice always makes my insides go all fluttery. Speaking of the devil himself appears to have invoked him. I turn around and stare straight into Lance's face.

"Hey." His smile is warm and inviting.

I return it, because seeing him makes me happy.

He reaches out and our fingers brush lightly. My body warms in anticipation but we're both being careful.

His gaze dips, taking in my outfit, and I feel exposed in my tight lycra leggings and my ripped crop top which reveals my stomach. His gaze slowly rolls up to my face and I see he's fighting to look calm. I can read those eyes well.

"You had a class?" he asks.

"Arla dragged me to spin."

He turns to Arla who is silent by my side. "Hey, Arla."

She nods. "Mr. Turner."

"You don't have to call me Mr. Turner." I can see the confusion on his face. Even he can sense Arla's iciness.

"You should try the spin class," I say, trying to lift the mood, because I was feeling elated until these two came face to face. Lance is wearing shorts and a t-shirt and I'm curious. "What are you doing here?"

"I was about to go and work out in the gym."

I catch a glimpse of his wiry forearms, and my gaze lowers to his legs. They're toned, muscular and hard.

We stare at one another, as if we're trying to get a read, a feel, as if each of us is waiting for the other to say something. A smile plays on his lips, but it's the way he looks at me, soft and reassuring, that makes my insides melt.

"I'm hungry." Arla chews off one end of her bar of chocolate and looks completely unimpressed.

"I'll see you around," I tell him, forcing my body to move.

He nods. "I'll call you."

I hope he will, because I'm still waiting.

"'Bye." Arla hooks her arm through me and shifts me away. I'm so mad, I try to count to ten. We walk along and I unhook my arm from her. What has changed? She used to be team Lance until recently.

"I noticed Chris helped you with the gears."

"You did?" I'm surprised she noticed there was anyone else in the room apart from Scott.

"He's hot and he's single," she says, as if we didn't meet Lance just a few moments ago. "He's hot and he's single," Arla repeats, when I remain silent. "He's nice. I could put in a word for you—"

I confront her. "Why are you so rude to Lance?"

"He's too old for you."

I'm too enraged to speak. We get in her car and she drives a short distance to the street where we usually find some great eating places. The mood is subdued and I'm on the way to losing the appetite I initially had.

"You can do better."

Better? She knows the heartache I've had with men. Hookups never end well. Anything more, anything substantial, I've mostly avoided. I never wanted to have a man take care of me because experience has taught me that I am better off alone.

Hookups I can do. Relationships I can't. But now, with Lance, I see the potential for something more meaningful, something precious and healing and good.

"We're going on a date soon," I announce, even though Lance hasn't been forthcoming with his intentions. I need to shut Arla up. I climb out of the car.

"You're *what?*" Arla gets out and slams the door hard.

"Going on a date. You were all team Lance before. I know you think he's lying and he's been cheating, but if I believe him about his wife, why can't you?" I get out of the car.

"Your mom will be mad. Your sister and brother won't be too happy, either, and, again, he's too old."

"Age is a number." We start walking towards our favorite tapas place.

"He's over forty!"

"I'm nearly thirty. It's no big deal. Not now."

"You just want to have sex with him," she hisses, just as an elderly couple walk towards us.

The woman looks at us and lifts an eyebrow.

But Arla isn't wrong.

I do.

CHAPTER THIRTY-ONE

LANCE

Megan's waiting on me to make a move and do something.

That's how we left things and I've been trying to figure it out. I haven't dated for years. I don't know how to, I don't know how to compete with the guys who are Megan's age, but I need to do something and fast, otherwise I'll lose her. I might not have her for too long, but at least I can try to make something of the time we have.

I am officially divorced now, and a single man again.

I am no longer married to Vivian.

But I will always be Cassie's father and I'm filled with dread that the thought of breaking the news to her. Vivian and I spoke about it and she agreed that I can tell Cassie in my own time when she next comes over to stay at my place.

I hope that Vivian will honor this as we navigate these new waters. Nothing has intrinsically changed. We've been leading such separate lives for so long that a piece of paper isn't going to make much difference but telling Cassie the truth—that's when things will change.

Cassie's away this week on a school trip, otherwise I'd tell her now. It's her reaction I fear for the most. Pretending I lived away to be closer to the college where I worked was easy enough to but I fear her reaction when she discovers I've lied to her.

My parents are still married and were high school sweethearts. I come from a loving family. Telling my little girl that her parents don't love one another enough to want to live together, will be hard. I won't phrase it like that, but as she grows up, she'll know the truth.

I'm at a loss for what to do this weekend. So, I pick up the phone and call the one person who truly makes me happy.

I've arranged to meet Megan at the coffee shop which is fast becoming our regular haunt.

It's a safe place to meet.

My life is at a crossroads, and even though I suggested that we try to get to know one another, properly this time, a part of me now wonders if this is wise. I can't think when she's close by, when her hands slip around my neck and she speaks all sexy and low, when there's a chance she can stroke my ego and much more ...

She's young, and gorgeous and probably moving to a new town soon when she gets a new job. She has her whole future ahead of her. I'm newly divorced, with a child and an ex-wife who will stick to me like a leech.

Is this wise, throwing myself into the dating game at my age? I know how to fend off interested students, but I don't know how to date.

"Thanks for coming," I tell her, when she slides effortlessly into the seat opposite from me. She's in casual clothes. A body-hugging t-shirt and jeans, over which she wears a long cardigan. It's going to be a mission to keep my eyes from wandering below her neck.

"Thanks for coming?" She blinks at me a few times. "This sounds official. Are you going to break up with me before we've even started?"

I cough in shock, and wonder what has gone on in her life that she has such little faith about relationships. There is so much unsaid between us. We stare at each other's faces, but there are no words. When I look at her, I sometimes catch a glimpse of the student she once was before I see the woman she has blossomed into. To have this perspective is strange. I seem to shift between two parallel universes, then and now, but I'm lucky enough to find her again.

"I never said anything about breaking up. You have such little faith."

She seems to consider what I've said. "You should have seen some of the guys I went out with."

"I'm happy not to have."

"Apart from Vivian, who else was in your life?" Her fingers grasp the ends of her cardigan sleeves as she brings her elbows onto the table.

"No one. Just you."

"Just me?" she asks, sounding surprised. I can't help but notice her long, long lashes.

"Yes."

"And before me, who was there?"

I cough lightly. "What is this? An interrogation?"

"I'm curious. Unless you have something more to hide."

"I won't hide anything from you, and, just to reiterate, I wasn't hiding anything before, the timing was never right." I pause, giving her time to make another barbed comment about Vivian but she doesn't.

"So, before me?" She doesn't want to let this go. I don't understand why she needs to know.

"There were women. Not many, but a couple."

"A couple? You're not very ... experienced then?"

"Experience has little to do with quantity."

This elicits a laugh. "You're very good, even with your limited experience."

I haven't done anything to her yet. "Thank you." My lips curl up at the edges. She amuses me. She's funny, and endearing. I am content just to sit here and talk to her all day long.

She swipes the menu from the small wooden menu stand and examines it. "You haven't asked me about the guys I've dated."

My gut hardens. "Because I don't want to know about them."

She looks up at me, then blinks again. "I'm sorry that Arla was so rude to you the other day."

The sudden change of subject once again derails my thoughts. Megan is the queen of subject changes, but it's a relief to know that I didn't imagine Arla's coldness towards me.

"Why was she? I only remember her as being a friendly, bubbly girl."

"She's being overly protective of me. She doesn't want me to get hurt again."

"I won't hurt you again."

We fall silent. I look at her. She looks at me. I remember her being in my classroom and staying back so that we could talk. I remember us going to the donut place. I can't remember how that transition came to be; how we moved from meeting at the library to eating donuts together. It was all so slow and innocent, until that last night. And now here we are a, decade later in a coffee shop. The years have passed and still our meeting places are low-key and normal.

"Are you free tonight?" I have ideas for other things we can do, other places we can meet at instead of coffee shops and donut places.

She makes a face that instantly tells me she's not. "My mom's coming over."

"Is this wise?" I whisper, conspiratorially, "Meeting now?"

"She's coming later. Make sure you lie low."

"She still hates me?"

"I think she'll always hate you."

I feel as if I've been punched. We hold our gazes, and I wonder if we're thinking the same things. "This doesn't bode well, does it?"

"We have now, Lance." She reaches across the table and takes my hand.

"Now?" It's too early to think of what we could be, but I want the option of tomorrow. I feel as if I've been living my life for other people—not that I would have done things any differently—for Sarah, for Vivian, for Cassie, who is my world. At forty-three, I've come to see that time is finite and that I don't have many chances at grabbing a future that is fulfilling in all parts of my life. I want to find and keep and cherish the things which make me happy.

I'm not content with just *now*.

"I'm not free this weekend," says Megan, setting down the menu and looking as if she's about to order. "but I am during the week. Are you going to surprise me?"

"Surprise you?"

"You suggested we should date, and I'm still waiting."

She's still waiting. She wants this.

I suppress the surge of a smile. A server comes to our table just then and Megan asks me if I want something. I order a hot chocolate before watching her chat to the server who is also a young woman. Megan tells her how much she likes her necklace and they proceed to have a conversation about it, while I look on and wonder what it is I can do for our first date.

CHAPTER THIRTY-TWO

MEGAN

"We're going to an art exhibition?" I exclaim in surprise when I meet Lance after work.

"You don't like art?"

"I'm not a pretentious person." I sound like a condescending bitch no less. "I didn't mean to sound so bitchy," I say, wanting him to like me.

"I didn't want to sit and watch a movie, or a show. I thought we could just walk around, and at least talk, while pretending to admire some art."

"I like the way you think."

He's thought it through, and I like that. Being with an older man is different. This date is different. It's not the type of place I would think to visit, not on a date. For me, it's the bar, and then bed. But tonight I feel sophisticated and grown up.

Is this what it will be like? Being with an older man? I'll

glide over my age range and slip into his. We'll have sedate dinners and watch shows and exhibitions. We'll make polite conversation when we meet his friends, and his family. Oh, my God. His family? What will they think?

What will mine?

He takes a hold of my hand then looks at me to see if I'm okay with him doing this. When I don't comment he tries to slowly slide his hand away, but I don't let him.

This feels *good*. It feels right. Like now is our time. It helps that my mom decided to only stay over for a few days. I can breathe easy now because she's in another state right now.

She worries about me and asked me if I'd met anyone nice. Erica is in a steady relationship, and Jensen might as well be married given that he's been with his girlfriend for a few years now. I'm the one who's always been in and out of relationships, and most of the time I've been single. Being asked about my relationship status is the part of my mom's visit I dread the most.

Still holding hands we go make our way to the art exhibition. Once there we walk around a large room staring at the painted offerings on the wall. It's contemporary art created by local artists, Lance tells me. The entire time we're going around admiring the works, he holds my hand.

I feel happy.

Cherished.

Every now and then I catch myself thinking that I'm with my high school teacher, with Mr. Turner. And then a pain goes through me when I wonder what my family would make of this.

I push the thought aside. I have a third job interview in a town which is about a two-hour drive outside of Boston. I'll have to move. We have this for now and that's all, so I should enjoy what I can of it.

"This is stunning." I stop to admire a painting of a sunset. The peachy blues mingle with the dusky pinks and bright juicy oranges. "It's gorgeous. I could lose myself in this." I stare in raw admiration and find myself falling deeper into the sunset. This is the type of artwork I admire; paintings of natural beauty. Lance is silent beside me as he squeezes my hand. I dare not look at him.

He has the patience of a saint, and he doesn't talk, or tell me to move on, or ruin the moment. He just lets me be. When I'm done I tug on his hand to move away, so that we can see the next work of art.

"You're done with this?" he asks, softly. "Don't feel you have to move on so fast just because of me."

"I could stare at this for ages," I confess.

"Then stare. Don't let me stop you."

My gaze slips to his mouth and his eyes meet mine as his fingers entangle with mine. A throbbing sensation pulses through my nether regions. His lips are so kissable, so perfect, but there's a gauntness around his eyes that I hadn't noticed before. Things can't be easy for him, with the divorce being so recent. I know how much he loves his daughter.

"Are you sure you want to do this?" I ask, because it seems like he picked something I would like. He hasn't really commented much on anything and seems to be content to walk around with me.

"I wouldn't do this if I wasn't sure. I'm with you, so this is already a great night for me."

It's back again, the humming between our bodies, the invisible, tenuous cord that ties me to him. "You always say the right things."

"I say what I feel when I'm with you."

"You're doing it again." I lean into him, feeling like we are a couple, after all.

"Did I surprise you? With this?" He gestures to the room around us.

"You did." I take another flute of champagne from a passing server, Lance declines, and we continue to walk around, taking our time, getting used to being with one another. Trying out this new relationship as if it's a luxurious new wool coat, something that will keep me warm and happy in cold, dark times.

We're examining another painting. This time it's of a wall of graffiti with flowerpots on the ground.

"Hey there ..." A light tap on my shoulder makes me turn around to look at a face I don't recognize.

"You're Arla's friend, from the spin class."

It's the guy who adjusted my gear level in the spin class even though I didn't ask for his help.

"Hey." We shake hands. "I didn't recognize you in the light. It's Chris, isn't it?" he looks so different without sweat trickling down his face. He grins, then looks from me to Lance.

"Yeah. Chris. You're Megan. Arla didn't introduce us but I've heard plenty about you."

I fight the urge to roll eyes. Something tells me that Lance isn't too happy with this interruption. An older couple look as if they're about to talk to this guy when they realize he's talking to us. "We'll be over by the entrance," the man says.

"My dad and stepmom," Chris explains. "It's my dad's birthday and he wanted to come here." His gaze bounces between me and Lance.

"This is Lance." I introduce them and the two men shake hands. There's a question in Chris's eyes and I feel wary.

"What brings you here?" he asks. I hesitate to answer.

"I wanted to surprise her." Lance beats me to it.

Chris's expression indicates that he is none the wiser. I'm about to say something.

"My dad's getting impatient. See you around." He nods at me then leaves.

"How do you know him?" Lance's voice is tight. I can feel the tension in the air and I try hard to fix my attention on the graffiti painting. Did Chris think Lance is my boyfriend, or my father? A young father, perhaps. Is this what it will be like, always?

"From the spin class I went to, that time me and Arla saw you."

"You must have made an impression if he remembers you."

I look at him. "Do you have a problem with him wanting to talk to me?"

He looks down. "No."

"It sure sounds like you do." I don't understand it. I care nothing for that guy. I wouldn't have remembered who he was had he not told me. But Lance acting like a possessive dick worries me.

"Were you embarrassed to be with me?" he asks, finally.

I spin my head to him so fast, in shock. "Embarrassed?" I wasn't, but there's a pause as I think about how awkward our interaction became. That I, too, wasn't sure who Chris thought Lance was. "No." I try to say it with as much indignation as I can, but Lance doesn't seem convinced. "You didn't say who I was."

"Because I don't know who you are."

"We're on our first date," he growls.

"Then why are we arguing?"

People are looking at us, because our voices have grown louder. We've almost come full circle, back to the portrait where we started.

He lifts his hand and palms the back of his neck. "I've got an early start tomorrow."

I don't like men who think they control me and own me and can dictate who I can talk to or not.

The hero side of him that once I found sexy, now makes me feel claustrophobic. I don't want a guy who's going to watch my every move and comment on everyone I talk to, especially men.

"Me, too. Let's call it a night."

CHAPTER THIRTY-THREE

MEGAN

My palms are sweaty and I feel out of place.

I'm sitting in a reception area with three guys who are suited and booted, their attire exuding confidence.

These men are my competition.

I'm in my not-so-high-heels and an expensive, new suit I bought over the weekend, hoping to look and feel super confident. These men look like Preston, and that immediately makes me uneasy.

Stressing over this interview kept me up last night, as it has done for the last two nights. It's the third interview and after this the managers will decide who to take on.

The job-hunting has been a good distraction, otherwise I'd have sat on my couch and gotten depressed about Lance and the perils of dating an older man. His superhero persona is now wearing thin and I'm beginning to see him as someone who is too controlling.

I don't want that.

I like being with him. He makes me feel special. It's undeniable, this attraction between us, and I like that he is older, wiser, decent. That he's caring and kind. He makes me feel special. To top that, he is hot and sexy and he's all the things I've not had in a man ever.

He's almost too good to be true, I often think, until I'm reminded of the fact that he has a wife—ex or not—and she'll always be a part of his life because of his daughter. These people will always be a part of his life, and I have to somehow fit into the jigsaw puzzle, but I'm not even sure if I'm the right piece. I don't even know if I want that. Lance comes with a lot of baggage, and I already have a truckload of my own. Once this magical beginning is over, once we are over the novelty of being together, things will fade, and we'll become jaded. Most people do. The things that gnaw at us now, will only get worse. Our date at the art exhibition has already uncovered some warts.

He won't be patient with me and my hangups about love and I won't want to be second place in his life.

Maybe I make a clean break. I'm looking to make a new life, with a new job and in a new town.

It's probably better that Lance isn't a part of it.

LANCE

Megan sounded tired and said she was staying in tonight because she just got back from work.

I didn't call her until now. I left it for a few days; I thought it might be best to give her some space especially after our date didn't end on such a great note. But she had an interview today, and I wanted to make sure she was okay.

Despite putting on a brave face and acting all hard-nosed, I can tell these things faze her, so I decide to surprise her.

I knock on her door while trying to balance a bag of groceries in one hand. She opens the door in her PJs—silk pyjamas and a thin sweatshirt on top. Surely it's not that late?

"You're going to bed?" I exclaim, waiting for permission to enter.

She eyes the groceries with suspicion. "What are you doing here?"

"I'm making you dinner."

"Why?"

"Because ... why not? Can I come in?" It's a bold imposition on my part, given how we left things, but that's all I have. I pray she hasn't eaten.

I wasn't expecting such coldness, not now. She wears her grudges for longer than is healthy. Maybe that's a generational subtlety. Younger people think they have more time, that they have forever. I have learned that time flies the older I get, and that it is limited, and scarce, and that holding grudges isn't wise because tomorrow isn't guaranteed.

"This is heavy. Can I come in?" I'm hoping to appeal to her good nature as I shuffle the bag from one hand to the other. She's in a mood, and she's tired. There's a chance that my good intentions might not be appreciated the way I had hoped.

"I don't want you to make dinner." But she opens the door and lets me in.

Her place is spacious and tastefully done, in silver and grey and white, contemporary colors, not pretty and girlish, but slick and smart. A quick glance around shows me a tidy little space, just like how I imagined. It's a cozy place, with cushions on the sofa, a table with a stack of books. A vase filled with pink carnations. She turns on a lamp and a honey colored glow bathes the room in a soft light.

"Have you eaten?" I ask, following her to a good-sized open plan kitchen area.

The firm set of her mouth tells me that she hasn't, and doesn't want to own up to it. On the countertop I see a box of cereal, an empty bowl and a spoon. "Is *that* dinner?"

"What if it is." She moves towards the bowl and stands in front of it, as if hiding it might make me forget all about it.

"I can do better than cereal." I start taking out the ingredients on the kitchen island. She doesn't stop me and, to my surprise, she pulls out a stool and sits down wearily. I set the ingredients over by the stovetop, and when I glance over my shoulder, I catch her gaze skimming my butt.

I take that as a good sign. "How was the interview?"

"I don't want to talk about it. What are you making?"

"Cheesy mushroom sauce with salmon fillets. It works, trust me," I tell her when she scrunches up her nose.

"Should I?"

"Should you what?"

"Trust you." Her eyes dim with suspicion.

"You can always trust me." What has she heard?

"Can I trust you not to have a hissy fit when someone—a guy—wants to talk to me?"

"Yes." I clamp down on my teeth, feeling foolish for the way I behaved. "I'm sorry."

"Just don't make a habit of it." She gets up to put her cereal and bowl away.

"Knives?" I ask, looking around the kitchen. She points to the knife stand, then tells me where the cutlery and the rest of her kitchenware is. I catch sight of an open bottle of wine and her half-filled wine glass.

"Shall I get you a glass?" she asks. I shake my head. I'm driving.

She sits silently behind me, while I get on with the cooking. I leave her alone, sensing that she's tired and perhaps a little worked up because I'm here.

"I don't think I got it," she says after a long time has passed. I've put the salmon fillets in the oven and I'm making the sauce. I'm boiling a whole heap of fresh veg on the side.

"Why don't you think you got it?" I walk over and place my hands on the kitchen island, then lean over slightly.

"Because the others were all men and they looked so much smarter and—"

"They looked smarter? Based on what?" She puts herself down so much. It's like the smart confident girl has vanished. I hate that I never once called her up to see how she was, but I truly thought it was for the best.

"They all looked like Ivy League grads."

"They can look like Ivy League grads all they want. You're smart, you just didn't have the chances, and what makes you think they're college grads? Why does it matter?"

"Because it does. Maybe not to you. You'll never know these struggles."

"Sounds to me like you've got a chip on your shoulder."

"A chip on my shoulder?" She takes a big sip of her wine.

I try to suppress my smile. I knew this would rile her up. "You're a smart girl. You always have been. Just because you didn't get to go to college it doesn't make you not smart. You're still applying for the same jobs, as those Ivy League guys, that's even if they are Ivy League people. You just did things your way, without a helping hand, without your parents giving you a hands up, and that makes you a fighter. I'd pick you any day over those candidates, simply because you've worked hard to prove yourself while they've just glided along on Daddy's coattails ... not unlike my ex-wife."

This makes her smile. "You can't stop thinking about her, can you?"

I raise an eyebrow. The tension has melted away and it feels like we're back to where we were before the spin class guy showed up. I clear my throat. "I was jealous. The other day at the art exhibition."

"Of what?"

"Of that younger, fitter, sexier guy. The one from your spin class."

"Why?"

"Because of those things I just said. He's younger, fitter and sexier. He's your age—"

"Age is just a number. Are you being serious?"

"I am."

"But I don't care about anyone else. I don't want anyone else, and you look way younger, fitter and sexier than him."

"Are *you* being serious?"

"I'm being serious." My lips form a slow smile at her words. She empties her wine glass and I refill it again.

"Are you trying to get me drunk so that you can have your wicked way with me?"

"I'm hoping it will relax you—"

"Enough for you to have your way with me?"

There she goes again. Being suggestive. I back away a few steps in case she reaches for me and runs her hands all over me, like she is prone to doing.

"I don't want to do anything hasty. I want to get to take things slowly, Megan, now that we can, now that we have a chance. I want to get to know you."

She stirs the sauce while I check the vegetables. She turns

to look at me, and her lips are parted, juicy, tempting. I force myself to focus on the vegetables again, fighting the urge to kiss her. Because one kiss won't be enough.

The timer for the salmon filets goes off, momentarily stealing my attention, and I start to take them out of the oven.

"Thanks for coming over, and cooking for me," she says, after a while. "That's the sweetest thing anyone's done for me."

Her words make me sad and angry. If that's the sweetest thing anyone's done for her, I hate to think of the bozos she's been with. All I can do is force a smile, but what I really want to do is take her in my arms, hug her close to my chest and hold her. I will do many sweet things for her, because she is so deserving of them. She looks at me as if she's waiting for me to make a move.

I swallow. "Shall we eat, before it all gets overcooked?"

She presses her lips together in a pout, and I start plating the food. Maybe tonight, I'll kiss her, and leave her wanting more.

Just one kiss.

I need, I would like, just one kiss.

I'm about to pour the sauce when I hear a ringing noise and it sounds like my ringtone. I rush over to my jacket and retrieve it.

It's Cassie. I answer it and she's babbling incoherently. Shock freezes me to the spot. I can't make out what she's saying.

"Calm down, Cassie. Honey. Calm down."

"You don't love us!" she wails, the words penetrate my body like shrapnel.

"What? Of course I love you, Sweetp—"

"You liar!" she screams. "Mommy says you're leaving us. Mommy says you lied."

"Mommy said ... what?" My insides whoosh out of my stomach. Cassie starts wailing again, and then she hangs up.

"What's wrong?" Megan looks worried.

"It's ... it's ... " My mouth turns dry.

Fucking Vivian.

I call back, but the line goes to voicemail. Two plates of food are sitting on the countertop.

"You should go to her," Megan says.

I hug her to me and hold her tight. Right now I need her more than she needs me. "I'm sorry."

"Don't be."

I press my lips to her forehead, and look into her eyes. "But I am."

She nods in understanding. I look around and grab my keys and my jacket. "Make sure you eat."

"I'm not a child, Lance."

My body feels hollow. "I'm sorry. That's not what I meant. I know you're not a child."

This isn't the first time I've had to rush off in the middle of things.

CHAPTER THIRTY-FOUR

LANCE

I try to tamp down the rush of anger which engulfs me.

Vivian promised me she wouldn't say anything, but I should never have trusted her. I should have known better.

When I arrive at the house Mila, the live-in nanny-and-housekeeper, lets me in. I hear voices coming from the living room. Vivian is sitting on the sofa and Cassie is lying with her head on her mother's lap.

At a distance I can already see that her face is red and she's been crying. The moment she sets eyes on me, she starts to holler. Vivian's face is hard. Her eyes wearing a what-did-you-expect expression.

"Sweetpea ..." I crouch on the floor, try to brush away a lock of her hair from Cassie's forehead.

"Go away! I hate you," she screams.

I buckle backwards, as if I've been hit. Vivian's eyes glitter. She's enjoying this.

"Cassie, baby." I try to plead with my daughter, my heart heavy, my insides in free fall.

"Go away!" Cassie shrieks again. "I hate you! You don't love us. Mommy says you don't want to live with us anymore."

I search Vivian's eyes. "That's not true." I attempt to stroke Cassie's face, but she pushes herself further against Vivian's stomach, as if she can't bear my touch. Shrieks and howls pierce the air.

"Goaway, goaway, goaway!" she yells, going into a full-blown tantrum. She has a temper on her, but I haven't witnessed anything like this since she was a toddler.

Mila, the housekeeper, rushes into the room, but Vivian dismisses her with a wave of her hand. I back away because me being near only makes the situation worse. I can't calm my daughter down.

She hates me.

"There, there." Vivian strokes Cassie's hair. "Mommy still loves you, baby. Mommy will *always* love you."

My ex-wife has always been a conniving shrew. My eyes fall to my daughter again, my insides splinter like broken glass. Vivian did this on purpose. She knows exactly how to hurt me.

"Can I have a word?" I hiss, and leave the room. There's nothing I can do. Me being around Cassie right now is only going to make things worse. I'll explain it to her soon, because she will calm down at some point, but I have to be prepared for my daughter to despise me. It's so obvious that Vivian has poisoned her against me.

She pads softly in bare feet into the hallway. Her thin, flimsy, silky night shirt leaving nothing to the imagination. Even this was staged. She tries every trick in the book. I stare into her cold-as-ice eyes. "You told her."

"I—"

I point my finger at her. "We agreed that I would tell her when she came to stay with me one weekend."

Vivian folds her arms and leans against the wall. "You're angry."

"Yes, I'm fucking angry. You're turning my daughter against me."

"She needed to hear the truth."

"But we agreed I would tell her when she came to my place."

Her gaze slips down my body and she sniffs. "You smell of butter and garlic."

Oh. Fuck. This hawk-eyed eagle can see and smell everything. I open my mouth to say something when she says it for me.

"Did you have a date? Did we disturb you?"

I can't lie. Even if I tried, she would know. This high priestess has always had the uncanny ability to sense things that others can't, maybe because she's fucked around so often she recognizes these things easily. Sniffs them out like a bloodhound.

"And what if I did?" I'm a free man now, and I can date, and it's okay. But I don't want her on my trail. She's dangerous.

"Is it that same one as the last time?"

I try not to swallow, even though I badly want to. I can't give Vivian any indication of my panic. More than anything, I need to keep Megan out of this mess.

"It's not like you," Vivian muses, admiring her painted nails, pretending this is a minor piece of information. Her eyes and ears and all her senses are fully engaged, searching for more data to confirm her suspicions. "This one must mean a lot to you. Is she a student?"

I despise her insinuation that there have been others.

"Nothing ever happened in college." Maybe she's heard the rumors. "I'm not you, Vivian. I have never been involved with anyone. I've been faithful when I should have walked away from this years ago."

"But it's different this time." She rubs her lips together, contemplating. "It is her, isn't it? The woman we caught you with?"

I try not to think about that time with Megan. But Vivian takes my silence as proof of something. "It must be ... serious," she says, her expression as hard as steel.

I've tried to stay calm, but she's tested my patience. "You are free to fuck the pool boys and gardeners and all the home help all day long."

Her hand lashes forward to slap me, but I grab her by the wrist. "Careful, Vivian. Your talons are showing." I glance over to my daughter. I still have to be nice to this woman. Because of Cassie she will be in my life forever.

CHAPTER THIRTY-FIVE

MEGAN

Lance makes me happy, and then he makes me realize how this isn't going to be easy for us, all in the same breath.

He is a remnant of my past, but he's suddenly in my future and I have a false sense of hope. He did a sweet thing for me by turning up at my place, not knowing what sort of a mood I'd be in, and making me dinner.

That's precious. I can't remember the last time anyone other than my mom, and maybe Erica when I've stayed over at her place, made me dinner. It could have been a lovely evening, us eating together and it was all going so well, until his daughter called.

He called me later and apologized for rushing off, but I told him he didn't need to. His daughter comes first, always, and I know that. His wife told Cassie that they were divorced, and she made Lance out to be a monster.

Something tells me his wife isn't going to make things easy for him. We stop and start, trying to get to know one another all over again. We take one step forward and then we're slapped back.

It's not easy, but nothing worth having ever is. Besides, what I have with him isn't love, yet, and maybe it never will be more than a crush. It feels so fragile. As if it can easily fizzle out and die because the odds are stacked against us.

He opened up and told me about how he felt when I ran into that guy at the art exhibition. The idea that a guy I didn't even remember could make Lance jealous, surprises me. All this time I've been worried about measuring up to Vivian, about being elegant and sophisticated enough for Lance, and he's worried about being enough for me.

He calls and arranges to meet again, and promises that this time there won't be other distractions. I tell him he can't promise me any such thing. I have been a child in a dysfunctional family and I recognize the similar pattern in Lance's family.

We go ice-skating one day, then sit outside in a park eating hotdogs and talking.

He tells me how much he likes this and, whenever we're together, my doubts vanish. I love spending time with him. People who knew us from our past would find this strange, but to me he's just another guy.

Not my teacher.

Just a sexy guy I am madly attracted to.

There's still nothing much going on other than us holding hands. He won't kiss me and it's infuriating how he's taking his goddamned time to do anything. He's way too chivalrous for my liking.

One evening we walk back from dinner at a restaurant, and thankfully we have no interruptions. It's just us talking about our past, reminiscing about the donut place we used to go to, and how we'd meet in the library. He takes me back to my memories and we remember them fondly, holding hands, going back in time. The connection now is magnified, and it feels as if we're on the precipice of something.

Then it begins to rain. Not just raindrops that will soon peter out, but the heavens have opened, and thick, heavy marbles of rain strike out of the sky. In no time at all we are soaked through. The deluge comes down unexpectedly, catching us off guard so that we're forced to seek refuge. The downpour is relentless and the water soaks through my sweatshirt to the tank top underneath, and also my jeans, making them stick to my skin. We stand under a canopy and I look up to see Lance swiping his hands across his hair. Water trickles down his smooth face, over those sculpted bones, and I admire him quietly while he doesn't notice.

He, too, is drenched. His suede jacket has turned a dark shade of brown and the dark blue shirt he's wearing sticks to him like a second skin. His jeans are thick and almost black where once they were blue.

That's when he catches me looking at him.

"You're soaked." He pulls me towards him puts his arms around me, as if that might ward off the rain.

I shiver. "So are you." My teeth are chattering. With my hair glued to my scalp, I dread to think how awful I must look. "This could go on for a while." I stare up at the heavens in despair. So much for our leisurely walk after dinner; walking and talking, holding hands, trying to navigate our way through our second chance.

"I'll call for an Uber, and we'll drop you off first." Lance lives further out from me and in this weather, many people will be getting lifts.

I have a better suggestion. "I'm not that far away. Let's walk."

"Walk? In this? I can't walk back in this."

"You can walk to my place and dry off there."

There's a knowing in his expression when he looks at me. Like he's not sure. Like he's realizing that this is also how that night began. Maybe this is how we'll come full circle.

"Let's go," I say, taking off at a fast speed, wanting to get home quickly. He's soon by my side.

"Are we walking or running?" he asks.

I haven't run for anything in recent years. "Fast walking."

We set off, power walking through the falling rain.

LANCE

This is how we began, that brief encounter that was the culmination of spending so much time outside the classroom.

It was a downpour just like this one when Megan came to me soaked to the skin, needing me.

She lets me in and I stand inside her apartment, conscious of the raindrops trickling off me. "I'm making a mess on your floor." I reach for the door.

"Where are you going?" she cries, taking off her wet sweatshirt.

"Home. I'll ... get a lift or something. I just wanted to make sure you got home okay."

"Don't be silly. I don't want you catching pneumonia and blaming me."

"I won't—"

But she's already disappeared and comes back with some towels. She hands me one, while she dries herself off.

Soon, we're no longer dripping, but we are most certainly still wet. My jeans aren't going to dry while I'm wearing them, and neither are hers.

"Ugh," she groans, and starts undoing her buttons as she walks away.

No.

This isn't happening.

"Don't just stand there," she says, throwing me a glance over her shoulder.

Well, maybe I can get dry … I follow her because my dick commands it. My brain has given up and left the room. I follow her into her laundry room. It's a good size with a washing machine and dryer and her cleaning utensils and products neatly stacked in a corner.

"I'll throw the wet clothes into the dryer." She strips down to her underwear. My eyes widen.

It's really happening.

She's gone there.

This time I won't be able to retreat so easily.

She throws me a look. "Don't be so shy. I've seen you naked before."

I'm wet and uncomfortable, and this has nothing to do with the rain. I could leave, but I'm here now and to leave would be … unthinkable.

"Now?" My voice is a pathetic high-pitched sound, stripped of any manliness.

She doesn't say a word.

"You had this planned." I unzip my jeans, feel my burgeoning manhood straining at my damp boxers.

"You think I commanded the heavens to open and pour?"

She folds her arms, which brings slight respite because her breasts are partially hidden from view.

My gaze drops and ... fuck me ... she's wearing the tiniest little triangle which barely covers her.

I have a déjà vu as I hand her the clothes.

"Your boxers look damp." She cups me through them, and I stiffen, my cock taking on a mind of its own.

"I'm not taking them off." My voice is still high-pitched, and at odds with my body which wants to lift this woman and pull her to me.

"You sure?" She gives my cock a squeeze through the fabric, and I swear the sucker mushrooms even more.

She bends down, turning her back to me, letting me see that only a string parts her butt cheeks. She's wearing a thong, and I can't take my eyes off her. I try to stifle a moan but I can't stop from reaching out and touching her. My hand slides over her soft-as-silk bottom. She shivers as soon as I touch her.

"Ooooooh ..." She stands up and leans her back against my chest. My manhood pokes her lower back. I can't stop from cupping her breast. Her pebbled nipple pokes through her flimsy bra and I run my thumb over it. Blood pools south to the place between my legs. Megan throws her head back and I inhale the fresh flowery scent of her shampoo.

I didn't set out to do this. But, damnit it. She's so irresistible. So sexy, so beautiful, and I can't restrain myself any longer. My boxers tent, and she giggles as she turns around and looks up at me.

"Are you sure you don't want me to dry your boxer briefs?"

In answer I lean down and lick her swollen lips. My tongue darts inside her mouth. She is sweet and soft. My mind is ablaze. I want to shove my cock into her mouth, but at the same time, I want to fall to my knees and feast on her pussy. I kiss her hard, and soon we're a medley of hands and groans. She breaks for air, then switches the dryer on; a slow hum fills the air as she props herself up on top of the vibrating machine.

"Ooohhh," she squirms, wrapping her legs around me, Venus fly trap style. Our bodies are damp, steam curling off them. My cock strains even more against the fabric, as she plants more hot, desperate, needy kisses on my face and neck. It's like we can't get enough of one another. We touch and stroke and feel, tongues lapping, mouths clamping. Her fingers wrap around my neck, and her ankles cross around my back. Her heels dig in and I grind my hips against her.

I want to sink inside her. I palm her pebbled nipple and, unsatisfied and greedy, pull down one of her straps and bra cup to expose a beautiful pert breast. My mouth suctions around it and I suck as if my life depends on it.

She throws her head back, giving me unfettered access to her neck and jawline. For a moment I stop and look at her, her eyes are half closed, lashes so long and curly. Her mouth is parted and she's semi topless. She looks like an erotic painting. Just then she opens her eyes and stares at me, as if she doesn't understand why I've stopped to stare.

"You can't ..." She shakes her head, disappointment veiling her features.

"Can't what?" My voice is hoarse with need, and pain, as if my engorged cock will wither and die if it doesn't get a release.

"You can't stop now..."

"What makes you think I have any intention of stopping?" No way do I ever want to stop. I want to do this forever. We kiss again, feverishly, hungrily, as if we're making up for all the lost years. She consumes me and all the things I've thought about, the things I've wanted to do to her and with her, now I can.

I pull her panties to the side and slide in a finger, making her shudder as she clenches around me. No, I do not want to stop.

I couldn't, unless she asked me to.

But she wants this, and she opens for me, widening her legs on the dryer. I slide in another finger and stroke her nub. She arches her back, moaning deep and dirty. I want to dive in and eat her out, but I also want much more. The torment of exploring and seeing her all over again is too much for me to take things slowly.

"You're so ready," I murmur, my thumb sliding over her easily.

I pull down the other bra cup so that her breasts are uncovered. She puts her hands behind her and leans back a little. With the dryer spinning, she jiggles around on top, vibrating with the spin cycle, her perky breasts bouncing. I pump my fingers in and out, like pistons. Each sweep elicits moans from her. She parts her legs wider, as if she wants more of me inside her. I hook my finger inside her and she lets out a squeal. My brain is in a haze. It's like I'm intoxicated. I rip the tiny little piece of fabric away. But doing it like this, so that it partly reveals her, and partly covers her, is sensual.

It's dirty.

She's *almost* naked, but not quite. She grinds herself against my hand and starts to shudder, as if she's on the edge of her orgasm.

Not yet.

I pull my fingers out and she whimpers, until I claim her mouth and kiss her hard. Our tongues stroke and taste and lick, and we go at it like two wild animals.

I need to fuck her here. *Now.* But in the distant edges of

my mind, I have enough awareness to think of her. It won't be comfortable for her, not like this, and I want space and softness for her. Not the cold hard edges of an appliance.

"Do you have condoms?" Her voice is raspy as I lift her off the dryer.

I'm embarrassed to admit that I do. "Will you hate me if I say 'yes'?"

"You do? Oh, thank God, thank God," she mumbles against my neck. In answer I palm her breasts roughly and devour her with another kiss. She's a smorgasbord of delight. I don't know what to taste or kiss or touch and stroke next., I'm spoiled for choice.

My cock could so easily slide inside her. I don't carry rubbers around with me because I don't expect to have sex with women other than my wife—and that fizzled out years ago. I'm not a guy who makes moves on women. But being with Megan, I had to be prepared. I've had to guardrail my heart and my emotions, because goodness knows this woman has tried to get me to make a move on her. She's been hard to resist.

Impossible.

Her ankles dig harder into my lower back as she tightens her grip around me.

Fuck.

I pull down my boxers, needing the release, needing to feel her. I have a mind to fuck her right here. Then I remember ... the condom is in the back pocket of my jeans which are in the dryer.

"I need a moment," I manage to mutter, as I bend to retrieve my jeans but her parted legs steal my attention. I want my cock inside her, filling her to the hilt, making her mine. I want to watch her come and fall apart under my gaze while I fuck her into oblivion. I want her to be mine forever, but she is so wet, glistening under the tawdry light that I can't help myself, and roll my tongue over her, lapping at her juices.

Oh, fuck.

The smell, the taste, it makes me want to come right now. I bury my nose against her, memories of her familiar scent reawakening. She tastes like an elixir I never want to stop drinking.

A gasp tumbles out of her. "Lance ..." It's her dirty, moany, soft sex voice. I'm tempted to lick her to an orgasm but my cock fights for attention. Her fingers graze my shoulders until I stand up with a warm foil packet.

"Do you think it will still be okay?" She's stroking my hard cock with her soft hands, her grip firm as she works it. I don't have the staying power to let her keep doing this. My pent-up frustration threatens to spill and I begrudgingly move her hand away before rolling a condom on. I don't have the time or patience to carry her to her bed, and as if she's not teased me enough already, she parts her legs even wider, opening like a flower.

I lose it, what flimsy shred of restraint I had. Positioning myself at her opening, I hold my breath. She stares at me, her eyes glazed. I push in, slowly at first, and the friction is beautiful.

Jesus.

She's tight.

And at this angle, Oh, fuck, fuck, fuck.

I slide in slowly then ram inside her to the hilt, losing control because she feels so good. She is soft and tight and hot and wet and I'm like a teenager on his first time, slamming into her with no finesse, only desperate need. A hunger that's lasted years is finally being sated.

I kiss her with abandon, then suckle her breasts, going from one to the other as if I can't make up my mind, as I thrust in and out of her. I want all of her. It's beautiful, the friction between us. She makes me come undone, makes me lose my mind. Makes me unravel.

It's all a blur, the dryer vibrating, Megan jiggling around on top of it, and me ramming into her, with my hands under her thighs, I shift her down towards me, and she leans back until she's almost horizontal. With her hands behind her for support, her naked breasts taunt me. I want to suck and lick them, and I will, I will but first ... I angle her upwards towards me, and then I fuck her hard. I ram into her, over and over and over again.

She hangs her head back, sighing, her chest rising and falling, and I... as if needing a final caress, suckle her breasts, first one, then the other; I feast like a greedy man, then bring her up flush with my chest so that I can go deeper inside her.

She moans. I'm so deep inside her, it's like we're conjoined at the hips, like we'll never come apart again, and then she convulses around my cock, her muscles tightening and shuddering, it's a marvel how I can feel her doing this. She cries out, her moans and satisfied mewls piquing my arousal. I'm still moving in and out of her, not completely done, taking every last ounce of pleasure from her. I groan then, and we hold each other, my arms around her, her legs around me. Years of longing spilling out, being spent. Falling into blissful satisfaction.

"Fuck," I mutter, because no other word comes to mind.

"Oh you did." She lifts her face to mine and kisses me. Our lazy tongues mesh and mingle. It's a messy kiss, wet and sloppy. "You fuck so good," she whispers.

"It's been years in the making, thinking about this." I lick her lips. Her warm breath kisses my skin. She moans, and we sigh and stare at one another, our foreheads pressed together.

"You said you never thought about me."

"That's not what I said. I said I didn't want to mess your life up by getting in touch with you. Didn't stop me from thinking about you."

She gives me her fullest smile. "Let's go to bed," she says, while I am still inside her. I want to stay like this for longer. Her legs begin to wrap firmly around my hips again. My manhood stirs to life.

I want to fuck her in bed this time. I need more room, more space to properly feast on her. I lift her easily and carry her through the living room. She directs me to her bedroom and once inside, I carefully put her down on the bed, disentangling myself from her.

She's covered in a layer of sweat, and her pussy is soft and wet and ... I just want to curl up against her for now. Hold her in my arms and enjoy the feel of having her.

She plants her foot on my thigh before moving it and stroking my already stiff cock with it. A mischievous gleam lights her eyes. "Come again?"

"Oh, yes." My hoarse reply coincides with the slamming of a door. Then I hear a voice and the hairs on the back of my neck lift as surely as my cock.

"It's meeeeeee!" We hear a young woman's cheerful voice. It's as welcome as a bucket of cold water.

Not her goddamn friend, again?

Megan looks at me in fear.

"Fucking timing," I growl, hating the interruption. Megan shoots out of bed, reaches for the duvet and wraps it around her while I stand confused, semi-hard and furious.

"Megan?"

The door opens and a young woman stares at me, her eyes falling to my cock as she gasps. I place my hands to recoup my modesty. It's not her friend.

"What are you doing here?" Megan asks. "You told me you were coming on Friday."

"I changed my mind."

"You could have told me!" Megan yells.

"I wanted to surprise you!"

I'm caught in the middle of this exchange. Not daring to move, or breathe. The woman snaps her head towards me. Then frowns. "Mr ... Mr...*Turner?*" She looks at Megan for a response.

Megan shifts back against the headboard, her hand glued to the duvet which thankfully covers her. I'm still standing with my hands covering my privates, trying to claw back some dignity.

It's then that I recognize her. This is Erica, Megan's younger sister.

"It *is* you," her sister insists.

"Could you ... leave and give me some privacy?" I feel powerless and pathetic.

"What the hell?" Erica hisses to Megan before closing the door.

"Fuck," I mutter, hating that we've been caught like this. A worried look settles over Megan's face, but it's her silence which concerns me. I walk over and cup her face, stroking her cheek with my thumb. "Hey."

"She told me she was coming on Friday. She had a course here for the entire week. She told me she'd come over on Friday.

"Are you going to be okay?" I'm worried about her. Her family doesn't like me, and this will make things worse for her. It's another obstacle we don't need.

"I'll deal with her." She jumps out of the bed and rifles through her closet, throwing on her clothes.

"My clothes are still in the dryer," I remind her.

She looks even more distraught. "Ugh. So they are. I'll get them for you." Then she disappears. I hear the two sisters squabbling and then Megan sticks her head through the door and gives me my clothes.

"I'm leaving," I tell her. She comes inside and with her back to the door, holding it firmly shut, she watches me getting dressed. She gives me an apologetic look.

"I have to talk to her."

"You're in my thoughts and prayers." I press my lips to her forehead before she leaves.

CHAPTER THIRTY-SIX

MEGAN

"What the hell are you doing with *Mr. Turner?* Are you insane?" Erica faces me with an angry look. I immediately have second thoughts about going home for Thanksgiving.

"I want my key back." I feel so humiliated, like I want the floor to open up and swallow me. Poor Lance.

"Here." Erica slaps into my proffered palm. "How long has this been going on?" I lead her into the kitchen so that Lance won't have to see her as he leaves. My sister stands facing me with her hands on her hips. I imagine soon enough she'll call my mom and tell her this juicy news.

"Not long. We only started dating recently. A few weeks ago."

"I don't believe you."

I scoff. "Well, it's true, whether you believe me or not." Not that I would tell her anything so personal, but this is the first time we've had sex. Full-blown sex. My body is still coming down from the high of our lovemaking.

It was *amazing*, and we would have done it again and again. I look away. There's no point thinking about what might have been if Erica hadn't turned up unannounced.

"Mom's going to be so angry," Erica points out.

"She won't know if you don't tell her."

My sister gives me an incredulous stare. "That man ruined your life. He brought shame and humiliation to you."

"He did nothing of the kind."

"I'm a grown woman now. I'm not a student. What we're doing isn't forbidden anymore."

"I'm not talking about now. Something happened that night. He brought your clothes back for chrissake. Why don't you just admit what everyone knows?"

"Nothing happened," I insist, but I start to wonder if she might have found out the truth, or if she's just projecting the wild rumors that flew around back then.

Erica throws her hands up in dismay as she paces around the room. "Were you ever going to tell us this? That you're seeing him? How? Why? I don't understand."

I clench my jaw. "Look, I don't even know what's going to happen. I'm looking for another job and I'll probably have to move away ..."

"You won't. Not now that he's here." Her face is still twisted in anger. "You're moving away with him, aren't you?"

"No, I told you—"

My sister looks around the room. "Does he live with you?"

"No! No. No. This isn't what you think. This is new. I didn't go looking for him and he didn't come looking for me. We met purely by chance." I tell her how Lance came into my life and the campus shooting. Erica lives a two hour car journey away, and I'm not sure the shooting would have made a big ripple on her local news network. She waves a hand at me. "One of my friends said something about that. Is this the shooting in the college?"

"Redmond College."

My sister's face is set hard, unrelenting. "I didn't realize it was him."

"It was. He was all over the news."

"He lives here?"

"I didn't know that until the shooting."

"And then he walked into your life? Just like that?"

"I walked into his," I say, softly, remembering the time at the crossing when I dropped my groceries.

I'm not going to tell her that this is the first time we've been fully intimate and I turn away from her and pretend to examine some paperwork lying on my coffee table but I can feel the heat on my face at the thought of what we've just done. My body starts to heat up just thinking about it. He's the best lover I've ever had, and he's a gentleman, and so good to me. I don't care about the opposition from my family.

"Don't make a mistake. Don't take it any further."

"What?" I can't believe my ears. I can't imagine not being with him again. I want to be with him again, in his bed, in his life, for as long as we have this time around.

"Walk away." Erica stares at me coldly. "You're moving away, getting a new job, a new start. Don't mess it up. He's caused trouble for you before, and he'll do it again. People don't change, Meg."

I don't know who Erica thinks she is. I know the reason Lance didn't come back, I know the real story of what happened and it's enough for me. "He's good to me."

"He ruined your life."

"No." I shake my head. "*Dad* ruined our lives. Lance helped me."

She smirks. "We all know how much Lance helped his favorite student."

"It wasn't like that." I fold my arms. "How long do you plan to stay here?" I have no desire to talk about my relationship anymore. It's none of her business.

"I was going to stay for a few days but I'll leave, because there's too much tension here for my liking."

"There doesn't have to be." I don't see her often, and, as much as she's pissed me off, my siblings and I are close. We get on. We have a good relationship, because we've had to look out for each other after my mother tried to take her own life. As much as I hate the advice she's offering, I don't want to fall out over this. "Are you going to be difficult?" I ask her.

"Am I going to get in the way of you and Mr. Turner?"

I bite my tongue. "He's not Mr. Turner anymore, and no, you're not."

"I was going to stay for the weekend."

"Then stay for the weekend," I reply.

She looks unsure.

"I won't see him while you're here."

"We'd all prefer it if you didn't see him at all," she grumbles. "He's so old. I don't know what you see in him."

"Shut. Up."

And she does. The color drains from her face and the message has obviously gotten through.

LANCE

Deflated, I drive home.

This isn't how I envisaged our date would go. I wasn't planning on ending up in bed with her, albeit it that I fucked her on the dryer. I didn't think we'd end up doing that today, but Megan has a way of making me do things I often wouldn't.

I tried to hold out for as long as I could, but I couldn't resist her anymore.

Fuck.

But we are victims of bad luck and bad timing. While I hate that her sister caught us, it's Megan I feel sorry for. She'll have lots to explain.

I am restless now and need to go out for a run or maybe hit the gym. I need to do *something*, because even though we had the best sex and I was ready for more, I was also just as ready to curl up beside her and fall asleep with her in my arms. Her sister appearing is like a bad omen that I would rather block out of my mind.

I plug my dead cell phone into the charger before grabbing a beer from the fridge. Then I slouch on the sofa; the idea of a run and gym session out of the window. That's when I hear the multiple beeps. I lean over and check my phone only to find that I have fifteen missed calls. Alarm spreads through me like a wildfire.

It's Vivian.

And my first thought is *Cassie.*

I call her, with my heart in my throat. "What's wrong?"

"What's wrong?" she echoes, her voice a little slurred.

"Is it Cassie? Is she okay?"

"Cassie?" Vivian cries, as though she's surprised by my question. She laughs, and it sends shivers up my spin. "She's fine!" She's got a sleepover at Tiffany's."

My heart relaxes. "So she's okay?"

"She's having a great time."

"You called me fifteen times."

"You didn't pick up."

"My phone died." Irritation skims across my chest. "Well, why?"

"What?

"Why did you call?" My resentment simmers. This woman is supposed to be out of my life, but I have a feeling, I know, that she'll always be a part of it. I don't want to be on the phone talking to her. All I want is to sit with my bottle of beer and just think. I want to think about what happened between me and Megan, and I want to try to imagine the type of future we could have.

We've been getting to know each other slowly, and I've managed to take down that walled barrier around her brick by brick. It's a rekindling of old feelings, yet with a touch of something new, because while we have the same heart, time and life have made us into different people. We're older and wiser and the most amazing thing of all is that the yearning is still there, growing stronger by the day.

With her I have another chance and I don't want to let her go.

"Come home, Lance." Vivian's voice cracks me out of my reverie.

"I *am* at home."

"Come home to me. I'm lonely."

"Vivian. Stop."

"Please?" She sounds on the verge of tears. I have to nip this now before she lures me into her web. "Is the pool boy not available?"

She says nothing. I wince. Maybe I shouldn't have said that. She is, after all, the mother of my daughter. But I'm already mad about the interruption we've had. Were it not for her sister, I would still be in Megan's bed. I wasn't done. Neither was she. We had time to take it slow. Now that I've tasted her again, and fucked her, and seen her face when she comes, I want more.

"I'm sorry," I say, when the line is still silent. "I shouldn't have said that."

"You're so cruel to me." I hear a sniffle. "I'm by myself. Don't you feel anything for me? We have a beautiful child. A piece of paper doesn't mean a thing. You're still her father, and I'm her mother, and that is a link we'll always have. You'll never be able to cut me out of your life, Lance."

"Stop." She's doing it again. Luring me in. Making me listen to her twisted, convoluted way of thinking.

"I miss you."

"No, Vivian." I don't miss her.

"I don't want us to break up. A piece of paper means nothing. You'll always have my heart."

She's a walking, talking mannequin with a plastic heart and the emotional intelligence of a pen. I grit my teeth together. "We're divorced."

"Some people get back together after a divorce."

I hate this, going round in circles with this pointless conversation. "You've had way too much to drink. Go to bed."

"I'm lonely."

"Drinking won't solve that problem."

"What are you doing tonight?" The pleading in her voice makes me pity her. "Can we just be friends? Can we try and stay friends?" she begs.

"We are friends, for the sake of our daughter, we will always be friends."

"Then come over. We can still talk. Friends talk."

"You might consider hiring a new butler," I say, feeling especially evil and vindictive.

"You're horrible."

"No, seriously. You've gone off the pool boy, and there is no one else in the house. I'm sure you had a fling with the last butler." I don't ask her outright because I don't care, but I remember he was a good few years older than Vivian. "To this day I can't figure out why your father fired him."

"You're evil."

"I'm not. I'm a good man, and I was good to you. I was loyal."

"How's your little student whore?"

My insides jerk as if she's stabbed me with a knife. "Don't call her that."

"Which one? The girl you saved, or the other one who was in your apartment? You like them young."

I swipe my hand across my forehead. "That's despicable. It's a new low, even for you."

"She looks too old to be a student." Vivian doesn't want to let it go.

I want to shut her up. "I'm in love with her." I hear a gasp. I continue. "I am. I'm falling for her and I can't help it."

"That ... that little ... slut?" she spits back.

"Hire a butler, Vivian. Go at it all you want."

I slam the phone down.

CHAPTER THIRTY-SEVEN

MEGAN

"Is it true?" My mom's voice drips acid. My cell phone is on loudspeaker so that I can still iron my clothes. It helps to be doing something when I talk to my mom.

"Is what true?" My guard tightens. I've been expecting this call all weekend but it didn't come. I know exactly what my mom is angry about.

"Your high school teacher, of all men," my mother snarls at me across the phone line. "What's possessed you?"

Barely thirty minutes have passed since Erica left. We've had a relatively good weekend, catching up, and awkwardly steering our conversations away from the opening blockbuster scene she witnessed when she first arrived.

I was hoping she would have kept this news to herself, but Lance Turner being back in my life is big news for my family. I pray Erica had the decency to leave out the details of how she discovered us together.

"He's not my teacher anymore, Mom. We're all grown up now."

"Lance Turner," she hisses. "That man should be locked up."

"For what?"

"Don't even get me started."

"For what, Mom?" I place the iron back on the stand, before I get so worked up over this and burn my silk blouse.

"For doing what he did."

I inhale and count to five. I'm not even going to lie. "He's good to me." I'm aware that this sounds weak.

It's also not enough. These words don't fully explain how I feel about him. How *he* makes *me* feel. I'm falling for him, and I may already have fallen face first onto the ground. I can't stop thinking about him, and my obsession now is worse than ever.

We've been texting while Erica was here. He wanted to see me, but he didn't want to get me in any more trouble. He's aware that my family aren't his biggest fans, and he's worried about me.

"Why him, Meg? Of all the men you could have gone out with, why *him?*"

I can't work out why she's still so angry all these years later. She seems to have forgotten what life was like for us. How the father we once knew disappeared forever and took no interest in our welfare and wanted nothing to do with us. How can she so conveniently forget that she overdosed and our family was thrown into further chaos? Or that she had to be nursed back to her sanity and health, and that I became responsible for my siblings.

Lance Turner made my life easier, not harder. And now that I know the full truth, that he didn't intend to leave, I am content with his explanation.

Maybe the rumors that spread around school like a contagious disease is karma I deserved, because I wasn't purely innocent. I seduced him. I went to Lance that night with all that need and unrequited love burning a hole in me. I needed a release and I made him give it to me.

"Lance didn't ruin my life, Mom. It was nothing that he did. It was you and dad fighting all the time. You not being able to cope when he left you, and everything that happened after that, that's what caused me pain."

My mother makes a noise at the other end, something like a gasp and a shock. My gut twists. It's too late to take my words back. "I'm sorry, Mom. I didn't mean it like that."

"Don't you dare put this on me. I was in a bad place. You have no idea of the hell I went through."

"I said I'm sorry. I'm a grown woman now. We're not at school."

"He's not to be trusted."

"For goodness' sake. Just leave it, Mom. Please."

Naturally, she doesn't. "How long has this been going on?"

I groan as if I'm in pain. "Why do you and Erica think this has been going on for years? I just met him a few months ago."

"I don't believe you. It sounds suspicious. It's too neat, you both ending up in the same place."

"I have no reason to lie!" I exclaim, thinking that my family's objection to Lance is too far-fetched and no longer valid.

"You always lie when it comes to him," my mother says with a huff.

"I don't know why you hate him so much."

"He's too old for you. I don't trust him."

"For being old?" I retort. "And he's not old. He's young at

heart and ..." I see Lance naked in my mind's eye. The man is beautiful.

"He was your teacher—"

"But he's not my teacher now!"

"This man is trouble."

"He's been very good for me, Mom. I didn't go into this lightly. I didn't rush into anything"

"You certainly know how to pick them," my mother snorts. "You're always so unlucky when it comes to men."

"Why do you think that is?" I snap. "Maybe it's because I saw you and dad and how your relationship worked out. You weren't the best role models."

"You keep blaming me! How can you think I caused all of this?" She's angry, and now she's making me angry. We'll just end up saying nasty things to one another if this continues.

"Let's not fight, Mom."

"Are you going to stop seeing him?"

I can't believe she's asking me that. "No." Nothing can stop me. Nothing and no one.

She hangs up on me.

Lately I feel more and more isolated, by Arla, by my family. Lance is the only solid, dependable person I have in my life.

I miss him. I miss being with him, I miss talking to him. I miss him but we've agreed to stay away from one another for a few more days. He's busy marking some papers and I need to pace myself because I have no resistance or willpower around him. Right now I'm tempted to go over to his place, or ask him to come to mine so that we can continue on from where we left off.

Texting is all we have right now, and when I jokingly—or maybe not so jokingly—suggest that we get together, he reminds me that he's taken a lot of work home. He tells me to practice restraint; that I don't need to jump into bed and throw myself at him. I have a sneaky suspicion that he finds me too forward. That's why he made me wait so long before we were intimate.

I also suspect that things are hard on him emotionally as well. I can't imagine that his ex-wife is going to let him go completely, and Lance still beats himself up about the way his daughter found out, even though it wasn't his fault that the poison witch went behind his back and told her when they'd already agreed that he would.

Even though we're just texting, it's nice to have someone in my life again, and Lance cares for me more than I'm used to having someone care for me. It takes some adjusting to having something other than work in my life.

In the days that follow, I work later than usual, slowly reverting to my long hours again just so that I have something to keep me distracted.

Then Preston walks in. I inwardly groan.

"I'm moving offices," he tells me, that smug self-satisfied look permanently plastered to his face.

"Yeah?" I smile at him and start putting my things away. I decided the moment I saw him come in that it's time to go home.

"I'll be really good to you when you're working for me."

"What if I don't want to work for you?"

His face sobers when I don't laugh and he realizes that I'm being serious. "Why? I'll give you all the best clients, and the most interesting work."

"Whatever." I turn my computer off.

"You're not still sore about it, are you?" He means about him getting the job.

"No." Because I'm still looking for jobs, and I have another interview lined up. It's a shame I've heard nothing back from my last interview, because I thought it went very well.

"You're acting weird. Ever since you met your new guy."

I ignore his comment.

"How the hell did you meet him?" he asks, poking his nose in my business again. When I don't answer, he probes some more. "Or are you just another one of his groupies?"

I give him a hard stare.

"He has women throwing themselves at him because of his heroic stunt." Preston says 'stunt' like it's a euphemism for something.

"And you would know this because ...?"

"He was telling one of the secretaries at the awards night. You know the superhot sexy young thing who just started in the Marketing department?"

I don't know who he's talking about, but it doesn't surprise me that he's aware of the 'hot young things' in other departments. Luckily my cell phone rings and I am saved from giving Preston a reply.

I grab my phone quickly and answer it. It's a call from the recruitment agent who tells me that the company I interviewed at want me. As in, they've offered me the job!

A burst of energy explodes inside me and my insides feel supercharged. This is the news I've been praying for.

"They're going to put an offer in writing, but I wanted to let you know," the agent says.

I'm so excited I squeal with delight and thank her for the news. Preston is watching me, listening in. He's nosy. He wants to know why I'm so happy, but I don't want to share my happiness and joy with him.

I try to contain my excitement. "Excuse me," I say to the agent, then to Preston, "Do you mind?"

He raises an eyebrow. I gesticulate with my hand for him

to leave. "And close the door behind you," I say, moving the cell phone away. I get back to the woman on the phone. "Are you sure they made an offer?"

"I'm staring at it now."

"Could you maybe scan and send it to me in an email?"

She laughs. "Of course. I just wanted to let you know because you were so enthusiastic about that company."

I immediately call Lance and break the news to him. The sound of his voice makes me happy. Even him saying a simple 'Hi.'

"I got the job!"

"The job? The one you really wanted?"

"Yes!"

"Congrats! That's awesome. Well done!"

"Thank you."

"I'm so happy for you. Which job is this?" It's only natural that he's confused as I haven't said much about the interviews I've been going for. I tell him, but he doesn't sound as happy as I'd expected.

"What's wrong?" I ask, tentatively on tenterhooks in case something's come up with Cassie, or his ex-wife.

"Nothing." A brief pause follows before he asks. "Is it out of state?"

My heart lifts, because he sounds sad, as if he doesn't want me to move away. "Yes." I tell him that the new job is too far away to do a daily commute. I'll have to move, and now I feel a little down, now that it's all real, now that I have the job, because it means I will be moving. I don't want to leave this behind me.

"We have to celebrate," he says, the tension in his voice palpable. I know the normal pitch and cadence of his voice, and I can tell that he's forcing himself to be excited.

"We don't have to celebrate tonight," I reply, seeing that it's late, and also because I sense his reticence.

"I've missed you. I want to see you." Now those words warm my heart and my lady parts. "I'll come over to your workplace."

He wants to see me.

I want to see him.

I'm sailing on air as I leave the office.

LANCE

'm happy for her. I am.

Megan's new job sounds like a huge step up, and I'm glad that it's the one she really wanted.

I met her at her workplace. She looked so gorgeous in her work clothes. So business like and professional. There's nothing as powerful as seeing someone who fills you with joy, who makes your heart sing, and causes a physical reaction in your body, than to know they are yours.

She is mine, for as long as we have this.

We went for a meal, and then I asked her to come back to my place. She jumped at the chance, and then she jumped at me as soon as we walked through the door.

It was only a matter of seconds before our clothes came off, and we rolled onto the bed and made love.

Maybe because we'd both been interrupted the last time, and had waited days before we saw one another but our lovemaking turned hard and fast. Animalistic. There's no softness, only pent-up need being sated. She moans beneath me, but she's feisty, and a fighter, and she wants control. We roll around fighting for dominance and soon she's straddling me and riding me for her pleasure. I lie back, watching her and my heart springboards off a ledge when she stares down at me through thick lashes, her pupils dilated, her lower lip rolled between her teeth, as if the ecstasy is too much.

We see one another every evening after that. Sometimes she stays at my place, and other times I go to hers.

We hold hands and talk in bed every night after we've used one another, after we've feasted, and worshipped and had our fill for the night.

I'll never tire of her.

Never.

One night she's in my bed and we talk about her family not liking me, and I tell her about Vivian still hounding me.

She falls silent, and now because she is moving away, we don't have things to say to one another. Maybe it doesn't matter that her family detests me, and that my ex-wife is still hanging around the edges of my life - because our worlds will never collide.

The threat of a long-distance relationship darkens the once blue sky of our hopeful future.

These things tend not to work out. We won't be in different countries, but we'll be in different states and it's not the same as being in the same town. It won't be like this, where we can meet easily; where we're so close to one another we don't even have to think about it.

I never thought our paths would cross again, let alone that we'd get another chance. I hate that life conspires against us and that this is all we have.

But, for now, we have tomorrow.

CHAPTER THIRTY-EIGHT

MEGAN

Thanksgiving comes and goes in a heartbeat.

Lance spends it with his ex and daughter and I don't ask about the details. I visit my mom and Erica and Jensen also come. My mom starts to talk about Mr. Turner, but thankfully Jensen stops her short. We've only got a few days together, he says, and we shouldn't bicker. I love my younger brother and I wish my sister would have his sense of diplomacy.

I start looking for friends to visit over Christmas so that I don't have to go home and live in fear of my mom asking more questions.

When I return to Boston, Lance and I do things a couple would do. We go bowling one evening and watch a show the next. Then one night we go for a walk after dinner, and this time there's no rain, so our walk is uninterrupted. We stop off for coffee and dessert in a cozy little diner that's open past midnight.

At work, and much to Preston's shock, I announce my resignation. He had no idea I was looking to leave, so naturally he's annoyed that not only haven't I told him, but that I've found a new job and I'm leaving.

I have a two-month notice period to work out at this place, and this gives me time. Time with Lance, and time to find a new home.

When I announce my good news to my family, they're happy, but then lots of questions follow, about Lance and where I'll be living. Secretly I sense that they're pleased my job is so far away and I'm moving, and they think Lance and I will fizzle out.

Lance and I don't talk about it much, the new job or that I'll be looking for a new place soon, or when I'll be leaving, but we see one another nearly every night.

A week ago he invited me to an informal event where he introduced me to his work colleagues. It took place in a wine bar and not at his college. I was surprised he invited me. I took it to mean that we're now officially an item. It was an interesting night and I had a chance to see Lance in a different environment with his peers. He's one of the youngest there. I even got to meet Lesley, the colleague he speaks of highly. She's the one who gave me his phone number when I had to return his pen. She was warm and friendly, but not a pushover. I could tell that she was assessing me; maybe our age gap was more apparent to her experienced eye. When she asked how we met, Lance and I looked at one another. We've never addressed how we were going to answer that question. After a hard-to-miss awkward and very pregnant pause, the reply tumbled out of my mouth. I told her that I was crossing the street when my groceries fell out and Lance came to my rescue.

It's partially true and a good enough story for how we met the second time around.

Christmas arrives like a whirlwind and, just as we did for Thanksgiving, we celebrate Christmas with our families. This time Jensen and his girlfriend are hosting and I feel a sense of relief because my mom won't ask any probing questions about Lance in front of Jensen's girlfriend. My mother is 'ashamed' of what happened in my past during high school—though she doesn't know the half of it—and there's no way she'll bring up anything about Lance.

Lance and I exchange small, practical gifts. Scents, chocolates and books. As soon as I return, we go out for dinner and spend the rest of the night and the next day in bed.

I love being with him. I love not being alone.

I love having someone to wake up with and planning our day together.

I love this new life we have.

Weekends are something I greatly look forward to, and my work and the desire to make a mark are no longer important to me. I concentrate more on the future and where I want to be, even though it is tinged with sadness because every day I spend with Lance means we're closer to the end. He can't move to where I am because he has Cassie here, and he won't want to disrupt her life.

I won't give up the new opportunity I have, and so, we are doomed. That's why we spend as much time together as we can. I'm not alone anymore, and I don't want to go back to the life I had before he was in it.

One evening, after we've bought the tickets to watch a movie, we're standing in line to get popcorn when Lance's phone rings.

The sharp *'What?'* coupled with the tone of his voice, catch my attention. But it's when his face turns pale that I get alarmed.

"Cassie, calm down. Slow down, Sweetpea. Now, tell me again." He turns his back to me and walks away. I'm left holding the tickets wondering what's going on. I move out of the line because it doesn't look like we'll be watching a movie. I watch and wait until Lance wanders back towards me. His phone is still stuck to his ear. "Don't worry. I'm coming."

"What's happened?" I ask, desperate to know, but I don't hold his attention. He's not even looking at me, his mind and his gaze is elsewhere as if he's lost, as if his world has imploded.

"Don't cry, honey. I'm on my way." He hangs up, his face tight with worry.

I tug his arm. "Lance?"

He finally looks at me. "It's Vivian. She's ... she's drunk too much, it sounds like. Cassie is panicking."

"You need to go. Do you want me to drive? I can take you?" I offer because I don't want him to drive in this state. I don't want anything to happen to him.

"I need to go. Cassie sounds worried. Vivian has a tendency to over drink sometimes." He gives me an apologetic look and rushes away.

He didn't even hear me. He wasn't even paying attention to what I said. I hope his ex-wife is okay, and I really hope that Cassie is, as well. I wouldn't wish that kind of trauma on anyone, especially a child. I can see why Lance is so concerned that he has to go to them.

Once again it becomes obvious that this man isn't free. The truth hits me like a sledgehammer. He might have a sheet of paper to say he's divorced, but his ex-wife still has a hold over him. She always will because she's not going anywhere, like my father did.

I understand this situation. She's probably drunk herself silly because, just like my mom, she can't come to terms with the fact that the man she loves has left her. My mother also didn't handle it well.

I reel back in shock when it hits me, how similar this is to what happened in my own life. I knows what it's like and I feel sorry for Cassie. The poor girl is caught up in this mess and it's not her fault.

I sit on one of the benches in the mall and wonder what I'm doing. Lance will never be free. He'll always be tied to his ex-wife because of Cassie. He needs Cassie in his life, but Vivian seems unable to process that she and Lance are over. She'll make his life miserable, and because of that, she'll make my life miserable.

I look around me and see couples walking around, arms hooked, hand-in-hand, like Lance and I were just now. A bitter thought twists inside my head. What if he goes back to Vivian? That woman is capable of finding a way to make this happen. She'll work on Cassie and pull Lance's emotional strings, because Cassie doesn't want them to split. No child wants their parents to ever split.

Maybe my mom is right.

Lance is no good for me, but now I'm in deep because I think I love him. Because he's the best friend and lover I've had.

My phone rings and I rush to answer it, expecting to hear Lance's voice. I'm momentarily confused when I hear Arla's instead.

"What are you doing? You look miserable sitting by yourself."

She's here?

I look around, searching for her in the crowd of people swarming around the mall. "Where are you?"

"Around," she says, in her teasing way. I cling to the warmth and familiarity of her voice. I need that, right now. I've missed her.

"Come on over," I tell her.

"Are you sure you're not waiting for a date or anything?"

"My date left me ..." The declaration feels dramatic, as if I'm feeling sorry for myself. The line goes dead and a few moments later, Arla is standing in front of me.

"He left you?"

"His wife needed him. His ex-wife," I say in air quotes.

"Oh, sweetie." She sits down beside me, her arm around my shoulder.

"I've got a spare ticket to the cinema. Want to come?"

It's like we've never argued. It's like we never had weeks of not getting in touch.

"Sure."

"I have other news." The movie is due to start so we head towards the movie theatre.

That catches her attention. Then I tell her about my new job, and that I'll be moving out of town in a few months. A rather theatrical response follows, with Arla throwing her hands around me and hugging me. "You can't leave me. You can't."

"I have to. It's too far to drive to."

She pouts.

"We'll talk about it later," I tell her as we take our seats. She hasn't asked more about Lance and why he left and I am glad. The movie is about to start so we head into the theatre. In the darkness, enveloped in my own misery, I pretend to watch the film, but I keep checking my phone for an update from Lance. There's nothing. He hasn't even read my message to him asking if everything was okay.

I enjoy my evening with Arla, and it's the distraction I need. When the movie ends, I still don't feel like going back to an empty home, so I make a suggestion and soon we're sitting in an ice cream parlor. That's when Arla asks me what's going on with me and Lance.

"I know you don't approve," I answer slowly, licking some chocolate ice cream off the back of my spoon. "But he makes me really happy."

"Are all his parts in full working order?"

I suppress a smile and lower my head, remembering. They're most definitely in full working order. "He's not that old," I retort. "And anyway, age isn't that important the older you get. It's not like we're at school anymore." "

"It's hypocrisy when people have such a hard time accepting an older woman with a younger man."

I raise an eyebrow. Who cares? But, yes. If the situation were reversed, if I were the older one and Lance was the younger man, people's attitudes would be different. Scathing. Disapproving. Loathsome.

I don't want to worry about such things, especially since it doesn't affect me. Our age now doesn't matter anymore. There's no Principal Fielding to warn us, but my family, on the other hand, are another matter.

"If he makes you happy, that's all that matters." Arla smiles, her eyes lingering on my face as if she's looking for something. In the back of my mind a niggling feeling grows. "But ... why did he leave you?"

I explain in the briefest of terms, that something came up for him with his family.

"You're going to have to get used to that." She scoops out another spoonful of ice cream.

"I'm trying."

"Will you always be content to be in second place?" There's a small blob of chocolate on her lower lip which irritates me. But her sentence irritates me more. I don't remember Arla ever not liking the guys I was with. Even the douchebags who left me waiting for meals and movies and events. Even the guy who borrowed money from me and never paid it back.

But Lance, who has never taken but has always given and who has always been here for me, she seems not to like.

"You have chocolate on your lip." I gesticulate by pointing to the exact location on my lower lip.

She licks it off. "Maybe it's not such a bad thing, you moving away." She's happy that I'll be away from Lance, and I'm suddenly eager to finish eating and leave here.

CHAPTER THIRTY-NINE

LANCE

The situation is far worse than Cassie led me to believe.

My ex-wife drank herself into a stupor and because that wasn't enough, she took a ton of pills.

By the time I got to the house, she'd been rushed to the hospital. Mila said Vivian was drowsy, and was talking a lot of nonsense, and she wasn't herself. The housekeeper got worried which was when Cassie called me, but soon after Vivian lost consciousness and that was when Mila called 911.

Because no one else was at home, Mila stayed with Cassie. My daughter was a mess. I felt like a failure. I'm supposed to keep this family together, but Vivian made it impossible, and now this has happened and my daughter's suffering. It's a big, stinking mess. Vivian likes to drink, but she's never taken pills before. It wasn't until Mila showed me the empty bottle that I believed her.

After calming my daughter down, trying to answer her

when she blames me for making Mommy sad, I go to the hospital to see my ex-wife.

To my relief there's no sign of her parents anywhere and I pray that they've left. I sit by Vivian's bedside. Her eyes are closed and she looks peaceful. The only motion is that of her chest rising and falling. It's a comfort, a huge relief, that she's breathing. That she will be okay. The doctor I spoke to told me that it was lucky my wife was found so quickly. That, this could have been fatal. The doctor goes on to tell me that this is a cry for help. I think it's a cry for attention, but I keep my thoughts to myself. They've pumped her stomach and put her on IV fluids. They want to keep her in overnight for observation, but she will be able to go home tomorrow.

Vivian will keep me dancing to her tune, which means having no life of my own, doing what she wants, because that is who Vivian is. A master manipulator.

I stare up at the ceiling, a loud exhale leaving my lungs as I try to figure out my life, and my short-lived new freedom.

Vivian will recover, she will be fine, she might need more therapy—Vivian is always in therapy—but it's my daughter I worry about more. I jolt when I look at her and find that she's been staring at me the whole time. It's creepy.

"How are you feeling?" I ask, sitting forward, wanting her to be okay.

"Happy now that you're here."

"Why did you do it?"

She stares at me.

"Why did you take the pills, Vivian?"

"I can't live without you, Lance. I want things to be how they were."

And how were they?

My ex-wife lives a glamorous life, and she has no remorse

for her infidelity or her behavior. She does what she wants with no regard for others.

Not even Cassie.

And now that I've chosen to walk away, to sever the ties that bind us, she can't cope. I won't be a part of her victimhood. "What were you thinking?"

"I can't live without you. I don't want to. I want you back in our lives. Think about our family, think about Cassie."

I cringe inside. I asked the wrong question. She interprets my silence as me being interested in what she has to say. Perhaps in her crazy deluded mind, she thinks I'm considering her words.

"It was a silly thing to do, Vivian. You scared us. You scared Cassie. Why would you do something like that?"

"Because I love you. Because I can't imagine my life without you."

I stare at this woman, and I feel so sorry for my daughter for having a mother such as her. All of a sudden it comes back. My feelings of bitterness. Being trapped and powerless. Frustrated and angry.

Is this my life? It will be, if I don't do as Vivian says; if I don't toe the line, this is how she'll keep her hooks in me. Threatening me with over drinking, overdosing, not caring about the effect it has on our daughter, as long as she can have me come running back to her.

"You should try to get some rest." I don't want to listen to her anymore. I can see right through her selfish attention seeking drama. It's cruel of me to think like this, but it's the truth. I know Vivian. I'm fully aware of what she's capable of. All I want is for her to get well and be a good mother to Cassie.

"Stay with me. Please. I don't want to be alone." She looks pale, and her gaunt eyes burn into me, stabbing me with guilt.

She's so good at this. I suppress my weary breath and nod. Her parents aren't here, and she has no one else. The pool boy and her other lovers don't care. Liaisons such as those don't have longevity, or loyalty, or love.

But I hate this, being reeled into doing something I don't want to. I don't want to spend the night here. I want to be with Cassie, and I'm only here out of pity.

Vivian seems appeased and closes her eyes, leaving me to sit and wonder what Megan is doing. I'm covered in guilt for ruining her evening yet again.

My thoughts float away, and even though I'm sitting by my ex-wife's side, it's Cassie who is on my mind, and Megan. I worry about my daughter. We didn't want to disrupt her world, but this has punctured an irreparable hole in the fabric of her existence.

Half an hour passes, and Vivian looks to be peacefully asleep. I've already gone back on my word and have decided to go home despite what I told Vivian. She's in good hands here and Cassie needs me.

But as soon as I walk out of the door, I almost crash into Vivian's parents. They visibly step back, in shock and surprise and rage at seeing me.

This is good. They can take over from me and keep watch over Vivian. I would have been civil and offered my hand. I would have hugged Aurora, my ex-mother-in-law, but I sense a new frostiness from them. They've never liked me. I've always been lacking for them. They would have preferred an investment banker—at the very least—for a son-in-law. They probably hoped that their daughter would marry an heir to a dynasty, or a scion of a powerful empire. Instead, she got me, a poor college professor. Those expensive private schools and Swiss finishing schools didn't result in their daughter making a suitable match.

There is a hardness in Richard's eyes which I haven't seen before. Maybe because the divorce is final. It's not just something tenuous like our broken marriage, a secret that we kept hidden from Cassie and therefore never talked about openly. Now its official, and they can officially hate me.

"Look what you've done to her." Megan's father has the audacity to look me in the eye. He knows of his daughter's behavior, of her affairs and her casual disrespect for our marriage.

"With all due respect, sir. I no more poured the alcohol into her mouth than I forced the tablets down her throat," I whisper-hiss back to him.

He looks affronted. "Show some goddamn respect. My daughter's almost on the verge of death."

My mother-in-law looks pained. "Stop it, Richard. It's not his fault."

I attempt a smile, but Aurora doesn't look directly at me.

"It could have been fatal. He did this to her. He pushed her over the edge." Richard's face turns red. He's seething with anger and seems to want to lash out and blame everyone but his beloved daughter. Vivian is an only child who has been the apple of her parents' eyes. She is Daddy's girl.

"Cassie's very upset about it all," Aurora says, and if she's trying to heap guilt on me, it's not going to work.

"She needs me. I'm going home to her now."

"Are you leaving?" Richard asks, his tone indicating that he doesn't think I should.

I fix him with an icy state. "There's no reason for me to stay by Vivian's side. She's in good hands and you're both here now. Cassie is the one who needs care."

They look at me as if I've announced that I'm taking one of the nurses on a date.

"My daughter has just taken an overdose—"

"She will be fine. She'll live." My words come out all gritted and as hard as nails. But it's true. I shouldn't feel so callous, but this is so Vivian-esque.

"You really are a monster," Aurora exclaims as if she's seeing me with new eyes. I wonder what Vivian's been telling them.

"I'm sorry I couldn't turn a blind eye to your daughter's affairs," I reply. Aurora blinks so fast, I wonder if she's got an eyelash in her eye. It's the first time I've ever addressed the situation. "I'm sorry if her weekends away, and spontaneous trips caused me to be suspicious. I'm not sorry for always being there for my daughter." I was always the stay-at-home parent for Cassie whenever Vivian went away, but I had no problem with that. I relished the time I had with just her. "You're here now," I say coldly, relieved to get this off my chest." "You can spend time with your precious daughter."

I don't wait for them to reply and make my way back to the sprawling home I shared with Vivian; the home Cassie has known all her life. I will stay with her tonight, and I pray that I won't have to move back here. Just because Vivian is having a hard time getting to grips with the situation doesn't mean that I cave in and let her dictate my life.

The divorce has tipped her over the edge. The separation was manageable because I was still married to her, but the divorce is final, and that's what she can't handle.

Mila is watching over Cassie who is asleep. "You go to sleep," I tell Mila. "I'll stay the night and keep an eye on her." I reach over, take my daughter's hand and kiss it. I'm going to stay with her. I will probably have to stay here for a while because I don't want to leave my child here with my wife.

I sit on the chair watching over Cassie in the dimly lit room. I've turned down the light on the lamp so that it's not too bright. I don't want to leave Cassie alone, not after what she's seen. But sometime in the middle of the night she wakes up and starts crying.

"Hey, hey." I lean over and hug her. "What's wrong, Sweetpea?"

"I want Mommy." She sits up and rubs her eyes and my insides turn to stone.

"I'm here, Sweetpea."

Angry, sleepy eyes glare back at me. "Mommy says you don't love us. You made Mommy sad."

I perch myself on the side of her bed. "No, honey. I love you both so very much."

"Then why are you leaving us? Mommy says you don't want to be my daddy anymore. She says you don't live here because you love someone else."

She might as well have punched me. "I'm not leaving you, Cassie."

"You don't want to be married to mommy anymore. You don't want to be my daddy."

"That's not true. I will always be your daddy. I will always love you."

"Then why don't you live here? Why don't you stay married to mommy?"

Words fail me. The silver unicorn printed on my daughter's mauve pyjama top stares back at me.

"Sometimes, it's better for parents to live apart. It doesn't mean they don't love one another, or you, it just means they are better friends when they aren't in the same house."

"But I want you to be in the same house. Lisa was so sad when her mommy and daddy broke up, and she ran away. I'm going to run away too."

This is what I was afraid of; Cassie being so upset she wouldn't be able to handle it, and I've messed up again. Gotten it all wrong. Her friend Lisa took it very hard when her parents got divorced. It didn't help that her father went on to have a child with another woman a few months later. The girl did run away, to her grandparent's house, but that story was one of the reasons we didn't feel ready to tell Cassie the truth just yet.

Now my angel threatens me with the same and it scares me.

"No, Sweetpea. That's a very bad thing to do."

"But you're being bad, Daddy. You don't love us, and you don't want us."

I can almost hear echoes of Vivian's voice, and I wonder what malicious words she must throw around for my daughter to pick up on and believe.

"I will always be here for you, Sweetpea."

"Promise?"

My heart breaks into pieces. "Promise."

It's the first glimmer of light I see in her eyes. "Always, Daddy? Promise you will always be with us?"

I swallow, push away my dreams and my future. "I promise." She throws her arms around me, and I scoop her up in my arms. She's getting heavier to carry, but I hold onto her and sit down with her on my lap. I hold her until her breathing turns deep and then I carefully tuck her back into her bed, but as I sit back, my heart is heavy. It feels like I'm being forced into a future I don't want.

I meet Megan in the coffee shop again.

Vivian came home a few days ago and her parents have been staying at the house. It's been awkward, but I've been worried about Cassie and have been watching her like a hawk. We've watched movies, and baked cupcakes and cookies, and made puzzles. I've spent quality time with her, and checked in on Vivian now and then, but mostly I've left her and her parents alone.

The house is big enough that we can all get lost in it without running into one another, but no space is big enough for me to avoid Vivian and her parents with ease. Yesterday was tough, the air fraught with friction, partly because I sense Vivian's parents want to go back to their home, but they don't quite trust me to fully look after their daughter.

I needed to get out and, after dropping Cassie to her friend's house for a playdate, I called Megan and told her I needed to see her.

I've kept her in the loop and called and told her what had happened, but maybe that was a mistake because I've felt her slowly slipping away from me in the days that followed. I didn't want to keep anything from her, I wanted to be upfront and tell her the truth but this face to face meeting fills me with anxiety.

When we meet, she doesn't hug me for long. She's the first to pull away and sit down, and when the server delivers our coffees straightaway, she busies herself in opening the sachets to pour the sugar into her coffee.

"How is your wife?" She stirs her coffee, and then when she at last looks up at me, I see something closed off in her. It's like a three-inch wall of concrete has been erected in the time we've been apart.

I begin to tell her about the events in more detail, while trying to figure out what's going on with her. She's a little stiff, a little guarded, a little distant. It's only when I finish recounting my story that the realization hits me like a lightning strike. "This is what happened with you," I say, softly. This is the same situation Megan dealt with as a teenager, that night she came to me looking for comfort.

She stares back, giving me a subtle nod. "How's Cassie?" she asks, clearly not wanting to discuss that further. I'm still shocked by the parallels in our lives. I tell her my daughter is handling it well, and that I will likely have to travel back and forth between the family home and the college. I'll have to go back to doing the long commute, but I will do it. I don't tell her that my daughter threatened to run away, or that she filled me with so much guilt I promised her I would come back and stay with her, with them, forever?

I made a promise I'm not sure I can keep, a promise I don't want to keep. I said something I didn't believe because it was what my daughter wanted.

I am dreading the next few weeks, or months or however long it will be before Vivian is able to accept our situation and let me be, let me go. I'm dreading living a life that is a lie but wanting to keep my daughter happy and feeling secure. I'm filled with resentment at what my life has become.

Vivian thinks she's won, with me living under the same roof. She doesn't need me here to take care of her, she just wants me here, in my place—at least this is how she would frame it in that devious mind of hers. I haven't even bothered to clarify to her or her parents that I'm staying for Cassie's sake.

All I know is that my life is a mess, and it doesn't feel *mine*.

Megan says she understands and knows what Cassie is going through. She surprises me with how flexible and understanding she's being, but then I realize it's the right reaction. The only reason I'm surprised is because I'm so accustomed to Vivian and her selfishness.

"My in-laws, my *ex*-in-laws," I clarify, "they assume I've moved back in to look after their daughter. I'm not doing it for Vivian. I'm doing it for my daughter."

Megan nods in agreement. "As you should. This is a really difficult time for her, and Cassie needs you. Vivian needs you."

My heart feels hollow because I didn't expect Megan to say this, to be this understanding. I have a feeling I know what's coming. "Vivian doesn't need me as much as she doesn't want you and I to be together." I reach across the table and take her hands. "I'm sorry."

"For what?"

"For this, for *all* of this, for leaving you that day, for always leaving you. I'm sorry for this mess."

"You have to do what's right, Lance. Cassie's so much younger than I was, and she's fragile and malleable."

She's so good, so understanding. I wish she wasn't. I wish in this instance that she was more like Vivian. Selfish, and self-obsessed, and wanting me no matter what the cost. But I'm also fearful that Cassie might do something stupid, and that fear keeps me captive.

"I hate the timing of all this." I press my palm against hers, relishing the warmth of her skin, loving the feel of her soft, thin fingers against mine.

"You need to always be there for your child."

"I will be." I tell her about Cassie and what she said, and the promise I made to her, to stay with her and Vivian. "I don't know what I was thinking. It's not what I want, but what I must do, for now. I hope you can understand."

"I understand."

"I want to be with you, but things are complicated again. My ex-wife and her parents seem to think they've succeeded in guilt-tripping me into moving back and being there for Vivian. That's not the future I want."

"Sometimes we have no say in our how lives will work

out. You're the captain of your destiny but right now your family needs you, so you have to change course."

Since when did she become so wise? She pulls her hands away. I'm confused by her actions, by her warm hand which she slides out from under mine.

"Maybe life is trying to send us a signal," she says stirring her coffee.

Dread kicks in. I hate what she might be thinking, what she might say. Is this how we end? Is that why she agreed to meet me?

"Life doesn't always go how we want. What happened to my sister, and how it affected all of our lives is proof enough of that, but we can always adjust course and slowly, slowly, get back to where we want to go, to what we want." It's not the best analogy, but I'm hoping I can tell her that she's the one I want. That after I have made sure Cassie is okay, and Vivian too, that she's the one I want a future with.

"I'm starting a new job in a few weeks, and I'll be moving away. I found a new apartment to rent."

My breath chokes in my throat. We've not fully discussed this, her moving and us ending. "Distance is nothing. We can make this work." I want her to tell me that she's joking. I keep waiting for her to smile and cry, 'Gotcha!' but she doesn't. "What are you saying?"

Her eyes turn shiny. Worryingly shiny, and when I push back my chair, and go to stand up, she puts her hand out, halting me. "Don't. Please. Let me say what I need to."

We are going there. She's breaking up with me. "You don't need to say anything. It's not going to be easy ..." Her eyes are downcast, and she's staring at the table.

My heart lurches to the base of my belly. "Are you breaking up with me?"

She nods, still not looking at me. "For now, maybe."

She's trying to soften the blow, but she's telling me a lie. 'For now,' will turn into forever. I've already tried something that was supposed to last forever, with a woman who was so wrong for me. "But we've only just found one another."

She lifts her head, her eyes narrowing and she's about to look away.

"Look at me." If she's going to lie, I want her to look me in the face before she breaks my heart. I don't want to give up on us. I want to look into those eyes forever.

"When things don't work out, maybe it's because they're not meant to," her voice is soft and sad.

She can't mean that.

"When things don't work out, when the world and events conspire against you, it means you have to fight harder. You have to keep at it and never give up."

"How are we going to do that?" she asks. "You'll be on eggshells every time the phone rings and you'll wonder what's happened to Cassie or your wife."

"My ex-wife."

But even as an ex-wife, Vivian seems to have won. She's got what she wanted. Me back, at whatever cost. I try to appeal to Megan, feeling desperate and on the edge of a precipice I'm not willing to jump off. I'm in love with this woman, and I can't lose her again. Not now. "Vivian will get used to it, slowly. This is a big shock to her, but she'll get used to it."

"And Cassie?"

"In time, Cassie will understand. Maybe as she gets to know you ... I'm never not going to be there for my daughter."

"You're going to have to be there for her more than ever. My father wasn't and look what happened to me."

We've truly come full circle. It's freaky how the things in our life now mirror how Megan and I began.

"I'm not walking out on Cassie. I'm not."

"My mother fell apart, just like Vivian has. You left her, just like my father left my mother."

"It's hardly the same situation. I've put up with Vivian's dalliances, turned a blind eye to them because my focus was on Cassie, but I'm not prepared to give up the rest of my life for something I don't want. In time Cassie will understand."

"But Vivian will always create drama. You have a child together and you'll never be free of your wife."

"My ex-wife."

I made Cassie a promise, but in the cold light of day I know I can't keep it forever. I hope that in time, when I explain things to her, she will come around to the idea of me with someone else. And as she grows up, she will, hopefully, one day understand why I can't be with her mother.

But while I know how things will work out with Cassie, it's Megan who worries me. I know we have to slow things down, but not this. Not a break. A split. Not now.

Tears well up in her eyes. "Do you have any idea what a parent overdosing does to a child? What it feels like to know that my mom so hated her life without my father that she wanted to kill herself? For years I felt that we weren't enough for her. Do you know what it's like to not feel loved, to not be wanted by your mother?"

I get up ready to scoot over to her, but she begs me not to. She sniffles. "I have sought comfort in men, just to feel worthy, just to know I can be loved; that someone wanted to be with me enough to let me into their bed and—"

I put a finger to her lips. "I don't want to give you up." This isn't the solution I came here for.

"You're not giving me up. *I'm* giving *you* up. I'm breaking up with you, Lance. I've been through this as a child, and I know this is the right thing to do."

"How can it be the right thing if I don't want to be with a woman who doesn't love me and only wants to manipulate me for her own convenience? I want to be with you, Megan. I thought you felt the same."

"Can't you see that history is repeating again?"

"But I didn't cheat on Vivian. We've been living separate lives for years. I'm a single man and the ring on my finger is only there to keep up the ruse for Cassie. It's not the same."

She lets out a weary breath. "I'm moving away. Long distance relationships don't work. I'm sorry, but you'll see one day that this is the right thing to do." She stands up, her cup of coffee still three-quarters full.

"Where are you going?" I manage to ask, even though the rest of my body is in shock.

"Erica and Jensen are coming to stay for a few days." She's made her mind up. She's leaving, and we are done. "'Bye, Lance. I hope things work out for you."

CHAPTER FORTY

MEGAN

Lance Turner has broken my heart for the second time. Only, this time around it's me who gets to leave and do the breaking up. My heart is in tatters, and what should have felt like a tiny victory rings hollow. An emptiness seeps into my body again, erasing the blood and guts and bone and muscle. That's what it feels like.

Because Lance gave me a burst of yellow in my blue, blue world. The world where a guy smiling at me and buying me a drink is all it takes for me to go home with him and make it up to him.

Lance loved that neediness out of me. He made me wait, and he showed me that I was worthy.

But we are not meant to be. When life shows you the signs, it's best to heed them.

So, I walk away with a breaking, aching heart and try to focus on my future. Erica and Jensen aren't coming to stay this weekend, nor the next. That was just something to tell Lance in order to keep him away. I'll need my family's help in moving out, and that's when I'll call them over.

As before, whenever I'm feeling lost and lonely, I turn up at Arla's door with a bottle of wine. She opens the door, her hair messy, her face flushed, and I immediately know I've made a mistake.

It didn't even occur to me to check that she might have company.

"You're busy." I take a step back, ready to leave.

"You've been crying." Arla's eyes fill with worry, and she quickly pulls me inside before I say another word. Scott walks through shirtless, wearing only his boxer briefs. It's hard to miss his abs and his physique, but I do a mental comparison and Lance definitely has the better body.

"Hey." I manage, stepping towards the door and getting ready to leave. "I'll come back another—"

"I should go." Scott disappears out of sight, re-emerging seconds later fully dressed. He sweeps Arla into his arms, and they kiss passionately, but I can tell it's a hurried passionate kiss, for my sake.

I feel a failure, and out of place. But more than that I feel like an extra. Before I can protest, Scott hurriedly says 'Bye' and disappears.

"I'm sorry," I blubber, my sadness welling up and threatening to overflow. I had something like this, and I've given it up, and worse, now I'm messing up Arla's love life.

She stares at me, her face twisted with worry. "What happened?"

"I broke up with him."

She blinks. "With Lance?"

"Yes."

The worry melts away from her face and for a second I

contemplate the wisdom in coming here and telling Arla.

"Sit, I'll get glasses." She says it like we're celebrating something. For reasons I still can't work out, Arla is not team Lance.

She fills our glasses and I wonder if she's going to make a toast.

"Why are you so happy?" Suspicion ties a knot in my gut.

"I love you, Megan, and I don't want to see you get hurt again, I know what you went through with that man last time."

I shake my head. "But this is different," I explain. "This is nothing like my schoolgirl obsession. Don't you want to know why we broke up?"

"He can't be trusted?"

"What? No!" I don't understand how she can come to that conclusion from the last time we met, when he left me holding two movie tickets.

I quickly tell her what happened, about his ex-wife taking an overdose and his daughter being disturbed about the divorce.

"I'm the one who broke it off."

Arla nods, as if agreeing that I did the right thing. "It's a good thing you did... She sounds like a volatile woman, someone who's not going to let go of him easily. You're better off without him."

"Why are you happy for me? I'm in love with the man."

"I don't want you to fall apart like you did before."

"I fell apart last time because of everything else that was going on in my life, with my mom getting depressed when my dad left. It was a tough time for my family, and then when my mom took an overdose, it was the worst, and then Lance left, and he was the one solid, dependable thing in my life." I roll my eyes when Arla tries to interject. "You have no idea how bad things were at home. My mom and dad were constantly at one another's throat, and I couldn't get my head together to study. But Lance Turner was always there for me. He was my salvation. He helped me. He was a place for me to go to and he made me better. He made my life better.

"It's a good thing," she waves her hand dismissively.

"What's a good thing?" My suspicions are aroused.

"You breaking up with him. Married men are complicated, and you shouldn't be getting involved with marr—"

"I have never gotten involved with a married man. And also, he's divorced."

"But you breaking up with him now is a good thing, especially as his wife has taken an overdose, and their daughter must be suffering. Oh, my goodness!" She slaps a hand to her forehead. "This is how it was for you! You definitely did the right thing."

"That's why I broke up with him, but it still doesn't explain why you're not fazed by it. I'm upset. I'm broken. You're supposed to be my friend and empathize with me. Lance wasn't a one-night stand. He's not just good sex, or a comfort for a night. We have a real connection. I feel it here." I place a hand on my chest. "Him reappearing in my life was weird, but when I finally let him in, he fit so right. I tried to fight the attraction. I tried not to get involved. I'm clear about the baggage he has, but he's been truthful about it. He's never tried to hide it. I can't explain it. I know him, Arla. I know him in my soul. The connection I have with him is something I've never had with anyone else."

The room falls awkwardly silent.

"He hasn't always told you the truth." Arla blinks a little too much. I know that face. That's Arla's I'm-telling-you-the-truth-you-will-hate face.

Fear crawls along my spine and I try to mentally brace for the impact of her hit.

"He was in a relationship with that student, the one he saved on the college campus and took a bullet for."

And there it is. Arla's words land like a bomb. I open my mouth to say something, but my voice has vanished.

"Remember those two guys in the bar? The ones Lance got into a fight with. You and Lance left, and they told me. They know someone at the college, and they said Lance and that student had been in a relationship, and the guy who shot him, was the girl's ex-boyfriend."

Her words were like a crack in the mirror. An ugly lie with veined forks, lies leading to other lies, spreading out, breaking all of my heart. It isn't until I take a breath that I realize I've been holding it in. "They said what?"

"They said the shooter hated that his girlfriend had cheated on him with her professor, so he wanted to kill her, or him."

"But I haven't heard that on the news."

"It's old news now. It's all gone quiet, but the investigation is on-going, and I'm sure we'll hear more."

I feel as if I've been hit in the face.

"I'm so sorry, Megan," Arla continues.

I force myself to take a sip of the wine, to appear unfazed, but it tastes bitter, like I've swallowed paint stripper.

Lance and the student were having an affair?

Panic stutters in my throat, blocking the air from reaching my lungs. I can't breathe, or talk, or move.

Arla pats me on my thigh. "You did the right thing to break up with him, and it's the best thing that you're moving away. Time to forget Mr. Turner and stick him where he belongs, well and truly in your past."

CHAPTER FORTY-ONE

MEGAN

Something is off. I can't focus. I can't think. I am restless and I'm not sleeping well.

I've been out of sorts ever since I broke up with Lance. I'm not happy and I can't stop thinking about him despite knowing the truth.

I hate myself for trusting him. He's such a good liar. He had me believing his lies and bullshit.

Are men really so deceitful?

That's why I avoid long-term relationships because they're so hard and demanding and require so much honesty and integrity to work.

Most people aren't honest, or decent, in my experience. A part of me now second guesses whether I want to move all the way to a new town. I'm not good with change.

A new town, a new job, new friends.

I don't want to give up what I have here, now. What I've finally found. A sense of belonging.

I looked down on women who needed a man to ground them, or bring them happiness, but I am now one of those women.

I hate that, but maybe it's not so much that I depend on Lance as the idea that he completes me.

I was safe and happy with Lance, and I'm giving it all up, pushing him away, because it's the right thing to do, for him, for his daughter, for his peace of mind and for her happiness.

It's in the middle of this restlessness that I get a call from another agency who tell me that a smaller firm, an hour away from Boston, is interested in me. I've been headhunted.

Do I want to have an interview?

I think about it. Would it be so wrong to go, even though I've accepted the new job?

Sure, I tell the agent. It can't hurt to look.

Arla wants me to meet Chris, the guy from the gym. The one who made Lance feel old and not good enough. Because I am struggling to forget Lance, even knowing what Arla told me, I go along with her and Scott one evening.

We go for drinks, but I find him so boring, and cannot relate to him. I don't feel how I felt when I was with Lance.

I don't feel with him what Lance made me feel—special and wanted. He looked at me as if I were his world. Chris looks at me as if I'm his for the night. I threaten to skip dinner until Arla leans into my ear and reminds me that Lance is a cheater. That I'm not the only one whose caught his eye.

Her words stab like a knife. To know that it wasn't just me. That he does this routinely. I start to see Vivian with sympathy.

I was on the verge of leaving after dinner, and not going to the movie they've decided to watch, but I'll be going home to what? An empty home, staring at four walls, with an emptiness that's consuming me.

LANCE

I'm living in hell, being back at the house I tried to leave, under the same roof as my ex-wife. The only saving grace is that I can see Cassie every day.

This is how it used to be before, with me doing mostly everything for her, the school runs, and homework and spend my evenings with her. We hang out at the mall on the weekend and we watch a movie. Her friend is having a birthday party at an ice-rink so I take Cassie there, then vanish for a few hours until I have to pick her up again.

I love this part of it, and it makes being under the same roof as Vivian's parents slightly more bearable.

But a life without Megan is hard to come to terms with. I can't accept that she has broken up with me, and if I wasn't here, dealing with Vivian and her parents while trying to take care of my daughter, I would have given into my temptation and gone over to Megan's place to tell her that splitting up doesn't make sense.

It's not fair that she can make the decision to split up because she believes it's the right thing for Cassie. It's noble of her to think of my daughter's wellbeing but I don't fully believe it.

Megan is scared, scared of commitment. Scared of getting hurt. Scared I'll walk out on her, again. Scared I'll be like her father.

I want to make a stand. I want to make her see. I want to win her back.

Megan doesn't get to make a decision about my life.

She didn't break up because it was the right thing to do for 'us'. I don't buy her reasons for it. What does she care about Cassie? I'm the one who decides what's best for Cassie, and while my daughter scared me to death by her notions of wanting to run away, now that I've been here, living this lie for a few weeks, I can't do this forever. I'll wait for her. For however long it takes. For Cassie to grow a little older and find her wings.

I can't, I won't walk away from Megan again. I did it once before and it was a mistake I've long regretted.

That's all I can think of while Cassie and I are watching a movie. She's making her way through a huge bag of popcorn, and I love this daddy and daughter time. I must focus on this daddy and daughter time.

I must move on.

When the film ends, we file out of the theatre and while Cassie is enthusiastically recounting the film she watched—because my mind was elsewhere—I see her. In a crowded theatre lobby teeming with people filing in and out of the big movie theatre, I see Megan. I laser in on her, and everyone and everything blurs into the background. She sees me at the same moment, her lips twisting as if she is in pain. That's when I note her unease comes not from seeing me so much as I will see who she's with. It's a cosy foursome, with her friend Arla and a man she is staring up at adoringly.

Megan is with the guy we saw at the art exhibition. The one who is younger, fitter. Younger, younger, younger. I almost stop walking because it feels like a bullet has hit me again.

But it's unavoidable. There's only one way down and we will have to walk past her to get the escalator.

"Daddy, it's your friend!" Cassie shouts, with the ignorance of a nine-year-old.

I can't now pretend I didn't see Megan. That's the path I was going to take. A nod of acknowledgement as I walked past her, but Cassie will find that odd. She tugs at my hand, which she's suddenly taken a hold off, this child who told me she's too old for us to hold hands the moment we got out of the car in the parking lot.

"Oh, so it is." I look away, pretending to be mesmerized by a movie poster showing next month's offering.

"She's looking at you, Daddy!" And to my horror Cassie waves at Megan.

"Why are you waving?" I growl.

"She's your friend, Daddy. Don't be rude."

By now, we're only inches apart. Her friend glares at me, and the guy from the art exhibition gives me a curious look. I have to veer away from the trail of people heading towards the escalator and I'm forced to take a few steps towards the group I don't want to talk to.

"Hey," I manage to say, nodding at them all, and focusing on no one.

"Hi!" Cassie says to Megan.

I don't understand her exuberance.

"Oh, hey." Megan's face breaks out into a smile that puts my heart back together again.

"Hey, Lance." Arla interrupts us. "This is Chris, I don't believe you've met."

"We've met." I don't offer a handshake, but it's obvious that Megan is here with this douchebag.

Megan bends down until her face is level with Cassie's "What film did you see?"

Cassie proceeds to tell her, and enthuses about how good it was. I stand in painful silence, as do the other three, while my daughter and my ex-lover exchange pleasantries.

A long, painful moment passes, until Megan stands up. Cassie waves to someone else then turns to me and asks if she can go and speak to her friend. "Sure." I'm about to follow, and make my escape, when my daughter runs off.

"Kids," I say, grinning, and examining Megan's face. The hardness is back. She looks pissed, more than I've ever seen her.

"We'll see you inside," her friend says, and the douchebag strokes her arm as he follows them, leaving me and Megan alone. I sense she wants to talk, so with one eye on Cassie, I turn my attention to Megan, my heart full of hope that she has changed her mind.

"Was it worth it?" she asks, venom in her voice.

"Was what-_"

"The student. The affair, the cheating on your wife. I found out. Were you ever going to tell me?"

I frown, and then as the words land and start to make sense, my eyes widen with astonishment. "The student? Heidi Byrne?"

"How many others were there?"

I shake my head. "It's not true. There was no affair, no cheating. I don't do that."

"You did that with me!"

Her face twists with anger.

"It was you her boyfriend intended to shoot, because he was jealous. Because you had a relationship with a student." She shrinks back in horror. "This is you. This is you all round. A serial cheater. This is how you operate. You prey on young women."

I flinch at the description. "Don't say that. Don't. It's not true." I knew this news would come out, and with it the rumors that would spread like a virus. I never thought they'd reach Megan, which is why I never thought to tell her, to prepare her for something which is pure lies.

"You lie with such ease." She shakes her head, looking at me as if I've shattered every nice thought she ever had of me. It was hard to win her over, and harder still to not give in to her the way she wanted. We had at last managed to find our happy place and now it's all come crashing down.

"I'm not lying to you." From over her shoulder I can see her friends looking in our direction. Cassie is making her way back to us slowly. I don't have much time. "I swear to you, nothing happened. I am not a serial cheater—"

"Your poor wife."

Fucking hell. Her taking sides with Vivian is too much to bear. "It's nothing like the picture you're being painted of me. I swear, Megan."

She will believe these lies as if they are a truth I tried to desperately to hide. She will see me for something I am not. The way she's looking at me now I can already tell that the damage has been done.

"Was she vulnerable, too? Did she have a hard home life?" She mocks me with ice in her tone.

"She used to come to me, too much, if I'm honest. Any excuse she could find, but she didn't have family problems. She didn't have any problems, as far as I could tell. She was just a flirt."

"She was pretty, and young, just like how you like them."

I feel the color drain from my face. "That's disgusting. I'm shocked you would say such a thing."

"I'm shocked you would do such a thing."

I press my lips together as I catch the guy she's with staring at me from a distance. "I see that you didn't waste any time." I jerk my chin in his direction. "Are you two double dating now?"

"I don't date," she throws back. "I fuck." Her words are like a hard slap. Her anger unleashes onto me. "You fuck, too. You fuck all the pretty young things."

"Don't swear." I feel my age telling her this.

"Don't judge me," she warns. There's a hardness in her gaze that pains me.

"Daddy, can I go to Arianne's house tomorrow?"

I glance down at my daughter. "Let's see what we've got going on tomorrow." I face Megan. "We need to talk," I whisper in a low voice.

"We're done talking," she says, smiling, her voice sweet, so that her voice and words don't match. "Nice to see you again, Cassie. Take care." She swivels on her heel and turns to walk away but not before I've grasped her wrist. "It's not true. I swear. These fucking rumors. Always rumors. It's not true."

Megan yanks her hand away. "I know exactly what you are, you monster."

"Who is she?" Cassie asks as we get into the car.

"Someone I used to know a long time ago."

"Really, Daddy?" she shrieks. "How long ago?"

I stare at her and weigh up my words. "Long before you came along, Sweetpea." I fasten my seatbelt and check that Cassie is fastening hers. "Why did you make me go and talk to her?"

"Because she's your friend, and you like her."

"What makes you think that?" I ask, sharply.

She stares at me with innocent eyes. "I can tell, Daddy."

She can tell? From that one awkward time when she and Vivian turned up, after Megan had just given me head? Given that I wasn't too happy to see Vivian, at that precise moment, I'm not sure I believe Cassie. "How can you tell?"

"Your face goes all soft, and your eyes smile."

"Eyes don't smile." I start the engine and drive away slowly, the exchange between me and Megan fresh and hurtful in my mind.

CHAPTER FORTY-TWO

MEGAN

Chris and I had a date last night. Just the two of us. I wanted to prove to myself that I didn't need to jump into bed with a guy just because he was good looking.

And I didn't.

We had dinner in a French bistro and talked about things I have no interest in.

I smiled and laughed and said appropriate things.

He thought I liked him, so much so that when we left the restaurant, he took my hand in his and when I pulled mine away he asked me what was wrong.

"Nothing," I told him.

"I thought we were having a nice time. I thought we were getting on."

He looked disappointed.

I was disappointed.

I'd just given up an evening of my life that I was never,

ever getting back. My speech was ready; I told him I wasn't ready, that I didn't feel the same, that I was getting ready to move. But what I didn't tell him was that I was having second thoughts about my new job and about moving away. I've got a third interview at the smaller firm near Boston.

Chris was gracious and sweet, and wished me well. What I also didn't tell him was that I'm no longer a girl who needs to feel that she owes a man something just because he bought her dinner.

When I get home I start my packing again. My family are coming to help me move out. There are boxes everywhere, and on the coffee table a book: *Applied Calculus and Mathematical Modeling*.

It's a book Lance left behind on one of the times he was here. A book that makes me remember the man I knew then, before I found out the truth of who he really is.

I lean back against the wall and slide down it, sitting with my arms hugging my knees, feeling lost, and forlorn, and abandoned.

And unlucky in love.

It has to be done. I walk into the quaint looking building which houses Lance's office and look around for cubbyholes. Somewhere I can leave his book.

But I don't find anything.

And a part of me wants to look into those eyes for one last time.

I make my way down the wood-panelled hallways, until I find his office, and all the while I'm preparing myself physically and mentally, to be cool and calm and be able to walk away for the last time.

Except when I get to his office, the door is open, but he's not there.

I exhale, my shoulders dropping, the tension in my neck loosening.

He's not here.

This makes it easier.

But a part of me is sad, because I'm prepared for a final goodbye and he's not letting me have it.

"He'll be back soon." I jump at the sound of a soft voice. A familiar voice. I turn around.

"Oh ... hi." It's Lesley, Lance's good friend. I can feel her looking at me, through me, seeing everything.

"He's got a one-to-one tutorial."

"A one-to-one tutorial?" I echo.

"It'll be finished in ten minutes."

"I'd rather not wait."

Lesley smiles at me. I wonder if she thinks we're still together, but surely, she must know what's happened to Vivian? In any case, she doesn't say anything. Her gentle smile, her air of being wise and all knowing, puts me on defense.

"No?"

I shake my head, fighting the urge to rush over to her and sob my heart out. To tell her everything that's wrong and wish that she can fix it.

"No, I was packing, and I found this and I just want to return it before ..."

"Before?"

"Before I move away."

"Ah, yes." She nods. "He told me."

I'm curious to know what he told her. Whether she knows of our history, and our breakup. She says everything and nothing and I am none the wiser.

"Are you okay?" she asks when I've still said nothing.

I waver between wanting to rush off, and staying here and asking her a million questions.

"Is it true? The rumors about the student he saved? About her boyfriend being jealous."

She takes a long, deep breath in. "What do you think?"

"I don't know."

"You must have an idea about it."

I scowl, hating her riddles, and hating her for making this such hard work. For not giving me an answer.

"Did you know that Lance and I met while I was in high school when he was my teacher?"

"I know."

I almost fold into myself. The weight of her knowing eases the guard that's been keeping me upright. Lesley's face is still soft and welcoming. Friendly.

She doesn't look at me with disdain.

"He told you everything?"

"Lance doesn't tell people everything. It took him a while, but yes, he told me about high school, and how you both recently connected."

My heart starts to thump as hope laces with fear. "Is it true? About the student?"

"He's not a serial cheater." Using his words tells me she knows about the last conversation between us. "I've always told him that his face and his body aren't made for teaching. Lance is gallant, to use an old-fashioned word. He's noble. He did the right thing by that young woman. She was always hounding him. She was always in here, knocking on his door. It's why he always keeps it open. She's not the first student who's come to him asking for help, claiming she hasn't understood what he's explained in a lecture. I doubt she'll be the last. His looks have landed him in trouble with some students; these young women and their desire to catch his eye. But, as you probably know, Lance isn't like that. He's not a player. He's no Casanova, even though he has the face and body of one. My daughters have always had a crush on him, so I know too well the effect that man has on the opposite sex. But Cassie is the apple of his eye."

I nod. "She is. She's his life," I say softly.

"Vivian has been a thorn in his side for as long as I've known him." Lesley looks away and lets out another sigh, pressing her lips together as if she's trying to keep her words about Vivian to herself. "But, he's been a lot happier these last few months, after the shooting." She gives me a pointed stare. "At first, I didn't understand, but then I met you on the drinks evening, and it all made sense."

I look at her trying to figure it out, what he's been telling her, what she's telling me.

"Lance is no more a serial cheater or purveyor of beautiful young women than I am a pole dancing stripper," she says.

I suppress a laugh.

"Do you want me to take that?" Lesley glances at the book in my hands.

My body feels lighter, but I am confused. "Yes, please. Could you give it to him?" What she's just told me makes it difficult to walk away, but it will be easier to look back on my time with him.

I'm moving on. A new chapter, a new start. Lance always complicates my life, after he makes things better, and I just can't deal with all the rollercoaster emotion that being with him entails.

CHAPTER FORTY-THREE

MEGAN

"Stop messing around!" I yell at my brother when he puts the empty cardboard box on his head, like a three-year-old.

Erica breaks out into a fit of giggles, and my mother is still going around with a Sharpie pen and labels.

It's nice that they've come to help me finish my packing, but most of it is done and now my siblings are just messing around.

I don't move for another week, but this is the last weekend that I will be here in this apartment.

My family wanted to help me but with everything else that's happened lately, my nerves are fried.

I finished at my workplace and got a great send off. I hardly did any work and most evenings there were drinks and dinners to go to with all the friends I've made during my time here.

Preston seems genuinely sad.

I kind of feel it too.

But I'm ready to move on.

Erica puts a bigger cardboard box on her head and my temper rises.

"How old are you?" I scream. My patience is wearing thin. I don't know how I'm going to put up with another night with my family here with me.

Mom still hasn't forgotten that Lance was here, and Erica I'm sure still has memories of catching us in bed together.

It's been tricky.

I feel the closing of one chapter and the start of something new, something scary and unknown.

It's what I wanted, right?

Then why don't I feel happy?

I keep going over Lesley's conversation in my head. Do I believe her or Arla? Do I trust Arla and her rumors from those guys we met in LuLu's or do I believe Lesley?

If anyone would know the truth about Lance, it would be Lesley. And that's the problem. I'd managed to extricate myself from Lance once before, but this second time is a warning that life isn't going to be easy.

The man has an ex-wife who refuses to let go. He has a child. He has a truckload of baggage.

There is so much stacked against us, and yet, I can't stop wallowing in my unease. I'm so eager to move on and being here starts to irritate me. My family adds to that irritation.

I've ordered pizza for dinner, and I just want to take a long bath and wallow in my sadness and self-pity.

I'm packing my CD collection when the doorbell rings. Erica and Jensen are still fooling around with my books. They're not packing them away as much as they are commenting on my taste in reading.

"It's the pizza delivery guy." I fish some change out of my pocket and hand it to my mom. "For the tip."

"Will you two grow up!" I yell, when Jensen drops one of my books. Sometimes I still feel like the only responsible adult around them. "Leave it. I'll pack my books." I rush to pick it up and dust it. Books are my prized possessions. I never bend the spine. I never fold a page. I treat my books as good as I'd treat my pets, if I had any. "You two go and clear the table and—"

My mom shrieks and I hear angry words, but I can't make them out. I wonder why she's having an altercation with the pizza guy. Rushing to the door, I stop in my tracks when I see Lance standing staring at me.

Oh. God. No.

"What is he doing here?" My mother snarls. Erica and Jensen come to the door.

"You said you broke up with him!" my sister cries.

Only Jensen stays quiet.

"What do you want?" I ask, noticing that his eyes are tired and more wrinkled than I remember.

"Can't you leave her alone?" my mom yells at him.

"Mom, stop it."

"I won't stop it. This man has been sniffing around you and I won't have it now."

"He's not—"

"Ma'am, with all due respect I would like to—"

My mother jabs a finger at him. "You can stick your due respect down your throat. You should have been locked away years ago for what you did."

"Mom!" This is unacceptable. Lance's face hardens at the accusation.

"Mom, give the man a chance." Jensen says.

"Why are you here?" I ask Lance again.

"You returned my book." There's a look in his eyes. A glimmer of something, hope, perhaps. Lesley has obviously told him about our conversation.

"And?" I school my expression to being blank and try not to focus too much on the way the thick wool sweater clings to his body. Or the way his suede coat contrasts with it. Or the way his eyes are an electric blue, and his lips are so red. He's too gorgeous for a man, and the extreme cold outside only accentuates his perfect features even more.

"You're leaving, and I wanted to say something."

"Goodbye, I hope." My mom again. She can't stop herself.

"I love your daughter, ma'am. I love her and nothing you say can change that."

Erica gasps.

"Oh, boy." Jensen rubs the back of his neck.

It doesn't stop my mother. "You're a disgusting man. You're old enough to be her—"

"I was worried about Megan at school, and if I made a mistake then it was that I—"

Oh. *No.* No. No. No. He doesn't need to come clean with my mother about what happened that night. He doesn't owe her an explanation or anything.

"You don't need to say anything," I tell him.

"If I made a mistake, it was that I walked away and left her to deal with the fall out. I've always regretted that."

Just then the pizza guy arrives and thankfully Jensen takes the pizzas, takes the money from my mom and hands it to the guy, and then herds my mom and sister into the kitchen.

Lance finally comes inside, and I close the door.

It's just the two of us, but I'm aware that three pairs of ears are listening albeit out of sight. "You didn't need to come and tell me that you got the book."

"I've regretted walking away from you that night, but even

if I could change things, I don't think I would do things differently."

"I know." My gaze falls to the scar along his jaw again. "That's because you always do the right thing." He's my Lance, and he's here.

"I'm getting ready to move," I say, confused about his appearance.

"You spoke to Lesley." It's hope I hear again in his voice.

I nod.

"I'm not the man your mother thinks I am. I'm not the guy you think I am. I don't get involved with my students. It's only ever been Vivian … and you."

I know this is the truth. My heart knows.

"Don't walk away." He's begging me to stay. "Don't walk away because you believe the lies. Walk away if you don't feel anything for me."

But that's the problem. I feel so much for this man. My mouth turns dry. My insides slowly climb out of the stupor they've been in ever since we broke up. He takes a step closer and now I can smell his cologne. I can feel the low thrum of electricity, the sparks, the fizz and zing of invisible energy that flows between us whenever he's near me.

My skin tingles.

This is what I was afraid of. A reminder of what we are, what we can be. I am tempted to fall into his embrace, to have him hold me and press me to him. It's so familiar and warm, like coming home.

I swallow. "But I'm … I'm moving away."

"And?" He sounds unfazed.

"And? We'll be so far apart."

He smiles.

"What?" I ask.

"You haven't said' no'. You haven't said it won't work, us

being together and living so far apart. You haven't yet pushed me away or made excuses, but you will and I'm prepared."

I frown at him.

"You can say what you like, Megan. You can swear and cuss and talk about liking hookups and that you like to ... you know ...the f-word."

Heat sears my cheeks and I shut my eyes. My mother probably heard that. Taking him by the hand, I lead him out and close the door behind us. I walk down the hallway and turn a corner until we're in a small nook. I back away from him into a corner.

"You can say what you want to try to push me away, but the only way I'll walk away is if you look me in the eyes and tell me that you don't have any feelings for me."

I look up at him, take in his soft, liquid eyes, the curve of his lips, the smooth skin along his cheekbones. I can't say that to him. He'll know I'm lying.

"I thought this was a second chance for us, and I wasn't prepared for Vivian to mess things up. If I have any regret, it's that I didn't tell you everything at the start, but I truthfully didn't expect anything to happen between us. You're so young, and beautiful, and you have a wonderful future ahead of you. I'm still surprised—but grateful—that you were single. I didn't want to be the old man from your past who got in the way."

I shiver at the description which conjures up an image of a bald and toothless eighty-year-old. "You're not old. Don't ever call yourself an old man." I raise my fingers and trace along his scar gently, feeling its bumpy outline against my fingertips.

He gives me a sexy grin.

He knows I've given in. Given up. Stopped holding back. He cups my face in that familiar way I love, and I automatically tilt my face against his palm. A knowing glimmer flashes across his eyes. "I love you so much, it's unreal what I feel for you."

My heart bursts with happiness. I want to tiptoe up and kiss him. He thumbs my lower lip. "Sometimes you can't control how things happen, and sometimes you have to grab the moment, and sometimes, you have to fight to make the truth be heard. I don't expect you to believe me. Why should you? I wouldn't expect Cassie to blindly follow anything a man said to her. He'd have to prove himself to her first, but Lesley thinks you might believe her."

I nod.

"If you want ... you can ... maybe I can get Heidi Byrne to talk to you."

"Who?"

"The student whose boyfriend shot me." He winces. "It would be a bit awkward but I could find a way for you two to talk—"

I wince on his behalf, trying to think of a situation in which he'd get his student to talk to me and tell me that nothing happened between them. I would never do such a thing because it wouldn't be right, especially for the student. I don't need to do that. I believe him.

"I love you, Megan. I've tried to slow down my feelings for you, but I can't. I'm in love with you, and it's new and different, and *allowed*."

I hold his gaze as my heart falters on the precipice of something new and unknown. A possible future.

One man, the only man who has ever cared about me and loved me and cherished me.

I'm suddenly afraid to take the leap but Lance Turner has proved himself to me time and time again.

"I think I believe you," I say.

"It's not enough to think you believe me. It has to be stronger than that."

But I do believe him now, because I believe Lesley, and things are falling in place. I remember how the other girls at school crushed on him when he was our teacher, but he always kept his distance. I'm also aware that Vivian will do whatever she can to stand in our way, but together, Lance and I can deal with her, because, when I look back on it all, Lance Turner has always been there for me.

"What about Cassie?"

He inhales a deep breath. "Cassie's starting to see that I'm happier when I'm around you."

"She has?"

"Enough for her to notice it. She's seen how demanding and difficult Vivian has been, and maybe she's picked up on how unhappy I am being back in the house. She's seeing things she didn't see before but also; she's noticed how Vivian comes to life whenever Joachim is around."

"Joachim?"

"Vivian's new therapist—a very expensive therapist her parents are paying for. He's been doing home visits."

"How is she?"

"Better. Almost back to her usual self. A few more visits from Joachim and I'm sure she'll be on form again."

I feel sorry for him, but something else comes to mind. I remember how enthused Cassie was when we met her at the cinema. "That wasn't a proper date, with Chris, the guy you met at the—"

"I know who you mean."

"He's not fitter, younger and more good looking." Eager to assure him, I lift up on my toes and plant a kiss on his lips. It's like a match has been lit to paper. Our kiss is hot and all-consuming. Heat rushes through me, blood charges through my veins as I feel the hard press of him against me. Our gazes hold, firm and steady. I want him, in my life, in my bed, in my future.

Many years ago this man helped me through a dark time in my life and now we get another chance to be together.

Second chances are for the taking; they're to be grabbed with both hands and never let go. I'm ready to take this chance because I've found the man who will always be there for me, no matter what.

EPILOGUE

Six weeks later ...

LANCE

Megan is doing the laundry at my place. Vivian came to pick up Cassie earlier, and now we have the place to ourselves.

I hover in the doorway admiring her in her satin shorts and tank top. Her wavy hair floats down past her shoulders, and she has her back to me which means I get to stare at her for the longest time. I thank my lucky stars for this woman who is finally in my life again. Hopefully for keeps.

As if she can feel me staring, she turns around. "What?"

"Nothing." I raise my arms and grasp the doorjamb above my head, in an attempt to resist her, otherwise my hands will wrap around her soft, silky skin and we'll end up in bed again.

She starts the washing machine then turns around. "Hey, handsome. Remember this?" She nods behind her, at the washing machine.

Remember? I will never forget. "Similar room, different appliance."

"Similar room, different apartment," she corrects me. Her breasts jiggle softly as she walks towards me. These are her bedtime clothes, but I usually manage to strip them off her within minutes of her climbing into bed alongside me. She's staying over tonight because Cassie has gone home after staying here for the weekend and Megan won't stay the night if Cassie is here. She thinks it's too soon for us to be sharing a bed with Cassie around.

"I love having you here." My voice has that familiar rasp, the gravelly undertone which hints at my arousal. Where before I was measured and restrained, not wanting to rush things, she was forward, eager and wanton. But now our roles have reversed. I went two years without sex and then I met Megan and now all I want is her, all the time. It's probably a good thing she stays at Arla's place on some nights.

"It's only temporary." Her hand reaches up to stroke my jaw and her finger traces along my scar. She only has to touch me, be near me, and my defenses weaken. My fingers loosen on the doorframe and my cock stiffens.

This is all it takes.

Her.

Near me.

I reach down and press my lips against hers, my hands tentatively wrapping around her waist, struggling not to drop lower and cup her sexy little bottom. She moans and nestles into my chest, her fresh flowery aroma wreaking havoc in my brain, sending signals to my excitable zones.

Cassie's tenth birthday is coming up and Megan and I

have planned a ton of things for her. Vivian is throwing a party to which Megan and I aren't invited. Cassie mentioned that Mommy's doctor friend is coming. I'm assuming it's still Joachim. That might be the reason we're not invited, but also, Vivian hates Megan.

It didn't help that Megan was here when Vivian came to pick Cassie up earlier. It didn't help that I put my arm lovingly around Megan's waist and reeled her close to me. It especially didn't help that Cassie hugged Megan and told her she couldn't wait to go girlie shopping with her again, and that she excitedly showed her mother the fishtail braid Megan had done on her.

I had to hold back a chuckle, even with Vivian's ice cold face in front of me.

This morning Megan enticed Cassie into helping her bake cupcakes and cookies for a local cancer charity. I read student dissertations while the two of them had fun in the kitchen and it occurred to me that Megan spends so much time with my daughter; time which her own mother never has for her.

The contrast is hurtful and reassuring at the same time. Megan is amazing with Cassie, and Cassie seems to have taken a shine to her.

Once Megan decided to change jobs again, I sat Cassie down and explained who Megan was to me and why I couldn't live with them anymore. Vivian's therapist helped me, by becoming Vivian's new plaything.

It hurt. It hurt like hell seeing Cassie's lips wobble and her face turn sad. But then she said, "It's okay, Daddy. Mommy laughs more when her doctor comes to see her. So, it's okay if you don't stay."

The first meeting between the two most important females in my life was the scariest for me, but I hadn't been prepared for Megan's charm, for her friendliness, for the way she put Cassie at ease and her ability to win her over.

Turns out I didn't have much to be worried about.

This weekend was the third time Cassie has come to stay and my two girls have been getting on just fine. Megan doesn't stay over on those nights when Cassie is here.

"It's too soon," she told me. I'll let her guide me. She's been through this scenario, and she knows the damage that ensues when parents split up.

For now Megan lives with me, but stays with Arla when Cassie is here. She didn't work out the probationary period at the new firm because she had an interview from another firm closer to Boston and she accepted their offer. It wasn't because the money was better. It was because it was run by women and she liked that. She also liked that it was small, and she said she got a better vibe from it.

I like to think that maybe being closer to me, distance wise, might have had a bearing on her decision but who am I kidding? Megan is focused, driven and ambitious. She is the woman I always knew she'd grow up to be, and I will support her in anything she chooses.

She's been looking for an apartment in Boston and when I touched on the idea of her living with me, she told me that it was too soon and she needed her own space; that our being together was wonderful, but she didn't want to rush things.

It crushed my hopes but I understand. She's with me. We're together. I won't rush her into anything because I don't need to. I'm just so happy that we met again.

Her hand dips down and she reaches straight for my cock. A devilish smile curls on her lips. "You're ready."

"I'm always ready when you're around." It doesn't take much for me. A glance at her in her night clothes will do it in a heartbeat. She kisses me slowly, tenderly, while her fingers stroke me through the fabric of my pants. I'll have her naked and in my bed in no time, and then we'll spend all night doing unspeakable things. Dirty and delicious.

"I need to order the balloon arch," she says, between kisses and strokes.

"The … what?" My brain is thick with fog.

She pulls back and looks up at me through thick lashes, her eyes dark with desire. "For Cassie's party."

She's thinking of Cassie's birthday party, in this moment?

"And who invites a psychotherapist to a children's party?" she cries. It takes a few seconds for my thoughts to adjust.

"Vivian. She can be conniving and manipulative like that."

"Cassie will have more fun at our party." Megan grins wickedly and my heart turns soft and gooey. She cares for Cassie, and I'll bet she's put more thought into this party than Vivian has.

It's too early to have any conversations about the future—about potential marriage and kids and my worries about being older. Would Megan even want marriage after all that she's been through? How would she feel about being a stepmother to a ten-year-old or a teen, whenever the time is right to have that conversation. There's so much to think about and right now, I don't want to think.

I slip my hand underneath her tank top and palm her warm breast.

Fuck.

My cock turns to steel.

I move my hand away, wanting to broach the subject. "You've never asked me what went wrong in my marriage."

Surprise lights up her eyes. "Because I've met Vivian, and it's self-explanatory." She's never been nosy. Never probed, but I feel the need to tell her and now seems as good a time as any. "Why are you bringing this up now?" She now looks confused.

"Because we've never talked about it. You've never once asked me what went wrong and you were angry when I first told you about Cassie. You were angry that I'd moved on with my life, that I'd gotten over you so quickly."

Her hands slink around my neck. "We don't have to talk about the past anymore, Lance. I've dwelt in it for too long and I want a new start. *We* want a new start."

"I know, but this is the one thing you need to know, and I never got a chance to tell you why it happened so soon. I don't want you to think I forgot about you, or that it was easy for me, meeting Vivian and getting married."

Her smile is soft, her expression tender. She splays a hand across my chest. "Then tell me."

"It was one night which turned into a week. It happened soon after I moved away from Nebraska, when it was time for me to let my brother-in-law and Sarah move on in and get used to a life with just the two of them. Sarah was a little madam by then. She was walking and talking and looking more like Anna every day. I'd been getting my accreditations while taking care of them both and during that time I didn't date. I didn't make friends. I didn't want to. But then I met Vivian at the college I started at before I worked at Redmond."

"She went to college?"

"No. It was the opening of a new library her father had paid for. He was a benefactor of the college because it was his alma mater. It was the first relationship after two intense years of looking after Brett and Sarah and grieving for my sister. You can imagine how stunning Vivian was to look at. She was charming. It was all so different from what my life had been like. The moment I saw Vivian, she made a beeline for me—"

"I bet she did," Megan snaps.

"Yeah, she made a beeline for me, and she was charming."

"You've said that twice."

"Are you jealous?"

"No."

"Good, you shouldn't be because there is no competition when it comes to you. You're my everything, Megan. We've come so far, we've gotten over so many obstacles and I believe this is fated, you and I being together after all this time. Back then, I had no intention of getting married. I'd put my life on hold and this was all so new and unexpected for me, meeting Vivian. She was beautiful and ..."

Megan folds her arms. "Is this supposed to make me feel better?"

"I just want to explain, and then I'll never talk about it again." Megan purses her lips. I'm going to make her come so hard once this conversation is over with. I'm going to fuck all this talk about Vivian out of her system. I stroke her lips, wanting to soothe her. "I didn't want to marry her. She said she was on birth control and I foolishly believed her."

"And you being a man you didn't think you had any responsibility for your actions. Silly risk to take, if you ask me."

I cough lightly, feeling sheepish. "I was irresponsible, and not thinking straight."

"You were probably also sex starved," Megan adds. "But you had Cassie, so ... it was a good thing." Her saying those words sends a rush of happiness through me.

"Yes. Cassie was the best thing to come of it." I'm tempted to kiss Megan now, but I force myself to behave. "I had no intention to get married. I didn't even think about settling down. We were only ... we only ... it was a few nights in the span of a week and then she disappeared. She went on a cruise to Italy, and when she came back she announced that she was pregnant. I'm not a man who walks away from his responsibility."

"Are you ..." Megan nibbles her lower lip but I know what she's thinking.

"Cassie's mine. I didn't even consider that she might not be. Not then. Not until a few years after we got married and Vivian's eye started to wander. That was a difficult time, seeing what she was really like. It wasn't a happy marriage because I didn't fit her parents' ideal of the type of partner they had in mind for her. At parties and formal occasions, when I'd meet her friends, I felt like a fish out of water. I didn't belong. We were truly happy for that first week, but after that, things went downhill fast. Later when I had my suspicions I demanded she take a paternity test. She did, which is why I know for a fact that Cassie is mine."

I pause to take a breath and try to gauge Megan's reaction. "That's it. That's all I wanted to tell you. She got pregnant and that's why we got married. Vivian wasn't too bad in the beginning, but things changed after Cassie's birth. She wasn't depressed. She had the best care, she was well looked after, her father saw to that. She wasn't the problem. I was. I wasn't enough for her. I wasn't charming enough, or funny enough, or like the other men, that's what she said." I press my eyes tightly. "But it didn't take me long to see that she was a narcissist, thinking only of herself, having delusions of grandeur, and no emotional empathy or understanding. She was at the center of her own world. She didn't even have much time for Cassie and that's when I realized what a huge mistake I'd made, sticking with her, staying married despite the cheating. But I stayed because of Cassie."

Megan puts her hands on my forearms. "You stayed

because you love your daughter and you wanted to do the right thing."

I let out a breath.

"You did it because you're a good guy, Lance." She puts her arms around me and presses her body to mine. She plops a kiss on my sweatshirt, right in the middle of my chest. "You're a good man. A responsible man. A kind and caring man who would do anything for those you love. You also happen to be hot and sexy, and gorgeous, and while Cassie's lucky to call you dad, I'm lucky to have you as my friend, my lover and my confidante."

I give her a smile that is almost as big as the one when I first held Cassie. It was a moment when I held back happy tears. A moment when I was vulnerable, and joyous and bursting full of gratitude. Kind of how I feel right now.

"I love you."

"I love you," she echoes back. "I love Cassie, too."

Maybe because I frown, maybe because I think it's too soon, but she sees it. "I understand her, and I want to make it all better for her, for whatever she's going through. I want her to know that she's safe and loved and that I'm not a threat just because I'm in your life."

I kiss her then, deeply, slowly, tenderly. I want to make this woman be mine forever, and when the time is right, I will. But for now I scoop her up in my arms and take her to my bed and toss her down.

"Oh, yes ..." she purrs, starting to slide off her satin shorts. I slap her hand gently, wanting to strip her myself.

"I'm in charge here. You will lie back and take it," I order.

"Oh, yes, pleeeease," she purrs, then watches as I strip my clothes off. I plant my thighs on either side of her waist, my hardness pointing upwards like a lightsaber. I salivate as I hook my fingers through her spaghetti straps and peel her top down slowly, revealing her bare skin.

I move away to kneel between her legs, knowing that I'm the luckiest man alive.

I found her again, and I'm not walking away, ever.

MEGAN

"Kiss me, up here," I whisper. He's about to sink to his knees and plant his face between my legs.

Heat coils inside my body as he moves over me, the delicious feel of his warm, smooth skin on mine as his lips feather my breasts. I feel drunk and in a haze. Dizzy, dazed, breathless because of what will follow. It's not only that he will have me screaming his name while he's inside me, or that my world will splinter when he takes me to the edge and waits for me to come back down. It's knowing that he will hold me in his arms and still be there in the morning. He is a steadying, solid, firm foundation in my life.

He is exactly who I need.

I will treasure and cherish this man the way he deserves. I believed that I was the only one who found love hard but Lance hasn't had things easy either. I never asked about his marriage because I didn't want to know. I wanted to look forward to the future, not dwell in the despair of the past but now that he's told me I feel at peace.

We are similar, he and I. Lance is my other half. The yang to my yin. The day to my night. The glitter to my darkness. He is the calm in my chaos.

A man who will stay.

A man I want to stay.

"I love you," I say again, wanting him to hear it, needing my words, my truth, to sink through his skin and lodge into his heart. I stroke the corner of his eyes and run my fingertips over the creases. I love his creases. They signify the passing of time. They signify wisdom and strength.

His eyes turn glassy, and his vulnerability is laid bare. It's not often he shows this side of himself. He worries that he's too old for me. He doesn't talk about it, but I know, I can tell because we are so connected.

I get him.

I don't want a guy who's going to treat me like a piece of meat. I don't want someone who's going to have fun and make me happy for one night, and then leave me.

In Lance I've met my soulmate.

My fingers flutter over the gunshot scar along his shoulder, before moving to the scar along his jaw. This man has lived, and loved, and protected. He is a keeper, and he is mine.

For tonight, tomorrow and for always.

Thank you for reading TOMORROW BELONGS TO US! I hope you enjoyed Megan and Lance's story!

I have some EXTENDED EPILOGUES for their story and you can get these by signing up for my newsletter: http://www.lilyzante.com/newsletter

Existing subscribers will automatically receive the bonus content. There's no need to sign up again.

If you loved Lance, you might like Dominic, a bossy billionaire who falls for a waitress in Greece:

When a jaded waitress meets an obnoxious billionaire, all hell breaks loose.

LOVE AMONG THE RUINS is an age-gap, grumpy meets sunshine, opposites-attract, slow-burn, steamy romcom.

I appreciate your help in spreading the word, including telling a friend, and I would be grateful if you could leave a review on your favorite book site.

Thank you and happy reading!

Lily

Eleni returned with Stefanos to the bustling taverna to find tables filled with people.

Laughter and chatter floated across the air along with the aroma of fresh coffee, the smoky, juicy scent of cooked meat and fresh bread.

"That was fast," she muttered, surveying the scene with trepidation. Lunchtimes this busy indicated a long, hard day would follow.

"He looks cute. Table in the corner." Stefanos gripped her hand, the way he often did when he insta-crushed on someone.

Eleni cast a glance in that direction to find a man sitting alone surrounded by a paperwork and a briefcase lying on the chair next to him. He wore aviators with attitude, dark slacks, expensive looking loafers, and a watch.

There was always a watch. Big, bold and brash.

Eleni's gaze traveled over his slim fit, short sleeved, cotton polo shirt. It was white with a thin blue stripe running across his shoulders; not that he needed to draw any more attention to them. Wide and thick, they hinted at more than his masculinity. They promised protection. Comfort. Strength.

She shook her head; certain she was coming down with something. But her gaze went back to the man whose short shirt sleeves strained slightly under biceps that teased her attention. Her eyes dropped lower, and she was in danger of drooling over his forearms: lean, veined, muscular and, for as long as he didn't notice her, hers to ogle freely.

One quick laser glance and she'd figured him out. Not because she was a fashionista. She wasn't, didn't care much for such things, but because Stefanos was a fashion whore who admired a well-dressed man as much as any hot-blooded woman.

The man's attire alone probably cost more than she earned in a year.

"I don't think anyone's seen to him yet." Stefanos' voice turned squeaky high with uncontained excitement.

"He's all yours." Eleni rushed to the kitchen and whipped on her half-apron, as did Stefanos. She tied the apron around her waist, before pulling out a notepad and pencil from one of the deep pockets. Then she got ready to tackle the customers.

Stefanos turned to her. "You can have him. You need the money more than I do." He veered off in the opposite direction before she had a chance to tell him that she didn't want this particular customer, but he'd left her with no choice.

She approached the man's table and saw him looking through notes and scribbling things down.

"Hello," she attempted a breezy greeting. Aviator sunglasses hid his expression, not that he was looking at her. She cleared her throat hoping to get his attention. "What can I get you?"

He looked up slowly. "You are open, then?"

An American.

She gave a small laugh, not understanding his comment. She even forced a smile. "Yes, sir. We open from—"

"I've been waiting for hours for someone to serve me." His voice was crisp and sharp, and he looked at his watch as if confirming how long he had waited.

She forced another small laugh. "It can't have been hours." He raised an eyebrow which, given that she found herself reflected in two shiny black lenses, didn't help her to gauge his expression. "Lunchtime is a busy time for us."

"Then get more staff."

She blinked. "I'll be sure to pass your advice on to our manager. What can I get you?"

"An espresso."

"Will that be all or would—"

"That's all." His attention returned to his cell phone again.

Rude.

And no 'please' or 'thank you', either. Another one of those rich, ill-mannered, arrogant ones. Eleni walked away, sliding her pencil into the front pocket of her apron, and gave the order to the barista.

Stefanos stopped to share his observations. "Have you seen the size of his hands?" he whispered. "He must be hung like –"

"Don't," she hissed.

"I wish I hadn't given him to you."

"It's not too late. You take his espresso," she offered. But Stefanos had already rushed off.

"Espresso." The barista slid the small cup across the counter to her. She placed it on a small tray with a napkin and walked back to the rude American. "Your espresso." She placed the cup on the table.

The man grunted. At least, she thought he did. He didn't

look up but seemed vexed by something on his cell phone and jabbed his finger, texting away.

She was about to walk away when he asked, "Do you have freshly squeezed orange juice?"

"Yes, would you like some?"

Still not looking at her, he nodded, making a noise in his throat. Something on this phone had grabbed his attention.

"Was that a 'Yes?'" she queried with a smile—hoping for a good tip—it was always for the tips.

He put the cell phone to his ear. "A large glass," he said, absentmindedly.

She had visions of throwing it at him. "Only the one glass, then?" She was about to turn away when his tone stopped her. "The Acropolis? Linus, are you fucking kidding me?" he barked. "It's a wasteland of ruins. What is wrong with the man?"

She frowned as she listened, unable to move.

"Tell him to go to hell," he snapped. Then, "Don't. Wait for me to get back." He slammed the phone on the table, before sitting back and resting his arms on the armrest. "Jesus." He raked his hand through his sandy brown hair. Eleni fought the urge to give it a good yank.

She couldn't help herself. "It's not a wasteland, and they are not ruins."

Dark shades stared back at her. "Were you listening to my conversation?"

"Does an elephant have ears?" It wasn't quite what she intended to say, but her anger had reached boiling point and rage simmered under her skin.

"You refer to yourself as an elephant. Interesting."

She was about to shoot back a response about his sunglasses, about him being visually impaired, but didn't want to stoop so low. Grounding down on her molars, she lifted her chin. "The Acropolis has ancient buildings which bear great historical and architectural significance."

She walked away, her heart in her chest, knowing she'd done it again. Being rude wasn't a part of who she was, but some people, like Mr. Arrogant and Rude, brought out the worst in her. She could not hear this man talking trash about the Acropolis and say nothing.

"Are you walking away?" He raised his voice, and she was sure people heard him two tables away. Customers turned to stare. She raced to the kitchen and poured out a glass of orange juice.

Maybe she had taken it too far this time.

"What's going on?" Stefanos hissed, glaring at her as he reached for a tray of food to deliver.

Eleni shook her head. She didn't know how he did it; took care of his customers and kept an eye on her at the same time. "The man is a nightmare. You should have served him."

"It's too late. Adamos is watching you, Leni. Don't mess it up."

"I'm going to fix it."

She would. Mr. Arrogant was just this side of being too grumpy and too rude. He grated on her like the sound of metal scraping across a squeaky-clean plate. She walked back to his table, a glass of ice-cold orange juice in her hands, mentally preparing to be submissive, to put on an apologetic demeanor without verbally begging for forgiveness. Bracing herself to be nice and friendly when she felt anything but that. These types of men responded well to women like that.

As she reached the table, something wrapped itself around her ankle and she went flying. The glass of orange juice slipped from her hand at the point of impact.

Thankfully, it didn't break but slammed to the ground with a thwack.

Meanwhile, her hands and face smacked against the American's chest. In her dazed state of shock, as another pair of hands helped her off him, her brain registered a body that had been hard. A wall of steel. There had been no give.

"I'm so sorry," she gushed, as Stefanos helped her to standing. The American also jumped up, picking at his wet shirt.

She looked down to find her foot trapped in the long strap of a handbag.

"I am so sorry. It was my bag you tripped over. Are you hurt?" A timid looking young woman holding a toddler stared at her. A stroller stood nearby, and another slightly older child sat at the next table.

"I'm fine," she replied. Eleni glanced behind her to see Stefanos helping the American. Wiping him down with napkins. A wet dream unfolding in real time.

The mother, face red and eyes popping, rained apologies on Eleni. Was she okay? Had she hurt herself? She looked so upset that Eleni forgave her on the spot, needing to hush her. She reassured the mother that she was okay, then untangled her foot from the bag and handed it back.

She and Stefanos had one goal; to make sure Adamos wouldn't hear the commotion.

Although, this really hadn't been her fault.

She hovered around and listened as Stefanos fretted and fussed over the American. "I'll get you another glass of juice, sir. Don't you worry. Is there anything else I can get you? On the house? No? Are you sure?"

"This place is a joke." The American gathered his papers together. "Get me your manager."

Stefanos smiled widely, quickly standing between Eleni and the American. "Please, sir. There's no need."

"Your manager." The American growled.

"Don't do that, sir. Please. She needs this job."

Eleni couldn't take this anymore. She couldn't let Stefanos beg on her behalf. It was time to plead, and to appeal to the American's better side, if he had one. She waded in. "I'm so sorry. I tripped, but it really wasn't my fault." That didn't help, but also, it was the truth.

"Jesus Christ. I'm soaked and I smell like an orange." The man pinched his shirt which now clung to his chest.

"At least it now has some color," Eleni countered, nodding at his shirt and trying to make light of the situation. The American removed his shades and this time when he glared at her, she felt his wrath. "Imagine if it had been the espresso, you might have suffered burns."

Stop talking.

It wasn't like her to ramble. She usually knew when to shut up. The American lifted his head, immediately drawing her attention to his angular jaw. Emerald green eyes—just like the water a stone's throw away—filled with fury and stared back at her. Her heart jolted.

In a panic, she stepped away, confounded by her reaction, by her noticing these very things. Something odd was happening to her. Her heart was racing in a way it had not for a long time.

The man squinted. His brow furrowed, his lips parted.

She waited for his tirade.

When he didn't speak, she rushed to fill the prickly silence, confusion mixing with trepidation and causing her brain to short circuit. "Not that there's anything wrong with your shirt but ..."

"But?" The word shot out like a bullet.

"It could have been much worse. You could be wearing Giouvetsi."

"What?" He gave her a look that could have harpooned a whale.

It didn't stop her from explaining. "Greek beef stew … with orzo pasta. We have it on our Specials menu today."

BOOKLIST

Honeymoon Series: Take a roller-coaster journey of emotional highs and lows in this story of love and loss, family and relationships. When Ava is dumped six weeks before her Valentine's Day wedding, she has no idea of the life that awaits her in Italy.

Honeymoon for One
Honeymoon for Three
Honeymoon Blues
Honeymoon Bliss
Baby Steps
Honeymoon Series (Books 1-3)

Italian Summer Series: This is a spin-off from the Honeymoon Series. These books tell the stories of the secondary characters who first appeared in the Honeymoon Series. Nico and Ava also appear in these books.

It Takes Two
All That Glitters

Fool's Gold

Roman Encounter

November Sun

New Beginnings

Italian Summer Series (Books 1-4)

The Billionaire's Love Story: This is a Cinderella story with a touch of Jerry Maguire. What happens when the billionaire with too much money meets the single mom with too much heart?

The Promise (FREE)

The Gift, Book 1

The Gift, Book 2

The Gift, Book 3

The Gift, Boxed Set (Books 1, 2 & 3)

The Offer, Book 1

The Offer, Book 2

The Offer, Book 3

The Offer, Boxed Set (Books 1, 2 & 3)

The Vow, Book 1

The Vow, Book 2

The Vow, Book 3

The Vow, Boxed Set (Books 1, 2 & 3)

Indecent Intentions: This is a spin-off from The Billionaire's Love story. This 2-book set consists of 2 standalone stories about the billionaire's playboy brother. The 2nd story is about a wealthy nightclub owner who shuns relationships.

The Bet

The Hookup

Indecent Intentions 2-Book Set

The Seven Sins: A series of seven standalone romances based on the seven sins. Emotional, and angsty romances which are loosely connected.

Underdog (FREE prequel)
The Wrath of Eli
The Problem with Lust
The Lies of Pride
The Price of Inertia
The Other Side of Greed
The Seven Sins Books 1-3

A Perfect Match Series: This is a seven book series in which the first four books feature the same couple. High-flying corporate executive Nadine has no time for romance but her life takes a turn for the better when she meets Ethan, a sexy and struggling metal sculptor five years younger. He works as an escort in order to make the rent. Books 4-6 are standalone romances based on characters from the earlier books. The main couple, Ethan and Nadine, appear in all books:

Lost in Solo (prequel)
The Proposal
Heart Sync
A Leap of Faith
A Perfect Match Series Books 1-3
Misplaced Love
Reclaiming Love
Embracing Love
A Perfect Match Series (Books 4-6)

Standalone Books:

Tomorrow Belongs to Us
Love Among the Ruins
Love Inc
An Unexpected Gift

ACKNOWLEDGMENTS

I owe a big 'Thank you' to the wonderful ladies in my proofreading group for their patience and support, as well as their tolerance for my ever-changing deadlines. They check my manuscript for errors, typos, inconsistencies and the many strange words and phrases which often find their way into my stories.

They give me the confidence to release each book and I am eternally grateful for their help and support:

Marcia Chamberlain
Dena Pugh
Charlotte Rebelein

I would also like to thank Tatiana Vila of Vila Design for creating this awesome cover.

ABOUT THE AUTHOR

Lily Zante lives with her husband and three children somewhere near London, UK.

Connect with Me

I love hearing from you – so please don't be shy! You can email me, message me on Facebook or connect with me on Twitter:

TikTok |Instagram | Website | Facebook | Twitter | Email

tiktok.com/@lilyzantebooks

instagram.com/authorlilyzante

facebook.com/LilyZanteRomanceAuthor

twitter.com/lilyzantebooks

goodreads.com/authorlilyzante

bookbub.com/authors/lily-zante

amazon.com/author/lilyzante